HUNT

Also by Alexandria Warwick

The Demon Race

The North Series
Below
Night

HUNT

ALEXANDRIA WARWICK

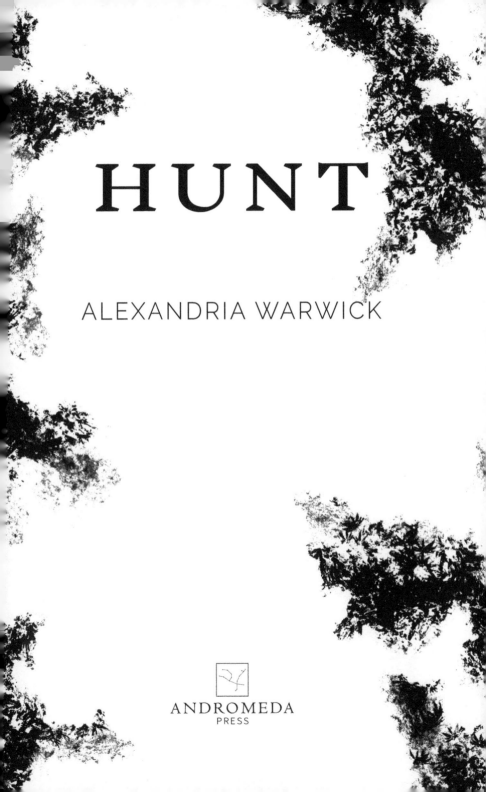

ANDROMEDA
PRESS

Published by Andromeda Press

Cover illustration by Faryn Hughes
Map art © Alexandria Warwick

978-1-7330334-4-2
First Edition

Quarantine 101: I wrote a book

The North

Iniga Fore

Nalwa

Tor

The Western Sea

Norther

Lun

Talguk

Western Territory

River Mitka

Central

Unana

The Atakana

The Dea

Kesikan
Pass

Southern

The
Banished
Lands

Auk

The Ira

☆ Nigun

Kunivik

The Island of Kir

erritory

Aatu Forest

Apaay's Village

Naga

The Eastern Sea

River Pak

erritory

☆ Sinika

River Iniak

Eastern Territory

• Nannek

☆ Ariviat

lains

erritory

☆ Nur

• Kaal

PART ONE

PREDATOR

← 1 →

In the highest reaches of the Atakana, bound and trembling between the roots of an ancient pine, Ila fought sleep.

The fourth hour had come and gone. The sun, trapped in its eternal summer throne, cast the land in a brilliant pale glow. Though her shoulders ached from lying atop the chilled permafrost, though every mile traversed these recent weeks throbbed through her blistered feet, her mind held a perfect, painful clarity. One slow breath, followed by its soft release. It was nearly time.

Shifting onto her side, Ila took in the slender man leaning against a nearby tree. The small, discreet fire tossed cruel shadows onto his face, making hollows of his eyes, cutting beneath the cliff of his jaw.

Tulimaq was a stranger.

Ila had carried this weight across snowy peaks, deep into plunging valleys as the distance between herself and the Wood grew vast and insurmountable, along with the knowledge that no one knew where she was. Not Apaay. Not the Face Stealer. Not Kaan or Ro. She'd left the Wood seeking answers, and she'd found them. A name: Matilaqaa of the Wolf Kingdom, first-born daughter to the Vaal and Narg, her parents. Dead now.

Unfortunately, she'd trusted the wrong person. Now that

Tulimaq knew her identity, he would use her to gain leverage with his tyrant father, Nanuq. War was approaching, and the Polar Bear Empire stood in the eye of that storm. Tulimaq may have fooled her, fooled them all, and bound her like a prisoner, but she was leaving. Tonight.

As Ila settled down to wait, she cleared her mind of the lingering betrayal and focused on what came next.

Her wrists were not actually bound. She had cut through the rope hours ago. Once free of Tulimaq, she would travel to the labor camp that held the wolf Unua—her people—captive. She did not know how she would free them. She only knew she would not rest until she did.

As the fifth hour waned, the fire died to embers. Ila's face slackened, her eyes slits beneath lowered eyelids. Her breathing fell into an even rhythm.

Tulimaq's gaze felt like a touch, elicit and forbidden. He thought she was asleep. She hadn't given him reason to suspect otherwise. He would assume she'd continue meekly onward. It would never come to pass, for he had acted with cruel intention. Drugged, bound, weaponless. He'd even taken all her supplies, including the small stone carvings she'd packed, a reminder of everything she had overcome. But it wouldn't be long now.

She knew the moment he fell asleep, with his staff curled in one hand, her mother's precious talq tucked into his waistband, and his cheek pressed against the ground. Ila perused the dips and planes of his face for only a moment before glancing away. She hated him for it, that he could sleep so easily after betraying her. He didn't care. He'd never cared. That hurt more than she was willing to admit.

To be safe, Ila let another hour pass. Her eyes burned with fatigue and the chill that lingered in the higher altitude. For every day she'd been bound, she had monitored his routine and sleep schedule. Tulimaq rose before the sun, but once he fell asleep, he didn't wake. Ila was prepared. She had her eyes, her intuition, the clothes on her back. She would have to trust in her ability to navigate the treacherous terrain. It was Tulimaq, after all, who had taught her how to survive.

Gaze never leaving the former combat master, Ila slowly sat up and began untying the rope binding her ankles. Her hands trembled. She discarded her mittens to quicken the process. The pads of her fingers explored the complex contouring where the pieces of rope crisscrossed, and she tugged hard. The cold stiffened the material and wouldn't budge.

The trouble with lack of hearing, Ila thought, was she never knew how much or how little noise she actually made. That notion slowed her frantic movements. Her skin prickled as she fumbled to pull one end through the loop, her lower lip caught between her teeth. Then the rope loosened around her ankles, and skin flared to life from the rush of blood.

Cramming the rope into her pocket, Ila climbed to her feet and stood tall on bruised ankles in the shaded half-dim, sunlight dappling her back, and a hard, coiled emotion burning behind her sternum.

The more Ila learned about the world, the more she noticed its insidious corners. Retribution—she understood it like never before. How easy would it be to snatch Tulimaq's staff and shove that blade into his chest? Wouldn't he deserve it? He, who led her to an unknown fate, who had earned her trust, who had betrayed her, and whose heart she did not know.

Still, she didn't move. As much as his deception hurt, she could not end his life. She could not.

Ila fled on shaky legs. Kept to the deepest, blackest shadows, branches whipping across her stomach and face. Attempting to steal back her mother's talq was too risky, so she left it behind. There, something scurried in the underbrush, but she was already darting past it, too full of adrenaline to slow.

The terrain transformed to protruding rock. The trees grew sparse. Tulimaq would expect her to follow the warmer air into the valleys, so she went up, scrambling along a mountain ridge full of loose shale, breath panting from her open mouth. Large granite outcroppings blurred to shade in her peripheral vision. Then they, too, fell away.

After three or four miles, the ridge leveled out before sloping into a wide, shallow valley. She was crossing into alpine meadow when the air grew charged. Ila, thinking of an approaching storm, glanced upward.

White light erupted across the landscape. The earth heaved, tossing her forward. Solid air slammed against her back.

Her vision returned to her in pieces: green needles piled at her feet, a large tear in the canopy that hadn't existed previously, like an open sore. The fallen tree yards away blocking her way forward.

A loping, shadowy figure materialized beyond the veil of swirling dust and debris, a glowing, slender object clutched in hand.

She ran as though fleeing death itself, clambering over the fallen tree, clawing through the compact branches. One of the smaller saplings whipped across her cheek. She freed herself of the tangle and sprinted across the open plain, seeking cover up ahead. The flash of brightness—had that come from Tulimaq? How had he found her so soon?

The ground lurched a second time, yet she managed to keep her footing. She pushed through the burn in her legs until she could run no farther, and slowed. Ahead, the ground had split to shape a massive canyon. Far beyond was the horizon, its pearled edge that never went completely dark. There was no way to cross. A band of white water lashed below, carving out rock, the river's current carrying eastward. Ila couldn't swim, but she had made her choice. She would not go back.

She jumped.

The shock of cold stole her breath. Ila plunged like a stone, sinking into darkness. Her feet hit the river's sandy bottom, and she pushed off hard. Her head broke the surface, time enough for one mouthful of air, before the current dragged her down.

Churning liquid sucked her deeper into the swollen rapids. Her shoulder slammed against a boulder, and she was tumbling. Another rock pounded her side before she could brace for impact. And as the pressure crushed her lungs, fanning the flames higher and brighter, she succumbed to the river's hold.

Water poured down her throat, and the torment cut open a line in her chest. The air had gone. There was no light to guide her. She rammed into a fallen tree but swept past it before she could grab onto the branches. Under she went, and stayed. The cold numbed her mind. Her heart, which beat with such ferocity, began to slow.

Ila did not want to die, but she was an animal in this old world. What she wanted meant nothing.

Eventually, something soft nudged her back. She'd drifted to a bend in the river. Her head tipped to the side, and she retched, every muscle clenching to rid her body of the water she'd inhaled.

Her head hung, spittle dripping from her partially open mouth. Her teeth chattered uncontrollably as she pushed to her feet, and the ground swayed as though she were still twisting and rolling and tumbling downstream. No time to build a fire. She had to keep moving.

Mile after mile, hour after hour, Ila stumbled toward a nameless, faceless, unknowable destination. The sky lightened further to the east. A vanishing opportunity to disappear with every mote of breath. Ila no longer cared about being quiet. She tore through the forest with mindless desperation.

Stumbling into a clearing, she froze.

The fallen caribou was massive. A swell of animal flesh packed in dense fur the color of pinecones. An arrow sprouted from its chest, blood darkening the fur to black. A second arrow had found its mark in one of its haunches. The antlers were so substantial they gouged deep scars into the soil. Short, shallow breaths pulsed through its nostrils. Its eyes were closed. Wounded, but still holding on to life.

Ila circled the animal before her skin prickled with the approach of that crackling energy. Her stamina was nearly depleted. She had run as far as she could, but no more.

Ducking behind a bramble patch, she crouched down and waited. Moments later, Tulimaq raced past her and vanished.

Ila held still and was glad of it, for Tulimaq returned almost immediately, moving with considerably more care. She noted the tilt of his head as he studied his surroundings: the disturbed earth, the felled caribou.

As he circled the animal, a dull light flattened his gaze. The curved, slender blade of bone attached to the end of his staff glowed whiter than its typical hue. A glow from *within*. This, she realized with dread, was no ordinary weapon.

Ila realized his intention almost too late. The staff swung toward the caribou's neck, its blade thin as a crescent moon. Ila burst from the bush. She vowed to keep her eyes open as the weapon sped toward her, but there was still cowardice in her heart. She let them close.

The strike never came. Cautiously, Ila opened her eyes. The blade's edge hovered a few inches from her throat, a glint of pale, beautiful and deadly both. Tulimaq's pupils shrank, giving way to the gold-brown of his irises, the white encircling them.

"Fool," he said, and she imagined his voice to be cold from how stiffly his mouth shaped the word. "It is dying. Best to put it out of its misery."

The caribou opened a single clouded eye, looking straight at her.

You don't know that, she signed. *It could still survive.* Though the arrow had pierced its side, it didn't appear to have hit any vital organs. Lather foamed the animal's mouth from its long, desperate run, but it was white, not red.

"Move, Ila."

No.

She lunged, her arm snaking out, fingers wrapping around the staff as he jerked it back, pulling her off balance. The heel of her palm shot out and connected with his nose. Bone crunched and blood sprayed. Ila grimaced through her teeth. He had taught her that move. The irony was not lost on her.

Tulimaq recovered quickly, knocking aside her next blow. They were nearly the same height and build, both slender, though Tulimaq's frame held tight to compact, wiry muscle, hidden strength. Lunging, he caught her hands, pinning them to her chest. Sweat gleamed in the hollow of his throat.

Ila thrashed in his hold, rage rising as a knot in her throat. Weeks of floundering toward a horrible, unknown fate, and Ila had not asked him the one thing she wished to know: *Why?* It shouldn't matter. He'd made his decision. This was Nanuq's son, her enemy, and he would use her to gain leverage with his father, and why did she care when he so clearly didn't?

Tulimaq wrenched her hands behind her back, binding them at the wrists. Then a strip of cloth slipped over her face, guttering her vision.

Ila's stomach bottomed out. He couldn't possibly know what had been done to her in the labyrinth. That pit of ice, the rumbling of something mammoth out there, beyond the fabric shuttering her eyes. To have no vision *or* hearing? For the first time since Tulimaq's betrayal, Ila was afraid.

The prick of a knife against her spine was the only motivation Ila needed to keep walking. She lost track of time stumbling across the peaks and gullies, the meadows with their long grasses scraping against her clothing. They traveled north, she thought, or northwest. Her limbs trembled with fatigue, hot sickness sliding through her, fear of their destination. Eventually, red light seeped through the dark cloth: the sun having finally breached the canopy.

When the ground shallowed out once more, they stopped, and Tulimaq removed the blindfold. Ila blinked against the brightness and froze in recognition at the sight before her. Peaked roofs. A clearing pocked with holes.

Digging the knife against her back, Tulimaq forced Ila into the labor camp.

← 2 →

Ila's legs pooled with blood. They proved useless as Tulimaq half-dragged her across the gray, colorless clearing where the prisoners toiled, his fingers digging into her upper arm. There was nowhere to look but at their hollowed faces. The flaky patches of frost-bitten skin, chunks missing from a nose or chin or ear. One by one, the prisoners slowed the lift and fall of their shovels, taking her in. They were nothing but eyes and bones.

The reality of Ila's situation hit her like a slap to the face. She recoiled from Tulimaq's proximity, but he only tightened his grip, and the knife dug a little deeper, warning her to settle. Many months had passed since she and Tulimaq had carried out the Face Stealer's mission. It had always been Ila's intention to return to the labor camp, but as a savior to her people, not as a captive.

They'd nearly reached the opposite side of the clearing when a guard stepped into their path. His eyes, pinched in his face, narrowed further in her presence. Smoke belched from one of the buildings at his back.

Ila was too dazed to keep track of their conversation. They took her to one of the buildings. The room held a single cell, bars slashing sooty lines into the floor from the meager sunlight squeezing through the singular window. Tulimaq locked her inside, leaving her alone save for her rising terror.

She paced and paced, and when she had worn a furrow into the floor, something inside her snapped. Ila lunged, rattling the cell bars. A faint growl caught in her throat.

Her legs folded, fingers curled around the chilled metal. A tremor wracked her body. *Pull yourself together.*

Distant words. A sense of heightened awareness. Sharpened eyesight adjusting to the void.

It was as if she had lost her mind, or rather, it had transformed.

Ila continued to pace. She understood this was a cage, and she could not escape except through the door, which she hadn't a means to open. She understood, too, that those beyond the door meant to harm her.

Her body twitched, and her bones ached and sang with pain, and her limbs stretched, and Ila lost more of herself.

At the end of the hall, light speared through the opening door.

Acute vibrations shuddered beneath the floor. The set of footsteps fell unevenly, thudding into place, followed by a drawn-out dragging sensation. Ila retreated from the door, crouched, tension curling through her body, and underneath the sensory overload, a vague sense of bones and muscles locking into place.

The cell door opened. Ila lunged.

A blast of power slammed her into the wall, knocking her out cold.

Ila came awake in stages. First, an acute throbbing at the base of her skull. An ache in her limbs, as if they had been stretched beyond the limit of her bone structure. An uncomfortable roughness to her tongue.

Cracking open her eyes, Ila let her surroundings sharpen into focus. A sparse room with wooden walls, a door leading elsewhere, and a single chair in which she sat, her wrists bound at its back.

Splotches darkened the packed dirt floor at her feet. The air felt clotted with old blood, and she wheezed, unable to remember how she'd gotten here. Her pulse beat so forcefully it hammered against her skin.

What did she remember? Very little. Something forceful tossing her backward, and pain rupturing down her spine. There had been a man. She could not remember what he looked like. Her thoughts drifted, pliant and unclear.

Across the room, the door opened. Tulimaq crossed the threshold, his focus latching onto her before he moved to stand against the opposite wall.

A second man limped in after him. One glimpse at his face, and ice branched through Ila's limbs. This was the guard whose leg had been crushed beneath an enormous statue during the Face Stealer's mission. It seemed the bones had never properly healed.

"Hello." One step, two, and the guard's face crammed her vision, a smile seeping across his fleshy mouth. He was so close she could count the clogged pores dotting his skin, trace the outline of the birthmark darkening his cheek. A thin, sleeveless maq displayed a set of bare arms that bulged with muscle, the raised veins running like tributaries beneath the coarse hair of his arms. "Do you remember me?"

Ila's gaze flicked to Tulimaq, but he stared straight ahead as if she were not present.

"I asked you a question," Birthmark said, spittle spraying her chin.

Ila yanked her wrists against the rope with a sound of frustration, trying to indicate she needed her hands to communicate. Tulimaq, who had come no closer than the far wall, said, "She's deaf."

That gave the guard pause. "She cannot understand me?"

"She can read your lips, but she will need her hands free to answer."

"She has the ability to nod or shake her head, does she not?"

Tulimaq said nothing.

"I will ask you again," said the man, his attention returning to Ila. "Do you remember me?"

Ila nodded.

"That's good, very good." His smile hadn't changed. "Because I definitely remember you. Do you think you can infiltrate my camp, disrupt its operation, ruin my leg, and walk away without consequences?" He laughed. "Little girl, we haven't even truly begun."

Memories of the mission resurfaced too lethargically for Ila to understand what was happening, but the way these men spoke of her, as if she wasn't there, as if she were an animal to be caged, cleared the clouded waters.

"Tulimaq informs me you are wolf Unua. Is this true?"

Ila feared what would happen if she lied. She nodded.

"You will fit right in." Birthmark studied her in closer detail. She shrank against the back of the chair.

"This is how it's going to work." Pressing the fingertips of both hands together, he tucked them beneath his chin in a gesture of deep contemplation. "I know the Face Stealer has been protecting you. I know there were other refugees with you, and that they now hide elsewhere. You're going to tell me where the rest of your people are. You're going to tell me where the Face Stealer hides, and his intentions toward Nanuq. If you cooperate, I promise no harm will come to you."

Her pulse pounded with increasing urgency. What had Tulimaq told this man? Everything? The Face Stealer's alliance with the Owl Clan? What about Ro and Kaan? Did they have targets on their backs as well?

"Nod if you understand."

He gave her little choice in the matter. She did.

The guard stepped in front of her. "Tulimaq."

The former combat master pushed off the wall.

"Remove her bindings. You will translate what she says to me."

Ila flinched as Tulimaq set to work untying the knots. Once the rope was loosened, he stepped neatly back, as if needing space from her. Ila rubbed her aching wrists.

The man said, "Where is the Face Stealer?"

I don't know.

Tulimaq communicated her response to the guard.

"How does he intend to stop Nanuq?"

I don't know.

Birthmark's sneer sent a wave of fear through her. It was a cold gesture, completely void of compassion.

"Oh, dear." He studied her as one would a particularly pathetic creature. "That does not sound very cooperative. Perhaps a simpler question is in order."

The slap cracked against the side of her face. Heat blazed across her cheek, then the throb sank beneath the skin. Blood leaked from where her teeth had cut into her lower lip. She struggled to control her breathing as the world spun. In her periphery, she noticed Tulimaq had frozen mid-step toward her, his eyes pinched.

The guard said, "Did that hurt?"

Her teeth started chattering.

"You expect me to believe the Face Stealer is not plotting against Nanuq this very moment?" Grabbing her by the collar, he shook her furiously. "I've heard things. Rumors. They say the Wolf Kingdom will rise again." He tossed her back into the chair so hard Ila tumbled over its back and crashed onto the floor. "Who will lead you, girl? The Face Stealer? Don't forget, many blame him for the death of the ruling family."

She pushed onto her knees, head dangling. Her stomach pitched into a slow roll. The guard didn't know her identity. For whatever reason, Tulimaq hadn't told him.

"Last chance, girl. Tell me where the Face Stealer is, and I will spare you."

Ila didn't want to lie. Somehow, it felt too close to weakness, as if she could not hold strong against a man.

Tell him, she signed to Tulimaq with shaking hands, *that I would rather die than give him the information.*

Tulimaq stared at her. She thought something flickered in his eyes, but they reverted to their cold, emotionless state.

"What did she say?" the guard snarled.

"She said—" Tulimaq's chin dipped a fraction. "—that she will consider your offer."

He was lying. Why would he lie?

Ila rapidly signed, *That's not what I said. Tell him the truth!*

Tulimaq added, "But if she is harmed, she will die before ever giving you that information."

Ila's heart skipped a beat. Her hands, which had lifted in anticipation of another lashing retort, dropped to her sides. Either he was trying to protect her, or Tulimaq had his own motives for stepping in. He had given her no reason to believe the former.

Birthmark laughed. A small mercy, to be spared that terrible sound. "Many die here." His lips stretched and his skin crinkled and cruel emotion hemorrhaged across his face. "But we do not make it easy."

He gestured to Tulimaq. "Take her to a holding cell. She'll talk. They always do."

Hauling Ila to her feet, Tulimaq escorted her, stumbling, from the building. An unmarked forest path led to a long, squat building hidden in the trees, no windows, a single entrance door. The interior revealed two lines of cells separated by a narrow walkway.

Ila recoiled from the sight. The darkness was complete. The reek of bodily neglect was so thick she could feel the particles in the air sticking to her skin. Strange, how one never really forgets.

After unlocking the cell farthest from the door, Tulimaq nudged her inside. Ila whirled and slammed her fists against the iron bars, biting back a scream. It was both demand and plea. Why had he betrayed her? What was his motivation? She raged against the metal until her skin split, feeling as if she toed an unknowable threshold, the long drop too frightening to study head-on.

Tulimaq stared at her without answer. Then he abandoned her to the dark.

← 3 →

"Tell me again why I've agreed to do this," Apaay said, studying the sweeping grassland separating her from the behemoth gates in the distance. It was a plain, it was a sea, beaten down by fierce winds.

"Because you don't want me to die."

The voice, though weak, still managed to hold a note of allure.

"You'd be surprised," she said dryly.

"I'm nice to look at."

Apaay shifted her attention to the demon sitting by her side. Irritatingly, he was right. Even in his deteriorated state, the Face Stealer was painfully beautiful, sharp-edged, with a mien of breathless cruelty.

Pale violet eyes regarded her, glossy with fever. Seven weeks they had trekked, from the abandoned port city of Talguk, through the Atakana's glacial peaks, to the one place that might stop the poison from reaching the demon's now-returned heart: Nigun, winter capital of the Northern Territory.

The journey had been exhausting at best, downright harrowing at worst. Apaay could not count the number of times she had been reduced to tears, forced to take cover from Nanuq's men, Yuki's army, all while caring for an ailing traveling companion on little to no sleep. The Face Stealer was weak—too weak. Their time was nearly up.

"Wolfling."

She focused on the rich timbre of his voice, the threat that was never far off. "What if I get caught?" she asked.

"So don't get caught."

He *would* say something like that. "May I remind you that while you remain safe in the forest, I'll be putting my neck on the line for *you.*"

"And what a lovely neck it is," he purred.

Scowling, she slapped his hand aside as he reached for her. "It's not like I can pretend to be someone else. We can't all have the gift of deception."

The Face Stealer's mouth drew flat. "Yes," he said, a strange note to his voice.

Apaay studied the grassy plain that lay at the foothills of the Ira, the olden, eroded mountain range casting rounded shadows against the sunlit ground. At long last, summer had come to the North. The ice coating the majority of the landmass was in full retreat, giving way to the mosses and lichens of the tundra, the bright, flowering plants of the taiga. For the Analak, the season of the skin tent was a time of rebirth. A time when the rivers rushed, full and swollen, toward the sea. This season, Apaay would not join Papa on the summer hunt. It was a little difficult to do that when running for your life.

How quickly things had gone wrong. With Yuki's—the Sea Mother's, she amended—true face having been returned to her, and the Wood forfeit, Nanuq growing in power, Kenai's betrayal . . . Nowhere was safe. She did not know what tomorrow would bring. For her family, whom she'd been separated from once again. For Ila.

A weighted pressure pinched her chest, as though a stone rested atop her sternum. She winced, rubbing the area with the heel of her palm. As much as she tried to avoid thinking about her friend, sometimes, in a moment of weakness, a thought slipped through. That was, assuming Ila still considered them friends. When the shadowy fog that had veiled her heart the last six months had at last begun to lift, Apaay had seen clearly how she'd wronged those who mattered most to her by acting as though they mattered not at all.

"What?" said the Face Stealer.

Apaay blinked. She hadn't realized she'd been staring at him.

"Do you regret what you did?" she asked, referring to the dark oath he had exchanged with the Raven, the god who reigned over Taggak. If he hadn't agreed to it, the Face Stealer would still have his power, and the Raven would still be trapped in the Shadow Realm, bound by whatever curse Nanuq had placed upon him, spending eternity ferrying the newly dead into the spirit world. With his newfound freedom, who knew where the dark god was now.

He stared at a point beyond her shoulder. In this light, his black lashes were so thick they looked painted on. "I regret a lot of things. I've had this power for so long I had forgotten who I was without it."

"And who were you before your power?" Apaay found she desperately wanted to know.

A slight tilt to his mouth. It did not look anything like a smile. "I was a boy who loved his brother more than anything, and was willing to go to any lengths to ensure his safety."

The admission made her chest twinge. Even if he rarely spoke of it, she knew Kenai's betrayal pained him.

Since there was no reason in putting off the inevitable, Apaay climbed to her feet, scanning the miles of swaying grass running from horizon to horizon. "I'll be back once I locate the hot spring."

The Face Stealer caught her hand in his. With the warmer weather, they had done away with their mittens. The scrape of his calluses puckered her skin. "Be safe."

Apaay searched his gaze before pulling away. "I didn't know you cared."

His smile was sharp. "You don't know a lot of things."

← →

The gates of Nigun were hewn from dense gray stone, and took shape as Apaay hurried across the hissing sea of yellow grass. They were as tall as the world was old, their twin arches curved like caribou antlers, too great to have been built in any one year. Apaay was just a girl. This was the earth: ancient, powerful beyond measure.

Apaay was halfway to the gates when something whined past her ear. She dropped, using the grass as a shield. A white object protruded from the dirt behind her. It was a blade of some sort, carved from an antler, and deadly sharp.

The grass hissed loudly, nudging her back and arms with their spindly bodies. Her ears pricked for a sound that did not belong. She couldn't stay here forever. Each passing moment dragged the Face Stealer a little closer to death. As much as she still grappled with their complicated relationship, she did not want him to die. The underground river leading to the city was located west of the gates. It wasn't much farther.

Squeezing her eyes shut, Apaay inhaled until her lungs strained and her ribs pinched, until it felt as if the North were inside her body, its strength flooding her limbs.

She sprung, bolting toward the safety of the cliff wall, ducking and swerving the objects that sliced through the air. The wind yanked at her messy braid, which had grown past her shoulders, wonderfully thick and dark and missed.

Apaay reached an opening in the rock. A rough, narrow squeeze between the stone led to a widened tunnel, an oblong cave with a curved ceiling, and cool, stale air.

The space was all dark, glistening rock and low light. Various-sized crates lined the walls. But the most unusual distinction was the river cutting through the cave's center.

Boats bumped against one another in the weak current, a hollow knocking of wood where she expected a whalebone frame and toughened walrus hide. It wasn't driftwood, as her people sometimes used. This wood was young and green, easily formed. Fascinatingly, the vessels were shaped like arrowheads, their fronts pointed, the backs abruptly blunt, and they perched high atop the water, unlike the umiaks she knew.

Moving to the nearest crate, she lifted the lid and peered inside.

It was filled with a white, powdery substance. Apaay weighed the likelihood that these boats would head into the city and hurriedly climbed inside, fitting the lid over her head.

Darkness pooled in her eyes and slid sweetly down her throat. Her breathing hitched, then eased. It spoke volumes of how far Apaay had come in her healing, because while she could not erase her memories of the labyrinth, only the faintest prickle of sweat now touched her brow in being held in total darkness.

It was a long wait. Apaay dozed, then woke to voices drifting from somewhere deep in the cave. Men, two of them. There came the sound of heavy objects being pushed across the floor. Water plunked and splashed.

Apaay froze as her container jerked forward.

One of the men grunted. "Why is this one so heavy?" He shoved the crate harder to get it moving. Then, with a few uttered curses, the man heaved the crate—and Apaay—into the boat.

The vessel dipped before settling. Aside from the water lapping against the boat's dense wooden hull and Apaay's slow breathing, all was quiet, tranquil. She couldn't sense the water as strongly, even when they pushed forward to merge with the current.

The river wound aimlessly in its search for the sea.

Pulling her legs closer to her chest, Apaay propped her chin on her knees. She didn't know how long the journey would take, as the Pale One hadn't mentioned it. A set of twin blue doors marked passage to the spring. That was all she knew.

Deeper and deeper they drifted into the rock.

A voice sounded from the void beyond. "You're late."

The boat rammed into something hard, causing the containers to slide forward. Apaay braced her hands against the walls and listened to see if anyone would approach. She had no idea where she was, how many men were out there, if they bore weapons, whether they were friend or foe.

"We're here now, so stop complaining and help me check for inventory."

Apaay wiped the sweat trickling from her hairline. They'd crack open her crate, spot her huddled among the powder, and then what?

Apaay shifted onto the balls of her feet. Pressing her hands against the wooden slats, she threw her body weight against the crate wall. The vessel rocked wildly. The men shouted in confusion.

"Something's in the water!"

The crate tipped, and the lid slid off, giving her a view of the damp tunnel wall a few feet away, the river below.

"Grab it before it goes over!"

Apaay curled her fingers over the lip, letting her body weight sink against the crate, and tumbled into the water with a splash.

She'd braced herself for excruciating cold, but the water was warm, pleasantly so, steam curling from its surface. Apaay disentangled herself from the container and swam in the opposite direction, coming up for air behind the furthest boat.

"Do you know how much powder that was?" one man snarled. "Who's going to tell the commander we'll be two hundred weapons short?"

Hugging the inside wall, Apaay followed the bends in the rock until the men's voices faded and all was still. Dark, drifting water and damp, glittering walls. When she reached a split in the river, she swam down the narrower passage and grabbed the rock face to stop her forward motion. Ahead, a wide platform bisected the water like an island. It smelled sweet, which was to say, it smelled of the earth.

Vines and flowers clambered over the island, its quaint bridge connecting it to the network of tunnels and caverns. The Caribou Nomads were a nation of agriculture. With the hot spring so near, Apaay imagined it remained warm enough for the caribou Unua to grow food during the long night, allowing them to sustain their population belowground.

She nearly overlooked the armed guard slouched against the wall. Short, red-brown hair curled tightly around his ears, his skin sharing a similar coloring. Small antlers protruded from the top of his skull. He was slender in the arms and legs. A narrow jaw was all she saw of his face. The rest was concealed by a mask.

Apaay wouldn't be able to pass under the bridge without the guard's notice, but his clothes would be of some use to her.

Apaay slipped beneath the surface and swam the short distance to the edge of the walkway. She held herself under, eyes open, staring upward, and made a small splash. The man arrived to peer into the river, his features distorted by ripples.

Lunging, Apaay snagged the front of his collar and hauled him into the water.

A loud splash echoed. The man thrashed in her grip, his strength overpowering. He shoved her under, and Apaay clawed at his neck, but he was too strong.

Her back hit the wall. Bubbles frothed around her head. Apaay caught one of his antlers, yanking him closer, and slammed his forehead against the rock. He thrashed more violently. She slammed his head against the rock a second time.

The man went limp as blood bloomed. Apaay clawed her way to the surface, one arm wrapped around his torso, and gulped air. Her body shook with adrenaline. That had been too close.

After some difficulty, Apaay managed to drag herself and the unconscious man out of the river and into a niche shielded from view. Her ears strained. Lapping water, echoes of far-off sounds. It meant nothing.

Apaay ignored the prickling unease and hurriedly stripped the man of his clothes. They were made of caribou skins, a smoky brown, with paler hairs speckled throughout. The hairs were short, thin, and lacked an undercoat, so they had been harvested in the summer months. Flowing trousers completed the ensemble. The shoes were too large. She didn't think anyone would be looking at her feet, so she kept her boots on and attached the man's nigana to her hip, the sharpened antler tips hanging downward to ensure she wouldn't accidentally stab herself. Not that she knew how to use it, but a weapon might prove useful.

Lastly, the mask. It was bizarre and had been made from an animal skull. The eyeholes were positioned in a way that did not allow her to see in her periphery. Her skin itched where the mask pressed against her jaw and mouth. That prickling sensation had occurred more often of late.

As she was not a Caribou Nomad, her lack of antlers was cause for concern, but for the wild caribou herds, the males and females shed them in alternating seasons. That might extend to the caribou Unua as well, in which case, it was likely the women were currently antlerless, for they dropped their antlers prior to the calving in late spring. She could only hope.

Apaay chose a tunnel at random, boots squelching with every step. To think she was doing this—infiltrating a stronghold, risking her *life*—for the one person she hated. Was Apaay aware that her actions did not align with her thoughts? Yes. Did she wish to reflect further on the matter? Absolutely not.

Eventually, Apaay realized she wasn't getting anywhere by remaining near the river. She hurried down a different tunnel, the wet hide of her trousers chafing her inner thighs.

"You there."

Apaay faltered, then quickened her pace. The raspy voice echoed from behind.

"Stop!"

Apaay had only a moment to compose herself before the man caught her arm. He was tall, gangly, with a sparse beard sprouting beneath the edge of his mask. A nigana hung from his waist. His antlers had been sharpened to points. "Who are you?"

"I'm new," Apaay stammered in a deeper voice. "They sent me from Nalwa."

Lowering his chin, he peered into her eyes with thinly-veiled suspicion. Then he noticed her dripping state. "Why are you soaked?"

"Oh." Apaay laughed, then broke off with a hacking cough. The man stepped back, grimacing. "Accidentally fell into the river."

She clamped her mouth shut. *Stupid.* If the Face Stealer were here, he'd push her into the river. She wasn't like him. Verbal manipulation did not come easily to her—or at all.

A long silence passed. The man, who she assumed to be a guard, appeared confused, but seemed to push it from his mind. "Well, you're going the wrong way. The gathering's this way."

A mixture of sweat and river water slithered down her back.

Apaay wet her lips, fighting the screaming panic closing her throat. That one misstep might have ruined everything.

"Come," he said. "You'll learn the routine soon enough."

Apaay blew out a silent breath as the guard strode ahead of her. The deeper they traveled underground, the harder it was for her to breathe. All this rock piled atop her head, and she trapped beneath its immense ceiling. Lamplight flickered along the walls. The world above felt far away, its troubles nonexistent.

"What is the gathering about?" she said tentatively as they followed a curved portion of the wall. Voices stretched thin and bare in the distance. "Does it have to do with the war?"

The man stopped and turned toward her. There was a pause. Then something very strange happened. The man's eyes blanked. His previous suspicion just . . . vanished.

In an odd, absent-minded voice, he said, "What war?"

4

Apaay stared at the guard in confusion. His puzzlement seemed genuine. "The war? The one that occurred twenty years ago?" She kept staring. Couldn't think of anything else to say as a queasy feeling slunk through her.

They stood in the middle of a corridor, the promise of brighter light at its end. A little life had returned to those dead eyes. "I don't know what you're talking about," he said in a voice slivered with fear, "but you will speak no more of it."

Apaay searched the man's gaze for any sign of deception. He was utterly serious. "You really have no idea what I'm talking about?"

He did not respond.

That was the first time she recognized something was not right. "Have you heard of Nanuq?"

His gaze cut right, then left. Dark eyes moving behind an otherwise stoic mask. He said, "Nanuq." Like a question. Like he was trying to remember.

"He invaded the Western Territory—"

"Stop." The command rang out. The man stepped close, dropped his voice to a hiss. His eyes were alive now, and crackling like flame. "One more word and I will speak to the commander about this. I don't know what sort of things they tell you in Nalwa, but you should forget them. There is no war." Something like serenity slid over him, and his jaw softened, his words slowed. "We are safe in Nigun."

The man's reprimand left her reeling. He turned heel, and Apaay hurried after him. What did he mean there was no war? He didn't truly believe that, did he? Had he not heard of Nanuq, or Yuki, or the decimation of the Wolf Kingdom? What about how Nanuq had stolen land from the Owl Clan? It must be a joke. It was the only explanation.

Moments later, they entered a massive cavern, so wide she could not see the walls.

It was a forest. *Underground.*

Apaay blinked in peculiarity. She recognized many of the trees—birch and willow and poplar—but with one extreme difference: they grew upside down.

Thousands of trees had rooted in the domed, cavernous ceiling. Below, cutting through the bed of grass, the sleek, mirrored surface of the river tossed back the image of the green ceiling above. It was wondrous. Strange. At least the mask allowed her to ogle the sight without drawing attention to herself.

Yet for the second time, Apaay felt that something wasn't right. The image should have been lovely. Apaay deeply appreciated the North's beauty, but she had never seen anything quite like this. It could not be real.

Apaay glanced around, trying to ignore the feeling of being watched as the atrium began to fill at a rapid pace. She had thought the mask was part of the guards' uniform, but no. Every single caribou Unua wore a mask as well. She saw not one face, only eyes, thousands of them. Approximately half the population lacked antlers, Apaay noted happily, so she wouldn't stand out. Most possessed that brown, curling hair, though many shared coloring like Apaay's. The rush didn't slow. A tight squeeze, shoulder to shoulder, until the air began to warm from the multitude of bodies.

"Keep an eye on them," said the guard she'd accompanied. "The commander hates when they don't cooperate."

Apaay nodded, though she had no idea what he meant by that. And what was his earlier nonsense about the lack of war?

The Caribou Nomads flooded the strange grassland with its strange ceiling and even stranger whispering power. In total, Apaay estimated upward of twenty thousand people in attendance. Everyone stood around in their masks and their human skins, looking at nothing in particular.

Across the atrium, two massive wooden doors opened, each pushed by three men.

The guard straightened, one hand resting on his nigana. Apaay rose onto her toes to see who had entered the room.

A man strode with confidence through the parting crowd. Though he was not particularly muscular, there was certainty in his smooth, dance-like gait. Enormous amber eyes rested beneath a delicate brow. His rack of antlers: proud, branching from the crown of his skull, coated in soft velvet.

He was the only Caribou Nomad not wearing a mask.

The man strode to a raised platform in the center of the room. Now that he stood taller than everyone, Apaay observed how perfectly his furs gleamed in the lamplight, not quite red, not quite gold, but a blending of the two.

"People of the Herd." His whisper held all the power of a roar. "We have reason to celebrate. The world has never been safer, and Nigun is the safest place of all."

Apaay observed the gathering from the corner of her eye. Her heart thumped unsteadily, yet everyone around her looked perfectly calm. An entire crowd of dark, sheened eyes, pupils blown. Every hair on her body prickled in foreboding. They were like stalks of grass swaying in the wind, content to bend or break, their feet rooted.

"The world looks to us for direction," the man continued. "Now more than ever, you hear people speak of our legacy. They speak of the great caribou Unua: master antlersmiths, master agriculturalists. They speak of our even temperament, our fair nature, our honor. The jewel of Nigun grants us these freedoms, just as the mountain's heart offers us sanctuary and peace."

Apaay wished she could see people's expressions behind their masks, but she had the uneasy sense they did not share the same shocked sentiment. The man spoke of peace as if war were not bearing down on them like a storm. Was this the commander the guard had spoken of?

"I ask you, People of the Herd," the man bellowed, "whether food is plentiful here. Are your bellies full each night?"

The room seemed to lean forward as one body. "Yes," said the crowd.

"And are your sleeps restful?"

"Yes."

"And are your children nurtured?"

"Yes."

"And is there anything to fear at the day's end?"

"No."

"And is there war?"

"There is no war," chanted the crowd. "We are safe in Nigun."

Apaay's stomach dropped, the shock of these words like cold water dashed over her skin.

The man went on. "My fellow councilmembers and I have decided that, due to our poor harvest, we will not complete the summer migration to Nalwa this year. Our fields must be plowed, our trees tended to. This is a time of growth. Know that your work is valued, your contributions valued, your presence valued. People of the Herd," he said, voice gaining strength, booming against the walls, "who will lead you to prosperity?"

"The Council," chanted the room. "The Council of Nine."

"Who will ensure no harm befalls your home?"

"The Council of Nine."

"Who will you look to in times of need?"

"The Council of Nine."

"Who always has your best interests at heart?"

"The Council of Nine."

"People of the Herd, who leads the Council?"

"You do, commander."

A pungent scent drifted to her nostrils. Everyone tilted back their heads. Apaay's skin crawled, but she, too, looked up, drawn by morbid curiosity. Something began to lower from the canopy. Long, dangling ropes that twitched with life. Vines, she realized, tipped with pretty white flowers.

The commander appraised the room with a small smile of satisfaction. "Drink," he said, "and let no worries trouble you."

As one, the horde shuffled toward the vines. Apaay watched, horrified, as the caribou Unua latched their mouths onto the flowers blooming from the ends of the vines and drank deeply, eyes fluttering shut in a gruesome form of ecstasy.

Their throats worked. Pale liquid seeped from their flushed mouths. The sight made Apaay's stomach slosh with bitter, churning bile. One woman slumped against the wall, the flower still caught in her mouth. When the woman didn't move, Apaay took a step toward her before realizing that might attract unwanted attention.

The woman's chest rose and fell shallowly. Her pupils were fully dilated.

Someone screamed.

Apaay's head snapped in the direction of the blood-curdling cry. Another scream wailed from behind, and another, and now the air teemed with them, each landing like a puncture wound against her skin. Where was the culprit? The crowd stirred, knocking her sideways. So many bodies. Too many. The mass of gatherers blurred, and shifted like a great wave, dragging Apaay into its undertow.

Someone shoved her forward. Her head slammed against an elbow, and pain ruptured through her skull. Apaay clapped a hand over the sting, bright beneath her palm. But then the pain migrated to her face, and it boiled and burned and she swore fire gnawed away the skin until only bone remained. She might have screamed, whimpered, but the sound was lost to the fear-riddled cries as, body by body, the Herd began to turn on themselves.

An arm torn from someone's shoulder. A throat ripped out, blood spraying in a red mist that coated her lips. It was chaos. Apaay could not take two steps forward without someone attempting to end her life. The Nomads had no awareness of their actions. Their eyes were vacant, their bodies seeking violence despite the numbed minds. A man with two niganas swung his weapons with feeling. Antler blades bit into skin. The guards watched it all unfold from a distance.

Pushing out of the screams came a chilling sound: laughter. Deep laughter that originated from low in the stomach, oily and cruel.

Her eyes cut to the commander. There he stood on the dais, an untouchable figure as the hall descended into madness.

Apaay stumbled backward as the crowd heaved and flowed around her, its current threatening to carry her downstream. Hands latched onto her arms. Apaay screamed, snapping her elbow back into whoever had grabbed hold of her. The grip loosened, and she tore free, only to narrowly avoid amputation as a woman slashed her talq toward those nearest to her. Whatever spell the commander had cast over the crowd, it burst open to reveal the rotting interior.

"Please," someone shouted. "Help me!"

The roaring in Apaay's head amplified. She couldn't think. Couldn't breathe. Where was the exit? How did she get back to the river? A sting drew her attention to the seeping cut on her thigh. *Focus, Apaay.*

Get to a safe place.

Find the spring.

Survive by any means necessary.

Apaay fumbled for the nigana at her waist and swung it wildly to keep others at a distance. Gouging a path through the thickest of the fighting, she managed to reach the edge of what was quickly transforming into a stampede. Blood darkened the river and smeared the high grass. There was an arm. Just an arm, lying there, no body to claim it. The protruding bone gleamed starkly white, the skin ragged like a torn seam.

Apaay vomited.

A man, in his attempt to avoid impalement on a pair of antlers, stumbled into her. She snapped upright. Slapped his face to get his attention.

"Get out," she screamed. "Go!" But the man's eyes, huge and black and swallowing, sparked no life.

In the end, she couldn't save him, or any of them. There was no time.

With the guards distracted by the abhorrent spectacle, Apaay slipped from the hall and down a deserted corridor, glancing over her shoulder to make sure she wasn't being followed. She selected the tunnels whose air grew heavy with water vapor. They took her from the butchering, down a winding, well-lit path, the yelps and groans growing distant. It lulled her into a feeling of safety. There was no violence here, no bloodshed.

Apaay was so distracted by the tranquility that she nearly walked right past the doors.

Like two panels of blue sky, the doors seemed to drink in the darkness. The Pale One had claimed the doors were guarded, but the gathering took precedent. An odd yearning spilled through her. Apaay could not look away. In her eyes, these doors were the world. And the world had never been so within reach.

"Lost, are you?"

The lilting voice came from behind, a question of quiet curiosity. She had not heard anyone approach.

Apaay slackened her mouth, let her eyes go unfocused as she turned to face the commander, who studied her with his head tilted slightly. The proud arch of his antlers rose upward and outward from his skull, dusky hair curling around his ears. Apaay counted the tines. Four branches with no less than five tines per branch. She had never seen antlers this large. Somehow, he managed to maintain his straight-backed posture as if the weight did not bother him.

"Oh." Apaay looked around, as if she hadn't noticed her wanderings. "I suppose I am." She laughed, though her heart did a rapid *tap, tap* against her breastbone. She bowed slightly. "Apologies, commander. I'm a new recruit sent from Nalwa."

He offered her a small smile. "How interesting. I was not aware they had sent new recruits." He inhaled deeply through his wide nostrils. "They are beautiful, are they not?" he asked, referring to the doors.

Apaay didn't know why the question spiked alarm. She considered her response carefully. "They are the world."

His eyes crinkled with surprise. "Come." He took her hand and looped it over his forearm, drawing her back down the hall. "This is no place for a young woman. You're missing the gathering."

A bead of sweat slid down Apaay's temple. He knew she was not a guard. Neither was she caribou Unua. Why was he the only one who had noticed? Why didn't he capture her? Question her? The raucous noise, the screams, drew nearer, and she feared this man would sense her fingers trembling against his skin. What would he do, now that he knew her secret?

They stood at the mouth of one of the chamber's many entrances, her hand clasped warmly atop the commander's arm, as if they shared an affection for one another. Beyond, the entirety of the Caribou Nomad population obliterated itself as if war was not stirring, was not evolving, shrouding the land in growing darkness. The lack of awareness was appalling. They had no idea what awaited them aboveground. And they would never learn, so long as the nectar made them forget.

"What do you think?" he asked.

Apaay cleared her throat and pushed up her mask as it began to slide down her sweaty nose. His grip on her hand tightened, as if sensing she might flee. "About what?" she whispered.

"About all this." He made a sweeping motion toward the bloodletting.

"I think it's . . ." She trailed off, unsure of what to say. Watched as bodies fell and did not rise.

"Frightening."

Apaay fought the urge to look at him, afraid of what she'd see. Yes, it was frightening. She did not understand it.

"I've heard rumors."

"Oh?" the commander said politely, scanning the room.

"They say Nanuq is on the move."

A muscle leaped beneath where the pads of her fingers rested against his forearm. Apaay stared straight ahead. This place felt like a sickness. Engorged, so full she thought it might burst, like a blister. Were these people with Nanuq, or against him?

The mask slid further down her face. Again, she pushed it up.

"Come, my dear." The commander led her to one of the vines hanging from the forest canopy. "You must be thirsty."

Before Apaay realized what was happening, he shoved a flower into her mouth.

Sweet, hot liquid splashed across her tongue. Apaay tried spitting it out, but she found herself swallowing instead. It tasted so pleasant that she swallowed again, hardly aware of the numbness spreading across her face.

The commander pulled the vine free. "How do you feel now?" he asked kindly. "Better?"

"This isn't right," Apaay slurred. "War is . . . here. Nanuq will come. Take your people. Become . . . fully man." While she may have believed the words once, she now wondered what they meant. There was such a thick haze to the air. Apaay reached up, trailing her fingers through the hanging vines. War? Nanuq who?

"There is no trouble," intoned the commander. "There is no war. Drink," he said, pressing the flower against her mouth.

She did.

5

The story of Naga and Tor began, as most stories do, with a birth. It ended with a knife in the back.

The tale went like so: Naga and Tor, sister and brother, twins. They lived on the coast where the water between the islands froze solid in winter, allowing travel between one community and the next. Growing up, they spent much time together. As they matured, however, their relationship changed. Tor could no longer ignore his sister's beauty. He grew jealous of the men she bedded, those she drew away from the nightly celebrations. So one evening, he snuck into her ice house, using the darkness to shield his transgression, and took what he believed to be his.

This continued for some time. Naga, who did not know what man continued to abuse her body, created a plan. After extinguishing her oil lamp one evening, she pinched her fingers around the wick so the soot transferred onto her skin. When the man entered her ice house, she rubbed the soot from her fingers onto his face, marking him as the offender.

Afterward, Naga rejoined the celebration, searching for the man with the soot-marked skin. And she found him. But when she looked into the eyes of her brother, shame twisting his features, she fled, so fast and so hard her feet lifted from the ground, and she flew into the sky. Tor, desperate to catch his sister before she disappeared forever, threw his knife, which caught her in the back.

Naga fell. She hit the water below, and the sea tossed her body into the rocks like driftwood. Tor watched his sister's blood water the coast with horror and guilt. If his family learned what he had done, they would never forgive him. So he fled, traveled west on his kayak, far from his village, never to be seen from again.

This was Naga: vindictive, never to be soothed, and frosty even in the summer months. On this day, she was especially violent. Standing atop the tallest turret of the sprawling cliffside edifice, Kenai peered over the sea wall to watch the waves thrash below. They hurled themselves bodily against the cliffside, again, again. As a boy, Kenai had played in Tor's surf. Its waters moved from southerly lands, dragging the warmth with it. He and Sita, his sister, would swim out until the rocky bottom dropped off, waiting for Numiak to paddle out to them. But that had been a long time ago, before everything had changed.

Mist clung to his bare arms. The sleeveless, sealskin maq beaded with droplets that could not penetrate the waterproof barrier. The extensive, seaside structure clung to the cliff like a barnacle. It was full of winding stairs and heightened columns, spreading courtyards and tiered balconies, the white stone glowing dimly amidst the low-hanging clouds. He would expect nothing less of Ariviat, capital of the Eastern Territory and home to the Sea Mother.

Kenai touched the scar puckering his upper back where Apaay had stabbed him. It had healed, though the skin remained tender to the touch. And it always would if his facial scarring, the ruination of his left eye, was any indication of how poorly his body healed itself.

Following the events that had unfolded on the outskirts of Talguk, he and Yuki had sheltered here for his recuperation. Had the Owl Clan not arrived with reinforcements, he would have killed the Face Stealer. Even now, Kenai could not say for certain whether Numiak was alive. The spear points had been tipped with poison made from urchin venom, but his brother had a way of cheating death time and again.

Two months he had been confined here. It was a home, but it

was not *his* home. He had been waiting all this time, and he was still waiting.

With one last glance toward the sea, Kenai descended the sea-slickened stairs that wrapped around the exterior of the spire to the lower level. In Unana and Talguk and the outlying towns in the Western Territory, the homes were constructed of gray stone. This structure imitated the texture of dead coral, its narrow grooves lending it an appearance of constant motion. Sea spray dampened the pathways and tossed pale reflections of the towering structures back at him.

His footsteps echoed sharply in the vaulted passage. This wide, open space lacked roofs, even walls on occasion, offering an uninterrupted view of the sea. No doors, only rounded openings that allowed one to pass between rooms. Shells and corals and barnacles crusted the walls, the floors.

As Kenai entered one of the courtyards, he noticed Yuki climbing the stairs from the shore below, her skin agleam with salt water. Quite helplessly, his pulse spiked. Twenty years they had been parted, and Kenai looked at her as if for the very first time.

Upon spotting Kenai, Yuki brushed aside a coil of dripping hair and came toward him. "Hello, Kenai." The edge in her expression softened.

He waited, unable to approach. She dictated the where and when and how of their meetings. When she rested her gloved hands on his waist, only then did he curve his fingers over her slender shoulders and dip his mouth to hers. The salt encrusting her lips passed onto his tongue.

Yuki pulled away first.

Wet, spiky black lashes shaded her oil-slick eyes. She was exquisite and cruel, with bone structure like the cut of broken coral, and sharp, even teeth. They were, after all this time, together. It was enough.

"I was hoping we could share dinner this evening," he said, though it was naught but a form of expression, considering the sun never set. The last few days she'd been absent, away on business. He'd asked the cook to prepare something special for the night of her return.

She offered him a smile that was uncomfortably pitying. "While that certainly sounds quaint, I must be leaving soon. Nanuq has requested my presence."

He ignored the sinking sensation in his gut. Yuki played an important role in the war effort. He refused to cage her, no matter how he wished she would stay. "You met with him last week."

"And now he has asked for me again."

The barnacles attached to the curve of her neck shimmered. He wanted to touch them, explore their unique texture, but the risk of her ire was too great. "Then I will join you."

"No."

Kenai frowned.

Yuki adjusted the netting draped across her shoulders, peering at him with the air of someone who studied a particularly complicated problem and had yet to think of a solution. "Now that I've returned to my roots, things will begin to move quickly. There can be no distractions."

He bristled at the implication. "I'm not a distraction." If not for him, Yuki would still be land-bound, wearing the face of a child, separated from the seals and whales and fish—her children, born from the severed tips of her fingers.

She smiled, briefly touched his arm, then pulled away. "Kenai, you have to understand. Nanuq has a vision. Everything and everyone has their place."

She spoke to him as if he were a child. He was not a child. He was a man. A man who had done much for her. He had given up everything—his home, his family, his life's work—for her. They had loved each other. They still loved each other.

"I have stayed by your side," he argued. "I returned your true face to you. I have never, not once, abandoned you."

Not like your father.

In the end, Kenai kept those words to himself. Yuki would punish him for the slight, but all knew the tale of how a man, desperate for his life, had selfishly cast his daughter out to sea.

"Kenai." Her blunted fingertips, encased in a sleek black material, rested on his arm. "You are not unimportant to me, but there is a clear hierarchy at work here. Nanuq is a king. I am the Sea Mother. This is the natural order of things."

The feeling of being caught in a storm swept through him, and there was no shelter for miles. How had this happened? Minutes ago, they'd been kissing, his heart the lightest it had been in months. Now, he wondered what had gone wrong. This wasn't their first argument. Each left an increasingly bitter taste in his mouth.

"I wish . . ." He shook his head.

Yuki turned his face toward hers. "What do you wish?"

He wondered if she would understand. "I wish you would find value in me the way you do Nanuq."

A moment passed before she spoke. "The question is not if I find you valuable. The question is if Nanuq finds you valuable. Prove your worth to him, and he will reward you in this new world he builds."

He'd hoped for a different response. Reassurance, at the very least. He didn't care for Nanuq's opinions. Yuki had always thought highly of the man who ruled the Polar Bear Empire. She had her own motives for aligning with him. There was unfinished business between the Sea Mother and her father. She had never spoken of her motives aloud, but Kenai had pieced together bits of information, the rare moment of vulnerability. In helping Nanuq conquer the North, Yuki would showcase her prowess and might. Always searching for her father's approval. They had that in common.

He turned to study the breaking waves. If this would please Yuki, maybe it was worth the attempt. "How?"

She pulled an oiled scroll from her kelp skirt and handed it to him. "You once bore the honor of Numiak's second-in-command, leading your Pack unit in his stead with valor and respect. Do so again, and Nanuq will reward you handsomely."

He studied the scroll with sudden weariness. Decades before, he'd been a soldier, green as a leaf in spring, willing to die for his Pack and nation.

After his father's murder, he'd been a soldier, weathered and hardened, with vengeance on his mind. He'd played Numiak easily. No one had suspected a traitor in their midst until the day of the Wolf Kingdom's invasion, and by then, it was too late.

Kenai was no longer that man. He was older, and tired. He had but one eye. He wondered, sometimes, what there was left to fight for.

Still, he unrolled the pieces of parchment. It consisted of a map, supplies, a list of recruits: Yuki's followers, the seal Unua, men and women both. The unit was stationed near the northern border of the Central Territory, about one hundred miles from its capital.

"The commander of this unit has been killed," Yuki said. "Tortured by the owl Unua for trespassing onto their territory. Thus, they are without a leader. I'd like for you to lead them. This task is very important. Nanuq seeks the polar bear Unua that fled their homeland. They must be brought to justice."

He ran his thumb across a corner of the parchment, considering. *Justice.* He had been here before. Even now, he still remembered the too-sharp taste of the word in his mouth. Should he accept this mission, it would take him far from his beloved. But should he succeed in his task, Nanuq would see him as worthy. More importantly, Yuki would see him as worthy, too.

"I will go," he said.

"Then make haste, my love. War waits for no one."

← 6 →

They began with a blade. A small, slender piece of metal that carved shapes into Ila's skin. They took turns, the men. That guard and his faceless men, who returned day after day until the pain reduced her to a mindless animal. Fists pounded flesh and snapped bones. A whip peeled open the skin of her back. They broke her into smaller and smaller pieces so she could not walk, not crawl, not sit, not move. Yet somehow, they never touched her hands. A small mercy.

The insults the men hurled at her were almost as severe as the physical assault. Horrible words meant to belittle her.

"Answer me, dog!" A blow to the face, and Ila momentarily blacked out.

Dog, she thought in a rare moment of lucidity. A dog was chained, but a wolf was free.

In the days or weeks that followed, Ila weathered the storm, the bitter, spewing poison.

Where is the Face Stealer?

What is he planning?

Where are the rest of your people?

She told him nothing. They could snap her bones, but never her spirit. If there was a chance, any chance at all, that the Face Stealer could organize a force large enough to stave off Nanuq, she would not be the reason why they failed.

Ila thought Tulimaq had lied to that guard to protect her, but something must have changed, or she had misinterpreted the situation. Sometimes, she thought she recognized him standing in the corner of her cell, a blurred shape, slender and rigid in his stance, but she could never focus long enough to be certain. Her eyes drifted closed. When she managed to pry them open again, the Tulimaq-shaped shadow was gone.

Ila didn't think the punishments could get any worse, but they did. They stripped her bare and led her by a looped collar around her neck to the clearing, the holes like hundreds of unmarked, unfilled graves, and mutilated her back until she slid to the ground, unconscious.

Had every prisoner endured the same horrific treatment? Although ignorant of many things, she was learning, opening her eyes to the fragmented edges of her reality. Time lost all meaning to her. They broke her legs so she could not run, then had a healer mend the breaks so they could do it all over again. She wouldn't break. No matter what she endured, she wouldn't break. She owed it to herself. They could not break her.

Ila, propped against the cell wall, sensed someone approaching. It may have been the sixth day or the sixteenth. A tremor moved through her useless arms. Her fingernails were torn bloody from trying to claw her way to freedom.

The door opened.

Fresh pain tore up her spine as she tried to shift upright. The puffy skin around her eyes reduced her vision to slits. Two figures. One large, one slim. The guard she'd named Birthmark jerked her up by the arm. Ila thought she might have screamed.

One moment, the man was lifting Ila to her feet, and the next, he was slammed against the wall by a wave of power that blasted from Tulimaq's staff, the former combat master pressing its fine blade to the older man's throat. Ila spat blood, fighting to lift her head as the world spun and the ground lurched.

The guard's expression splintered into one of insanity. A fine line opened beneath the shard of bone, and a single drop of blood rolled down the brown skin of his neck. "Tulimaq."

Two heartbeats passed before Tulimaq stepped back, lowering his weapon with a glance at his hands, as if he had not been fully aware of his actions. Birthmark lashed out, the blow knocking Tulimaq into the back wall. "Overstep again, and I will put a blade through her chest." He stepped toe to toe with the smaller man. "Am I clear?"

After a pause, Tulimaq nodded.

The man shoved him aside. "Get me a nigana," he said.

How many ways could a person break?

Just one more.

← →

The reverberation of a door slamming open startled Ila awake. She lay curled in a ball, wheezing, her arms covered in old scabs from where they had mangled the flesh. It was too painful to sit, too painful to stand, but she managed to turn her head a fraction, squinting.

Tulimaq stood beyond the bars, flamelight outlining him in red.

A slow breath rattled her lungs as she sucked in air. At least three ribs were broken. The guards had beaten her within an inch of her life because she still, after days or weeks or an eternity enduring this pain in silence, would not reveal the Face Stealer's whereabouts or his intentions. But Ila wondered if soon it wouldn't matter anymore.

"I did not think you were this foolish of a person."

With only a single torch burning on the wall, it was difficult to read Tulimaq's lips through the gloom, so she struggled to piece together his words. He held his staff at his side. No sign of her mother's talq, though he'd no doubt stashed it somewhere far from her reach. She hated that he had touched something so precious to her.

Ila would not speak to him. She would not acknowledge him. She would lie here and wish him away, and close her eyes and think of Apaay, and Kaan, and Ro, and the Wood and its enchantments, and maybe, *maybe* it would grant her a shred of peace.

"All you have to do is tell the guards where the Face Stealer is," Tulimaq went on. "The pain would stop."

Ila pushed into a seated position. As it turned out, she was too angry to remain complacent. She had much to say to Tulimaq. This seemed as good a time as any. *And turn traitor like you did?* If she'd had the energy to scoff, she would have. *No.*

"Then you choose suffering."

Ila remembered the give of Kimmir's flesh beneath her fingers as she attempted to stop the Face Stealer's spy from bleeding to death, a man who had spent almost a decade of his life posing as the enemy. Courage was a choice. She was choosing it now, and she would choose it tomorrow, and she would choose it until the day she died.

She had not seen Tulimaq in all the days of her torture. How cowardly of him. She remembered seeing him for the first time, the ease in which he'd swung his staff. She had thought he looked strong then.

Do you know, she signed, *what my life was like before the Wood?* Her hands were the only things that did not pain her. *It was like this.* She gestured to her surroundings: an overflowing pail of fecal matter, rough stone floor, and a darkness so complete she no longer knew whether it was night or day. Imprisonment, that old acquaintance.

I came to the Wood, naive and frightened, but open to what the world could teach me. I did not know the world as you did. I did not see its dark corners. But I learned. My heart opened, slowly. Her eyes lifted and held his, and in them, there sparked a question. *I thought we were friends.*

She had communicated not one word to Tulimaq in nearly two months of travel. She was speaking to him now.

"You thought wrong," he said.

It wasn't the first time Ila wished she could hear his voice. She wondered how his anger or frustration would translate into sound.

He said, "You're willing to die for people you hardly know? Because these men will kill you. They will draw out the pain and make you wish for death. Is that what you want? Numiak, Kaan, Ro—you owe them nothing. You can free yourself. You can make this stop."

She clenched her teeth as she straightened against the wall. *I owe them everything. I was given a home, a chance to start over. Kaan is my mentor and friend.*

"And Apaay?" He knew how easily their friendship had crumbled when placed under pressure. It was he, after all, who had suggested she let go.

It had hurt. Of course it had. Maybe it always would to some extent. Apaay had chosen her path. Ila could not change that. She had accepted the path would lead her friend to a better place, even if Ila could not follow. *Without Apaay, I would not have made it out of the labyrinth alive. I owe her everything.*

He looked away. She managed to catch the shape of his mouth when he said, "Tomorrow, the men will use the whip if you do not give them answers." He turned back. A shock rolled through her at the intensity of his stare. "You have a choice."

What is the choice, exactly? It didn't feel like a choice. It felt like an inevitability.

"You can choose to save yourself."

Save herself? What would it matter if those she loved were dead? Ila shook her head. She was tired. She wanted to rest.

You had a choice, too, she said. *You chose to betray the Face Stealer, betray me.* Her next breath felt strangled. *You chose not to step in when those men were ripping me apart.*

His throat worked, the skin sheened in sweat, smooth and unblemished. She sensed his need to speak, the hesitation that indicated one response had been exchanged for another. "I once told you the world was cruel. Now do you believe me?"

He was not wrong. The world *was* cruel, and Ila could not have imagined it to this extent. But it was also lovely and soft and tender. The world could not choose to be. It just *was*.

Ila stood on the threshold of understanding. A revelation.

Tulimaq did not know how to connect with others. Isolation had taught him to always remain on guard, had shown a single, narrow, unchanging view, which he held tighter than anything. He stood with people and felt alone because the world as he saw it told him he was alone.

Ila found that thought terribly sad.

I don't know anything about the Face Stealer's whereabouts.

He curled his fingers around the bars. From this angle, it looked as if he were the one imprisoned, not Ila. "I'm not here about the Face Stealer," he said without breaking eye contact.

Tulimaq unlocked the door, stepped into her space, and strode forward until the toes of his boots hit her bent legs.

Reaching down, he grabbed the front of her grubby attire and hauled her upright, shoving her against the wall. Ila whimpered as her body throbbed from the ache of many beatings.

"This is what's going to happen," he said. "You're going to tell me where your family is. If you're alive, then there are others as well."

Ila struggled to process the change in subject. He wasn't inquiring about the Face Stealer, but rather her family. Did that guard, Birthmark, know of Tulimaq's whereabouts? Was this why he had brought her to the labor camp—to torture information from her?

He shook her so hard her mouth fell open. "Look at me."

She did. The trouble was, Ila no longer knew who she was looking at.

Tulimaq produced a knife, tucking the point under her chin. "Tell me."

She spat in his face.

He didn't flinch, though the tip dug in a little deeper. "I will do it, Ila. I will hurt you if you don't tell me the truth. Tell me where they are!" He slammed a palm against the wall above her head.

They're dead! I already told you! Those words gave her the strength to shove him back a step.

"I don't believe you."

His fist caught the edge of her jaw.

Her head throbbed, her eyes burned, but she bared her teeth and lunged at Tulimaq, fingernails sharpening, burying past clothes and into skin. Ila hardly noticed the change. Power ruptured from the end of Tulimaq's staff and plowed into her sternum, sending her crashing into the bars. She felt neither pain, nor weakness, nor fatigue. Ila was up, charging toward him, swinging a fist toward his face.

Tulimaq slapped it aside easily. "Sloppy."

He redirected Ila's next attack, this one wilder than the first. Her shoulder slammed into the wall, and she ducked to avoid Tulimaq's counterattack, dropping and rolling to her feet behind him, huffing for breath. He appeared almost bored by the scuffle. Ila knew better. The less emotion he displayed, the deeper and more complete was his rage.

She struck low toward his abdomen. He twisted, and her fist glanced off. The light caught his mouth, the disapproving frown.

"Weeks of training and this is all you have to show for it?"

With every insult tossed her way, that fury honed to a deadlier point. Ila imagined her mind as a blade. She sought flaws in Tulimaq's shield, and when she finally landed a blow that made him stumble, dark pleasure rippled through her.

Not once did his face change during their scuffle. That only enraged Ila further. What did he feel? *Did* he feel? She thought he did, sometimes, when he allowed himself to. When he did not view that vulnerability as a weakness.

A hard, fast strike cut toward his face. Even as his forearm snapped up to block, Ila was sinking low, slamming up, driving her elbow into his abdomen. She landed two more hits before Tulimaq caught her arms. "Enough. You remember. I know you remember."

What are you talking about? she demanded, panting for air. *Remember what?* Truly, she hadn't a clue.

He caught her jaw, forcing her to stare at the roiling tumult in his eyes. It hurt to do so. How had she never seen this level of pain from him before? It was as if she had finally breached a wall and could now see the shredded heart of that fortified interior.

"I told you the story of a little boy, how he and his mother fled their home to seek a new life. But one day the boy's mother left camp—and didn't come back."

Ila's eyes widened.

"Night and day, the boy waited. Weeks after her disappearance, the camp received a message. His mother had gone searching for food that morning because the stores were low, but didn't realize she had crossed into wolf Unua territory. Your people—your parents—" He was visibly shaking. "—thought she was a spy sent from Nanuq."

Ila tried to swallow. In a way, it felt as if she were seeing him for the very first time.

"They didn't believe her when she pleaded her innocence. Why would they, when she smelled of the enemy? They tore out her throat, never knowing she'd left behind a young son who hadn't a chance to say goodbye."

Seconds before his fist made contact with her cheek, she saw it. Something glittering in his burning gaze, something behind the mask that had broken through.

Pain ricocheted through her. Ila's back slammed against the wall, and she forced her eyes open, wanting to see him, wanting proof that what he felt was real, that he *did* feel something.

Tulimaq, listen to me. I'm sorry about your mother, but it wasn't—me.

His fingers crushed her windpipe. Her throat seared with the need to inhale. Ila didn't know how to fight him like this. Anything she said, he either discounted or thought to be a lie. A numbing sensation spread through her face as she took her last gasp of air and lifted her hands.

I suppose . . . I shouldn't be surprised. Her fingers twitched as the world darkened. *After all, you are your father's son.*

← 7 →

Apaay's head pounded as if someone had taken a hammer to her skull. A thick, gloopy substance pasted her eyes shut, and heat picked at the skin of her face. She groaned, pressing her cheek to the damp earth. It didn't help. If anything, the pain worsened. It ravaged and tore deep. It was agony, it was—

Gone. It was gone.

A great, rasping breath expelled from her lungs. Apaay opened her eyes.

It was a dream. A dream of hanging trees bursting with sweet blossoms, and cricket song, and tender green.

But the dream didn't last. It warped as the salted odor of recent bloodshed invaded her nostrils. Cautiously, Apaay sat up and looked around. The perfect, glassy surface of the river. Bodies sprawled in the grass, heavy and pliant in sleep. The lingering taste of sugar on her tongue. Rancid, now.

She didn't see any blood. It was utterly peaceful here, her heart light and free of worry. So why did she smell it?

Unless . . . *Was* she dreaming? Apaay pinched her arm. No, this was real. She shook her head. Strange. How very strange.

Memories of the night before returned, piece by piece. She was in the underground city of Nigun. There had been a gathering.

For what, she could not recall, but it had been a merry time, and welcome.

Apaay pushed to her feet, which throbbed with tenderness. She was barefoot. Another oddity. The caribou Unua didn't stir as she searched and found her boots in the grass, along with many abandoned articles of clothing. The initial confusion of what had occurred last night faded, and only a sense of urgency to return to the Face Stealer lingered.

She slipped from the hall, turning left and right, tension rising with each footfall. It was as though her body knew something her mind had forgotten. Something about this place. The strange lack of wind.

Once Apaay reached the river, she slipped into the warm current and followed it upstream to the supply area. Then she was crossing the grassland, plunging into the shaded Aatu, swerving past patchy undergrowth, hopping over roots that heaved from the ground like waves. She couldn't remember where they had made camp. Only knew it was somewhere nearby.

"Apaay?"

There he was. She crashed through a bush, found the Face Stealer nestled between the roots of an old pine. His eyes shone a muted silver in the half-light of the forest floor, as though a layer of dust coated them. Apaay sighed in relief.

"Where were you?" he demanded.

"What?" She plopped onto the ground, breathless. The forest greens were deeply saturated, swollen with color, and the warm breeze lay cool against her wet skin. "I was in Nigun."

"Apaay." He bit off her name like a piece of rotten meat. "You said you'd be back within a day."

Wherever this venomous tone came from, she didn't appreciate it. "I was." Wet strands of hair adhered to her neck. She peeled them free, wringing out the dripping water.

The Face Stealer stared at her in deepening alarm. "It's been three."

"What?" That was impossible. It was evening, or as close to evening as one could get when the sun never set. No more than half a day had passed since her departure. She thought of the revelers, asleep in the grass. Three days. The absurdity of that statement made her smile. "Numiak, it's still the same day—"

A sharp inhalation. He struggled to straighten against the trunk, his movements sluggish with pain. "Look at me."

Apaay laughed.

"I said look at me," he barked.

Finally, she did, her amusement dimming.

"Your pupils are dilated. What happened to you?"

Now *she* was confused. "Nothing. I don't know why you're getting upset."

"You never call me Numiak."

Of course she called him Numiak. That was his name. What else would she call him?

Apaay felt the skin of her face scrunching into tight, painful folds. An image glimmered as though in her periphery: the shape of a name in her mouth. Face Stealer. Demon. He was right. She never called him by his given name. The eagerness to move faded, and her limbs settled.

"Tell me exactly what happened," he said.

"Nothing happened. I found the river. It goes straight into the city. The water is warm, the plants plentiful." She smiled at him, hardly noticing how his gaze narrowed further, a cautious perusal of her face before it caught, briefly, on her mouth. "The thing is, we were all wrong. There is no war." And what a relief it was to discover this. "We are safe in Nigun."

"Safe." He was still staring at her. Black strands of hair lay tangled on his shoulders, stuck through with leaves and twigs, and dirt smudged his chin, the side of his neck.

Her lips sank into a deep curve. More laughter fizzled out, and when his fingers curled around her wrist, a different form of pleasure overcame her, the sparks igniting where his skin touched hers. Apaay's breath hitched.

He stiffened.

Their eyes locked. The motion snapped something in her,

brought her a little closer to clarity, to the why and how of where she was.

The Face Stealer pulled his hand away, gazing at the spot where he had touched her. "You have heightened sensitivity," he murmured. "Did you eat or drink anything while you were there?"

Apaay recalled a spinning sensation, sweetness exploding on her tongue. Again, she smelled blood. "I did." She felt his tension as if it were inside her own skin. What exactly had she consumed, and why was the Face Stealer so adamant about receiving an answer?

"Apaay."

"I'm trying," she snapped. The answer appeared as flashes of light and shade. "They had these . . . vines. With white flowers on the ends." Peculiar, serpentine forms. "Everyone drank from them."

"What did they drink?"

"I don't know. Nectar? It tasted sweet."

"How much did you drink?"

"I don't know." Apaay rubbed a tender spot on her forehead. "The trees grow from the ceiling in Nigun, did you know?"

"Really." He sounded more concerned than intrigued.

Something else tugged at her. The color red. Why couldn't she remember?

"Why are you looking at me like that?" Apaay asked.

He waited a moment before answering. She suspected it pained him to speak. A few days ago he had been complaining of a swollen throat. "You were drugged."

"Drugged? That's—" *Absurd*, she nearly said, but he wouldn't lie to her, and she felt the shadows gathering at her back.

"When I touched you . . ." He trailed off, though his eyes didn't stray from hers. "Did anything else happen?"

"I don't remember." Whatever pleasantness she'd experienced after wakening, it was fading. There were the forest sounds, overly harsh, scraping against her ears, the air like claws on her skin. "No, wait." Apaay touched her cheeks. Without the mask, she expected her skin to be cool to the touch, but it singed as though from fever. "There was pain in my face. An itchy, tingling feeling, like a burn."

When she had first slipped on the guard's mask. A second time, moments before waking in the grass.

"Has this happened before?" Cool, careful words.

"Once," Apaay said in surprise. "In the Wood. Before I entered the door that held your memories in the library."

Worry flashed in the shifting hues of the Face Stealer's eyes and died like roots under frost. "I need you to remember what else happened, Apaay. Think about what you heard. About Nanuq, the war—"

"There is no war."

"Yes, there is." He circled those long fingers around her wrist again. The Face Stealer's skin was a shade darker than hers, the hair on his forearm crisp and black. It was a strong-looking wrist. She wanted to snort her amusement at thinking such a thought, and couldn't, because he was touching her, and she wasn't sure that she wanted him to remove his fingers. "Try to remember."

A new, seductive quality threaded his voice. "Maybe I could," Apaay shot back, her heartbeat loud in her ears, "if you stopped distracting me."

His mouth softened, on the cusp of folding into a smile. "This is distracting you?" He loosened his hold, the fingers looped like bracelets: warm, heavy, firm. He trailed one fingertip up the inside of her arm.

The need to shift away from him clapped through her. Why did she want to recoil? Apaay clamped her eyes shut, trying to remember. Her skin puckered at his touch. Pleasure on the point of pain.

With a gasp, Apaay yanked her arm away. She remembered.

"The war. I mentioned the war to one of the guards. He didn't know what I was talking about." She had a disturbing notion that the entire population of Nigun had no idea. "There was a man. They called him the commander. He said the North has never been safer. He said Nigun was the safest place of all. And then . . ." Her stomach roiled. Apaay repressed that old fear. She wouldn't be able to think clearly otherwise. "It was awful."

"What was?" The words, clipped with impatience.

Apaay didn't want to relive that moment, but she must. Moving forward, she and the Face Stealer needed to know exactly what kind of situation they were walking into. A violent one, certainly. "It was a massacre. I don't know how it happened. One moment people were drinking from the vines, and the next, they were tearing each other apart." The blood. She could not forget the blood.

"Did you see what caused the massacre?"

"No. I was trying to get away. I found the doors to the spring, but the commander stopped me before I could enter. He knew I wasn't caribou Unua."

Numiak's eyebrows crept toward his sweat-dampened hairline. "He still let you go?"

It was strange. The deeper she dug into this mystery, the more Apaay believed something terrible had befallen Nigun. "Maybe he didn't think I would remember anything."

"Or he is curious of you."

Which might place her in further danger. She knew nothing of this commander, but clearly, he knew something of her.

The Face Stealer asked, "Who was the man who spoke and what did he look like?"

She described his manner of dress, how he commanded the room. *People of the Herd*, he'd said.

"There was no one else?"

She shook her head. "Should there have been?"

The Face Stealer closed his eyes. A muscle twitched in his cheek. "The Council of Nine governs the Caribou Nomads. The absence of the other councilmembers does not bode well."

"You think something happened to them."

"Yes. I just don't know what. The caribou Unua have been isolated for many decades. It is difficult to say whether the councilmembers' absence occurred at the beginning of their isolation, or only recently. If this commander is leading them astray, we might have to look for reinforcements elsewhere."

Except there were none. They had the Owl Clan on their side, but the Seal Colonies would side with Yuki, who had aligned herself with Nanuq and the Polar Bear Empire. And the Wolf Kingdom was no more.

Apaay studied his wan face, weighed their options, and reached a decision. "I'm going back." For the spring water, and to learn more of whatever sickness plagued this nation. With Nanuq growing in power, every able-bodied person had the potential to serve as an ally to their cause, and to turn the tide of this war.

Currently, Ro acted as their intermediary to the Owl Clan. As the Avi's general, he worked closely with his father to secure additional forces, however thinly spread they might be, and to oversee the Flock. Ro had also promised to secure a translator for the note Numiak carried, the one they'd found clutched in the stiff, frozen fingers of a dead man from Across the Sea months and months ago. But they hadn't heard from Ro in weeks.

"I know." With agonizing lethargy, Numiak shifted to a more comfortable position. By the end, he was a sweaty, shaky mess.

Apaay knelt at his side. "I'm going to check your wounds." He grunted, and she carefully peeled away the front of his maq, the thin hide sticking momentarily to the coagulation of blood, bandages, and puffy, inflamed skin. The stomach wound seeped continually, no matter how many times Apaay drained the infection. Another wound marked his thigh, his calf. Three separate points where Kenai had stabbed Numiak with poison-tipped harpoons. She wondered what would kill him first: the infection, or the poison.

"That bad?"

Apaay pulled down the hem so it covered the gruesome sight. "I could change the bandages, but I don't know if it will make a difference." When he didn't reply, she said, "Numiak."

A faint, pained smile shadowed his mouth. "It sounds nice when you say it," he murmured, eyelashes fanned against the high planes of his cheekbones. "My name."

Apaay didn't know what to say to that unexpected admittance. "You really are dying, aren't you?"

A chuckle rasped out and faded like dew under sun. "Will you miss me when I'm gone?"

Her heartbeat throbbed in her ears, the tips of her fingers. It was a question she could not answer. "You're not going to die," she said. "I won't let you." Then: "At least, not until you fulfill the blood oath."

"Is that so?" Even circling death, Apaay heard the menace lace his tone. "I think I would die just to spite you."

← 8 →

Apaay spent the next three days traveling between Nigun and the Aatu. The river, the gathering, the blood, the exhaustion—all led to a blanketing numbness, her heartbeat never steady, always spiking in sporadic intervals. She must save the Face Stealer. She must ensure her own survival. Above all, she must not despair.

With Numiak's strength waning, Apaay set a few snares, which she checked morning and evening. After the near-disaster of her first infiltration, Apaay had more care the second time around. As if on a hunt, she would wait. She would breathe anticipation and let the passing time rest upon her shoulders. She would not think about how precious that time was. Or how little of it remained.

In contrast, there was no sense of urgency among the caribou Unua. They spent mornings in the gardens, digging into the rich, fertile earth or clipping away deadened brush, which they piled up and left to rot, for reasons unknown. They drifted on the river and collected antlers from some distant place to forge weaponry, mouths slack, eyes slack, faces slack. Their day-to-day routine was odd, listless, with a drowsy feel that never truly lifted.

Apaay wondered about Nalwa, their sister capital and summer residence. With no migration this season, did that mean the city sat empty? Did Nigun provide enough food to sustain them through the long night, and beyond?

As Apaay formulated a plan to gain access to the spring, she witnessed the evening's routine atrocities. The Herd downed the sweet nectar, bloodlust pooling in their black eyes, and though Apaay never again drank from the vines, she was pulled into the horrifyingly violent displays regardless. When she awoke the next morning, body stiff with fatigue in the grass, she was alone in her disquiet.

It had become clear that their ignorance concerning the war was no farce. They truly did not believe it was real. This life of theirs—this safe, perfect, easy life—was a lie.

And now it was evening. Apaay pressed herself against the outer wall of the packed chamber as the caribou Unua fell, body against water, against grass, sharpened antlers coated scarlet. She fidgeted, the mask sticking to her sweaty face. It would all be over soon.

The commander surveyed the spectacle from the dais as he always did. When his predatory gaze snagged on her, Apaay met his eyes squarely. He knew who she was behind the mask. A woman dressed as a guard. She only wondered why he allowed her to remain.

Her attention shifted to the Herd, or what was left of them. Soon, the survivors would drop into dreamless sleep, heaped atop one another in the field. Apaay had learned how they removed all evidence of the violence. While the Herd slept, the corpses were collected, and the grass regenerated overnight. Come morning, nothing remained of the night's activity but a sense of confusion.

She asked herself why. What was the point of all this death? She understood, in some twisted way, that this fear-hazed bloodlust allowed the commander to control his people. But what was his ultimate objective?

One of the guards barked at a group of stragglers to move along when a woman passed nearby. It was only a glimpse: the crescent curve of a cheekbone, the dent bisecting a stubborn chin. It wasn't the woman's appearance that caught Apaay's attention. It was her eyes.

They had been perfectly, brutally clear.

← →

It was late by the time the woman slipped from the main chamber down one of the tunnels of dark stone. She didn't weave or amble like those under the influence of the nectar. Apaay, following at a clipped walk, called out, "Excuse me."

The woman, who gave no indication of having heard, kept walking. But at the next turn, she bolted.

Apaay gave chase, the crash of their footsteps reverberating in the enclosed space. Bit by bit, she closed the distance. Snagged the back of the woman's parka. The woman swung. Apaay caught her arm, slammed the woman against the wall, and whispered into her ear, "You don't drink the nectar."

The woman froze under Apaay's hold. She had the look of the caribou Unua. Brown, curly hair cropped close to the scalp and slender limbs. The mask shielded all facial features except her eyes, which crinkled as she laughed. It was a good act. Apaay would have been convinced, were it not for the white encircling her pinprick pupils. Apaay knew a panicked animal when she saw one.

"I don't either," Apaay said, and the laughter died.

A moment of silence followed as the woman appraised her with suspicion. "Who are you?"

"Is there somewhere we can talk?"

She hesitated. But Apaay imagined she had questions of her own, because she said, "This way."

The woman led Apaay over one of the garden bridges where the dwellings were located. Spaces carved from the rock, large and hollow and full of grass. Somewhere deep in one of these hollows, antlers clacked. On a lower level, they passed one or two rooms that belched an uncomfortable amount of heat. Inside, she glimpsed crates, men sharpening the multi-tined niganas or small, dagger-like talqs, the weapons coated in a strange, iridescent sheen.

At the next bridge, the woman crawled into a hollow tucked beneath the arch, gesturing Apaay inside the space large enough for two, out of sight from any passersby. Then she sat back on her heels, pulled the mask from her head, and tossed it aside with a satisfied sigh.

Apaay stared. "You're not caribou Unua."

Light from the wall lamps flared against the woman's wide cheekbones and tapered chin. "Neither are you."

Apaay removed the burdensome mask from her face. Her sweaty skin prickled against the cool air. No point in continuing the charade now. "Are you wolf Unua or polar bear Unua?" The woman wasn't owl Unua—no white hair. She wasn't seal Unua—eyes neither rounded nor oily black, and she didn't smell of the sea. She definitely wasn't Analak—because this was something Apaay knew, a truth of the world, hard as polished stone.

"Where I come from, we start with our names." She pressed a hand to her sternum. "Kirimat."

"Apaay."

"Well, Apaay." The woman linked her fingers, tilted her head. "Now that we've met, I must ask if you have any meat."

Apaay blinked in perplexity. "Excuse me?"

Kirimat slowed her words. "Do you. Have any. Meat."

"No." Still confused.

Kirimat cried out as if Apaay had spoken of tragedy in its highest form. Her fingers tore through her sweaty hair, head bowed. Her back heaved. "I've spent the last three months eating leaves, and I think I'm going mad."

"That's . . . unfortunate."

The woman's laughter rang out, a low, raspy sound that revealed the noticeable gap between her two front teeth. "Yes, it is." She sighed wistfully.

Apaay decided she liked this woman. If she had to survive on only grass, she might go mad, too.

Kimirat pushed back the hair from her face, briefly fingering the blue beads attached to one of the braids. "You are here for the spring. So am I." A brief, albeit tired, smile. "I believe we can help each other."

Truthfully, she cared little for this woman's motives. She hadn't time for questions. At least, those she considered irrelevant. "What do you know about the commander?"

Kirimat gifted her with the most dour of expressions. "Yet another man bloated on power. He has weaponized the fear and ignorance of his people. They are innocent in this."

"Why does he want to control them?"

"I have yet to figure that out." She scratched a few symbols in the dirt before brushing them clear. "He works them like dogs down in the forges. The nectar helps them forget." Kirimat shifted her attention back to Apaay, resigned. "How far are you willing to go to gain access to the spring?"

Apaay studied her dirt-creased palms, the short, ragged nails she'd bitten to the quick. They were strong hands. Capable. She could do what needed to be done. "Far enough."

Kimirat nodded. "Then here is what we'll do."

Later that evening, Apaay returned to the Face Stealer with her plan. She and Kirimat had discussed in depth the steps they would take to access the spring. They'd strike during the gathering when the guards, and the commander, were preoccupied. Tonight, Apaay would lay out each detail over dinner, bringing the Face Stealer up to date. Except when she stepped into the clearing where they'd made camp, he was gone.

Apaay's skin prickled. Leaves swarmed the ground as wind gusted through the canopy. Had he gone to check the snares? She found that unlikely, considering his declining health. She'd never revealed their locations either.

That's when she noticed a foot sticking out from behind a tree.

Apaay's heart ceased.

When she rounded the tangled roots, Apaay found the Face Stealer on his back, having collapsed. The warmth of his skin had leached away to the pallor of fetid whale blubber. Eyes closed. Utterly still.

Apaay cupped his cheek. "Numiak." The skin beneath the pads of her fingers was chilled. She searched for a pulse, her hands trembling, her heart careening forward with no intention of slowing, her body readying itself for an outcome she could not control. But—there. A shallow flutter beneath his skin.

Apaay pulled back the hem of his maq, exposing his stomach, and gagged at the heinous reek. His bandages were soaked in fluid and pus. Fine lines branched from around the dressing, darkly violet. When she tugged down his trousers to check his thigh wound, she discovered a similar sight. The infection had spread to his bloodstream.

Carefully, Apaay fixed his clothes with shaking hands. Her chin wobbled. Her eyes stung. It was too much for one person to endure. The journey had taken its toll, and she was exhausted beyond reason, and how much longer would she have to carry herself and Numiak through the unknown before she just . . . cracked?

Her breath hitched. Her chest squeezed until she thought she'd choke. She was alone. She was so alone, and in her moment of weakness, she allowed herself to think of Mama and Papa and most especially Eska. Her family. They were safe in the Analak village where Chena's brother, Muktuk, lived, but she was not with them. She was entirely separate. Did they worry, as she did? Did they await the day they'd be reunited again?

And then she thought of Ila, because in these dark times, she felt that absence like a limb, her warmth, her positivity, her generosity, her compassion. Apaay had wronged her. Had pushed Ila away. Had treated her as if she meant nothing. Everything they had built in the labyrinth had crumbled due to Apaay's negligence. She would not be surprised if Ila never wanted to see her again. If that was to be her punishment, then she deserved it. She deserved so much worse.

Her fingers strayed to her pocket, as they sometimes did, but the stone carving Ila had gifted her, the one shaped like a wolf, was not there. Apaay didn't know when she had lost it. The stone pressing down her heart seemed to weigh greater on this day, and each subsequent sun.

She buried it. Buried all that hard, knotted emotion, the shame, the guilt. Shoved it so far down it had no hope of reaching the light anytime soon. Then she rekindled the fire, because it had to be done. After this—healing the Face Stealer, convincing the Caribou Nomads to ally with them—then she could break. But not yet.

Not yet.

She checked the snare and returned to camp to skin the hare she'd caught, watching the labored rise and fall of the Face Stealer's chest while she worked. The skin bubbled and crisped as it roasted above the flames. While it cooked, she repaired a small hole in her trousers near the knee, and the feel of a needle in her hand, the motion of pulling the stitch tight with sinew, soothed her further. As children, she and Eska had learned to sew by making doll clothing. They had also helped Mama chew and soften the sealskin used for boot soles. Eska wasn't here to point out Apaay's crooked stitches. She wished otherwise, if only to hear her sister's voice.

With her trousers fixed, Apaay focused on her unconscious companion. Another thing that had to be done. Grabbing the waterskin, Apaay pried open his mouth and poured a mouthful of liquid down his throat. His brow twitched. Another mouthful.

A low groan slipped out. His eyes cracked open—green and blue and gold and gray—and rested on Apaay, the stick she'd used to stoke the fire clutched in her hand.

The Face Stealer said, "Why do you look like you want to skewer me with that?"

"I was considering it." With some regret, she tossed the stick into the flames and helped him sit up.

He looked from Apaay to the fire in confusion. His gaze, which normally missed very little, was slow to clear. "What happened?"

She shoved a piece of the cooked rabbit into his hand. "I don't know. You were unconscious when I found you. We can't wait any longer. I'm getting you the spring water. Tomorrow."

"You've been crying."

The knot in her throat swelled, lodging there. She hadn't let the tears fall. "I don't want to talk about it."

"Is it your family? Ila?"

"I said I don't want to talk about it," she snapped, and instantly felt that old shame rise and swallow her. She'd never learn.

Apaay sucked in a breath, sensing his interest, the impulse to ask additional questions contained at the moment. "Sorry. Can we please not talk about it right now?" As she spoke, Numiak picked at the meat she'd roasted over their small, indiscernible fire before setting it aside. Too quiet.

"You need to eat something." He hadn't eaten last night or the night before due to pain in his abdomen. The bones of his face were beginning to protrude, the skin beneath his eyes sunken. The pile of mushrooms she'd foraged for yesterday sat untouched.

"I'm feeling impartial to rabbit at the moment. I'll eat tomorrow." The words came slow, as though it took every bit of concentration to speak.

Apaay couldn't control how quickly the poison moved through his bloodstream, but she could ensure he had a full stomach at the end of the day. "You said that yesterday," she snapped.

"And now I'm saying it again."

Growling in frustration, Apaay picked up the neglected skewer. "You remember all those times you forced me to eat back in the Wood? Well, now I'm returning the favor. *Eat.*" She shoved the rabbit back into his hand with a cold glare.

That seemed to wake him up. "So demanding," he crooned. The tips of his canines flashed. "I think I like you this way."

"Deranged?"

His gaze softened. "Strong."

Drat it all, her cheeks warmed. Apaay wasn't sure if she entirely believed the sentiment. She had faced so much darkness in recent months, yet somehow, she'd clawed her way back to the light. "Do you mean that?" she asked, wishing her insecurity would die the most painful of deaths.

"Yes, I hate rabbit." He rubbed his chin in thought. "I'm rather partial to squirrel."

Well then.

She turned away.

"Apaay."

She wished she had never asked such a foolish question. With so much of the future unknown, she discovered her defenses drastically weakened. Apaay wanted to believe she was strong above all else. But with the separation from her family, which had felt like slow strangulation over the passing months, she struggled.

Reluctantly, she turned back to the Face Stealer.

His smile was the warmest thing she had seen from him in days. "You are strong. Do not doubt that." The smile then turned indulgent. "You could stand to compliment me a little more."

"And inflate your already bloated ego? I don't think so." Dismissive words, yet her heart raced.

"Come on. One *tiny* compliment."

"Fine." She crossed her arms and lifted her chin, because what else was she supposed to do when he turned that charm onto her? "You're looking a little less skeletal today."

He huffed in amusement, eyes soft and twinkling.

Apaay watched him from her periphery to make sure he didn't suddenly die on her. She'd experienced enough turmoil of late to last a lifetime. She didn't need to add to it.

The Face Stealer leaned his head against a log and stretched out his legs, one hand resting on his uninjured thigh. The slightest movement pinched the skin around his eyes.

The violet glow of dusk: the point where the sun kissed the horizon, having completed its curved descent, but sank no lower. A weak tendril of sunlight highlighted the bridge of his nose, and beneath, the cracked, peeling skin of his lips. She added another stick to the fire. "How are you feeling?"

His fingers twitched. "I'm not dead yet."

Apaay bit the inside of her cheek. And why, she wondered, did she ask him this? Maybe she felt responsible for his well-being after single-handedly dragging his body through the Atakana and beyond. "I meant about Kenai," she said, voice sinking to a whisper.

The twitching of his fingers stilled. The looseness fled from his torso. Apaay nearly apologized for bringing it up. He didn't sleep well nowadays.

"My brother tried to kill me." The Face Stealer's mouth compressed into a bloodless line. "What else is there to know? That is the world. We lose things. Yet sometimes," he whispered, the intensity of his gaze almost too much, "we find things, too."

"He hurt you," she said.

A fatigued sigh. "He hurt me a long time ago. I guess I thought—" He went quiet, staring at the sparks flaring against the shaded canopy like the stars they couldn't see.

"You thought you could save him." Because hadn't she believed the same?

Numiak touched one of his cheeks in confusion. "Maybe I did."

"You did all you could. He made his choice."

"What if my actions weren't enough?"

He continued to stare into the fire. One's actions might never be enough, and it did not reflect poorly on him. Kenai was a man grown. He alone could shape his future. But she found herself saying something else.

"You said you became the Face Stealer to save your brother," she murmured. The past weighed heavily on him, but if she could help lighten this burden, the strain on his failing body, she would. "Will you tell me about it?"

He eyed her waterskin, which she passed to him. Apaay watched his throat work as he drained it.

"How much did you hear?" he asked, and she knew he was referring to the conversation with his brother that took place a few miles outside of Talguk, moments before Apaay plunged a dagger into Kenai's back.

"Kenai said you killed your father."

He passed a hand over his eyes wearily. Released a fatigued sigh. "Kenai blames me for our father's poor treatment of him after our mother's passing. I can't say he's wrong." A pause. "But as much as Kenai claims to have loved our father, a part of him resented our father, too. One night he just . . . snapped." He lifted his gaze to hers. "The truth is, Kenai killed our father, not me."

Apaay blinked at the unexpected information. "How?"

When he next spoke, it sounded as though he had aged many

decades. "He returned late one evening, distraught and near hysteria. He led me to our father's body. I knew what would happen once it was discovered. Kenai was all I had left. They would have taken him from me, so I manipulated the scene to make it look like I was the one responsible. I paid my life savings for a slip of memory powder, which I mixed into Kenai's tea that night. His memories were wiped. That evening, our Packmates appeared on our doorstep. They took me away instead, none the wiser."

Apaay tried to process the Face Stealer's admission. She couldn't, quite. Because if what he said was true—and she didn't think he lied—then Kenai truly believed his brother had killed their father, and his hatred toward Numiak was for naught.

"Why didn't you tell him the truth?" she asked, searching his gaze.

"By then, it was too late. He thought me a monster. The Pack cast me out, my honors and titles stripped. I was cursed to live with the darkness of Taggak as punishment for my alleged crime. Numiak of the Wolf Kingdom was gone. From that day forward, I was simply, *Demon*."

9

Ila cracked open her eyes. Shadows made the darkness around her complete. After days of absence, Tulimaq had not returned. It felt as if a broken rib had punctured a lung, every breath splintering through her. The pain lived inside her these days.

She lay on the ground in her own filth and blood because she was too weak to move, too awash in agony to even consider the idea. Her thoughts drifted to Apaay. Was she safe? Frightened? Ila thought of the Wood, the first home she had ever known. She'd left it all behind to seek her destiny. It was not enough to belong to a people if she did nothing to help them.

What began as a series of faint vibrations morphed into the clipped tread of an approaching guard. Ila didn't bother sitting up. If they planned to resume her torture, they'd drag her wherever they wished.

The guard tossed something small and round between the bars of her cell. It bounced and skidded across the stone floor, hit the sole of Ila's foot, and stopped. She stared at it warily. It wasn't food. Her attention wandered back to the guard with his protruding nose.

"Healing salve," the man said, and left.

Healing salve?

Gingerly, Ila sat up. The wooden container rested in one of the cracks between the stones. She picked it up, still wary of a possible trap, but no one came. The cell contained only herself, her drifting thoughts. Removing the top, Ila brought the salve to her nose and inhaled. It smelled of crushed pine needles. The sharp odor broke through the fog, and she stared at the brown substance in confusion. Someone did not want her to suffer.

The salve cooled her feverish skin as she spread it over a particularly gruesome wound on her thigh. The cool relief morphed into a faint prickling. The prickling froze to a burning cold. Ila gritted her teeth, expelling air through her nostrils as the fire spread. She could bear the pain. It was nothing compared to what she had endured. It drew to a painful point, and then the ice subsided and warmed. Blessed heat sank deep into her brutalized flesh, the tender muscles, and seeped down into her bloodstream. A broken cry crumbled in her mouth at how good it felt. Ila managed to coat the rest of her body in the healing salve before her strength gave out and she slumped against the wall from the effort.

After a time, the darkness lessened. Hours passed. She massaged the salve into the worst of her wounds. Her bruises began to fade, blue-black to violet to a sickly yellow-green, and she regained her range of movement. No one visited except to bring her the gruel they considered food. For whatever reason, the beatings that day had ceased.

Ila slept most of the following day. When she woke, she wasn't alone.

A figure sat against the wall outside the bars, caught in the area of illumination cast by the torch. With one knee pulled to his chest, Tulimaq studied her with careful stoicism. The fingers of one hand dangled down. The knuckles were scraped raw.

Her nostrils flared. He smelled of blood and man-sweat and *violence*. She flinched, a little growl catching in her throat. Light and shade fell in amorphous shapes across his brow. Ila stared in surprise, for his hair was no longer pulled back tightly against his scalp. Dark strands fell around his face, which was drawn, bruised crescents beneath the eyes.

The hollow in Ila's gut seemed to stretch and eat away at her stomach lining. Tulimaq's story hadn't abandoned her in sleep. It came alive, and grew teeth in her mind. That, she finally understood, was the root of his pain—her family's responsibility for his mother's murder.

Ila shut her eyes. She was not her mother. She was not her father. She didn't remember them, or her home, or her sister, or anything. And yet, she *did* feel in part responsible for what had transpired. But that didn't mean his actions were justified.

He began to speak. "You couldn't possibly know what my father was like. The Great Bear, who single-handedly ended a civil war between our people. Nanuq, who is almost a man."

He stared at the black space above her head, and there was nothing in his eyes. An empty wasteland. Two holes in his face. Ila was almost certain he had sent the healing salve. An apology? A peace offering?

"He was my father," Tulimaq continued after a time. "But firstly, always, he was a king."

She feigned sleep as Tulimaq's past took shape in her cramped cell. He had told her little of his life prior to this moment. What had changed, that he now divulged these things freely? What would he have said had he known she was awake, if anything?

"You should have died in that invasion with your parents. That you survived, well, I imagine you must feel some gratitude toward them, that they would place your life above their own. But the truth is, you never knew your father. Not enough to remember him, or your mother." He still stared into the blackness, yet something in his face changed. "I think it must be better, to not know. Then you are never disappointed."

There was power in knowing. But, Ila amended, there was freedom in not knowing. She did not know if one was better—only different.

Clearly, Tulimaq thought otherwise.

He went on, the bones of his face pressing harshly against his skin in agitation.

"I know what you must think. How could I find disappointment in a god?" The smooth, unblemished skin of his throat dipped with his swallow. "It turns out I know much about disappointment. I am the youngest of Nanuq's children. My brother and sister were conceived legitimately. My mother, a common whore in his service, birthed me in the filth of one of the lower cells in secrecy. A bastard—that's what I am. I was born one, and I'll likely die as one.

"My father found out, of course. There is nothing you can hide from the Great Bear. In a rare gesture of mercy, he did not kill me, nor did he kill my mother. Should I thank him for that? For sparing my life when he is responsible for its existence?"

He went quiet for a time. The hard ground kept Ila awake. She imagined Tulimaq telling her this in awareness. They were having a discussion, a conversation.

How do you feel about that? Ila might ask.

She continued to feign sleep, her eyes mere slits as she studied him and the hunch to his posture.

"As soon as I was old enough, I was given a position in my father's service. I was six years old, scrubbing waste. I was told to keep my head down. A bastard, he said, should never be seen." His head dipped, and one hand lifted to rub his eyes. "I didn't care about the throne. I never did. I wanted to know my father. That was all."

Ila inhaled, and a sharp pain arrowed between her cracked ribs. Her gasp rang free.

Tulimaq's head snapped up as she shut her eyes. Her heart pounded, hammering into her sternum with enough force to bruise.

After some time, she peeked into the gloom. He sat in the same position, having resumed his one-sided conversation. He must have assumed she was having a nightmare.

"My mother and I left before my seventh birthday. Stole away on a wagon carrying quartz northward. The week prior, my father broke my hand for speaking out of turn. My mother wanted a better life for me, a freer life. And yet, when we left Nur, I begged her to take me back."

Tulimaq pressed his thumb to his lower lip, his features pinched, caught in the memories of old. "I know it doesn't make sense, but the heart wants what the heart wants."

Ila feared that he would go on, that he would stop. She wanted his story, however twisted and naive were her desires, because above all, she wanted to understand the world around her, and he, this man who had a child's heart, was a part of it. He wasn't offering his story, not really. Not when he thought she wouldn't remember it. Ila took it anyway.

"After so many years of wondering, wishing, obsessing over home, you showed up." He looked straight at her. It took every bit of strength not to flinch. "You were weak and afraid. Pathetic, really. But there was something in you. A need to better yourself. I could respect that. But you trusted too easily. Your heart is too soft. Can I fault you for that? No, because it led you to me. Matilaqaa," he said. "Heir to the Wolf Kingdom, yet so much more. You are my redemption. You," he said, "are my salvation."

Tulimaq's salvation. And, if she didn't escape this hellhole soon, her own downfall.

"Nanuq moves his forces west. In a few weeks, his general will reach camp, and when I tell him who I have in my possession, I will be granted a place at my father's side."

He carded his fingers through his disheveled hair, dropped them. There it was—great walls rising around him, a fortress built of mistrust. Ila searched for a sign of it weakening. Tulimaq had come here in the dark hours, given her these highly protected pieces of himself. It did not mean nothing.

"I don't know why I'm telling you this." He stared at the floor. "It's not like you care one way or another."

I care, she wanted to scream at him. *I have always cared. It is you who does not.*

Tulimaq uncoiled to his feet. She felt his gaze trace her bloodied face, which was partially covered by her unbound hair.

"I should hate you," he said, the muscles of his jaw clenched in undeniable loathing. "Your parents took away the person I loved most in the world. But I don't hate you. No," he said. "I don't hate you at all."

10

"Ready?"

Crouched at a bend in the tunnel, Apaay glanced at Kirimat beside her. The woman's mask made dark jewels of her eyes. In the distance, there were killing sounds. Revolting half-screams that came to an abrupt end as the caribou Unua spilled the blood of their own.

On the other side of the bend, four guards stood watch, the sky-blue doors at their backs. They hadn't anticipated guards, having assumed they'd monitor the gathering. So they'd improvised. Kirimat's plan seemed mostly foolproof. Apaay would distract the men, allowing for Kirimat to strike them down. They'd slip through the doors, nab some of the spring water in the vials they each carried, and flee.

Like she said: mostly foolproof.

With a silent acknowledgement, they rounded the corner, a boneless sway to their bodies, as if firmly under the nectar's influence.

The guards' attention latched onto Kirimat first. She was taller, curvier. She better understood the angles of her body, how to position herself to emphasize the swell of her breasts. Apaay was practically an afterthought.

"Hello," Kirimat murmured in a musical tone. Apaay followed her lead, face flaming behind her mask. Her job? Look like a helpless, simpering fool. Briefly, the men tracked the roll of her hips—though Apaay hadn't much hips to speak of. The whole thing made her want to melt into a puddle. If Eska were here, she'd be laughing herself hoarse.

"This corridor is off-limits," one of the guards stated tonelessly, his hand drifting to the nigana at his waist. "You will need to return to the hall."

Kirimat slithered up to his side with an impressive pout. He had the shoulders of a bull caribou and perhaps the intelligence of a lemming. Apaay, meanwhile, drifted to the guard nearest to the doors. He smelled like man, which was to say, foreign.

"But we're lost," Kirimat purred. "And *lonely*." Her eyes were liquid dark, full of sensual promise.

"And I'm unimpressed." He peeled Kirimat off him with a grimace.

The woman shot Apaay a look that said, *Do something*.

As if Apaay had any idea what to do. Sometimes women from her village would flutter their eyelashes to attract an admirer's attention. Apaay attempted to do the same.

The guard frowned at her. "Do you have something in your eye?" He reached for her, and two things happened at once.

First, the man's fingers caught on the edge of her mask. Second, Apaay stepped back, and the mask slid free, revealing her long black hair and lack of caribou Unua heritage.

There was a silence.

Apaay bolted, Kirimat not far behind.

The guards gave chase. Apaay sped down the corridor and cut left, left again. Kirimat screamed, her words lost to the echo. By the time Apaay glanced over her shoulder, the woman had vanished.

Something whipped by her arm, hitting the wall, and dust sprayed, small rocks tumbling free. Apaay swerved around the next corner. If she backtracked to the central chamber, she could disappear among the Herd. There was safety in numbers.

The men pushed forward with resolve, yet she grew sluggish

with each passing footfall. At the next turn, a field of tall grass nearly twice her height blocked passage through. Apaay didn't think. She dove in headfirst, whacking aside the wide, yellow stalks.

A loud hissing sound filled her ears. *Listen*, sighed the grass. She did.

Crashing footsteps reverberated in the tunnel. Sweat leaked heavily from her skin. Crouched, Apaay made herself as small of a target as possible. As long as she didn't move, the guards wouldn't find her. How many had chased Kirimat? And what about that scream? Was the woman injured? Was she still alive, for that matter?

Eventually, the men moved off. Apaay waited until her pulse slowed before weaving her way out of the grass and circling back to the blue doors.

The tunnel was deserted.

Her skin prickled. Had Kirimat managed to take out the remainder of the guards?

Apaay reached for one of the ornately carved handles when one of the doors creaked open. Kirimat poked her head through the opening.

Apaay stared. "Are they—?"

"Indisposed." She pushed the door open wider for Apaay to slip through.

She and Kirimat hurried down the lamp-lit path. The atmosphere thickened—heavy, sopping air. Apaay swiped at the tendrils of hair sticking to her sweaty neck and tried not to think of how little time they truly had.

The air around her pulsed.

It said, *Welcome.*

It said, *Safe.*

It said, *You are here I am here you are here—*

The walkway softened into grass. Ahead, the stone walls transitioned to triangular-shaped panes of glass through which she viewed an image of quiet serenity.

Apaay knew a sacred place when she saw one.

A small body of clear water, surrounded by grass on all sides, glimmered from the room's center. The ceiling soared high above and was lost. The earth didn't feel so crushing here. Aside from the gentle lapping water, it was quiet.

"Do you feel it?" whispered Kirimat.

"Yes." Whatever gods the caribou Unua worshipped, they were in the water, in the air, in the rock. It was old, this place.

Moving to the water's edge, she dipped her vial into the spring. When held to the light, the water flashed blue and pink and green.

"I wondered when you would make your move."

Apaay leaped to her feet and whirled. The commander had Kirimat crowded against the wall, a knife tucked beneath her chin, his enormous rack of antlers branching overhead. The woman glowered at him with pure loathing.

"Do you think," he said conversationally, gaze on Apaay, "I didn't notice a stranger in our midst? Do you think I didn't notice the poor fit of your clothing or the uncomfortable way you walked among us, as if you did not belong?" His teeth were strange, large and square in his mouth. Apaay couldn't stop staring at them. "I know everything about Nigun, down to the last weed. I thank you, though, for bringing this one to me." He dug the knife deeper, and Kirimat hissed out a pained breath. "I've been chasing her for months."

Apaay looked to Kirimat in panic. She could fix this somehow.

"I'm not here to endanger your people," Apaay said, stepping toward him. "I'd heard of the spring—"

"Do you think you are the first to seek the spring for its healing properties?" He smiled condescendingly. "If we allowed one person to take from it, we would have to allow everyone the same opportunity. Not only would it destroy the peace I've worked so hard to maintain, but it would sully the spring's purity."

Apaay tightened her grip on the vial. "Peace?" Revulsion bled through every facet of her expression. "Your people tear into each other nightly. You wear the skins of those slain!" The commander spoke of peace, yet blood saturated the soil and the river writhed through the rock like an engorged vein.

"Population control," he explained. "You understand the mechanics, I'm sure. Too many people, not enough food. It ensures their survival, so I let it be. The Herd is content."

"They are brainwashed!"

The commander sighed, as if he were dealing with a petulant child. "My dear, I'd avoid making gross generalizations. It's rather unbecoming." His eyes narrowed. "Now, set down the water, please. It doesn't belong to you."

Apaay glanced at his dagger. Kirimat's nostrils flared, as though scenting the blood rolling down her neck. "As far as I'm concerned, it doesn't belong to you either. It belongs to all of your people."

He inclined his head. "The Council and I have an understanding. They trust me to make decisions for the good of the Herd."

Apaay was so sickened by this man's selfishness she briefly considered chucking the vial at his head. Growing up, she'd been taught to act like water, to always seek the path of least resistance, but now she must be hard, she must be unwilling to bend, she must remain steadfast. "The People of the Herd are being lied to. They have no idea what lies outside of Nigun."

"What a stubborn child you are. Do you think the Herd wishes to involve themselves in a conflict they cannot win? I am doing these people a favor."

"And when the conflict reaches Nigun—and beyond? They will not survive if they cannot fight Nanuq. They are helpless in their ignorance."

"Nanuq is the least of my worries." His mouth puckered in displeasure as four guards appeared at his back. "The water, child."

"I won't give it to you."

Baring his teeth, he deepened the incision in Kirimat's neck. "The water, or she dies."

"Don't give it to him," Kirimat spat.

Apaay bit the inside of her cheek. There had to be a way out of this. Whose death would she bear—Kirimat's, Numiak's, her own? She had not traveled hundreds of miles, faced impossible odds, to let one more obstacle stand in her way. Numiak didn't have time. It was seeping out of him day by day, and it was almost gone.

The commander was a man with an organized mind. He liked his pieces orderly and his people compliant. Above all, he thrived on acting as the guiding hand. If she gave him what he wanted, she did not think he would kill her—yet. It might grant her time.

"I need the water to heal someone."

"You try my patience, child."

"You may have heard of him." Apaay let faith lead her blindly. Despite fear. Despite everything. "The Face Stealer," she whispered.

The commander pulled back the knife with an expression of unexpected intrigue. Kirimat's eyes widened.

"How interesting." He flicked a glance at his men. "Where is he?"

Whatever he had silently communicated to his guards, it couldn't be good. "I will tell you if you promise not to harm him. And if you let Kirimat go." She did not think the commander would refute her. The Face Stealer was a powerful individual, a potent adversary. Someone of far greater value than Kirimat.

The commander considered her request. The lure of the North's most notorious demon? No one could resist that. "Very well. You have my word."

← →

Four men carried the Face Stealer through the entrance by his arms and legs, dumping him like a sack of bones by the edge of the spring. He gasped in pain. Twigs and leaves made a mess of his hair. His eyes, though dull, still managed to retain some clarity despite the poison's hold.

Apaay curled her fingers into her maq and asked for strength.

"He looks exactly the same," Kirimat whispered.

Apaay whipped her head around. "You know Numiak?"

The skin around the woman's eyes pinched. "It's been years. He doesn't look well."

Yes, well, dying could do that to a person.

Grass whispered beneath the commander's boots. He wasn't a large man, but that sturdy tread demanded they listen. "I have questions, which you will answer. If I'm satisfied with your answers, I might let you live. And don't try to lie. I'll know." His gaze swung to Apaay. "First: who are you?"

She said, only a little uneasy, "Apaay of the Analak."

The commander glanced at the water before returning his attention to her. "Very well, Apaay of the Analak. Why are you here?"

"To heal the Face Stealer."

The man must have found her answer satisfactory, because he strode to where Numiak lay in the grass, staring down his nose in thinly-veiled disgust. The Face Stealer twitched, his pallor similar to that of a corpse. "And you, Face Stealer. I've heard of you."

"All horrible things, I hope." He flashed his teeth, and to Apaay's horror, she noticed they were edged in blood.

In a clipped tone, the commander demanded, "Why are you here?"

Three rattling breaths passed before the Face Stealer could respond. "To rid my body of this poison."

The spring shimmered a pale, luminescent pink before returning to its azure hue.

A measured smile stretched the edges of the commander's mouth. His thick, fleshy lips reminded Apaay of seal blubber. "A likely story. Your friend believes you come to the spring for healing, and that is obviously true—to her. But to you, that is only a half-truth."

Anger swelled as a knot in her throat. Numiak shied from her gaze, staring into the water instead. She had thought they were past the lies. They were in the middle of a war. How could Apaay stand tall when his lies weakened her?

"Tell me why you are here, demon. Tell me," he said, slanting a look in Apaay's direction, "and I will spare her life."

A knife point pricked the soft skin of her throat.

The Face Stealer's nostrils flared. Two of the guards took hold of Kirimat's arms.

Apaay's throat bobbed against the sharpened tip. She hadn't

seen the commander move, so swiftly had he appeared at her side, dagger in hand. Now he was unraveling the bond she and Numiak had formed these past two months in the alpine range, the lower valleys, the plains and shade-darkened woods. All he needed to do was introduce a sliver of doubt.

He dug the blade deeper. Apaay bared her teeth at him. The commander only laughed. It was a gentle, pleasant sound, and it was *wrong*.

The Face Stealer growled, "You are treading on dangerous ground."

"Hear me, demon, for I will say this only once. Keep silent, and she dies."

His attention slid to the red line trickling down Apaay's neck. He looked unimpressed, the bastard. "Kill her, and you will meet the same fate."

The fury fanned higher, crackling through Apaay's chest. How dare he weigh her life against the assumption that the commander would spare it? Had he forgotten it was she who had brought him here, carried him all this way, hundreds of miles, thousands of miles, to save his wretched skin?

The commander deepened the incision, and the Face Stealer's eyes flashed in warning. "Choose, demon."

The air seethed with unseen energy. A throb pulsed through Apaay's blood. Something cracked, and shimmering white power exploded from the Face Stealer's body and struck the commander square in the chest, sending him crashing against the wall. Apaay didn't understand. The Face Stealer's power had been depleted, transferred to the Raven in their exchange of the dark oath. How was it able to manifest and why had it taken the color of snow instead of the shadows he so dearly loved?

Trembling, Apaay touched her neck. Blood slicked her fingers.

"Touch her again," Numiak hissed, his eyes alive with glittering, sharp-edged emotion, "and I will rip out your heart and feed it to your precious followers. Push me, Nomad. I *dare* you."

It was the first she had seen of the commander's fear as he

climbed gingerly to his feet and brushed dust from his trousers. For someone to come into *his* territory, make him question his power over the situation—the commander had not expected that.

The Face Stealer said, "Our presence will bring no harm to the caribou Unua, yourself, or your city. On the contrary, I wish to discuss a possible alliance with your nation. Is that satisfactory?"

The water remained steadily blue. After a pause, the commander dipped his chin in affirmation. "Very well. I will allow you to be healed by the spring and remain here throughout your recovery, my stipulations being that you will not speak of the war, or of Nanuq, inside these walls. It has taken decades to cultivate this level of peace among the Herd, and I will not have it disrupted."

"You don't know, commander?" The Face Stealer's response wheezed out. "There is no such thing as peace for the North."

Only when Apaay felt certain the commander wouldn't kill her did she kneel at Numiak's side. She had the unexplainable urge to hit him. Nothing new, really. But the hurt she bore at his secrets— that was. "I'm angry with you," she whispered furiously.

"Apaay." His eyes closed. "Please."

"Coward," she muttered, and tipped the vial of spring water into his mouth.

A few moments passed with no change. Apaay looked to the commander. Lamplight cast his antlers in shadow against the wall, the tines particularly sharp. "Is something supposed to happen?"

He answered curiously, "Theoretically, he should be healed by now, his strength restored."

But Numiak's complexion was as sallow as ever. Apaay asked him, "Do you feel any different?"

"No."

"Maybe he needs more water," Kirimat offered, still detained in the guard's grip.

"The spring is so potent you need only a drop to heal the gravest of injuries," the commander remarked scathingly. "If it's not working, then something is wrong. You said he was poisoned?" Apaay nodded. "I will fetch our herbalist."

One of the guards jogged off and returned with a spry,

slender man. His eyes, while a pretty gold-brown, were clouded. "Commander."

He gestured to the Face Stealer, who had curled onto his side. "Our guest here was poisoned by—?" He looked at Apaay expectantly.

"We don't know."

The herbalist smiled at her in confusion. "All right then. Do you mind if I take a blood sample?"

An uncomfortable scratching sensation marked the back of Apaay's neck. The shamans, whose work required an extensive knowledge of blood's properties, warned that one's blood falling into the wrong hands could have dire consequences. But the Face Stealer had little choice.

Numiak stretched out his arm on the grass. A thin line appeared across his wrist as the herbalist sliced into his skin. The blood, which seeped rapidly from the incision, was red—deep red—but as soon as it touched the air, it rippled into smoke.

The herbalist was so startled he dropped the vial. Clarity chased the fog from his eyes. Awareness of the world and the truths surrounding him. "What are you?" he whispered in horror.

What, not *who*.

Numiak's expression flattened.

Casually, the commander strode over and curved a hand over the herbalist's shoulder. His fingertips dug hard into the muscle, and Apaay wondered what would become of this man after learning of the Face Stealer. She thought of how easily the Caribou Nomads butchered their own kind, succumbing to the bloodlust brought about by the nectar.

"I am the Face Stealer. I was made from the shadows of Taggak."

"Face Stealer." The words, hissed as though uttering a curse. Apaay knew better than anyone how names held power. Should a spirit or demon hear its call, there was no telling when it might appear. "I have heard of Taggak, I think."

"My people believe it is a waiting place for the souls that have yet to pass on to the spirit world," Apaay said.

The herbalist lifted his head. "Your people?"

"The Analak."

"The Analak." A bit more of the fog receded. "Yes. Your people live off the land, as we do."

The commander had yet to remove his hand from the herbalist's shoulder.

Out of curiosity, Apaay rested the backs of her fingers against Numiak's forehead. The skin was so hot she recoiled. "Do you know why the water won't heal him?" she asked the herbalist, though her attention never shifted from Numiak's face.

"I believe so. The spring is pure light. Taggak is pure dark. Because he is made from Taggak, there is too much darkness inside him for the water's healing properties to take effect."

"Then what do we do?" she demanded. "How do we save him?"

"Perhaps he is not meant to be saved," said the commander. "A tragedy, certainly."

Yes, Apaay decided, she most definitely hated this man.

"There might be another way. Our people tell stories of the kitska. They are a species of bear that crafts incredible healing remedies. Though, I'm not sure how I know that." He sounded deeply unsettled. "They are said to dwell near water."

"Thank you, Ulm, for your help," the commander cut in, giving him a gentle prod toward the exit. "Please wait out in the hall. I will be there momentarily."

The herbalist glanced over his shoulder, unaware of the commander's men trailing him, closing in. Apaay had the ill sense he wouldn't be returning. "I'm sorry about your friend. I advise keeping him as comfortable as possible in the coming days." He rounded the corner and was gone, the guards with him.

Apaay looked to Numiak. She looked to the commander. Her heart hurt. Her head throbbed. She didn't know what to do.

"My dear." The commander smiled his creepy smile. "You wish to save this man when he has been lying to you? I suggest you learn what he is keeping hidden. It might not be to your liking." With those parting words, he left them.

Kirimat came forward next. "If needed, I can find the kitska."

"No." Apaay pinched the bridge of her nose. Peace felt far away in this moment.

Numiak sighed. "Kirimat, can you give us a moment?"

A look of understanding passed between them that Apaay wasn't comfortable with. Then she took her leave, and Apaay and Numiak were alone, nothing but the thoughts swirling inside her head, all the questions she would never have time to ask.

"How do you know Kirimat?" Pushing to her feet, Apaay crossed her arms and glared down at the Face Stealer.

"From childhood."

It was perhaps the vaguest, most unsatisfactory answer she could have received. *Enough*, she wanted to scream. *Enough of the lies.* But it was useless. It was who he was. He wouldn't change, not for anyone. Had she been a fool then, to trust him? If Apaay could not trust someone's word, she could not trust them at all.

One way or another, she would get to the bottom of his deceit.

"What was the real reason you wanted to come here?" Apaay demanded. "Why do you need the spring?"

The Face Stealer scrubbed both hands over his face. Strands of black hair tangled in his fingers like wisps of emerging darkness. "I didn't want it to be this way. I wanted to wait for a better time, when I wasn't—"

"Dying? Helpless? Weak?" She punctuated that last word with a single arched eyebrow. Kaan would have been proud. My, but she missed that woman.

He huffed, though it sounded nothing like a laugh. "Let's go with *dying*."

"Useless?"

"Apaay." He leveled her a look that said he wasn't in the mood for verbal sparring. Well, too bad. He shouldn't have lied.

"Just get on with it," she gritted out.

The Face Stealer hissed a word under his breath. It sounded remarkably like, *Shit.*

For some insane reason, Apaay wanted to laugh.

He said, "Tell me what you know of the Creator."

Judging by his tone of voice, it almost sounded as though she *should* know something, which frightened her. "Not much. I found a document in your library, but it didn't tell me anything." Sketches. A vague sense of knowing. "Is that . . . the object of power Nanuq seeks?"

"It is." Such gravity in those eyes. "It's located inside this room."

Her attention snapped to the spring. Of course. What was it the Raven had told them? Nanuq sought to become fully man. He sought to shed his animal skin—permanently. The spring's unique properties could do that for him, surely.

"Apaay." The way Numiak drew out her name gave her pause, as if he knew where her mind had gone. "What if the object of power wasn't an object. What if it was a person? And what if that person is you?"

← 11 →

Silence thunked between them like a stone dropped from a large height. "What are you talking about?"

"I didn't want you finding out like this. I wanted to give you time to get used to the idea." He closed his eyes. "At first—"

"Look at me."

He did, albeit reluctantly. The rings encircling his pupils weren't gray, she was relieved to note. Neither were they the still-water aqua of his flirtations. They were the green of new growth, pale and brittle. The same color they'd been moments before he'd taken a knife to her scalp in the labyrinth, removed every strand of hair that had marked her as Analak.

And suddenly, Apaay understood. It was the color of having to hurt someone when, she thought, you would have preferred to do anything else.

"You were a newborn at the time," he rushed to say. "Nanuq was close to discovering your identity. I gave you a face—another girl's face—to shield you."

Her eyes watered uncontrollably. "No." She shook her head. "No."

"Apaay—"

"Stop. Stop *talking*. I don't want to hear this anymore." She turned heel, paced, stopped, whirled around to face him. "You're lying, you're—you're trying to manipulate me into doing something . . ."

As she spoke, Apaay stared into the water. Waiting, waiting, waiting for it to change. It never did, never strayed from the blue. He had killed the lies, every single one of them. He was setting them all free.

"It was the only way to protect you from Nanuq," he said.

Her ears rang and her face went numb and prickly. Apaay stared down at him, at his weakened, prone form. Sweat beading on his brow and eyes sheened. Every word spoken sounded bitten off.

"I know what this is." How hadn't she seen it sooner? "This is a punishment." She stabbed a finger at him. "You're trying to punish me for the blood oath, for the dark oath and your lack of powers. Some part of you blames me for what happened at Talguk. You told me to run and I didn't . . ."

I didn't.

"And for whatever reason, you think to play this trick on me, and I won't have it." She returned to pacing. Another ploy? A betrayal? Apaay couldn't figure out the *why*. Why go through such lengths to hurt her? "If I hadn't returned, Kenai would have killed you. Without me, you never would have reached the spring."

"Apaay." He waited until her attention swung back to him before continuing. "I am not lessening your contribution toward my survival. Without you, I absolutely would have died. But this is not a punishment. This is not a lie. This is not manipulation. This is the truth, in all its ugly, unwanted form."

Her chin wobbled. No change to the water. It was impossible. It was enormous. It was the truth? No. It couldn't be. It wasn't.

"If what you say is true, why didn't you tell me this sooner? Why keep this from me?" It was Apaay's greatest hurt. He knew how she feared the dark, yet he'd chosen to keep her locked away until a time of convenience for *himself.*

The Face Stealer sucked in a rattling breath. His body twitched with what may have been a convulsion. He said, "I could not risk telling you in the labyrinth, and you would not have trusted me anyway. I didn't give you a reason to." Another ragged inhale. "Later, you needed time to heal from your trauma. Then you were focused on reaching Nigun, and I didn't want to stray from that."

Apaay crossed her arms. "So when were you planning on telling me?"

"Soon. Nanuq's power grows. It would be a danger to keep you ignorant."

Sweat prickled her brow. She wiped her forehead with a shaky hand. "What exactly are you saying? I'm not who I thought I was?" Then who was she? Another girl bound inside a stranger's body, as Yuki had been? Apaay couldn't process that notion. "Whose face am I wearing?" she snapped. "Someone's you stole?"

His lack of response affirmed her suspicion.

Someone else's skin. Someone else's nose and mouth and chin. Where was the girl now? Dead? Apaay pressed two fingers against her forehead, feeling its smoothness and gentle slope. She had always wondered why she didn't look like her parents, or Eska. Now she knew.

"Give me the face," Apaay said. "I know you have it."

Wariness darkened his eyes, as it should be. For the first time ever, she thought the Face Stealer feared what she might do. "You need more time to process this—"

"Show me."

Still, he didn't move.

A blinding, ravenous fury rose up, bashing the remainder of her patience to splinters. "You have no right to make decisions for me. You lie, over and over again. Enough. Give me the face."

He did.

The face splayed out in her hands: gaping eye sockets; warm, malleable skin; and black, black eyebrows. It was one of the five faces Numiak had taken from the labyrinth, as if each held some significance. Apaay inspected it in recognition. The girl with the high brow, whose skin had hummed at her touch.

This was her face? It looked nothing like her. It was all Apaay could think of. *This is not me.*

She jerked away. The face dropped onto the ground. "You're lying." She didn't care if the spring said otherwise.

"I'm not." He attempted to prop himself up on one elbow,

grimaced, then lowered himself back down. "When you told me about your face stinging, I knew that your body was trying to reject the face I gave you." His mouth firmed. "Your powers trying to free themselves."

Powers?

No. Just . . . no. This was not her world. Her world was safe. Her world was her village and her family's ice house, that huddle of warmth amidst the cold long night. Its face never changed. It was steadfast.

Except it wasn't. That's what her world used to be, before the Face Stealer—this man—had ripped away her sister's face, forced Apaay to endure horrible torture in Yuki's labyrinth. It hadn't been safe for a long time.

"Wolfling."

The endearment sent a twinge through her. She had trusted him. She had *trusted* him and he still could not let go of his lies. "I can't right now." She stumbled in her haste to put distance between them. His eyes welled with a terrible sadness. "I need space."

Turning, Apaay bolted from the room, turned a corner, and nearly crashed into the commander. He braced her by the arms, a look of polite interest on his face. He didn't say anything. He didn't need to.

"Do what you will with him," she said, and left.

Apaay fled Nigun not by the river, but by the main entrance gates. At her request, they groaned open, and she was through. She ran south, across the plains separating Nigun from the Aatu, into cool, encompassing shade, leaving her confusion, that betrayal, behind.

Miles and miles passed, streaks of brown and green and gold and the occasional flash of pink, her feet flying over tufted grasses and unhurried streams. Apaay moved without thought, without destination. When she grew tired, she walked. When she felt the truth at her back, she picked up her pace. But there was no escaping it. She was the Creator? What did that even mean?

Her parents couldn't have known of this deception. The Analak lived honestly. When they were hungry, they ate. When they were tired, they slept. As well, her people hadn't taken part in the war. So how did the Face Stealer know of her existence? She, a young woman from a small village, with almost no connection to the outside world. Pieces, always pieces of information, but never the whole. After everything they had overcome, it wasn't unreasonable to expect the truth from him. She deserved that much. And when she returned to Nigun, she would demand it of him. Without the truth, they could not move forward. Simple as that.

The sun dipped low by the time Apaay stopped for the evening. Her feet throbbed. Her body ached as if she shouldered a great burden. With a weary sigh, she knelt at the River Pak and splashed water onto her face, rinsing the stickiness from her skin.

The wind shifted direction, carrying a new scent on its airy tendrils. Apaay lifted her head. Blood. It smelled of blood.

A set of eyes glowed from the wooded dim.

A man burst out of the brush. Apaay caught only a glimpse of him, the nasty scar slicing through his cheek, before he was upon her. Panic had her scrambling toward the water before someone crashed into her from behind.

Apaay slammed face-first into the river. Icy glacial melt rushed up her nose. She choked, swallowed, her lungs and head on fire. Someone dragged her up by the collar. Apaay retched as her head broke the surface, and there were armed men, and women, ten, twenty, maybe more, and then a scented cloth clamped over her nose and mouth, darkness falling into her eyes.

← 12 →

Vibrations warned Ila of approaching footsteps. The uneven gait announced Birthmark's return. Pushing into a seated position, Ila watched him limp into the room, slot a torch into the wall. Sweat prickled her palms, which she wiped onto her thighs. To watch her tormentor approach, step by step, the distance disappearing in an instant. It was a particular kind of cruelty.

With crossed arms, Birthmark studied her through the bars. "I know you can understand me. What I want to know," he said, "is what makes you so special. It has been ten days, yet I still have no answers from you." A smile ghosted across his mouth, though his gaze remained flat as stagnant water.

Ila glanced over the man's shoulder. He was alone.

"Tulimaq isn't here. Oh, don't give me that look. Please don't. I see how you watch him. I'm sorry to say the feelings are not reciprocated. Tulimaq is a cold one, isn't he?"

The only thing she knew about Tulimaq was that she didn't know him at all.

He said, "Are you ready to talk?"

The guard was mistaken. No matter how they broke her body, she would not give him the information he wanted. She had not escaped a cage only to die in one. This man, whether he knew it or not, was her way out.

Do you know sign language?

Birthmark's stony expression didn't change. "If you have something to say, you will wait until I retrieve Tulimaq."

Ila lunged forward, rattling the cell bars.

His eyebrows lifted in barely-concealed surprise. "You don't want me to get Tulimaq."

Ila shook her head.

A shrewd gaze as he took her in. Torchlight cast the man's wavering shadow onto the ground and darkened the splotchy birthmark on his cheek to purple. He left for an indeterminate amount of time before returning with an elderly woman, her back hunched and her fingers bent like old tree roots. Another prisoner. Ila felt as if she stared at her reflection. The sensation of fear clogging one's throat, but desperately trying not to let it show. The woman appraised Ila's broken state. Her look said, *We are the same, you and I.*

"All right." The guard shoved the woman forward. "Start talking."

If this was to be her only opportunity to escape, she would not squander it.

To the woman, Ila signed, *This man wants information from me. You are to translate what I'm saying, word for word. Do you understand?*

The woman nodded, though the stiffness of the gesture exposed her terror. Ila wished to say everything would be well, but she did not want to lie.

Tell him that Tulimaq has been lying to him.

Reluctance on the translator's face.

The guard's large shadow cloaked the front of the cell. Ila felt how her heart strained, the shallow pulse fluttering in her neck and migrating to her temples. She was afraid. She did not want to die here. If this woman did not cooperate, or if she translated the message incorrectly, Ila might never again see the sun.

She bared her teeth. It turned out she was a fierce thing when cornered. *Tell him.* Adamant.

Birthmark glanced between them in keen observation. When the woman relayed the message, his nostrils flared. "How so?"

She had the guard's attention. Good. *He's been keeping information from you. Namely, my identity. I am Matilaqaa of the Wolf Kingdom.*

The old woman gaped at Ila with wide eyes, searching. For the truth?

The truth was this: Matilaqaa was not dead.

"Well?" said the guard, slamming a fist against the bars. "What did she say?"

When the translator communicated the message, the man's mouth slackened. A knife-sharp realization gained clarity as the seconds passed and he stared at her.

Did Tulimaq expect her to sit meekly in this cage, awaiting more punishment, an uncertain future? That girl no longer existed. Whether this man knew it or not, he would let her walk free.

Imagine the reward Nanuq would give you, she went on, *were you to bring him the heir of a long-dead enemy.*

Greed lit the man's eyes. She knew little of Nanuq aside from his quest for power, the fear he sowed. Many would go to great lengths to be granted the tyrant's favor.

Birthmark said, "How do I know you're not lying?"

You don't. You will have to trust me.

The guard laughed. "Why should I trust you? The Wolf Kingdom has been gone for decades."

Or so you believe.

With her eyes steady on the man, she watched doubt creep into his expression. He did not know what to believe.

Think about it, Ila said. *For what reason would Tulimaq want to keep my identity a secret?*

The man waited for the translation, then answered, "The Great Bear is his father. As a bastard child, this would grant Tulimaq favor."

Ila allowed herself a small smile. The man was no fool. *There's something else.*

This time, Birthmark waited.

Good.

Very good.

Are you familiar with the object of power?

From the gleam in his eye, she interpreted that as a yes.

What if I told you I knew where and what it was?

"Then I would say tell me if you wish to live." He squeezed the bars. There was strength in those hands.

Lifting her chin, Ila signed, *The object of power is Tulimaq's staff.*

The guard's frown was deep enough to cut creases into the sides of his mouth. "You want me to believe the object of power is none other than a stick?" A ring of white showed around his lips. "Do you take me for a fool?"

Have you noticed how he is never without it? What better way to hide something valuable than in plain sight? One more push, and she would have him. *Imagine what it could do in the right hands.*

And there it was.

Let this man believe wild, unimaginable things awaited him, should he take the staff into his possession. Potential: all floods began with a single drop.

"If you're trying to lead me astray—"

I'm not.

The old woman spoke Ila's assurance, and the man said nothing.

Tulimaq is too protective of the staff to allow anyone to take it from him directly. I can help you. She'd help him—right off a cliff. *But I want something in return.*

Birthmark grinned at this. "Look at you, making demands. Was your previous lashing not enough?"

The thought of more pain kicked her heart into an uneven beat. The fresh scabs on her back tugged in reminder of what awaited her, should she fail. *Do you want the staff or not?*

"What do you request?"

I want to join my people in the labor camp. The time of solitude was over.

Upon hearing the translation, he smiled. "I will take what you've told me into consideration." He looked to the old woman. "Speak a word of this to anyone, Old One, and I will have your head. Is that clear?"

The woman nodded with a frightened glance in Ila's direction.

"When I've thought of a way to take Tulimaq's staff," Birthmark said, "you will know." He shoved the woman toward the door. "Come along, dog."

The object of power was not, of course, Tulimaq's staff.

But the guard did not need to know that.

← 13 →

That was the last of Ila's solitude. The next day, she was moved to a different cell, one of many crammed into a stout building. It stunk of defecation, pails and pails of it spilling over onto the ground. Bars upon bars, and emptiness, but not for long. For the first time in many weeks, Ila felt hopeful.

Hours later, the door opened. Ila sat absolutely still as a line of women entered the torch-lined space. The knot in her throat bobbed with her swallow. Her pulse quickened, surging against hot skin.

One by one, the prisoners returned to their cells. The guard unlocked Ila's door. An old woman stepped inside, the door locked behind her. Ila's stomach flipped in both excitement and terror.

In the cells adjacent to her, women young and old crowded against the bars, faces pressed into the gaps between. They wore rags—worse than rags. As such, Ila could see every scar, every bruise, every fresh split in skin, and the twisted shapes of their hands, grotesque and broken. Women—and wolves.

Lupine shapes paced, heads lowered and ears flattened, tails tucked between hind legs. Yellow eyes gleamed through the dark. Long, white, piercing canines flashed. She sucked in a startled breath. Surprised, but not afraid. There was so much she might say.

How sorry she was that it had taken her so long to get here. How she vowed to make amends.

Ila had never been good with words.

Torchlight limned the old woman's eyes at her approach. "Oh, dear." She knelt with some difficult. Her body had weathered things no person should. She cradled her left arm against her chest, as if an old injury prevented her from extending it. "Water," she said.

Someone passed a bucket and cloth through the bars. Wetting the cloth, the woman began to wipe the grime from Ila's face, working gently around what remained of her bruises. The cloth smelled awful. She couldn't imagine it having ever been washed.

One wolf, scrawny with matted gray fur, paced in the adjacent cell. Every few turns, its lips rolled back to reveal its saliva-coated teeth. Ila was glad of the bars separating them.

The cool water felt pleasant against her skin. As the woman rinsed the cloth, she said, "It has been a long time since we've had a visitor."

"It could be a trap."

The pacing wolf had transformed into a skinny woman perhaps a decade older than Ila, her sunken brown eyes narrowed in mistrust. Kaan had once told Ila about the Unua's extended lifespan, so she assumed this woman was older than she appeared.

The old woman only smiled. "Oh, I don't think that's true, Malina." She was studying Ila's face with such care. "All you have to do is look into her eyes. See?"

Ila didn't know what her eyes held aside from the struggles she'd experienced of late. But maybe that's what the woman meant.

"What is your name, child?"

A harmless enough question. Except Ila had two names, two lives. There was Ila: prisoner, forgotten, coward, overlooked. There was Matilaqaa: heir, purposeful, stranger, alone. What could she say? Her identity might be too dangerous a thing.

She wasn't afraid they would hurt her. She was afraid of their disappointment. She wanted to know them, learn from them, and build something, if at all possible, from their shared heritage.

"Your name," Malina snapped.

"If she does not want to give her name," the old woman said, sitting back as she finished cleaning Ila's face, "then she will do no such thing."

Most of the prisoners had returned to their human forms, faces pressed to bars, curious and wary both. Ila avoided their eyes for fear of what she might see. Suspicion. Blame, even. A multiplying of the anger radiating from the woman, Malina, whose body stiffened with continuous tension.

Ila asked, keeping her hand motions slow and clear, *Can you understand me?*

A new light entered the old woman's eyes. *Ah*, it said. *Now I see.*

Malina's mouth pinched as though having ingested something rotten. "No wonder she didn't answer. She can't understand what we're saying."

The words drove in their sharp points, and Ila, who was not prepared for the attack, flinched.

"Malina." Disapproval wrinkled the old woman's brow, and the younger woman leaned one shoulder against the bars petulantly. "Not all of us can sign fluently, but Tipki has taught us over the years," she said, gesturing to a woman across the walkway. Unlike Malina, the old woman didn't assume Ila was slow to comprehend, and Ila might have kissed her for it.

You'll have to excuse Malina, Tipki signed. The shape of her eyes reminded Ila of the thinnest crescent moons, and crinkled with a rare, unexpected humor in a place so dreadful. *She has control issues. You'd be wise to give her space.*

Malina banged on the bars. "Hush, Tipki."

Tipki raised her eyebrows as if to say, *See?* But she was grinning as she responded, "Malina, maybe you should sit down. You might hurt yourself."

Ila, torn between humor and fascination, watched as gray hair sprouted over the woman's face, her teeth lengthening. Strangely enough, Malina's no-nonsense brashness reminded her of Kaan. Disregarding the fur, of course. And that only served to remind Ila that she hadn't seen her friend, the weapon's master, in many months, or Ro, or Apaay. Most especially Apaay.

"You forget your place, pup." With the bulky teeth crowding Malina's mouth, Ila found it difficult to read her lips.

"And you have forgotten how to laugh." Tipki was no longer smiling. "The world is dark enough. I don't need your surly attitude added to it." Pointedly, she settled her attention on Ila. *As I said, that's Malina. Pili,* she added, gesturing to the old woman who had cleaned Ila's face. She signed with sweeping motions, as though to release excess energy. *The woman to your right is Saniraq, and I'm Tipki. You'll get to know the others in time.*

"How do we know we can trust her?" Malina demanded. "What if someone sent her—"

"Enough," Pili snapped. "You will speak no more of this."

No. Ila lifted her hands. *She's right.*

Trust was an exchange, not an expectation. She remembered the first time she'd ever met Apaay. It seemed like a lifetime ago. She'd sat in that cell beneath the labyrinth and watched this new girl enter her space, her sanctuary, mistrust in her eyes.

"Who are you?" Malina demanded with a flash of teeth.

She thought, *I am Ila.*

She thought, *I am no one.*

I am Matilaqaa, she signed, *and I am here to set you free.*

A paay awoke in a cage.

She lay curled on the bottom of the confined contraption, the walls punched through with small, round holes. The floor was metal. And the ceiling. And the lock, blocky and square. The sleek gray floor, chilled against her cheek, was so startling a sensation it sent Apaay's thoughts spinning.

Pain pulsed in her temples. The last thing she remembered was slamming face-first into the freezing river. Her soaked furs stuck to her skin, gooseflesh pimpling her arms.

Prey.

A single word, hissed in the deep recesses of her mind.

The cage was positioned in the center of a large tent constructed from worn, yellowing hide, which was so tightly bound not a single sliver of light slipped through. Her pulse spiked in panic. How long had she been unconscious? There was so much to be done. Find one of the kitska so she could heal Numiak. Convince the commander to side with them against Nanuq. Find a way to remove the Raven's tattoo so they could learn whatever secret or weakness the dark god had discovered that would drive Nanuq to bind the Raven to secrecy. Anything and everything to stand against the Polar Bear Empire, to weaken his force, to prevent further corruption from sullying the North's purity. All of this to secure her family's safety, her people's survival, so that one day she could return home to Naga's shores and rebuild.

Sounds beyond the tent drew her attention: hammering and clanging metal and shuffling footsteps. Apaay heard neither the river nor the birds. Instead, there was this: the voices of men, hundreds, possibly thousands. They were gathering for war.

The hide darkened with the sun that never completely set. Hours later, a man entered the tent, tall and broad, a silhouette that melted away the moment the oil lamp was lit. Apaay stared into a single shining eye, the pupil pooling to the ring of brown.

Kenai.

Apaay pushed to her knees, for the cage was too cramped to allow her to stand. She thought, *Traitor*. She thought, *Friend*.

Kenai approached cautiously. He looked unwell, and that was being kind. His scarring appeared more pronounced than ever, lumpy and misshapen. He'd pulled his lank hair back into a messy tail. She was quite certain he'd lost weight.

A strip of yellowing polar bear fur edged his collar and trailed a line down his stomach, like the shaft of an arrow. The white stripe lay in contrast to the red fabric of his thin parka. The man with the pale hair from Across the Sea, whom they'd found dead, had worn something similar. Yet another task she and Numiak must complete: translate the dead man's message. Another potential connection to Nanuq.

"So you're in business of capture as well as attempted fratricide," she said scathingly.

His pupil wavered like a dying star. "I know you hate me."

She should hate him. But his statement felt like it took something from her, just as it took something from him. "I don't hate you, Kenai," Apaay said, because it was true, and because she thought a part of him needed to hear it, for whatever reason. "I don't understand you."

A slow hiss expelled from his chapped lips. "What about this situation don't you understand? You are captured, in a cage. My soldiers will kill you if given the order."

The air clattered and clanked. A foreign sound of shaping metal into hard, sharp things. Apaay gritted her teeth against the intrusion. "So that's it? You side with Yuki and suddenly I am your enemy?"

Kenai looked away. "It was never my intention to hurt you."

"Maybe it wasn't your *intention*," she hissed, curling her fingers through the small openings of the cage, "but that does not excuse the reality. You lied. You hurt me, and others. It is no excuse."

"And I told you I did what I had to do," he bit out, head snapping back in her direction. "As someone who had everything taken from me, to take something for myself for once? I do not regret it."

His fury clashed with hers, stifling the tent. Look at this cold, hardened man. This angry young woman. This stranger, this foe. Apaay was the one caged, but she thought Kenai looked small.

"And attempting to kill Numiak?" she asked, voice softening. "Do you regret that?" She could not imagine ever laying a hand on Eska. Unless, of course, they were wrestling, in which case Apaay remained undefeated.

Kenai fisted his hands and shoved them into his pockets. He glanced at the tent flaps as a man called out for a weapon count. "Where is Numiak? I'm surprised to not find him with you."

"He's not my keeper."

"But he cares for you."

"And this surprises you."

"Are you telling me this doesn't surprise you?"

She wasn't saying anything of the sort. Most days, Apaay pretended it wasn't actually a thing in hopes that it would all . . . float away.

"Ah," he said sadly. "I understand."

"How can you understand?" she snapped. "I haven't said anything."

"You didn't need to. It's written all over your face."

Apaay curled her fingers tighter around the metal wiring. "Faces can lie." A lesson she had learned too frequently of late. Faces could lie, but the heart was true.

"Then you know the Face Stealer is the greatest liar of all."

The statement struck her with extreme force. She remembered why she had run. And yet, she acknowledged with reluctance, Numiak's lie had likely saved her life. It did not excuse the fact that he'd kept that information from her, but it softened the blow a little.

"You can call him your brother, you know." She returned to speaking in a softer tone. Kenai seemed more receptive to it.

His lips slitted into a line that tugged his scarring into gruesome shapes. "That man is not my brother. That man is a demon, and he took from me until there was nothing left."

Wrong. The Face Stealer had sacrificed everything to *save* his brother, and Kenai had no idea.

"You need to let me go," she said.

"And why would I do that?"

"Numiak's sick."

"A likely story."

"It's true." She lifted her head. The metal crisscrossed his form, cutting his shape into repeated, geometric pieces: a shoulder, his left cheek, his knees. "He'll be dead soon." If he wasn't already. She refused to consider that possibility, even as a pit opened in her stomach. She had left him at the commander's mercy due to her own cowardice and hypocrisy.

There was no North without the Face Stealer.

Apaay said, "Don't you care?"

"Should I?"

Somewhere inside him was a child, hurt and abandonment having rooted in his heart. Kenai had been forced to become a man before his time. "I think you do," she said, softly and with pity. "But I think you feel so much resentment toward him it clouds your judgment. It hurts too much."

She expected Kenai to brush her aside. She did not expect him to flinch, as though she'd announced that everyone he loved was dead. Maybe that's why Apaay said what she did.

"Growing up," she murmured, "my sister could do no wrong." It no longer hurt to speak of. This was who Apaay was. She wasn't good at any one thing. She was someone who tried and tried until her heart gave out. "Then her face was taken." She rested her forehead against the cage, the slender metal strips gouging imprints into her skin. "When you lose what is precious to you, you realize the small things don't matter."

"Numiak stole your sister's face," Kenai stated, trying to make a point.

"He did," she agreed. "But I'm coming to terms with what has been done."

A range of emotions passed fleetingly across his face. By the time she pinned one down it was already gone, and Apaay questioned what she had seen.

Kenai paced in front of her cage. It was as if his body needed to move, but his mind remained elsewhere, a separate entity, unaware of his actions. "My relationship with Numiak is not the same as the relationship between you and your sister. The thread between sisters is soft. The blood between brothers is nothing short of violent."

She disagreed. Kenai was a man, yes, but his needs were no different than hers.

Before she could respond, the tent flaps flew open, pushed aside by the broad shoulders of a man in fighting garb. One side of his head had been shorn. He wore a crisscrossing garment the color of algae that provided extra padding on his chest. "Sir, our departure?"

Kenai kept his gaze on Apaay as he responded, "Within the hour."

The man left. He was a soldier, one of many, if the gathering of voices was any indication. On his belt, there had been a long, sharp weapon caked with protruding coral. On his back, urchin-spine arrows. Yuki's children, the seal Unua. They had killing on their minds.

Apaay searched Kenai's shining eye and found nothing, not one sliver of the captive for whom she had bestowed a name—Masuk—because she had wanted the memory of his namesake to infuse him with great strength. His expression was so barren she might have believed he felt nothing were it not for the force of rage simmering beneath. A wounded animal fought back.

Apaay had thought it before, and she thought it again. A person wasn't their face. A person was their heart. And Kenai's heart had yet to mend.

Twenty years was a long time to live with a broken heart.

"Kenai." His name fell flat against her ears, drowned out by the camp sounds beyond. "If you don't let me go, Numiak will die."

"Why should he not die?" he growled, baring his canines. "He killed our family. Our mother. Our sister. Our father."

If Kenai didn't learn the truth, accept it, he would continue to make decisions based on a lie. He would continue down this dark path alone. "Your mother died in childbirth. That's not the same thing. Numiak killed Sita to end her suffering. And your father—"

"Dead by my brother's hand."

"That's not what happened. Numiak was trying to protect you."

"Do you think I wanted this?" he hissed. "Do you think I wanted the burden of caring for someone who took so much from me at an age so young?"

"It was your duty."

"No!" he roared, slashing an arm through the air. "My duty— my only duty—was to be my father's son. And I could not be even that."

The wave of adrenaline that followed was so powerful Apaay thought it might actually be possible to tear this cage apart with her bare hands.

Turning, Kenai made for the exit.

"Kenai," she cried, rattling the cage as her desperation peaked. If he walked out, it was over. "Kenai, please! You can't do this. You can't let him die. He was a child!" she cried to his retreating back.

Without turning around, Kenai said, "So was I."

← →

Kenai burst from the tent in a rush, needing space. Cool air hit his overheated skin. His surroundings blurred—trees, soldiers, weapons—for the only clarity was Apaay's parting words.

He was a child.

Without realizing it, he took the trail leading to the swollen banks of the River Pak. The chilled mountain runoff rushed eastward. The water frothed white foam, making it impossible to catch a clear reflection of himself. Everything Apaay had said was wrong. Numiak had killed their father.

He remembered that night clearly.

A man at the door, gruff and bearing weapons. A fellow Packmate. "Where is your brother, Kenai?"

It was late. That was his first thought. Late with a black sky, and stars like holes poked through cloth. No Packmate visited a private residence unless on official business. "Is something wrong?"

The man, whose name was Iniqit, said nothing.

He opened his mouth to respond when Numiak's footsteps sounded behind him. He would know the rhythm of his brother's tread anywhere.

"What is it?" Numiak said. "What happened?"

Iniqit lunged, slamming Numiak face-first into the nearest wall.

The image fractured into fragments of confusion. A span of rope. A painful grunt. The long tail of Numiak's braid. Kenai didn't realize he had moved. "Stop!" He grabbed for Iniqit, but another Packmate jerked him backward. "What are you doing?"

Numiak managed to turn his head. Blood dripped from what was undoubtedly a broken nose. "It's all right, Kenai," he whispered sadly. For whatever reason, he wasn't resisting.

Something strained inside Kenai's chest, a feeling like tearing muscle. He and Numiak had not been close in many years, it was true, but they shared the same blood, the same father, and once, the same mother. What did it mean that he wanted to hurt these men, who were his brothers-in-arms, because of how they had hurt Numiak?

"What is this about?" he asked quietly. He glanced from Iniqit to Numiak and back.

No one would meet his eye.

"What is this about?" he roared, his fear like a hand squeezing his throat.

As soon as the words left him, Kenai realized he had not

prepared himself for the answer. He had not considered how his world might change.

"I'm sorry, Kenai." Iniqit's voice. "Your father is dead."

Dead.

That couldn't be true. When had he last seen Father? Yesterday morning. He said he would be gone for the day. He hadn't said why, but then, he rarely did.

His stomach roiled in sickening waves. Kenai had to lean against the wall to remain upright. *That's not true*, he thought. But Iniqit, his Packmate, held nothing but pity in his gaze.

"How?" The word was a croak. He could not wrap his mind around this information. Not half a day ago, his father had eaten at their dinner table.

Iniqit's gaze flicked to Numiak, and Kenai suffered a greater pain in his chest, a rising pressure, a budding horror.

The man said, speaking in a halting tone, "Numiak has been convicted for the murder of your father."

What? No. *No.* He was lying. He was lying and how dare he come into his home, come into their home and spread this false information like it was nothing.

"How dare you," he seethed, chest heaving. "How *dare* you."

"Numiak's dagger was found imbedded in your father's chest."

The words sucked the air right out of him.

In this moment, Kenai had never felt more like a child. He was hurting, and where was Father? Where was Mother?

"That can't be," he quavered. "Numiak was asleep. I was—"

What? He was what?

"This has nothing to do with you, Kenai." Numiak's tone contained a strange, reassuring quality he'd never heard before. "You were sleeping, remember?"

He couldn't remember a damn thing. He'd left home a few hours before, right? Determined to complete something important, though he could not remember what. Except Numiak claimed he'd been sleeping. Had it been a dream? He believed his brother. It was an almost instinctive reaction, and he did not understand why.

Kenai sagged more heavily against the wall. "That's—" He peered at his younger brother, remembering a time when Numiak had been small enough to perch on his knee. "It wasn't you. It was . . . someone else . . ."

"I killed Father," Numiak said, and his eyes, his *eyes*. How had he never noticed how cold they were, how *other*? "I'm sorry, Kenai."

He fell to his knees. Time blinked out. It wasn't possible. It was—why had the men come here? He'd seen Father yesterday, and Numiak . . . he'd—

Kenai was seconds away from spewing his dinner all over his Packmates' boots.

He lifted his head, breath frail in his overworked lungs. "Why?" he whispered.

It was the detail he recalled above all else that night: Numiak's lack of reply right before the men hauled him away.

← 15 →

Two hundred armed men and women marched into a tiny, ramshackle camp. The cluster of shelters sagged, the homes sticks and hide, the people lean and hungry. A foul, rancid odor of unwashed hair and skin nearly bowled him over. Once, these people had been warriors of the earth. Now they were ghosts in the wood, fading into obscurity.

The refugees congregated nervously. Kenai and his unit surrounded the area. How many, he wondered, had deserted Nanuq's army? How many more worked against Nanuq's and, by extension, Yuki's cause? Justice guided him. If he could not convince these people to fight for Nanuq, they would not live to see the morning.

Kenai stepped forward, raising his voice. "Refugees. The Great Bear seeks those who will fight for him. I come here offering you an opportunity, a new life. One that will replace the shame of your desertion with pride, security, and greater purpose."

No one spoke. Terror thickened the atmosphere, and it was clear Kenai and his soldiers were not welcome.

He had not expected their immediate agreement. They did not know how they would yet benefit from this new arrangement.

"Join us," he said, "and share in Nanuq's vision for a united North."

"And if we refuse?"

The query came from a hunched elder who pushed to the front of the crowd. His wooden cane thumped dully against the packed dirt.

"You have little reason to refuse," he said confidently. "You will be fed and clothed and trained, at no expense to you. Your families will be provided for, so long as you return to the Southern Territory." They would not live in squalor as they did now. It was, to Kenai, an easy decision.

"Yet we would not be free," replied the man with contempt.

"Nanuq is agreeable—"

"Nanuq is a tyrant. You are wolf Unua, no?" The man bared his teeth. Two of them were missing. "I remember what happened the last time Nanuq rose to power. He is the reason you no longer have a home. He is the reason *we* no longer have a home. You are a disgrace to your nation."

A flush made furious red of his cheeks. The spat insult came as a shock. He did not know how to respond, not at first. That word, *disgrace*, held him firmly in thrall.

He raised a hand. One of Kenai's soldiers beheaded the elder in one calm swipe. As Kenai knew, the sword was an illicit thrill, an alien feel to the hand, weighted and agleam. The man's head bounced and rolled, coming to a halt at the crowd's edge.

Fear was impetus. It would make them choose.

Kenai said, "Take the camp."

They fought back. It was stupid and brave, so they died stupid and brave. What was there to defend? Why would they risk so much for so little? They had nothing. Dirt and disease, a half-life. They died by his blade, and with every swing, a fury ripped and roared through him, one of suffocation, of strangulation.

It was your duty.

What could Apaay, a woman, know of duty? What would she understand of hierarchy and sacrifice? The Analak had not fought in the war. The whole of Apaay's community offered her support, but it was not so with the wolf Unua. One must pick and choose loyalty.

It was because of duty he was here. Gathering the refugees was his responsibility. To stand beside Yuki, he must be worthy of it, a man of strength, and honor, and integrity. This would please her. And when he returned with his vow unbroken, she would know, without any doubt, the vast extent of his capabilities. An asset.

And if she does not?

Kenai swung blindly. There were now more bodies dead than alive, but so long as people stood, he continued to attack. Except one memory had been exchanged for another, and it was not the refugees he cut down in his mind, but his own men, his Packmates, who had trained with him and bled with him, as Unana caught fire in the distance, the deep snows of Kesikan Pass erecting walls around him.

At the time, he had believed their deaths to be necessary, though he had mourned them. Yet nothing had gone as planned. He'd been captured, separated from Yuki for twenty long years. If they could be together now, then surely he was making the right choice.

He faltered under the weight of his sword.

Silence.

His vision cleared. One survivor remained, a young boy on the edge of manhood. For Kenai, it was the age he had gone off to war.

The boy's lips peeled back. He smelled of wolf. "Traitor," he hissed, hacking at Kenai's side. "Traitor, traitor, traitor—" Tears streamed down his face as he struck Kenai again.

He beheaded the boy with a single blow.

← 16 →

Apaay slept fitfully that night. Curled into a ball at the bottom of the cage, she dreamed of clashing weapons and butchered remains, and the smell of damp stone, the phantom sound of skittering rats, was never far off. After eight hours of continual dusk, the day brightened, and she awoke stiffly, a cramp in one leg. Someone had brought her water overnight, which she drank.

Each passing hour was a crawling agony. Her mind began to turn on itself. She thought of Numiak obsessively. The long, clever fingers. The potency of his laughter. And his eyes, every shade of them. How she'd abandoned him to the commander and his brainwashed followers. Apaay rattled the cage and screamed until her voice grew hoarse. No one came.

Apaay must have dozed, because she woke to the sound of men, a herd of shuffling, dragging feet. The flaps snapped aside as Kenai tromped into the tent, his skin spattered red, his hair, the fringe brushing his shoulders, soiled with signs of battle.

Apaay stared at him in horror. "What did you do?"

Pulling a piece of cloth from his pocket, he mopped his face. It was some time before he spoke. "There was a refugee camp. We gave them a choice: follow Nanuq, or die. They decided their own fate."

"So you killed them." Apaay thought she'd sick herself. The iron-salt odor of the blood coating him permeated the space. "You don't get to tell people who to follow or how to live. You have no right."

"They made their choice. They betrayed Nanuq by fleeing instead of fighting."

"They were fleeing *him*," she spat. "And you betrayed your people, too."

"That was different," he said stiffly. "I knew we couldn't win against Nanuq."

Apaay turned away. She couldn't stand the sight of him.

The air cooled with the approaching twilight. Apaay leaned back against the wall, trying to ignore the increasingly awful stink of her excrement. Now wasn't the time to panic. She must remain clearheaded. A clouded mind led to mistakes.

"What would it take for you to let me go?"

"I'm not letting you go."

"So I will die here in this cage?" Further contemplation exposed what had been previously hidden. Ah. Now she understood. "You don't know what to do with me. You weren't expecting this. Your only option is to kill me or let me go."

"Or keep you as a captive."

Emotion coursed through her, black and livid. "You forget who freed you from the labyrinth . . . Masuk." And as his eye cleared of the bloodlust, Apaay reacquainted herself with the man who was not so strong, or certain.

Numiak's condition would not sway Kenai's decision. This—bars between them—spoke far greater volumes. She must remind him of a hand reaching through the dark, the healing touch it could bring.

"Do you remember when we were traveling to visit the First Man, and you said everyone leaves you?"

His mouth thinned. "Yes."

"I didn't leave you," she whispered. "I didn't leave you then, and I didn't leave you in the labyrinth, and I won't leave you to throw away your life. That's not who I am. But I am begging you. If any part of our friendship mattered to you, if any of it was real, please, *please* let me go." Sweat slicked her palms at the thought of returning to Nigun, finding the Face Stealer dead. "Then there will be nothing owed between us."

He did not release her. And yet, something kept him here. "You think me a horrible person," Kenai whispered.

"When have I ever spoken those words?"

Briefly, he turned away. He no longer stood tall with certainty. "Never," he said. "But you think it."

"Do I?" Apaay asked. "Or is that what *you* think?" When he didn't respond, she went on. "Why do you love Yuki?"

"You mock me."

"I asked you a question, nothing more."

As though he could not stand still, as though movement gave his words shape and power and purpose, Kenai strode from one end of the tent to the other. "She cares for me."

"How?"

"Everything she does, it is so that we may one day live in peace together."

That was what Kenai saw, but that was not what Yuki showed the world. "She sent you to lead those soldiers, didn't she. If she wanted you by her side, why would she order you so far from her?"

From the lift of his chin, Apaay reasoned Kenai had asked himself this same question. Had somehow pieced together an explanation that would support his unfaltering beliefs. "I am the only one she can trust to gather the refugees to Nanuq's cause."

"Or she wants you out of the way. Yuki aligns herself with Nanuq because of his influence. What do you offer her that she cannot get from Nanuq?"

He paced and paced. He could not be still. "You don't understand."

"I understand Yuki will use you for her own gain. She is a vengeful god, Kenai, and she has pitted you against the very people who might help you."

He halted. Listening. Something in the air hinted at change. The earlier noise—metal, footsteps, voices—had fallen silent.

Something crunched outside.

Apaay sat up straighter, her skin tingling with foreboding. Kenai touched the pommel of his sword.

Then she heard it: the wet, dull thunk of a blade cleaving flesh. A cry rang out, warning of an intruder. Kenai whirled to face whoever burst into the tent, his sword sliding free of its sheath, metal singing. It wasn't a person. It was a bird, an owl, and it arrowed through the flaps and dove for his face, talons extended, white wings flaring wide. Kenai swung faster than she could blink, but the raptor swooped out of reach and transformed into a tall, lithe man, hair moon pale, bow in hand. In a single gesture of fluidity, the owl Unua nocked his arrow and released.

Kenai slapped aside the arrow with his blade, countered with a vicious swipe toward the man's unprotected stomach, pushing him back. The man evaded, firing yet another arrow. Apaay couldn't believe it. Allies, but how many? Were Ro and Kaan present?

A second scream directed her attention to the tent flaps. The air rang with battle sounds, raptor cries, the final pleas of wounded soldiers. All the while, Kenai was lunging, swinging, arcing his sword toward the intruder, a wayward strike rattling the cage wall. Apaay shrunk against the floor.

The owl Unua whirled, ducked under the swing of Kenai's weapon, rolling to his feet a safer distance away. His arrows punctured holes through the hide. Kenai deflected and performed a series of blunt strikes, moving with the awkwardness of one who had forgotten and was trying desperately to remember. Yet there flashed brief moments of harmony, man and sword, pieces that had once been whole. This man, power incinerating his limbs, standing atop the highest pinnacle, never to believe he might one day fall far.

A horn blew in three successive bursts. Kenai's opponent faltered.

He plunged his blade into the owl Unua's chest.

Apaay heard bone breaking on impact. He crumpled, the waves of his white hair splayed out, blood seeping into the beige arm wrappings that marked him as a member of the Flock.

A second owl dove through the flaps. Keeping to the ceiling as it surveyed the sight below: a man dead, a woman captured, the enemy standing free. Apaay assumed Kenai would attack. He had much to prove of himself. Instead, he unlocked the cage. The door swung wide.

"Go," he said tonelessly, watching the owl circle out of reach. Blood flecked his face and neck.

Apaay stared, wide-eyed. A trap?

"Now!" He rattled the cage, which got her moving. Apaay crawled into the open, skirting the dead man. Her knees and ankles cracked painfully, but she managed to push to her feet, using the cage for support.

"You have to know, Kenai. The truth. Numiak didn't kill your father. It wasn't real. He took your memory away, made you believe—"

"Enough!" he roared, sidestepping the raptor as it attempted to whip its spike-wrapped legs against his back. The blade nicked one of its wings, and it screamed and flew off. Apaay watched it go, wondered if it was anyone she knew, if it would survive. Even if Ro and Kaan were present, she couldn't waste time trying to find them. Numiak's health came first.

Kenai lowered his sword, his single eye wild, and pulled her close. "You will pass on a message for me," he panted into her ear. The hand curling around Apaay's upper arm trembled. "Tell Numiak I am coming for him. Tell him there is no place he can hide that I won't find him. Tell him when we meet again, it will be for the very last time." A hard shove forced Apaay toward the exit. "A life for a life," he said. "Consider my debt repaid."

← 17 →

After fleeing the camp, Apaay fought her way back toward the River Pak. Patches of soft, muted sky foretold the day's end. The trees flashed like slivers of light. Her fingertips flitted against the roughened bark, trailed through the abundant leaves in strange familiarity. How odd. How very odd that she might know this place, know exactly where to go.

The wind gusted at her back, quickening her feet as she leaped over roots and disturbed the blanket of dried vegetation. She thought of Numiak on his knees before the Avi. She thought of his body curling around hers seconds before they slammed into a tree, Tor's coastal waters erupting at their backs. She thought of two lulling words—*Sleep, Apaay*—and how easy it had been to obey, dark power in his voice.

Apaay followed the wide, glittering band of the river until she reached a cave partially concealed by drooping, broad-leafed trees. By then, her chest ached with the force of her exertion, and cramps seized the muscles in her thighs. The water lay placid here. The cave was a dark mouth, and a pleasant, herbaceous scent drifted from its depths.

"Hello?" Apaay called, taking a cautious step forward.

Something shifted in the cave's shadows. Something massive.

A great bear lumbered forth. A shaggy, russet brown pelt coated a body that rippled with pure flesh on muscle, a pale mark in the shape of an arrowhead lightening its brow. It was perhaps half the size of a polar bear, but that did not make it any less formidable. This creature the Caribou Nomads called a kitska. Apaay could not help but stare. It walked upright on two legs, not four. Vines and overgrowth tangled with its fur, as if it were something grown from the forest, an animal with rooted legs and an earthen pelt, a trunked body.

Apaay brought moisture to her dry mouth. Green eyes met her brown ones with human intelligence. The color was too intense to be real. The longer Apaay held its gaze, the more she believed those eyes to be mirrors, or windows, for images appeared to shift inside the pupils—branches, perhaps, or leaves.

The kitska took her in. She, a young woman wearing a coat of sweat and a coat of skin. Marks of the forest upon her arms. As well, a single, unspoken word suspended between them.

Please.

The bear blinked. Apaay felt something probe the inside of her mind, seeking, digging, defiling. She trembled from the need to run, fast and far, but she could not. Everything would be all right. Apaay did not think this kitska meant to hurt her. It showed no outward signs of aggression. There was, however, something clearly *other* about it. Not a bear. Not Unua. Something more. Something strange.

Lowering itself onto four legs, the creature turned and vanished into the cave. And Apaay, against her better judgment, followed.

It was a small room, made smaller by the many shelves chipped from the black obsidian walls. Glass bottles cluttered the uneven surfaces, bowls stuffed with feathers and powders and colored liquids, including the long plumes of a bird she'd never seen before, the feathers gold tipped in blue.

A large vat of water boiled in the room's center. It smelled pungent and sweet. Apaay spotted tools used for tattooing resting on a table: needles of bone, and ink.

At the far end of the cave, the bear stopped and said, *I know why you have come.*

A woman's voice filled the space, but the bear's mouth never moved.

Apaay, caught in the peculiar power, answered, "I don't have much time. My friend is dying."

The kitska dipped its head, and Apaay swore the motion caused leaves to sprout from its shoulder blades, but when she blinked, the image had vanished. The air felt thick with haze. She pressed a hand to her throbbing eyes.

A cold, wet nose touched the base of her throat. *Your friend fights against a poison produced from the venom of the ghost urchin.* The bear plodded to the shelves of herbs. *How long ago since the poisoning?*

Apaay wondered how the kitska knew this information. Perhaps the scent of the poison clung to her skin, since she had spent so much time in Numiak's company. She thought of their journey from the Atakana to Nigun—a harrowing flight—and the time since arriving at the capital gates. "Almost nine weeks."

Then your companion should be dead.

Apaay caught her breath. She would not believe it. "My companion isn't human. He's a demon who hails from Taggak."

The bear pushed onto its hind legs to rifle through its stores. For such a massive animal, it moved gracefully. *There are only two people I know of who are made from Taggak, and I assume you are not speaking of its god. The one you call the Face Stealer, then.* Her voice, cool and melodious and slow as a drifting pool, sounded distant.

"Yes," said Apaay.

The kitska materialized in front of her. Its massive shoulders dwarfed her body, even standing on four legs. Apaay hadn't seen it move.

That's when she noticed a small vial full of chalky white liquid hanging from a cord around its neck. "What is that?"

Does it matter? It will cure him—for a price.

Apaay hadn't thought she would be given the cure so freely, but she was learning some things came with too high a price. Time and again she had given too much of herself. She must protect the most important pieces so that she would always remember: Apaay, Analak, sister, daughter, friend.

"What do you want?" she asked warily, knowing she would likely give whatever the kitska demanded outright. Numiak's life meant more to her than she realized. It meant quite a lot.

Apaay thought the kitska's eyes might have crinkled. *Surely you can spare five drops of your blood.*

She nearly recoiled from the suggestion.

One's blood was never to be trifled with. Sometimes, Analak were born with special gifts such as the power to interpret dreams or the ability to make marine life appear—indeed, one man from her village had the gift of healing wounds by licking them—and the power of another's blood could potentially amplify those gifts, but only at the cost of corrupting the individual whose blood they exploited. That this kitska asked for Apaay's blood . . . A feeling of foreboding wormed through her, warning her to tread carefully.

"Why do you need my blood?"

It is of no concern to you. A slight shift of the bear's head, and one of the vines wrapped around its neck uncoiled. *It would be mine to use as I wish.*

Apaay told herself the blood didn't matter. Curing Numiak—that mattered. Gathering the Caribou Nomads to their side—that mattered, too. Five drops of blood seemed like such a small thing. If it would save Numiak, then she had little choice, hadn't she?

Apaay couldn't know it then, but that day, the North witnessed a great change. It wasn't the first occurrence. Nor would it be the last. Sometimes, the change was subtle: a waning or waxing moon, or snow melting into spring. Sometimes, the change was of a blunter nature, uncomfortable and unfamiliar: a man with pale features and an indecipherable message.

And sometimes, change was five drops of blood.

← →

The sun had fallen to the horizon's edge by the time Apaay reached Nigun. The entrance gates beseeched her with an ominous groan, opening like a great maw. Apaay descended into the entrance tunnel, her feet slapping against rock. The first guard she came across, she stopped. "Where is he?"

The man stared at her blankly. A fleck of blood marred the edge of his jaw beneath his mask.

Her hands shook, and her knees. Her heart lurched as though carried on waves toward shore. Again, she demanded, "Where is he?"

A bit of clarity returned to the guard's face. He ushered her to a room overflowing with plants, vines climbing the walls, and water spreading on all sides: an island in the heart of an underground lake.

The Face Stealer rested on a bed amidst the wild tangle of plants, blankets pooling around his waist. His chest was bare, the skin smooth and taut, but far too pale, his flat abdomen marred by the gruesome puncture wound. It lifted only a hairsbreadth. A frail, rattling wheeze hissed out with each exhale.

The shaking grew worse as she moved to his bedside. Apaay felt as if she were dangling over a cliff's edge, clinging to a rope that was swiftly unraveling. His eyes were deep bruises. His lips were like cracked snow, white residue clumped at the corners. He looked halfway to the spirit world.

Unstopping the vial, she pried open the Face Stealer's mouth. His jaw cracked. An agonized groan tore from his chest, and he jerked in her hold. She tipped the liquid into his open mouth, closed it, forcing him to swallow.

Then she waited.

His breathing eased. Color seeped into his skin, returning it to a warm, healthy glow. She watched in uncomfortable fascination as the black veins around his stomach wound disappeared and the skin began to knit itself back together.

At last, he opened his eyes. His muddled gaze gained lucidity as the moments passed. The emotion behind it was quiet, contemplative, and maybe, she thought with a pulse of trepidation, happy.

His mouth softened into a rare smile that revealed his dimples. He said simply, "Wolfling."

Relief hit her as hard and sudden as a wave breaking ashore. Then came the fury, frothing beneath her skin. How dare Numiak put her through something like this. He hadn't any idea what she'd endured to return to him in time. He was so . . . so . . .

To her horror, tears stung her eyes. "I'm still angry with you," she hissed.

His gaze roamed her face with far too much leisure. "There's the warm welcome I was expecting." The smile remained, but the dimples had gone. "You are nothing if not consistent."

Apaay huffed, suddenly cured of her outward worry. "I should have let you die."

His laughter lulled into a drifting sound. His eyes were the liquid blue of dark waters. "Admit it. You would have missed me otherwise."

If she refuted his statement, did that make it false? "I would have missed not calling in your blood oath."

"The blood oath. How could I forget?" He reached out, brushing the tips of his fingers against hers. Apaay studied their hands in surprise. It was a gentle touch, unassuming and without pressure. "Let me remind you that I am very hard to kill."

"That's not—" Her voice strained from her tightening airway, because what if she hadn't returned in time? "That's not funny."

"For what it's worth," Numiak said, clasping her hand more firmly and brushing his callused thumb along her palm, "I was waiting for you to return before I died."

Every thought emptied out at his touch. The slow back and forth motion was driving her mad. "How polite of you." Apaay lifted her chin.

The dimples returned. He'd noticed the hitch in her voice, damn him.

A moment of silence passed before he asked, "What took you so long?"

Apaay hesitated before pulling her hand away. The plants hung like a veil around them, laden with fat blossoms dripping sweetness. Kenai's message was as fresh as if he had told her moments ago.

She should pass on the message. Doubtless, Numiak would want to know. Yet she could not purge herself of the memory, he and Kenai, the woods beyond Talguk's ruined city, and betrayal, poison-coated harpoon heads imbedded in Numiak's skin. Would it be a kindness to tell him, or a burden?

She said, "It took me longer to find the cure, that's all," and left it at that.

For the second time in many minutes, Apaay did not know what to say. Something had shifted between them. Had she ever feared for his life as she had while contained in that cage? And the relief at knowing he was safe and well—what of that? And the way Numiak looked at her, the affection in his gaze . . . She shied away.

"I know you're angry with me," he murmured, "but I'd like a chance to explain."

Her face warmed uncomfortably. Apaay cleared her throat and stared into the water. She waited for the fury, the rage that had sent her across the grasslands. It didn't come.

"I don't know," Apaay said. "I kind of like it when you grovel."

The Face Stealer pushed into a seated position. There was nothing left of the wound except a taut white scar. "Like seeing me in pain, do you?" The bones of his face pushed sharply against his skin from the weight he had lost.

It took everything in her not to flinch. That wasn't what she meant, and Apaay thought he knew that, despite his question. Perhaps they were both navigating uncomfortable emotions in relation to the ordeal.

Apaay whispered, sensing she had hit a nerve, "You know the answer to that."

"Do I?" His gaze held hers until she dropped her eyes. Sometimes it felt like looking into a mirror, and that was almost as frightening as the idea that he might not have survived.

"Apaay," he said when the quiet grew strained. "We need to discuss this."

As usual, he was right. And, as usual, she wished he weren't.

Sighing deeply, she sank into the vine-covered chair near his bed and rubbed her eyes. "I wanted to believe what you told me was a lie. I was angry. I felt you had betrayed my trust. But more than that, I was afraid of what it might mean were it true." Apaay lifted her face as if she might feel the sea breeze against it, but she was far from Naga's shores. "I never wanted to be involved with this war. I traveled to the labyrinth to find Eska's face, that was all. Now I learn my role is greater—vital, even—and I want to run. I want to run and keep running until these thoughts no longer trouble me. Can you understand that?"

"Yes," said Numiak. His expression softened a touch.

"If we're to move forward on this, I need your word. No more secrets. No more lies." She leveled him with a serious gaze. "Promise me."

His tongue darted out to wet his lips. At last, he nodded. "No more secrets."

She narrowed her eyes. He'd given his word, so why didn't she believe him? "You mentioned powers." The word tasted forbidden, potent. "What are they, exactly?"

"You are essentially my antithesis. The Creator has power over identities, but whereas I'm restricted to stealing them, you have the ability to create new faces, new identities entirely."

Apaay considered this . . . impossibility. It made sense. The North was a land of balance, convergence, a push and pull of greater forces. There was the sky and the earth and the sun and the moon and the cold and the warmth and life and death. It had always been so.

It felt as if a current of energy ran beneath her skin, prickly and uncomfortable. This was the truth—the unknown. Everything else was the lie.

Her head hurt just thinking about it.

"Your powers are beginning to manifest themselves. They are becoming too strong for the protections I placed on you."

Apaay caught the Face Stealer's voice in snatches. Words like *power* and *manifest* and *protection*, and she began to feel lightheaded. There it was again, that urge to run fast and far until her legs gave out. "Why does this matter to Nanuq?" Because it always came back to Nanuq, didn't it? The man who would shape the world in his image, no matter how depraved that image might be.

"When the Raven mentioned Nanuq sought to become fully man, I knew. He seeks for you to make him a new identity. A completely *human* face, without animal features, without any tether to his polar bear form."

Apaay gaped at him, dumbstruck. "I can do that?"

"You have the ability to make faces permanent, so that even I can't remove them. Nanuq believes man is the superior species. With a new human identity, he will conquer the North in its entirety."

Why did she have the horrible desire to laugh when, really, her throat ached with oncoming tears? Look at what had become of Yuki. Nanuq. The commander. Look at how quickly power corrupted. All of it leading to turmoil and torment, and peace nothing but a dream.

"Apaay—"

She lifted a hand, halting the rest of his thought. "Give me a minute. Please."

His expression folded into one of concern, but he remained quiet as she strode a few paces away, her back to him, and tried to reach a conclusion.

What did she want, truly? Apaay could not remember when she had last asked herself this question. Since escaping the labyrinth, she'd been swept up in conflict against her will. So she asked herself now. *What do I want?*

To return home. To stitch boots with Mama, hunt with Papa, wrestle with Eska, croon soft melodies to Chena's newborn daughter. To lose herself in the oral traditions of their people as darkness encroached. It was a dream, these thoughts, for there was no home to return to. Apaay found herself surrounded by things completely unfamiliar: rock and boiling water and eerie vines and men with antlers growing from their skulls, their tines honed for battle. Yes, these thoughts were indeed a dream.

Those days were gone. Now she must decide how to move forward. How much responsibility did she want in the war? It would reach them soon. Would she cower while others fought? Would she take a stand?

"How did this happen?" Apaay asked, turning back around to search his veiled gaze. "Start from the beginning. How did Nanuq know the Creator existed? And how did you know these powers manifested in me?"

He said, "You mentioned you found a document in my library. Describe that document to me."

"There were illustrations of the five Unua nations in their animal forms. Beneath was the silhouette of a human. They seemed to be connected somehow."

Numiak studied her carefully. "I have answers, but I do not have all of them. The most common interpretation is that a person might be granted special gifts as to what I just described. I do not know why. Meddlesome gods, perhaps. The document you found is ancient. It precedes my life by many millennia.

"My belief is that Nanuq found this document and brought it with him when he returned from Across the Sea. During one of my missions, before the Wolf Kingdom's fall, I was sent to retrieve it from his stores, and it has been in my possession ever since. As to how I know these powers lie in you, I imagine you know. Someone or something, old as the gods, that has witnessed the North's change, told me."

Apaay immediately knew of whom he spoke. "The First Man." The eyes and ears of the world.

"Yes."

It explained much, but not all. Apaay recalled talk of Nanuq, the object of power he'd believed to be held in the Western Territory. If she truly was the Creator, why would Nanuq have thought her to be located in the Western Territory? That was the reason for his invasion all those years ago, was it not? Unless that, too, had been a lie. A misdirection to protect Apaay, keep Nanuq from the Analak villages.

"Do my parents know? Why would they agree to this?" The possibility of their deceit hurt worse than this newfound knowledge, the Face Stealer's lies.

"Your parents are not aware of this. Your safety depended on your anonymity. No one knows except me."

Something didn't sit right with the idea. It felt incomplete.

That's when he pulled the scrap of skin from his pocket. It drooped over the pads of his fingers. How could he expect her to accept this with no hesitation, as if she wasn't having an internal crisis related to her identity? As if there were not enough things in the world to worry about.

"Take it," he coaxed. "It's yours."

Apaay studied the face with borderline revulsion. The eyes, nose, and mouth, so different from the girl in the water's reflection. In her hands was the face of a stranger.

Why should she accept this face anyway? Because the Face Stealer said so? It didn't seem like a good enough reason. What would he know of it? He barked orders and people jumped to do his bidding, but it wasn't his life in upheaval. He did not lose sleep over the words, *Who am I?*

The Face Stealer was wrong. This persona wasn't *hers*, as if an identity was something to possess, like a pair of trousers or a harpoon. It was not a *thing*. It was greater than that. It was something given life. It lived and died as she did. To accept this identity was to give up another, one she had spent her entire life coming to know.

Quietly, Numiak said, "Sometimes we must think of the world and our place in it, unselfishly."

Apaay bristled at the implication: that to refuse was an act of selfishness. At what point did Apaay think of herself, separate to the world? She had never asked for this. She did not owe anything to the world. And for him to push this enormous responsibility onto her, to say it was not enough, she was not enough, this old shape did not fit into this new world, after everything she had been through?

Apaay stepped back. "I'm sorry," she whispered, "but that's just not me."

← 18 →

Word spread like wildfire among the camp. Someone had come for them. A girl: Matilaqaa. Heir to the Wolf Kingdom.

Ila did her best to accommodate the questions, as she had many of them herself. It was her hope that she and these women would learn from one another. They told her about their lives in Unana and the outlying cities. In return, she told them about hers. About the labyrinth, then the Wood, anyone who would listen. Tipki asked about the Face Stealer with wide-eyed fascination, for they had fought in the Pack together, she and Malina and Numiak, though in different units. Malina asked no questions of her own, choosing instead to retreat to the back of her cell in wolf form, curling up.

On the third day, the guards arrived. Lumbering, mean, careless, fatted. The building shook as the door slammed open against the wall.

One by one, Ila and the rest of the prisoners filed from the dark, damp, dreary hole, out into the chill, down an uneven path, Ila bringing up the rear.

She knew what to expect. Pili had explained their schedule. Hours upon hours upon hours spent digging holes—searching for something these guards and Nanuq could never hope to find, this object of extreme power. She would get through this day. But first, breakfast.

The long, rectangular room was crammed end to end with tables and benches, guards stationed against the walls, weapons held close to their bodies.

The women filed inside first. Then came the children. Ila took in their dull-eyed appearances, lines of exhaustion cutting so deeply they were all but imprinted onto their skin. Somehow, the guards managed to cram hundreds of bodies into the tiny space. Ila received her food, gruel slopped into a bowl with a wooden spoon, and joined the others at a rickety table. The air reeked of sweat layered upon filth and dirt, and more sweat, and more dirt.

Pili rapped the side of Ila's bowl. "Eat. You haven't much time."

Lifting the bowl, Ila sucked in a mouthful of the watery liquid and promptly spat it out.

Four pairs of eyes locked onto her.

What is this? Because it certainly wasn't edible.

"Food," said Saniraq. Her hair was pinned in twin braids along the sides of her head, and her gaze had a piercing quality to it, though far more tempered than Malina's.

Hare. At least, that's what I tell myself, Tipki signed with a most unhelpful grin. *Goes down easier than human flesh.* She made a show of scooping a large spoonful into her mouth, gagging only a little. Ila's mouth twitched.

Malina slammed her bowl against the table. "Tipki."

The younger woman smiled, batting her curled lashes. "Yes, Mother?"

Shooting Ila a sour expression, she said, "Have care with who you speak to."

"I know who I'm speaking to. My Vaal, and yours. You should try it sometime." She turned away from Malina's scowling face.

Is she your mother, truly? Ila signed to Tipki.

No, though she certainly acts like it. With that, Tipki drew her bench mate into conversation, leaving Ila to observe the women at her table. They interacted with ease, yet the tension that thickened as breakfast drew to an end could not be missed. Ila looked to the guards. The door.

Saniraq touched her arm. "He's not here."

Something squeezed in her chest. *Who?*

The woman leveled her with a long look, saying nothing.

Ila glanced down at her gruel. It had the exact consistency of vomit.

In your story, Saniraq said, switching to signing, *you mentioned a man named Tulimaq. There is a Tulimaq here as well.* She wasn't completely fluent in her gestures, but Ila understood well enough. She appreciated the effort. More so, she appreciated that Saniraq cared enough to try.

In her story, she hadn't revealed everything, only details related to her time in the labyrinth, and then the Wood. She hadn't mentioned Tulimaq's betrayal, having felt foolish for trusting him so easily. They didn't know it was he who had captured her and brought her to the labor camp. *You are very observant,* Ila said.

She didn't mean it as an insult, but luckily, Saniraq did not interpret it as one.

"Everyone talks," she said, scooping up the pieces of gray meat with her spoon and watching them float in the murk. "Not everyone listens."

Unconsciously, Ila's attention slid to the end of the table. She thought it purposeful that Malina had placed so much space between them, though she had hardly spoken five words to the taciturn woman. Then she focused again on Saniraq, who said, "I assume you have a plan?" That was all she dared to say. The rest was implied.

It was a work-in-progress. *I will need everyone's cooperation if it is to succeed.* And that, too, was implied.

Saniraq sighed, resting her spoon in her bowl. *It will not be easy. Before the invasion, Malina was a unit—* She faltered, searching for the correct hand gesture. She looked to Ila for help. "Commander?"

Ila signed, *Commander.*

Commander, the woman continued, replicating the motion, *in the Pack. You cannot expect her to follow you without cause.*

And Ila had given little evidence of leading with conviction. It was a coat she wore that did not fit to her exact measurements.

You can train your body to become strong, but if your heart is weak, it will make no difference. Tulimaq had said that to her long ago. It was time again to put that into practice. If she wanted to lead, she must first become worthy of it.

"If you're not going to eat that," Malina said with a pointed glare at Ila's mostly-untouched food, "give it to me."

Ila swallowed down the vile contents of her meal.

← →

They gave Ila something called a shovel. She was to dig a hole of her exact height. If she found something, Pili told her, she was to report to one of the guards. Ila asked what she was supposed to be looking for. Pili said, "Anything."

The prisoners shoveled and did not speak. They gouged the field, piled up the dark, soft earth. Again. And again.

Ila worked the dirt tirelessly. The hole grew: wider, deeper, a swallowing mouth, a plunging chasm.

Pili nudged her. Ila lifted her head, blinking away the bright spots. Sweat slithered down her temples and slipped into her partially open mouth.

"You need to dig faster."

Faster? She was going as fast as possible. The blisters on her palms had burst, and clear fluid trickled over her wrists.

Ila shoveled until her shoulders throbbed. Her hunger gnashed its teeth before retreating with its tail between its legs. She knew only of her burning hands and throbbing feet and the sun baking any exposed skin. Beside her, Tipki shoveled hole after hole, seemingly immune to exhaustion.

It was mid-afternoon when she caught sight of a woman at the far end of the clearing. The prisoner had been struggling all morning, fighting to keep up with the brutal pace. She was still digging her first hole. Ila was on her fourth.

The whip came down across the woman's back.

Ila flinched. She kept digging. The women, all of them, kept digging.

It didn't cease. Frozen in horror, Ila watched the black serpent coil and strike, coil and strike, back and legs and shoulders. The woman curled into a ball to protect her face from the lash. Her skin split like a flower bursting open from the bud.

Another guard snarled at Ila, "Keep digging, filth!"

Saniraq interrupted her line of vision, face carefully blank. "You can't stop."

The woman was no longer moving.

Agony ripped open her back. Ila jerked forward, falling into her partially dug hole as hot liquid slipped down her skin.

A second strike followed, this one so deep she swore it hit bone. She screamed, feeling as though the pain were bleeding into her brain.

Then it was over. Her back burned and burned, a torment. Breathing labored, Ila grabbed her shovel and used it to help her stand. The guard snapped his whip against the ground in warning. "You are here to work, not stare into the trees. Next time, I will break bone."

Ila plunged her shovel into the dirt, biting the inside of her cheek so she wouldn't faint.

She didn't stop digging for the rest of the day.

← →

"Sit still so I can see how deep the wounds are."

Ila gasped as Pili tugged the shredded cloth from her equally shredded back. *How bad?* she signed.

The old woman wrapped her back with strips of an old blanket. Afterward, she sat. "The wounds are deep, but none hit bone."

If only she hadn't left that salve in her old cell. It wouldn't change her situation though. This was not a life. This was existence, spare and wanting.

The guard, Birthmark, had not returned with information regarding her plan. She feared he never would.

I would like to ask you something.

Pili, as if sensing the significance of the statement, offered Ila her undivided attention.

I would like to know . . . how you came to be here. What happened on the day of the invasion? Her only recollection of that tragic day was what she had witnessed in the Face Stealer's memory. Soot and flame, and a beam collapsing overhead, and the split in her skull, which had eventually healed into the knotted scar that parted the smoky brown curls of her hair. *I admit, I have been kept in the dark for much of it.*

"Then I should probably start from the beginning. I knew who you were the moment I saw you."

Ila stared at the old woman's mouth in confusion. Then all at once, her heart lurched forward. She had not misinterpreted the speech. She was certain.

I don't understand.

Pili smiled. "Your mother was one of my very good friends. You have her eyes. Qumiq and I met one afternoon in one of the markets. She was bored. I was bored. We were sixteen."

Her vision was too blurry to take in Pili's expression. Her mother at sixteen was a world away.

"Qumiq was of the lowest rank, as was I. Your father was heir. It was pure happenstance that he was visiting the market the same day we were. Oh, he was handsome. A man of eighteen years. He saw your mother and was immediately smitten. Of course, Qumiq did not know who he was," Pili said. "Your father was stupefied."

Ila found herself smiling.

"Urumak never forgot your mother. He tracked her down, revealed his identity. When he asked her to return with him to the capital, she refused." Her eyes twinkled.

What did my father do?

"He was wise not to press your mother. She was too strong-willed for that. So he waited. For three years, he visited her almost weekly, and in that time, they fell in love. When they were mated, it was perhaps the happiest union I had ever seen."

Did my mother ever visit you once she was wed?

"Actually," Pili said, "I became your mother's caretaker. I cared for you as a child."

Then you knew my sister.

Pili hesitated, as if sensing how important this answer was to Ila. "Only briefly. The invasion was . . . well. I cannot properly describe what it is like to lose your home and the people you love so suddenly and violently. I managed to escape the capital, but I did not get far before I was captured and brought here. That was twenty years ago. I've been here ever since."

And Malina?

Pili glanced at the sleeping wolf, and something in her eyes softened. "Malina carries a lot of guilt over the invasion. Many of her Packmates did not make it out. She trained her entire life to serve. Now she is caged. You can imagine what that might do to someone."

I feel as though she blames me for what happened.

"Blames you?" Pili frowned. "All I can say is nothing with Malina is ever given. It must be earned."

← 19 →

Days later, Kirimat found Apaay hiding in one of the vegetable gardens. Though Apaay noticed her approach, she continued to rip leaves from the climbing vines as the woman studied her with no small amount of concern. Admittedly, the leaves were rather mutilated. And if she imagined them as pieces of the Face Stealer's dismembered body, she'd keep that information to herself.

"Numiak says you're avoiding him," said Kirimat.

"Numiak is a coward." Curt.

The older woman sighed. "Will you look at me?"

Apaay had spent enough time in the Face Stealer's company to never take what he said or did at face value. Truths wrapped in lies wrapped in truths. His enigma of a mind. And so she looked into this woman's eyes and asked herself why she had come.

"What was the first thing I said to you when we met?" Apaay demanded, dropping the remainder of the leaves onto the ground.

Kirimat's brow wrinkled, collapsing onto itself. She had done away with her mask, as had Apaay. A small allowance from the commander, but only when out of sight from the brainwashed caribou Unua. "Where is this coming from?"

"Answer the question. Please."

"You told me I don't drink the nectar."

Tension ebbed from her body, and Apaay leaned back onto her hands. "Sorry. I had to make sure you weren't Numiak in disguise." Never mind that he'd been stripped of his powers.

Kirimat snorted, settling against the base of a tree laden with fruits the color of a warm sunset. "I'd gut Numiak before I ever let him take my face."

Good to know. In her opinion, it was wise to have a friend willing to gut a man. "How do you know Numiak anyway?" She hadn't spent much time speaking with Kirimat privately. And she hadn't bothered to ask Numiak out of anger, though his attempts at speaking with the commander caused his absences of late.

"Numiak and I go way back. We served in the Pack together. After the invasion, I went into hiding. It wasn't safe for my people."

"So what brought you here?"

Kirimat paused, as though she considered a reply, then promptly discarded it. "I'm here on a mission, which I cannot discuss, unfortunately."

Numiak once served on an elite, special operations unit, which completed highly confidential assignments for the good of the Wolf Kingdom. But Apaay didn't know how Kirimat could carry out a Pack mission, since her nation was disbanded, unless this was something completely unrelated.

"What do you know of the Creator?" Apaay asked. Tree canopies capped them in an interwoven ceiling, the stagnant air a constant reminder they were nowhere near aboveground.

"Nothing," she admitted, drawing her knees to her chest. "Why? What's bothering you?"

Reason warned her to keep this knowledge private, but what say did reason have in matters of the heart?

"Oh, nothing," Apaay said bitterly. "Except I recently learned the last eighteen years of my life have been a lie. Well, nineteen," she amended, recalling her birthday had passed a few weeks back. She'd celebrated by forcing food into Numiak's mouth when he'd been too weak to feed himself.

"Really." Kirimat straightened, appraising her with a critical eye. "How so?"

Apaay took care with her response, for she did not want to give away too much information, if only for her own protection. The Creator was cause enough for a twice-fought war. "I guess I now have this . . . responsibility to uphold, but I don't want it. So much has changed." It weighed on her. Apaay had not felt grounded since the day she'd left home for the labyrinth, and it frightened her that she might never feel stable again. "I miss the simplicity of my life *before*. I want—" Her throat spasmed, and she swallowed. To want was to dream, but Apaay could not let go of hope, no matter how dire her situation became. She would not go back to the dark. She would not. "I want to live without fear. I want to return to Naga's shores and rebuild. The Creator would allow for none of those things."

Kirimat asked, not unkindly, "Why not?" She seemed genuinely curious.

"Because as soon as I accept that role, I put a target on my back." It was to accept that the person she'd been did not exist, had perhaps never existed. The thought was breaking open her mind.

"Don't you already have a target on your back?" At Apaay's look of puzzlement, Kirimat explained, "Numiak told me of Yuki."

"Yes," Apaay replied tersely, "but this is different. This is . . ."
Permanent.

"I do not know what this Creator is," said Kirimat, "but do you think refusing the role will grant you peace? Do you think it will protect you from war? Will you live your life on the run?"

She bristled at the implication, the feeling of a light cast upon her, and not a favorable one. Did Kirimat imply Apaay was selfish in desiring a different life, or choosing to build one, rather than existing in one that had been built for her? "You don't have to be cruel about it."

"I'm not," Kirimat soothed. "But this has been my life for the past two decades. I settle, and then, for whatever reason, I'm forced to leave. Do you know how hard it is to plant roots in places where they will not grow? My people were captured, forced into labor camps, and I was free of that life, but was I?" Her voice softened. "I ask myself that sometimes—if it would have been better in the camps, because at least I'd have my people. Instead, I am alone."

"Kirimat, I didn't know."

The older woman said, "The peace you wish for will not be gained through avoidance, because the truth is this war never ended. Nanuq will conquer whether you accept this responsibility or not."

The black of Apaay's hair sifted through her fingers. It lacked the rocks and feathers and bones it had once displayed. It was a wound. It would always be a wound. But Apaay had come to terms with what had been done. "If I become the Creator, then what? Will I still be *me*?"

"We like to do that," Kirimat said, looking out. It felt as if the plants were breathing, and their exhale was the woman's inhale, and all the air was shared. "Put ourselves into rooms with walls. I am this, we say, or I am that." Compassion softened her expression, and the girl drew toward it, opened like a flower to the sun. "Why do we have to be only one thing?"

Apaay accepted this quietly, as though it were her own heartbeat, unshakeable and strong. Kirimat's comfort had the warm softness of Ila's touch, and Apaay wanted to believe she deserved it. She wanted to believe she deserved forgiveness, too, in her behavior toward Ila, but had been unable to take that step.

"I am Analak," she said. "I'm a sister, a daughter, a friend, a giver, a fighter, a survivor." The words sang with internal harmony. "And," she added, suddenly remembering, "the most important part of all."

"Oh?"

Apaay fought a smile, because here, too, was another forgotten piece of herself. A bit neglected, yes, but that did not make it any less valuable.

"The greatest joke-teller who ever lived."

← →

Apaay found Numiak deep in one of Nigun's many caverns, sparring with one of the Caribou Nomads. *Clack, clack, clack*—their staffs beat a hollow rhythm. They sparred on a narrow path cutting through a body of dark, placid water, trading blows, an ease to the motions, and a joy. Numiak's opponent bore graceful antlers poking from his tightly curled brown hair. Green streaks shifted beneath his skin like leaves on a bracing wind. Strange, how he did not wear a mask.

They had stripped from the waist up and wore loose trousers, their feet bare. Sweat gleamed in the hollows of their torsos, both masterpieces of warm, oaken skin. Lamplight flowed from wide, shallow dishes tucked into the rock. Muscle flexed: thigh, back, abdomen. Numiak brought his staff down with whistling force. The man blocked and struck low, forcing his opponent back, nearer to the water's edge. Judging by the fluidity of Numiak's movements, he had recovered well enough from the poisoning.

It was a pleasure to watch him fight, truthfully. Apaay had believed his predatory grace to derive from his wolf Unua heritage, but she saw now, as she had not seen before, that his movements were intentional, his limbs exploding forward with great force, then retreating, always with strategy in mind.

The antlered weapons shimmered in the low light. The Face Stealer blocked a strike near his head and retaliated with a downward slash, which his rival deflected. Both toed the edge of the walkway. During the next round of blows, the Face Stealer overstepped, plunging into the water below.

Apaay bit back a smile as the splash echoed. Breaking the surface, Numiak grinned at his opponent, treading water. "Well fought. You're even better than I remember."

The other man smirked, resting the butt of his staff on the ground. "And you're worse. No offense."

Numiak snorted before swimming back to the path and hauling himself clear of the lake. Water poured onto the stone, catching light in its dark spread as it pooled at his feet. "Two months of near-death will do that to you."

"Sounds like an excuse to me."

That's when Numiak caught sight of Apaay loitering near the entrance. His focus sharpened. A predator's stare. Without breaking eye contact, he said, "Let's take a break," and strode toward her, dripping, while the other man looked on curiously. His quick appraisal was over before Apaay could dredge up the indignation. "You're in a pleasant mood."

Apaay crossed her arms over her chest. "What can I say? I enjoy watching you get knocked down." His answering smile reminded her of dark things. Forbidden things. She wet her mouth. "You're training again?"

"I never stopped." At her surprise, he said, "Once a soldier, always a soldier."

"But—" Her gaze flicked to his opponent, who drank deeply from a waterskin. "I never saw you train in the Wood."

"You wouldn't have. You were always in the library." He didn't speak unkindly. Truly, Apaay *had* spent most of her waking hours with the books, if only to avoid him and the rest of her problems.

Her gaze returned to the handsome caribou Unua. "So who's your friend?" Obviously, they knew one another.

His smile changed. It widened and grew fangs. Apaay's heart skipped a beat. "Why? See something you like?"

Before she could snap a retort, his sparring partner ambled over. This close, she was better able to appreciate the exquisite symmetry of his face. He was, simply put, too pretty.

"Hello." His voice held the warm baritone of far-off thunder, and his hands were equally warm as they fit over one of hers. "My name is Pilan."

"Apaay." She was so focused on the man's touch that she didn't notice Numiak's frown. There was something about this man's mouth. It was very pleasant to look at.

"Apaay." The resonance of that word made her shiver. "I've heard much about you."

"Oh?" She looked at Numiak, surprised and a little pleased. "Good things I hope."

His grin held an edge. "Mostly."

She nearly hit him.

"Thank you," she told Pilan.

"For what?"

"For knocking this one—" She jerked a thumb in the Face Stealer's direction. "—down a notch."

He laughed. The Face Stealer narrowed his eyes.

"Apaay. I hope we shall see one another around, no?"

Now that Numiak was healed, there was the matter of winning

the caribou Unua over to their side. Since they were staying a while, she supposed that would be a yes.

After sharing a wordless look with the Face Stealer, Pilan slid on his mask and left them alone, the muscles of his back shifting as he went. Not that Apaay stared. Much. "He seems . . . nice."

"To look at, you mean."

"I didn't say that."

"You didn't have to."

She said, "He's not brainwashed." Eyes clear as the water, and as bright.

"No," Numiak agreed.

Apaay waited for an explanation. In vain, she knew.

"What did you say about me? Did you tell him you would have died a slow and painful death without my help?" She spoke teasingly, poking fun as he often did with her, but he replied with a surprising amount of severity.

"I did."

Apaay didn't know what to say except, "Oh."

Numiak leaned forward, perusing the curves of her face in greater detail. He was always doing that—infiltrating her personal space. Apaay took a step back when he caught her arm.

"Careful," he murmured, gesturing to the walkway's edge. "That would be a nasty fall."

Apaay inhaled slowly through her nose, for the press of his fingers against her skin held all the heat of a banked fire. "You would know."

A slight curl to his mouth. Apaay wished she could stop staring at it. "Yes. Now that I think of it, I might have broken something. Maybe you should take a look."

Damn her stupid, racing heart. "Maybe you should reconsider asking someone to hit you with a large stick."

"It could be serious."

"I'm sure."

"I have a concussion, I think."

"Try to stay awake."

And just like that, there they were.

Too close.

The heat of his body collided with hers, and spread, and curved like soft hide around her, so that its warmth became her warmth as well. The smoky scent of his skin licked at her awareness. It wasn't the first time Apaay had resisted the pull to lean into Numiak, body to body, but it was the first time she considered the consequences of letting go, giving in.

Surprisingly, Numiak pulled away first. Lean muscle shifted beneath the smooth tapestry of his skin as he pivoted, stalked to the opposite side of the cavern, and collected his maq where it hung on the wall, shrugging it on.

"How did negotiations go?" she asked.

"They didn't. I attempted to speak with the commander. He refused to see me. Tomorrow, he said, we could discuss the matter of an alliance."

"There's no way the Council gave the commander free rein of the city." It wasn't right. The Herd, drunk with forgetfulness. The soldiers solidly in his grip.

"I know." The words were drawn out, as if he had considered this often. "I'm going about this cautiously. We need the Caribou Nomads' support, but the commander cannot be trusted."

Apaay wandered to the edge of the lake. She had sought out Numiak for a reason. Kirimat was right. Turning away from violence didn't stop violence. Rather, it offered it room to root and grow.

The North was her land, and Nanuq sought to corrupt it. Wasn't it her responsibility then, to protect this land, her home? And if that meant defending it, acting as a shield against a greater evil, might that also be in her character as well? There were many types of bravery, after all.

"I want you to train me," Apaay said as her lungs squeezed with reluctance, acceptance, of doing what needed to be done.

Whether she was ready for it or not.

Numiak returned to her side, peering down at her. "You're sure?"

No, but when was anyone sure? She was willing. That had to count for something. "Can I see it?"

And there it was, resting peacefully in his hand. Apaay's true face, the one she had been born with, the one that had been stolen, the one that would now be returned to her. Apaay reminded herself of something she had always known: a person wasn't their face. A person was their heart. Apaay's heart hadn't changed.

She traced the shape of the eyes—spaced farther apart, slightly rounder—and the nose with its upturned end. It was strange and it was a stranger.

"I'm afraid," Apaay admitted, the whisper fading beneath the sound of lapping water.

"Of?"

She lifted her eyes to his. "Of forgetting who I am." After months of drowning in that dark water, she had only wanted to return to who she'd been prior to captivity in the labyrinth. As it turned out, that wasn't possible. So Apaay had faced a new challenge: discovering who this new person might be. She was facing it still. But it was time to move forward. Create this identity for herself.

For a moment, she thought Numiak might reach out to take her hand, but he only said, "I'll remind you."

20

They went to the spring, with its clouded air dripping with heat. It was there Apaay stared at her reflection for what would likely be the last time.

How often had she peered at her reflection over the years? Not enough. Apaay wondered why that was. Beauty, except of the heart, was not something that had ever mattered to her. But as she took in her narrow chin and fierce eyes, she could see the strength there. It eased the burden of what she would lose.

"Will it hurt?" she asked.

"No." The face splayed like cloth over Numiak's hands. He traced the arch of one eyebrow, and Apaay swore she felt a ghostly touch against her own skin.

"Very well." She knelt on the damp bank, hands curled into the sweetly scented grass. "Get on with it."

"Dip your head into the water."

Stinging heat enclosed her skull. Numiak's hand curved around the back of her neck, stabilizing her. Then the world fled to darkness. There was nothing. An absence of feeling, blindness, that swallowing abyss. Identical to the time he'd briefly stolen her face in the labyrinth. Seconds later, he lifted her head from the water, and sensation returned.

"Open your eyes."

Apaay braced herself for what she might find. "It looks the same," she said with shock. Colors were no darker or brighter, lines no sharper or duller. The only difference was the shape of her face, which she explored with a tentative touch as she stared at her reflection. It seemed as if she had seen this face before, or one like it, though she could not remember where.

"Did you think because you are changed on the outside, you would be changed on the inside?" he asked with a surprising amount of insight.

Maybe she'd thought that, a little.

"When dealing with faces," Numiak said, "you must consider them temporary. A face is about perception, hence why I am able to take people's faces and give them different ones."

Apaay considered this. She touched her cheeks, marveled at their new roundness. "Essentially, I look at you and imagine something different, and it appears?"

"For yourself, yes. You are not constrained as I am. Now." He shifted closer. "I want you to study my face. Think about how differently it might look were it altered in some way. It can be anything. The shape of my chin, the length of my eyelashes."

"The color of your eyes?"

"No. One's true eye color does not change."

"Yours does."

"It does," he agreed without explanation.

Apaay refocused on her task. It seemed simple enough. "Then what?"

"Then I want you to physically alter whatever feature you've chosen."

Apaay's gaze swept his bone structure. Had she ever taken the time to examine the contours of his features in depth? Dewy heat pinked his skin, and sweat rolled down the column of his throat, gathering in the hollow between his collarbones. Eyelashes like soot and cheekbones like blades. She eventually settled on his nose, since it was the most prominent facial feature. The trouble was, she didn't know how to mandate a change.

"Nothing's happening," she said after a long stretch of concentration.

"It might help if you touched my face."

Apaay stepped back. "What?" The word was borderline shrill. "Why? Isn't it enough that I'm staring at you?"

"Wolfling," he crooned with hooded eyes, "would I ever lead you astray?"

"Yes," she retorted, slapping his hand aside when he reached for her. "Should I count the ways?"

He chuckled. "I don't bite," he assured. "Unless you ask me to." White teeth shone against his brown face: hungry, gleaming points.

"Do it and see what happens," she muttered.

The Face Stealer's grin turned downright perilous.

"Stand up straight," Apaay snapped, chin angled haughtily. "And tilt down your head so I can reach."

She studied Numiak's nose—straight, symmetrical, narrow at the tip. How would he look if his nose were crooked, wider, bulbous? Apaay frowned in her effort of concentration. This was his face. It wasn't easy to change how she viewed him. Yet his philosophy on the matter made sense. Learning the shape of something would deepen her understanding of it, and might aid in the transformation process. No matter that it was an intimate affair.

Just get it over with.

Apaay dragged a fingertip from his eyebrow to the outer edge of his right cheekbone, focusing on the trailing path. She was distinctly aware of the stifling heat, the sweat dripping down her inner arms. Always, his heavy gaze upon her.

"Can't you look somewhere else?" she gritted out.

"Where would you like me to look?" A honeyed tone.

"I just said: somewhere else."

He fought a smile. "You don't like it when I look at you?"

"There's nothing to look at," she replied, if only to distract herself from the skittish nature of her nerves.

"On the contrary, I think there is something to look at." His gaze all but scorched her skin, this lazy, seeking-after pleasure. "Some*one*," he amended.

Flattery came easy to him. Apaay didn't actually think he meant it. She concentrated on her task, on the finger's exploratory trail.

As her touch passed along his chin, Numiak murmured, with a distinct purr to his voice, "Did you enjoy ogling my chest earlier?"

Considering she'd spent all but the last few months despising him, it wasn't difficult to feign disinterest.

"I wouldn't know," Apaay responded blandly. "I was too busy looking at your friend's." It wasn't a complete lie.

The skin around his eyes crinkled, though his gaze honed in on her mouth with voracious intensity. Apaay licked her lips. She worried he could hear her heartbeat with his keen animal senses, wondered if the accelerated pulse transferred through her fingertips to his face. "I'm sure he would be interested in getting to know you on a more intimate level, should you desire it." A suggestion ripe with promise.

It felt like a test, one Apaay didn't appreciate. Her fury rose to accept the challenge. "I'll be sure to ask him," she answered sweetly, pulling her hand away so he wouldn't see how it shook.

Except Numiak caught her wrist like a bird in a trap. Apaay startled at the touch, at how he leaned forward with the utmost leisure, and she couldn't help how her eyelids drooped as the warmth of his breath caressed the shell of her ear, puckering her skin despite the oppressive heat. "You do that."

She thought he would step back, give her room to breathe. He shifted closer, head tilting inward so his nose brushed the strands of her hair.

Was he *smelling* her?

With each inhalation, Apaay's shoulder brushed his chest. His presence was, simply put, overwhelming. Was this flirtation? Manipulation? Something else?

And if this was flirtation, so what? It felt good. There was no need to analyze it. Unless . . .

Unless he used this flirtation as a distraction, an obstacle to test her resolve. Was it all a game to him?

And, if so, why did she care?

← →

The butchering came early the following night.

A thick mist saturated the air, shrouding the moist, bloody soil, and above, the fat white blossoms swayed from their vines, their nectar a sweet perfume. Bodies lay half-submerged in the placid river: an arm here, a leg there, and bones like scattered sticks. The inside of Apaay's mouth tasted bitterly of stomach bile. The Herd was safe in their ignorance, though they had never been in more danger. Indeed, they had already forgotten the bloodlust. But not Apaay. Not Numiak, who stood next to her. Not Kirimat. No, they had watched from the outer edges, unwilling to interfere and risk the tentative sanctuary they'd been granted.

The commander's warning persisted. Keep her business to herself. Forget these nights as the Herd did.

Apaay could not forget.

Four days they had slept here. By day, Apaay trained with Numiak in altering her identity. Or she attempted to, rather. By night, she lay awake, tucked into a carved-out room, listening to the distant wails of the Caribou Nomads tearing themselves apart.

"I hate this," Apaay whispered, and yet did nothing to stop the atrocious spectacle. She feared she was becoming conditioned to violence.

Numiak, positioned at her back, rested a hand on her shoulder and squeezed. "I know."

Until Numiak convinced the commander to join his force with theirs, they could do nothing. "They have to know. They must know this isn't natural." The Herd was all dreamy smiles as they drifted, masked, throughout the room—those still alive, at least. Their nights lurked with horror, their waking hours spent producing weapons in a timely manner. "It's exhausting," she said. "Not knowing who to trust." Funny that she would express this to the very demon whom she hadn't trusted months ago.

He spoke quietly, as if he did not want to distress her further.

"There are good people in the world. People who fight for balance and peace. Do not let the actions of a few dictate the character of many."

"What of your friend, Pilan?"

He paused, then said, with a curious amount of irritation, "What about him?"

"Can we trust him?" Pilan wandered the room as they spoke. He participated in the killings. But he did not drink the nectar. Numiak had misplaced his trust in others before, namely his brother.

"Yes." The gray of his eyes roved her face. "It's the commander I'm concerned with."

The man in question conversed with three of his guards, directing them to various posts around the hall. Apaay touched the edge of her mask self-consciously. The commander did not know of her new face, and she wanted to keep it that way. His interest was far too lethal a thing. And yet, they needed his cooperation.

Apaay asked Numiak, "Have you made headway yet?"

"Working on it."

"You need to speak with him. This is a game, don't you see? Convince the commander he needs our support."

"I'm aware of the game." He scanned the room's activity carefully behind his mask. "Men like the commander cannot be pushed. They must be coaxed. I will not risk our safety."

"Numiak, we are the furthest thing from safe. Any moment, the commander could decide to kill us off."

"I'm aware of that, too."

"The sooner we convince him this alliance is of value to him, the sooner we can leave. We can't afford to wait."

One moment bled into the next. As the commander sent off his three guards, four more took their place. "You focus on training," Numiak murmured. "I'll deal with the commander."

"Or," she said pleasantly, "we both speak with the commander and forget my training." It had gone exactly nowhere anyway. She couldn't expect to master something in four days, but she thought she'd at least feel some connection to whatever power lay dormant inside her. *The thread*, he'd emphasize during their lessons. *Feel the thread.* What thread? She didn't feel a thread. Didn't feel anything, for that matter. Whatever abilities Numiak referred to, Apaay sensed no sign of them.

He answered in a slow drawl, "I did not think you were someone to give up so easily."

"I know what you're doing. It won't work." She wasn't so easily goaded.

"Suit yourself." Languorous, with a hint of knowing.

Or maybe she was.

The Face Stealer's chuckle trailed her as she stormed through the gathering, shoving aside any caribou Unua blocking her path. Cool air awaited in the tunnels branching from the atrium. Her sweaty face prickled beneath the mask. With the area deserted, Apaay felt safe to remove it, tucking herself into a natural alcove in the rock. Here, the air did not reek of blood.

It wasn't as though Apaay could snap her fingers, suddenly manifesting these face-altering powers. Days before, she had believed herself to be perfectly ordinary. Now, Numiak mentioned aiding their cause against Nanuq once she grasped the extent of her capabilities. It didn't seem promising.

Apaay closed her eyes. She had the will, but did she have the belief? Maybe the issue was she didn't feel like herself with this face. Deep down, she'd yet to accept it.

Or maybe it was this internal block, hard and unyielding. That stone on her chest when she allowed herself to think of Ila, but only briefly, for the pain was too great, having augmented over time.

Nothing had ever come easy to her, and this proved it. Apaay had never felt more out of place, wearing this face that was not hers and her family so far, the sea so far, the Analak so far. She couldn't focus. She couldn't think. Couldn't even add freckles to her skin.

"Excuse me, but do I know you?"

Apaay turned around. A middle-aged woman bearing elegant, three-pronged antlers had wandered into the tunnel. She stared at Apaay blearily for an uncomfortably long time. That's right. Apaay had done away with the mask. The woman couldn't know who she was. Didn't seem to notice the lack of antlers. "I don't believe so."

The woman took a closer look. "No, I believe we've met before. I remember—" The woman shook her head, glanced away. *Why can't I remember?* her pinched expression seemed to say. "There was a forest. You were traveling with a young man." Closer she stepped, invading Apaay's space. "I was wounded."

"You must have me confused with someone else," Apaay said, trying to back away. The wall hit her back, chilled stone against her spine.

The woman's confusion deepened, but she came no closer. "I thought—" She shook her head again. "My apologies." Then she, too, was gone.

Slipping the mask over her face, Apaay reentered the forested chamber. Numiak was wrong. They could not afford to wait. Her people could not afford to wait, or the North. And so she strode all the way up to the dais where the commander stood and said, "I'd like to speak with you. In private."

The commander waved his dull-eyed guards elsewhere, peering down at her with a combination of irritation and intrigue. "Are you not enjoying yourself this evening, Apaay of the Analak?"

"More so than those dead." She paused, then said, "Will you hear what I have to say?"

A fleeting touch against the back of her hand distracted Apaay from his answer. Numiak had appeared at her side and looked at her as if to say, *Really? We're doing this now?* Yes, Apaay thought. They were.

"Surely you can spare a few moments, commander," said Numiak in a voice that would accept no argument. "We have been patient thus far, but our time is valuable."

"I know what you're going to say," declared the commander, observing with faint interest as his guards began dragging the corpses from the chamber. "I am interested in your appeal for an alliance. I wonder what the Caribou Nomads could offer you, and what you, in turn, could offer me."

His smile was only slightly more unsettling than his ravenous, black-eyed gaze.

"All I ask," he went on, "is that you give me a little more time to consider. This is not a decision I make lightly. I must think of the Herd, and of their future."

Apaay looked to Numiak. If she opened her mouth, she was afraid she'd spit on this horrible, manipulative man.

"When?" Numiak demanded.

"Tomorrow," said the commander. "Tomorrow we will discuss."

← →

Tomorrow came and went. There was no discussion.

Nor on the following day, nor the day after.

The commander was an exceptional evader. He managed to be exactly where he was needed, yet vanished the moment Apaay or Numiak attempted to speak with him. After the third failed attempt, they decided to shift their attention to Apaay's training instead.

In the mornings, she and Numiak practiced what he called meditation. A deeper understanding of physicality began with the internal, he said, and that began with her breath. Surprisingly, Apaay was already familiar with this concept. To let the knot of time unwind so that she slipped deeper into herself, as she did perched on the edge of breathing holes, the world narrowing to water and her breath. From breath came awareness of other things: the pores on her nose, the weight of her eyelids as they sank down, the new fullness of her mouth, even the difference in her skin elasticity. Apaay had yet to accept that she could be all things, not just one, narrow and singular.

It proved to be the greatest obstacle in her attempts to grasp this slippery power, and the lack of time granted to them, each day hinting at burgeoning war, led to further frustration. Once Nanuq learned the power he sought lay in not an object, but a person, he would come for her.

"So do I have power like yours? Or like you had," Apaay amended one afternoon.

"Thank you for the reminder," Numiak drawled. Together, they lounged on the grassy riverbank in the great hall, taking a break after many hours of fruitless practice, Kirimat having made herself scarce to speak with Pilan. "Yes, you have power. No, your power is not like mine. Rather, they complement each other. When we exchanged the second blood oath, I was able to borrow some of your power to help us escape Yuki."

So that pale, shimmering power hadn't been his, as she had originally suspected. Now she knew it had been hers.

"Is this power separate from your ability to steal faces?"

He pondered for a time. "It is connected," he said slowly, staring up at the upside-down trees. "I'm not sure if my ability to steal faces manifested from my power or the other way around. Since your power does not originate from Taggak, I cannot say for certain the extent of your abilities."

Everything in this world was connected to something else. The Face Stealer's power was connected to Taggak, and those shadows served as a tool, something malleable, which he could shape into whatever he desired. He could only control objects he had called into existence—ones tethered to his power, and thus tethered to Taggak. So what was her power tethered to? How did she find that connection, that commonality?

Eventually, discussion moved to other matters.

"I made contact with Ro yesterday. No news of Ila or Tulimaq," he said, his eyes too knowing.

Apaay bristled even as her stomach tightened. "I didn't ask about Ila." That they hadn't reached Sinika, however, concerned her. Nanuq's roaming troops might have caused delays.

He shrugged from his reclining position, as if it was of no concern to him. "Just thought maybe you'd like to know."

Apaay sat up in the grass. "What I'd like to know is what's happening at Sinika."

Numiak followed her example, watching as she gulped from her waterskin. "Very well. The Avi worries Nanuq will attempt to launch an attack against Sinika using Nannek as a base."

Nannek, she recalled, was a former Owl Clan city Nanuq had sacked in the war, claiming it for the Polar Bear Empire. This was dire news indeed. "How do they know this?"

"The Avi's men were able to intercept one of his messages. He is transferring more of his kirn to the Dead Plains. It is my assumption Nanuq knows of our alliance with the Owl Clan through Yuki, who was likely informed by my brother."

"What are they doing to prepare?" Apaay asked. This was Kaan and Ro's home, their people. She worried.

"Ro has dispatched additional border patrols, and he's called back the men stationed at the western front." When he noticed the tension lining Apaay's features, his eyes softened. "I would not worry, wolfling. Ro is an excellent strategist, well-trained in military tactics."

"So are you, but the Wood fell anyway." Though she had played a part in that. A rather large one.

"You give me too much credit. Ro is far more knowledgeable than me. There is a reason he serves as the Avi's general, and it has nothing to do with his birthright. If Nanuq plans to attack Sinika, all is not lost. The owl Unua share a connection with the Aatu—a symbiotic relationship. The forest allows them to build their cities among its trees. The owl Unua, in turn, protect the woods from invaders. In case of war, the Aatu will do its part to protect its inhabitants."

Apaay trailed the tips of her fingers into the warm, steaming water of the river. "What do you mean?"

Numiak tracked the ripples unfurling across the water's surface. His dark eyes glimmered in the low light spilling from the oil lamps placed throughout the room. "The Avi's spirit is twined with that of the Aatu. He is both guide and vessel. The Aatu will wake from its slumber if needed, but only in times of great need."

"Is that what happened in the last war?"

"Yes." And now the light in his eyes dimmed, fog sliding across cool irises, like the sun in hiding. He had never looked more grave. "When Nannek was under attack, the Avi called upon the forest. But our forces were too few. In the end, we lost the city.

"The problem," Numiak continued, "is that we are blind to Nanuq's movements. We need someone on the inside."

Apaay asked, "Couldn't you put another spy in his army?"

"That's not an option, unfortunately. Not enough time."

And Kimmir couldn't return. The man was lucky to be alive. Last she'd heard, he'd traveled with Ro and Kaan to Sinika following the Wood's breach.

She caught the Face Stealer studying her. "What?"

"Ro finally secured a translator. He's located in Kunivik. I'm meeting with him so we can put the mystery of this note to rest."

"Oh." Apaay pulled her hand free of the water, frowning. Kunivik was a village to the east. The whales ended their summer migration off its coast. "When do you leave?"

"Tonight."

So soon. It was ridiculous to feel disappointed. As with everything else, it had to be done.

"Of course," he went on casually, "this isn't a task I can complete alone."

She slanted him a look of deep skepticism. "What about the commander?"

"It's clear he is avoiding us. We cannot change that. I think some distance from Nigun would benefit everyone. Perhaps the change in scenery will spark something in your training. And when we return, we will offer the commander a conversation he will be unable to ignore. Kirimat will keep watch in our absence."

"Wouldn't the commander interpret our absence as a slight?" The man was proud. "What if we aren't allowed back?"

"It would benefit him to allow us reentry," said Numiak, "if only to keep an eye on our whereabouts."

He had a point. Still, she had her doubts.

"Think of the enemies, wolfling." He appraised her with playful, blue-green eyes. "A dangerous job for a single person."

Sometimes it struck her anew how far they had come, across tundra and taiga, over mountains and streams, yet all that distance felt so trivial compared to this: partnership. A marvel, really, considering their history. But change, she thought, was not always a bad thing.

Apaay said, "I will go."

21

Ariviat, soaked in the salt water of Naga's fury, rose like a white spire in the distance. After a week of hard travel, Kenai had arrived in one piece on the shores of the Eastern Territory, having at last reached the outskirts of the salt-coated city, its foliage wilted and shrunken, having grown minute from what little fresh water existed in these parts.

His heart beat unsteadily and grew increasingly erratic as he crossed the last span of distance, until he reached the Sea Mother's home. It was separated from the rest of the capital by coastal seas, and a single bridge caked in bunches of gray-green barnacles was his only means of passage. Once lowered, Kenai crossed onto the cliffside that held the white edifice, with its span of high walls and spiraling turrets, and crumbling bridges leading nowhere, and shells lining the walkways. He ascended one of the outer staircases to the second level, where Yuki often spent time studying the horizon. He didn't see her, so he climbed to the third level and glanced below from his bird's-eye view.

Naga hammered blows into the cliffside. The water hissed its retreat before hurling forward in a brutal display of salt spray. From his position, he caught movement on the beach below. Yuki, returning from her time spent beneath the water.

He hurried to meet her on the first level. Despite his excitement at seeing her, he wasn't looking forward to this conversation. So he waited in the middle of the courtyard. When the top of her head appeared, her bared, wet shoulders, her slender waist, he remembered what it felt like to forget to breathe.

"Kenai." Yuki hesitated at the top of the stairs as though surprised by his presence. Kenai didn't understand. He had always intended to return. "Have you completed your task then?"

Saliva pooled in his mouth. His pulse spiked in dread as he prepared himself for her disappointment. "Not exactly. The refugees are dead."

"Dead?" Head tilted, she studied him in displeasure. "And why would they be dead?"

His throat dipped as he remembered the boy, the last refugee standing in a field of corpses. There must be a sickness in him to have done that. "I killed them."

Her eyebrows lifted in twin elegant curves. "I see."

It was as he had feared. "They refused to submit," he rushed to say. "I gave them a choice. I was angry. I . . . couldn't control it."

"What were you angry about?"

He did not respond, for he wasn't entirely sure of the reason himself. Was he angry at those who'd stood in the way of his goal? Or was he angry at himself for taking more lives, for betraying his nation, for all the horrible things he had done?

Yuki looked at him pityingly. "Not every problem can be solved with a blade, Kenai. I had hoped you were someone I could depend on." She drifted to the coral-encrusted wall and looked beyond it. "But you fell into the same trap my father did. You let your emotions cloud your judgment, you chose yourself over others, and now I must tell Nanuq that the refugees he expects will not be coming because they no longer live."

She turned to leave.

"Wait."

The Sea Mother strode two more steps before halting, then pivoted to face him. Once, Yuki had thought highly of him. Kenai wondered what had happened to that man.

"There might be another way," he said, because Kenai was coming to realize something else: she *would* leave, if he did not give her a reason to stay. "There is the Banished Lands."

"I'm aware of the Banished Lands." Curt.

"Then you know it contains a large population of outcasts who would happily fight for Nanuq so long as they were able to leave the island."

People did not voluntarily travel to the Banished Lands. They were sent. As Numiak's second-in-command, he had sentenced thieves and bandits to the Banished Lands on multiple occasions. There they lived, and there they died. No one ever left.

Her mouth pursed. He'd piqued her interest. As Yuki canted her head, weak sunlight caught her enlarged black pupils, flaming them to shining ebony. He had always thought her beautiful, but every so often, he was reminded of how they differed, she a god, ruler of the seas beneath, he a mortal man.

Kenai went on. "If I traveled to the Banished Lands, I could recruit people for Nanuq's cause. I know they would be willing." He had failed her once. He would not do so again.

"While the offer is tempting," she said throatily, "I am not sure if it would be in my best interest to allocate resources to this *ambition* of yours. That would require a ship. Supplies. A crew. I have already promised these things to Nanuq."

"I know," he hurried to say, hoping his remorse would appease her. "But I wasn't thinking clearly before. I understand how important these recruits are to Nanuq's cause and, in extension, to yours. I would like to do this for you." Kenai hesitated, then let his last arrow fly true. "Let your father see the greatness I have always known to lie in you."

The Sea Mother's eyes narrowed to slits. No matter how he displeased her, she could never resist flattery. "I'm listening."

←　→

It was a three-day journey thrashed by rough seas. The sour odor of sickness permeated the lower level of the ship where Kenai spent the majority of his time curled on a narrow cot. As his mind spun out with the tossing waves, he closed his eye and waited for the worst to pass.

The splash of oars sounded beyond the wooden frame. He was alone, Yuki back at Ariviat. Their parting lingered as a foul taste in his mouth. She didn't trust him to find the recruits they needed. Somewhere along the way, she'd lost faith in him. The realization sickened Kenai. He had two weeks to gather followers from the Banished Lands. She'd send a ship to pick him up, take him back to the mainland when the time came. He vowed to keep his promise, whatever the cost.

When the ship sighted land, Kenai climbed onto the upper deck, grateful for the clean air to clear his head. The shore wasn't far. The crew tossed a rope ladder over the side of the ship, which he descended. Warm water greeted him as he began to swim, the waves helping propel him to shore.

His bare feet touched sand. The surf was violent, cold—a mad thing. Foam hissed and the water sucked around his ankles. Kenai stumbled to a hilltop on higher ground that offered a view of the surrounding town, though *town* was being kind.

Those banished had used the forgotten pieces of whatever had washed ashore to build their places of residence. Driftwood and mud homes, holes for windows, curtains for doors. The structures closest to the shoreline perched precariously atop stilts, far above the storm surge.

He followed the path of a wet, muddy road, shivering as the wind plastered the sopping fabric against his chilled skin. The stink hit him first: refuse and body odor, yet compounded. His nostrils burned from the stench, and he covered his nose with one arm, trying to imagine how many unwashed bodies it would take to create an odor this intense.

Prior to his journey, he had done away with any manner of dress that would distinguish him as wolf Unua. He assumed many of the prisoners he had sentenced still lived, and while his scar offered him some manner of anonymity—he'd received the injury following the invasion when Numiak had captured him—he didn't want anyone to look too closely at him. As it turned out, his injury was not the gravest he observed among those wandering the street. For the first time in his life, his scar allowed him to blend in.

Kenai caught the eye of a man with a hunched back and a club foot leaning against one of the water-logged structures. He jerked his head in the direction of a nearby alleyway, wandered down the lane, and waited for the man to follow.

The man hobbled into the gloomy space, wary, yet curious. The looseness of his jowls suggested he lacked teeth.

"You interested in a way off the island?" Kenai asked. "I can make it happen."

"Oh really?" He smiled. Kenai had been right: no teeth. He scratched at the sparse beard patched across his face. His hand reminded Kenai of the driftwood cluttering the shore. Roughened, broken at the edges, not quite whole. Grime creased the lines of his palm. "No one can get onto the ships dropping off the banished from the mainland. It's a lost cause."

"This is a different ship. Private. It'll be here in a few weeks."

The man narrowed his gaze as though against his better judgment. "What are you trying to sell, boy?"

"I'm looking for recruits. Nanuq needs men to fight for him. He'll provide shelter and housing in exchange for your loyalty."

The man's interest immediately extinguished. "Nanuq," he spat, turning away. "Like I'd offer anything to that tyrant."

"Wait." Kenai reached for his arm, but the man moved with the reflexes of someone thirty years younger, slipping underneath his outstretched arms and behind, until Kenai slammed into the side of the building, the man's mouth at his ear. A knife pricked the skin above his artery, the one that flowed beneath his jaw. Kenai froze.

"You're clearly new here, so let me offer you some advice. Here, everyone's a murderer, a thief, a whore." The edge of the blade sliced a shallow cut into his skin. A single bead of blood welled. "I'd watch yourself, unless you want your other eye gone as well."

The knife lifted from his neck. He turned, but the man had vanished.

Kenai returned to the street, shaken up more than he cared to admit. The Banished Lands lacked laws save one: eat, or be eaten. A relentless prickle against the back of his neck forced him forward. If he stopped, he would attract unwanted attention. Once he figured out how to approach his mission, he could begin gathering recruits for Nanuq's cause—ones that wouldn't carve out his other eye for sport.

The smell announced his arrival to the slums. Filth, piss, grime, blood, and defecation—all amassed to create a repulsive concoction. His eye watered and his nostrils burned, and not even the sea breeze could drive it off. Kenai pressed his forearm to his nose to block the worst of it. Mud squelched around his boots, runny and red.

The stilted establishments—if one could call them that—gradually fell out of disrepair, and soon the main road ran parallel to structures that sagged into the ground, until the people decided to do away with them altogether. Instead of buildings on stilts, they dug inward, deep into the earth.

A roar of noise blew in from the end of the street. The structure—four low, leaning walls and a roof pocked with holes—was so overrun with people it was splitting open like torn flesh. He stood across the street, studying the packed staircase that obviously led to a place of excitement. Curiosity deemed he follow the crowd.

After some maneuvering, he managed to squeeze past a few dead-eyed vagrants, down the short staircase to a spiked, driftwood fence encircling the hollowed-out ground below, offering a view to the spectators above.

It was an arena.

There had been a place such as this, as large and as wide, in the training facilities back in Unana. It offered Packmates the opportunity to hone their skills, whether with blade or staff or fists. Kenai remembered facing off with Numiak a time or two, prior to their father's death. The crowd jostled him. Bets were made. A chance to earn a bit of coin. He would need a way to barter food during his time on the island. This seemed as good an opportunity as any.

This arena differed from what he was used to. An oblong shape as opposed to a square. Floors of mud as opposed to stone.

Two contenders occupied its center: a man of behemoth proportions and a petite, slender woman, the right side of her skull shaved to stubble. It had been decades, but Kenai knew the look of a soldier. Something about the set of one's posture. This woman was used to battle.

A bell rang.

The man snatched the woman close before she could dart away. His hand was so large it completely swallowed her forearm. He lifted her up as if she weighed no more than a leaf and swung, then let go. The crowd roared its approval.

Except as the women careened toward the wall, she twisted her body and ran along the curve, one, two, three steps, and dropped harmlessly to the ground. Kenai wondered if she had allowed that man to touch her to give him a false sense of confidence. She dashed toward her opponent, struck out low with her open palm slamming into the man's pelvis. Kenai winced. The lumbering bear attempted to snatch her, but she was too quick, flouncing away with seemingly little effort.

Judging by the woman's combat style—favoring low kicks and open-handed strikes—she might have been wolf Unua. But then she flowed into fast-paced punches targeting the abdomen and lower back—a distinctly polar bear Unua technique. Kenai imagined one could acquire a variety of fighting techniques in this fractured, forgotten place.

At one point, the man managed to grab the back of the woman's neck. She sagged in his hold, let him toss her in whatever direction he desired, and once his grip loosened, managed to twist in midair, wrap her legs around the man's shoulders, and yank her body weight downward.

They hit the ground. The woman rolled to her feet, fists snapping out to hit various pressure points. The man bellowed as the arm he'd lifted went limp. His knee collapsed, and Kenai heard the pop of his tendon snapping. A blood-curdling shriek erupted as the man's enormous mass fell forward, dragged down by the weight of his shoulders, his trunked arms.

The woman beat the man's face until it was a pulped, bloody mess.

← 22 →

Ila felt restless. She paced her cell throughout the evening when she couldn't sleep, though the hours of digging holes left her drained. Pili watched her in silence.

Have you shifted yet?

Ila closed her eyes. She had thought of this often. How to transform from woman to wolf and back as she observed the other captives nuzzling each other's necks with their muzzles. She said, speaking with her hands and shaping the word with her mouth, *No.*

"As a wolf, there is no separation from the other members in your pack. We communicate through a special mind-speak, which allows us into the thoughts and emotions of those we're closest to. To become a wolf, you must think like one. Which is to say, you must embrace your animal half." Pili touched her nose. "Concentrate on your senses: sight, smell, touch. Brush all those distracting thoughts aside. You don't need to think. You need to feel. In wolf form, instinct comes first. Everything else comes second."

That seemed logical enough. Ila focused on sight, touch. The air against her skin. She ran the tip of her tongue against the edges of her teeth and imagined them sharpening, lengthening. But nothing happened.

Ila opened her eyes as a feeling of shame moved through her. *Anything?*

"Have patience with yourself," said Saniraq from the adjacent cell. "I was not able to shift my first attempt."

Nor could I, signed Tipki across the way. *Now that I think about it, I couldn't shift the second attempt either. Or the third.* Her face fell. *Or the fourth.*

"But you didn't give up," said Pili with a pressing look. "Right?"

Tipki wiggled her eyebrows. Ila thought she did it to annoy Malina, mostly. "I didn't."

Saniraq said, "And neither will Ila."

It helps to think of things that remind you of your wolf. Me, I always think about the feel of a hare's neck snapping in my jaws. Tipki licked her lips with gusto.

Ila winced. Saniraq said, "That would be helpful, Tipki, except Ila has never transformed before." She was the calm to Tipki's storm.

"Oh." A chagrined smile. "Right."

Try again, said Saniraq.

Except the atmosphere shifted. It felt as though the air had fallen abruptly silent, though Ila would not have been able to discern the change. In the next cell, Malina had shifted to her human form.

Ila glanced from Tipki, who had lowered her eyes guiltily, to Saniraq, who was glaring at Malina. *What is it?* But she knew, somehow. A part of her had expected it.

Turning to Malina, she hammered out, *Whatever you must say, speak plainly. Only cowards strike when one's back is turned.*

The scrawny woman straightened. Her mouth shaped an ugly, disparaging scowl. "I said if you cannot change into your wolf skins, can you really be considered wolf Unua?"

Heat crawled up her neck. Shame, but not her own. Shame placed upon her as though it were a punishment by someone else. And Ila wondered, when was enough . . . enough?

She was tired of Malina's combativeness, tired of her derision. She had reached her limit. No more.

Stand up, she demanded.

Malina leveled her with the frostiest glower in existence. Ila almost laughed. She had been through too much to let a little dislike intimidate her. But, eventually, the woman rose, arms locked at her sides. That was good. It meant respect was not completely out of the realm of possibility.

I know you dislike me, Malina. I also know some part of you blames me for your misfortune, and the misfortune of our people. You must understand I did not avoid this. I tell you this, and yet I owe you no explanation. You have been nothing but rude toward me since my arrival, when I have only acted kindly toward you. Truthfully, I am not even sure you deserve that. Her hand gestures were slow, without any outward frustration shown.

You may not like me, but you will respect me. Ila paused. *You will respect me as heir to the Wolf Kingdom, and your Vaal.*

Malina's lips whitened from how hard they pressed together. Ila went on. She could not lose momentum.

I promised I would set you all free, but I cannot do it alone. You once served as a commander of the Pack, a protector of our nation. I ask you now if you are willing to do so again, to guide me in forming an escape plan, and getting us out, and moving forward, reclaiming our history.

Tipki gazed at Ila with awe-filled eyes as she chewed on the end of her thumbnail. Saniraq nodded her approval of the composed handling of this conversation.

Malina said, upper lip curling, "You were not there. You did not fight in the invasion. You did not see."

How could I? I was but a child. She did not invalidate Malina's feelings, but Malina hadn't witnessed the flame devouring her childhood bedroom, a girl tangled in blankets, a fallen beam, and blood, and broken skin, a scar, old tough skin. Ila had lost, too, though she could not have known it then. Her family, of course, including a sister she could not remember, but who still lived. And her hearing.

I cannot live up to your impossible standards, and I am not going to try. If you're expecting a battle-hardened soldier, who also knows exactly what to do and what to say, you will be disappointed. That is not me. I am not perfect, but you know something, Malina? Ila signed the next statement with high satisfaction. *Neither are you.*

Malina's black mood seemed to shift. She no longer looked as if she'd consumed rotten meat.

You have a choice, Ila went on. *You can choose to help me. We will walk out of this camp as free women.* A pause for consideration. *Or you can laugh at my attempts to better understand myself. You can hiss insults beneath your breath thinking I do not know what hurtful things you're saying because I cannot hear. You can do nothing. And when Tipki and Saniraq and Pili and everyone else goes free, you can stay here, digging holes, trapped beneath the thumbs of men.*

Malina's pale, sweaty face glowed in the dark. Her mouth tightened. Wordlessly, she turned her attention elsewhere. Only then did Ila allow herself to slump against the wall, knees shaking. Standing up to Malina had been absolutely terrifying, but she'd done it. And she hoped to never do it again.

Pili looked on with pride. "You did well."

Ila settled next to her on the ground. *But Malina is right. I don't know what I'm doing.*

"The girls don't care about that. If you fight for them, they will fight for you. Simple."

Even if I'm unable to shift?

"Give it time." She patted Ila's hand in comfort, as a mother might. "Nothing worthwhile ever comes easy."

And if it did not come at all? Could she lead her people while barred from the other half of herself?

Pili pointed to Ila's right, drawing attention to where Malina stood expectantly on the other side of the bars separating their cells. Ila stood and approached, wary. She half-expected the older woman to lash out with a clawed hand.

They stared at each other for an indeterminate amount of time. Ila refused to speak first.

Malina's nostrils flared, the only tell of her distaste. "About what you said . . ." She looked to Tipki and Saniraq, both watching curiously. Tipki made a hand gesture as if to say, *Go on. What are you waiting for?*

"I will think about it," she said. "About helping you. It will not be easy."

No, Ila agreed. *But it will be easier with your help. You and Tipki served on the Pack. You have experience dealing with crises.*

"True," said Malina, though she didn't look happy about it. A moment passed before she said, "Get some rest. Otherwise you're useless to me." She shifted back into a wolf and curled on the ground, tail covering her nose. Ila shook her head in exasperation. It was a start, at least.

Hours later, Pili, Malina, and the rest of the prisoners slept. Ila, however, remained awake. She paced from corner to corner and back in the contained space, trying to piece together an escape plan. The guard hadn't returned. She accepted he had forgotten. They must find another way.

She was so distracted she didn't notice the figure that stepped inside the building.

It was Ila who made her home in the filth on the ground, yet she no longer felt small in the former combat master's presence. His haggard appearance alluded to lack of sleep. She didn't pity Tulimaq. He didn't deserve it.

She didn't ask why he had come. She knew why. It was the same reason he'd disappeared for weeks, unable to meet her eye as the guards broke her body into pieces. It was why he'd sent her that salve, yet had been unable to offer it himself.

Instead, she asked him something else.

Ila approached him from the back wall of the cell. *Are you happy, Tulimaq?*

As expected, his expression didn't alter in the slightest. It told her little, by which she meant, it told her enough.

She smiled a sad smile. *I don't think you are. I think you brought me here because you thought it would prove something. Fix something. Change something.* In the end, it had only hurt her. And, she thought to some extent, him as well.

But it hasn't changed anything, has it? He had come to her cell because he was searching for something, but didn't Tulimaq know? Ila didn't have answers.

She wondered if he might speak, but that would indicate he had something to say, a thought or opinion on the matter when, truly, he couldn't express his feelings if his life depended on it.

You feel trapped. She took a step closer. *But no one has trapped you, Tulimaq. You've done that to yourself.*

"Stop talking."

Ila laughed. He no longer held control over her. He had given it up the moment he'd brought her here.

You told me once that my heart was weak. That I was weak. I'm not the weak one here. Her fingers curled around the black, frosted metal, the cold painful against her blistered palms. *You are.*

Arm snaking through the bars, he snatched a handful of her filthy attire and hauled her forward so they were nearly mouth to mouth.

"I said—" His hot breath brushed her chilled cheek. "Stop talking."

Ila's gaze narrowed. *What are you going to do with me?* she asked. *You steal me away, take me to your father's empire, and then what?* Ila suspected Nanuq would kill her. He had no reason to keep her alive when she was an obstacle to his plans. As for Tulimaq, he had grown up forgotten and unloved by a father in name only.

You can't change the past, Ila went on. *Your father is who he is. I think you know that. You feel helpless because of what happened to your mother. You want to* feel *something.* She let her hands hang for a moment. *But you don't feel much of anything, do you? You're afraid to. You're afraid to open yourself up to pain again.*

Tulimaq's eyes were all pupil and flame. Ila wished he would say something. Pain lingered when it came to Tulimaq's betrayal, but that wound had scabbed over—mostly. Her only thought was to escape and never return.

When I leave this place, she signed into the space between their bodies, *I will forget you. I will think of you no more when I am gone.* The lie coated her tongue, thick and chalky as ash. She wanted to believe he could be hurt by her, wanted to believe she meant something. More than nothing. *But I guarantee you will not forget me.*

Tulimaq's eyes glowed with frightening intensity. He shoved away from the bars as if he'd burned his hands. Seconds later, the door opened and the guard, Birthmark, entered, stopping when he caught sight of Tulimaq. He studied the younger man curiously. Behind him lurked the woman who had translated for Ila weeks ago.

The man said, "Leave."

Tulimaq left without a backward glance.

Ila met Birthmark at her cell door. She had assumed he wouldn't show.

"In four days," he said, shadows slithering across one side of his face, "officers from the neighboring camp will arrive with new recruits. That is when you will make your move."

Ila processed this information, then said, *What do you want me to do?*

The woman translated. Birthmark responded, "You are going to create a distraction. Pretend to escape. One of my guards will capture you. I'll make sure Tulimaq overhears. He'll come for you."

Would he? She wasn't so sure.

"Your job is to convince him to enter your cell. You need to be close enough to take his staff."

What if it won't work?

"You don't know?" The guard shook his head, as if he hadn't the patience for her ignorance. "The boy cares for you. Use it to your advantage."

← 23 →

"I explained to you before how the cairns are connected through place of origin," Numiak said. "What you need to do is open your mind, sense the spirit inside the rock, and let it channel through your body."

It was early evening. A curved, pearlescent shade between blush and violet, and pale stars sharpening into gradual focus. Apaay considered the landmark of large, stacked stones built in the shape of a man located some five miles south of Nigun among the twisted trees of the Aatu. Blocky thighs, and torso, and arms extended. It was heavily eroded, tangled in vines. Built, perhaps, by the Iskra before their disappearance, either for navigational purposes or to mark a food cache. They had inhabited the North for a thousand years before the Analak settled, having arrived in silence. And having left in silence as well.

Due to Numiak's lack of power, it would be Apaay's responsibility to transport them to Kunivik. She touched the cairn. Nothing. She felt nothing.

Her hand dropped away. "I don't think it will work for me."

"It will." Catching her hand in his, he pressed it to the rough surface, his palm cupped over the back. "It takes practice."

Apaay wasn't thinking of the cairn's spirit. She was thinking of his hand on hers. She was thinking of his voice and its delicious depth.

"Do you miss your power?" Looking at him, she would never guess the Face Stealer lacked the frightening shadows that made him so *other*. His eyes flickered, every hue, every shade, yet none belonged to him.

He replied, "I realize now that I'd grown too dependent on my power. It became a crutch. A weakness." His gaze dropped to her mouth, where it lingered.

Apaay swallowed around the knot in her throat. This thing between them . . . it was like watching a far-out wave approach shore. First, it was but shallow bumps. The bumps grew to hills. The hills swelled to mountains with plunging valleys, and suddenly white foam snarled around her legs and the earth suctioned her feet. The need to fall was so much stronger than before, an erosive force. One of these days, she would not have the will to resist.

Apaay refocused on the cairn's spirit, that pathway that would lead her hundreds of miles from Nigun, all the way to Naga's doorstep. A hum vibrated against her palm. Apaay let herself go, let herself sink into the well of energy, let its spirit carry her and Numiak into suffocating dark, as if they were being sucked through an airless tunnel, and hurl them out onto the other side.

With Kunivik north of the tree line, Apaay expected open tundra, a sweep of red and gold, of willow and lichen both. Summer was a time when the colors of the earth rivaled those of the sky. The months were brief, a radiant bursting of color that died under autumn's frost, though it would be weeks yet until the North witnessed those changes. Apaay, however, saw none of those things. She saw not the coastal waves either.

Instead, there was this: gray. The earth trodden into mush. A sky that emitted feeble violet light. And everywhere, everywhere, a sculpted disorder of pointed structures that blocked her view of the sky, of the horizon, of the sea.

She and Numiak stood among a jumble of crates piled at the back of an alleyway where the cairn was located, crushed between two buildings. They emerged from the cramped space onto a road bisecting the collection of structures, which protruded around them like many broken teeth. There was little space to move, much less breathe the air soaked in the odors of salt and fish, for the houses were piled atop each other like weeds in a narrow patch of sunlight. Around them, amassing bodies teemed, men and women and children all moving in various directions, carrying baskets or hauling meat by sled or stopping traffic to complete a trade in the middle of the road. They were many, and they were *loud*. Their boots, she realized with a small amount of unease, were not made of sealskin. They were dark brown, the color of animal hide, though the animal itself was unfamiliar to her.

Papa had visited Kunivik on occasion. He would trade meat and pelts for goods that came from distant lands. Upon his return, when Apaay asked what it was like to travel to such a place, he always gave the same answer: suffocating.

Numiak, who shifted nearer to her side, said, "Look up."

She did and . . . oh. Overarching white beams sank into the ground on either side of them. Familiar, though she had never seen them used in this context.

A whale. Or rather, the skeleton of a whale, its backbone spanning the stretch of road, the vertebrae gradually decreasing in size as they neared the tail end. Farther down, Apaay spotted additional skeletons running parallel and perpendicular to this road, creating a map of interlocking spines and ribs. Somewhere beyond the buildings, the skeletal infrastructure, lay the sea.

Kunivik was built of bones.

Numiak tugged her against the side of a building that sagged at the edges, away from the thickest of the activity. He tipped his chin at a group of men and women with shaved heads and green uniforms, seal Unua who carried barnacle-tipped swords, the occasional talq. They prowled the streets, obviously searching for something.

"There's an inn not far from here," he said. "We'll stay there for the night. Best to keep out of sight for now."

They moved deeper into the crooked passage, drawing the stark shadows around them like a cloak. Apaay glanced over her shoulder to see if the soldiers had followed them. They hadn't.

"Look." Numiak pointed to a piece of parchment displayed on the wall of the building.

She did. "What is it?" Perplexed.

"That's supposed to be us."

The charcoal illustration looked nothing like her—a girl with all of her old features and none of her new ones. But Numiak's sketch didn't resemble him at all.

He looked like . . . well. His head was massive. His mouth was full of teeth, sharp and puncturing. His nose was a hole in his face. Long, black hair stuck upright, spiked and severe. The only trait they had depicted correctly was his eyes. The coldness and the cunning.

"Seeking," Numiak drawled, "demon known as the Face Stealer. Traveling with a young Analak woman. Generous compensation if captured alive." A deep scowl folded his brow, and he tore the paper from the wall, studying it in closer detail. "This is Yuki's doing. She always was too clever by half." Crumpling the paper, he tossed it onto the ground in disgust.

"You have to admit," Apaay said, fighting laughter, "it has a certain likeness." Her grin stretched. "Why, I'd say it's in your exact image."

A dry quirk of lips. "Hilarious." He scanned the area to ensure all was clear, then gestured her to follow.

Their destination was a tall building with the door cracked open and the smell of cooked whale meat drifting through the window. Numiak entered first. The inside was like nothing she had ever seen, with the enclosed walls so far from one another, and the ceiling so high, and the windows so square. Brightly patterned furniture cluttered the room. Shelves displayed various objects that Apaay assumed had been acquired from Across the Sea.

A rotund man waddled toward the doorway. He had the look of the Analak, but there was a disconnect between how he dressed and how he moved within his environment. He did not wear their traditional clothing. Shorter black hair poked from his scalp, and metal winked in his ears.

Papa once mentioned a shaman who had left the village long ago, after having rejected the old rules, their traditional way of life, leaving his powers behind. The man had become suuniq—an

Analak who adopts a way of life that is not Analak. This innkeeper, it appeared, had become suuniq, too.

"May I help you?" The innkeeper glanced at Apaay before his gaze inevitably locked onto her companion.

"You may," said Numiak, stepping forward with an air of expectation. He moved the way one did in the dark: slow, deliberate motions, each pause holding weight. "My companion and I are in need of housing for the night. A room on the second floor will do. With a window."

The man's mouth opened, then closed. He cleared his throat, and the fleshy skin of his jowls wobbled. "Sir, unfortunately all of our rooms are occupied."

Numiak gave a pleasant sort of smile as he moved to one of the shelves, picking up book after book and handling them as if he had every right to. "Now we both know that's a lie." He studied the innkeeper over the book he held, and his eyes flashed from green to gold.

His face reddening with nerves, the man eased back toward his desk. *Demon*, his mind might whisper to him. "A room on the second floor," he repeated in a hoarse voice. "Yes. I believe there is one room available that I had forgotten about."

With a pleased expression, Numiak returned the book to its shelf. "Excellent. My companion and I require a certain amount of discretion. I'm sure you understand." He slid Apaay a warm look that might have been *too* convincing.

Stepping forward, he passed payment to the innkeeper, who recoiled from the touch. Apaay imagined a horror ripping open his mind, one where that hand flashed, tearing face from bone.

The man's throat worked. "Of course." He fumbled to grab a key from its hook on the wall. His hand trembled so severely he dropped it twice before regaining his composure. "This way."

Driftwood stairs and walls of packed sand constructed the inn's second level. It held that fermented seaweed smell Apaay was fond of. The innkeeper led them to a door at the end of the crooked hallway. Once Numiak searched the room and deemed it safe, they closed the door and locked it behind them.

The room was small, simple. It included a bathing area tucked behind a half-wall, a hearth in the far corner, two chairs, and a stack of firewood.

There was only one bed.

The Face Stealer, broad and oozing menace beside her, was near enough that Apaay caught the woodsmoke scent drifting from his skin. She looked away from the bed, stared out the window.

She should say something, or he should. Or someone. Or anyone.

"I'll take the floor," Numiak announced, brushing past her. He pulled one of the pillows from the mattress, a blanket, tossed them onto the ground.

The announcement broke Apaay's momentary paralysis. She rushed to build a fire, and soon the flame chased away the chill. The days were warm, but the cold blew in with the sinking sun, the moon's arrival. In a few months, the long night would be upon them, and the world returned to darkness.

"We'll stay here for the night." Numiak spoke to her back.

Apaay nodded. Then, realizing he might not notice, said, "Grood."

There was a silence.

"Grood?" It sounded as though Numiak was trying not to laugh.

She winced. "I meant *good*, but then I thought *great*, and it all . . ." She flapped her arms, focusing on the burning wood so she would not have to look at him, and seriously considered throwing herself into the fire. ". . . smushed together."

Then he did laugh, and that was even more mortifying.

Apaay leaped to her feet, hissing, "It's not my fault you're so . . . you." More arm flapping. "And there's only one bed!"

His dimples deepened as he braced his hands on his knees and released great, bellowing guffaws that reached down her throat and nearly strangled her lungs. Apaay sputtered helplessly. Really, this would be so much easier if she could stop staring at him.

"Wolfling." Once he calmed down, he chuckled, "I said I would take the floor." A twinkling gaze. "Unless you'd rather I didn't?" he purred, hunger rippling across his features.

"No! No, you're definitely sleeping on the floor." The thought of his hard body pressed against hers was having a strange effect on her heart. She poked at the fire to distract herself, then said, with impressive serenity, "When are we meeting the translator?"

Numiak glanced out the window. Both sun and moon hung low on opposite horizons. "Soon. It will be safer once it grows darker."

Until then, they would wait.

"This could be a good time to practice," he suggested.

Apaay grimaced as she settled on the ground before the crackling flames, legs folded beneath her. "I've been unsuccessful in my previous attempts. I see this one as no different."

Numiak glided to a chair and settled, one wrist balanced on the arm, one leg stretched out arrogantly, the toe of his boot pointed at her. "And why do you think that is?"

"If I knew, do you think I would be in this predicament?"

His eyes flashed. "Touchy." Elongated canines poked into his lower lip. "Here is what I know. Mind, body, and spirit are not separate. Think of the North. What happens when a tree dams a river?"

"The water cannot flow."

"Yes. If you are unable to connect with yourself, then something is causing a block or interruption." A long moment of scrutiny. "What's on your mind, wolfing? Do you worry about your family?"

Apaay answered, voice strained, "Of course I worry about them." Her eyes stung. She blamed the wayward smoke. "It's hard to feel connected to them. Will they even recognize me when I see them? Will I still be their daughter? I think about . . ." The words pushed at her chest. "Stories. I think about stories and all that I knew, and it is like nothing I know now. It's not fair. I know it doesn't matter. I didn't ask for this. That doesn't matter either. But sometimes, I wish . . ."

"You wish I had never stolen your sister's face," Numiak said quietly.

"Maybe." She shook her head, looked at the ceiling until the tears cleared, except they never did. "I don't know."

The silence lasted so long it began to grow uncomfortable. She thought her admission would bring some relief. If anything, the ache in Apaay's chest worsened.

"You've been carrying something heavy with you since we left the Wood," came his murmured voice.

Apaay's fingers paused in fiddling with a split in her trousers. The one she had recently mended, she noticed. "I'd rather not talk about it."

There was a pause, as if he considered whether to push or not. In the end, she was not surprised to find that he did. The only business Numiak liked more than his own was someone else's. "Why don't you want to talk about it?"

It's none of your concern.

It's not important.

It doesn't matter.

Lies, all of them.

"Because—" Her voice cracked. "It *hurts.*"

Except it went deeper than hurt. It was as though a piece of her core self had fissured in two. Just snapped like a frail winter branch. When she loved, it was with the whole of her heart, yet she'd managed to poison the bond she'd shared with Ila. In order to come to terms with the fallout of her actions, she had to stop running. She must face it. Otherwise she could not move forward.

When Apaay gathered enough courage to meet Numiak's gaze, she found his eyes sheened like her own, volatile, as though the thought of her pain distressed him. "What hurts, wolfling?"

Her throat was so swollen with emotion she couldn't squeeze the words past the barrier. She pressed a hand to her heart to show him.

"Ila," she choked out. "I think about Ila," she whispered, and then tears fell freely, they fell fast and hard as the pressure against her forehead throbbed. "I think about how poorly I treated her, and I feel horrible. Sick with guilt. She knew I was struggling. She tried to help me. She kept reaching out her hand, and every time she did, I just . . ." Didn't take it. Didn't want to. Didn't know how. "I spit in her face. That's what I did. Like she was nothing to me, like I didn't need her, even though I did need her, and yet instead of trying to breach that gap I kept pushing her away. I couldn't stop."

Now that Apaay had begun to speak, the words poured forth with no intention of slowing. And she let them. At last, she let everything she'd suppressed since having wakened from that numb existence go free, because she thought maybe relief, a lightened heart, awaited her at the end of this torrent, if only the gods would grant her that grace.

"I kept telling myself she had no idea what I suffered through, yet I never gave her a chance. She was trapped in the labyrinth, too, for *years*. Years and years." It was awful. So, so awful, and heartbreaking. "Why did I never ask Ila how she was coping? Why did I assume her pain could never be as great as mine?"

Because she had felt alone, and lost, unable to find her way back to herself. Because she'd been drowning for months with no sight of land.

"I lashed out, said horrible things to her." Apaay couldn't remember them. She only remembered the sight of Ila's face, crushed and betrayed. A woman who stared not into the eyes of a friend, but a stranger.

Who are you? What happened to my friend?

Ila had said that moments after Apaay had pronounced something she couldn't take back. Cruel—she'd been unfairly cruel.

"The worst part is I can't do anything about it. I can't apologize. She m-must think I hate her. I was so horrible—" One sob rolled into the next, until she completely dissolved under the mountain of strain.

Apaay couldn't remember the last time she had cried so thoroughly. She was broken. Breaking. Like so many pieces of her life. Her lungs felt crumpled and ineffective, unable to contain her gasping breath. It wasn't despair she felt. It was just a deep, unending sadness, shame for her actions, and guilt at being unable to change them.

Strong arms suddenly banded at her back, tugging her against a wide, solid chest. As one large palm cupped the back of her head, Apaay broke in Numiak's arms.

ALEXANDRIA WARWICK

Her fingers clawed into the soft hide of the maq warmed by his body. Her face, pressed into the curve between his shoulder and neck, burned from the force of this purging. Tears soaked his collar. She trembled violently, yet he embraced her tighter, the whole of his body acting as a shelter able to weather the tumult of her emotions.

"You're all right, wolfling," Numiak whispered into her ear. "You're all right." Pressing his lips against her temple, he rocked her, the rich depths of his voice like peace, the crooning darkness that had once terrified her, now a comfort.

"I miss her," Apaay whispered hoarsely, the words distorted. "I miss her and I want her to know I'm so s-sorry for everything I did."

"I know," he said.

The tremors gradually lessened, and that coiling sensation that had tightened her skin and twisted her insides released its hold. She slumped in the circle of Numiak's arms, spent.

"I'm sorry," she whispered.

"Don't apologize." A command, yet his tone was somehow gentle. He tucked her head beneath his chin. "Never apologize for how you feel."

"I feel like I didn't go through all of that—" She waved a hand in reference to those dark months. "—just to end up at a place where I'm struggling again." Even if the darkness never went away completely, she had learned how to live with it, manage it. It no longer made her feel small.

"In my mind, they're not separate issues. You addressed your trauma, but the shame you feel over your treatment of Ila, that's new."

"I was selfish."

"You weren't selfish," Numiak broke in calmly. "You experienced a traumatizing event and coped the only way you knew how. You faced an unbelievable amount of suffering and pain. I don't know how anyone goes through what you did and comes out of it with their humanity still intact." Pulling back, he searched her teary gaze, then wiped her damp cheeks with the palm of one hand, the gesture so tender she felt something shatter inside her. "If Ila loves you, she will forgive you, in time, when she is ready. You can't control that.

What you can control is how you treat yourself. Choosing whether you will extend yourself the same compassion you would extend anyone else."

Their faces drifted closer. "What if I'm not worthy of it?"

He tucked a strand of hair behind her ear, his fingertips hovering over the outer shell. "That is for you to decide. But I think Ila would not want you to suffer. You are worthy of forgiveness, just as you are worthy of love."

Her breath hitched. Tears blurred her sight save the pale green of Numiak's eyes.

"Sometimes," he said softly, "we must let go of our past selves in order to make room for all that we could be."

Let go. Apaay's hand went to her braid, the strands free of the carvings and shells she had once worn with honor. Numiak tracked the motion, and when their eyes locked with mutual awareness, they were no longer present in the tiny room of a coastal inn, but an impenetrable labyrinth of ice, as though reality had been traded for memory, a moment in time when a thread connecting Apaay to her culture had been severed by force.

Numiak blew out a breath and drew back, putting space between them. Scrubbed a rough hand over his face. "I didn't mean it like that."

Apaay suspected as much, but the memory lingered. "I know," she said. "I guess I was hurting myself because I didn't want to be that person. I'm trying to be . . . better. Someone I can be proud of. And I guess I'm still coming to terms with this new me, this face, this responsibility. It's connected in ways I didn't realize."

He nodded in a quiet, introspective way. "You can always talk to me about these things, you know. I don't have to say anything. I can listen, if that's what you need."

Apaay had never feared the Face Stealer's manipulative nature. It was his kindness she needed to watch out for. "Thank you," she said. "I appreciate that."

"You know who you are, Apaay. I know you do. It's reasonable to feel afraid. Change is scary. But the North does not remain stagnant, and neither will you, neither will any of us." He turned away. "At the end of the day, it's just a face. What lies in your heart, that's what truly matters. That you express remorse for your actions, don't you think it's reason enough to forgive yourself?"

Yes, she thought. And again: *yes*. She didn't want to continue carrying these burdens. But why was it so difficult to forgive herself? Why couldn't she be kind to herself, nurturing? Apaay knew she was enough. The struggle lay in remembering during the difficult times. Keeping faith. Looking toward the light.

She thought, *I forgive you.*

She thought, *You are not perfect.*

She thought, *You are a child in this world, learning how to walk, and then to run without faltering. You are worthy of love. You are worthy of so many things. I love you. I forgive you.*

Apaay touched her cheeks. Just a face. A tool. Changeable.

Temporary.

But her heart, her culture, that was forever.

The knot of all she had held close loosened and slipped free. Apaay, eyes closed, felt the weight ease from her chest. Something glowed behind her eyelids, in the pit of her stomach, pale as moonlight. A tangle of pulsating threads. She pulled on one experimentally. Her face tingled. It happened very quickly. The fallen tree shifted, dammed water rushing free at last. When she opened her eyes, eyelashes spiked with tears, Numiak was studying her work with glowing pride.

"So?" said Apaay tentatively. "How did I do?"

"See for yourself."

He passed her a shallow bowl of water. Apaay lifted her eyebrows, impressed by the likeness. Except it was not her eyebrows in the reflection but Numiak's, though without the cunning gray irises beneath. Her eyes remained brown.

"I can't tell the difference," she said.

"It is a convincing likeness. How do you feel?"

He wasn't speaking of the external, but the internal, she knew. Her palm pressed to her sternum. "My heart still hurts, but I feel lighter. Like maybe there's hope for Ila and me whenever we next see one another, to repair the damage of our pasts."

"I'm glad to hear that." He smiled warmly. "Now can you change back?"

That took a little more time. She was used to her old features. Eventually though, she felt things slide into place, naturally.

Numiak said, "Very good."

A wave of fatigue overcame her. "It drains me."

"That is to be expected. You are exerting energy in a way you are unused to. Rest while I get us something to eat."

He disappeared downstairs and returned with dinner. They ate in silence. The fire burned low and Apaay built it up again. As the hours lengthened, she felt the tension rise in her, though she could not explain why.

"Wolfling." Gently.

"Hm?" She lifted her head, which had slumped sideways to rest against the wall.

"It's time."

Quietly, they went downstairs, out onto the street. They traveled east, toward the sea.

Apaay smelled the water before she saw it. Her nose, her lungs, burned. Yet when she finally beheld Naga, disappointment and confusion rose in her throat. The view was not as she had expected: an open expanse, white-capped waves. It was blocked by massive boats thrice the size of the surrounding buildings. Their wooden hulls were as wide as they were deep, spotted with barnacles. How they didn't sink from the weight was beyond her. Strange sheets hung from tall columns and rippled in the coarse wind. The boats looked foreign, with their ugly bulk, and in Apaay's mind, they did not belong.

The road slithered into a path, which meandered to the lapping water, the behemoth vessels that blocked the sky. The docks were bustling with activity, ropes thumping against wood, the occasional exchange of an unfamiliar language. Apaay studied the curved planks that shaped the boats' hulls. Who were these people? Why were their boats built larger than life?

"They are whaling ships," said Numiak.

Whaling ships. She did not speak those words aloud.

"They use these boats to catch whales? Do they eat them?"

She felt his hesitation at her back. "They sell the meat to other traders."

"From Across the Sea?"

"Yes."

Apaay stepped onto one of the docks and stared into the water. An oily sheen lay atop the swirling current, and the sight of her new face gave her pause. She was still getting used to it. "What about the blubber? The skin?" Every part of the animal could be utilized in some way. For her people, the successful capture of a bowhead whale—a rare but joyous occurrence—could provide a village food, tools, shelter, heat, and light for an entire year.

When Numiak spoke, she knew he had chosen his words with care, as if sensing how this information upset her. "I don't think these men respect the land as your people do, wolfling."

The coastal Analak hunted beluga during the summer in their umiaks when the sea ice was in full retreat. If they were lucky, they'd harpoon a narwhal. Due to its clear-burning properties, rendered narwhal blubber was the preferred fuel for lamps, whereas seal blubber tended to leave soot marks on the inside of their ice houses.

But it had been many years since anyone in her village had captured a whale. The elders had believed the Sea Mother's disappearance to cause a decrease in the whale population, her spite toward their failings to follow the old rules or bring her offerings. With the truth of the Sea Mother's identity and whereabouts revealed, it was possible, but Apaay wondered if these traders with their colossal ships hadn't contributed to the decrease in whale pods as well.

"I don't like this place." Her voice was hoarse. "It makes me sad." Was that even the right word? Defiled felt like a more apt description. These men from Across the Sea had taken something that had never belonged to them. And they didn't care.

They boarded one of the vessels via a plank of wood connecting the hull to the dock. The ship shifted from the rocking motion of the waves, and Apaay's stomach lurched unhappily.

Numiak took them down a set of stairs leading into the ship's underbelly. Inside the candle-lit darkness, a man with pale features glanced up from where he was working at his desk. Eyes of the palest, most translucent blue, and yellow hair. Apaay stared.

Numiak strode forward. "You are the translator?"

In answer, the man held out his hand. Once Numiak dropped the crumpled note into it, he skimmed the writing. "How did you come by this?" His accent was foreign, sharp like burning wood, yet he spoke Analak without hindrance.

"That is my business."

The man peered at his guests warily, for the Face Stealer's voice had gone soft with malice.

He tapped the tip of his forefinger against the dark-grained wood. His mouth twisted, as if he were about to say something against his better judgment. "I ask because I have seen this handwriting before, though it was long ago."

"What did the handwriting say?"

"I do not remember." He gestured to the note. "It's not often I translate Svald. The penmanship is distinct."

Might it be possible the man from Across the Sea had passed through Kunivik before his death? Had he been looking for something, or someone?

The Face Stealer gestured to the paper. "The translation, please."

The man again read the note, this time aloud.

My son,

You were taken from me too soon. I know the bear was responsible. He watched you sometimes, after the fights. The hatred, the love. Then one day you were gone, and he was, too.

If you are alive, I will find you. I will not rest until you are returned to me.

Warmly,

Your dearest Papa

Apaay and Numiak exchanged a wordless glance. Here was an answer, but it was to a question they had yet to ask.

Numiak tossed the translator a gold piece, which he caught. "For your silence."

← 24 →

Later, when the moon had partially risen and violet dusk chased them back to the inn, Apaay and Numiak sat before the hearth discussing what they had learned, trying to find a common thread. A father believed Nanuq had taken his son. If that was true, why? For what purpose? Every detail, however slight, helped shape his plan: to cloak the North in his darkness. To plant the seeds of war and water them with blood.

Apaay said, "Tell me about when Nanuq traveled to Across the Sea."

Numiak lay outstretched, having propped himself up on one arm. "No one knows much about his time away. But there were rumors of his return. Apparently, he was initially denied acceptance as a kirn of the Empire due to his small stature. Days later, the captain who had rejected his request took ill and died. The army's general extended Nanuq a personal invitation to join his force."

Apaay stared into the fire, then shifted her attention back to the Face Stealer, observing the war of light and darkness shift across his face. Come morning, they would return to Nigun and demand that the commander side against Nanuq's force. "You think Nanuq killed that captain."

"Of that, I have no doubt."

Something had stood in Nanuq's way. And he had removed it.

Which brought Apaay back to the note. If Nanuq had stolen this man's son, was it because the boy had stood in his way? And what was it the note had mentioned about fights?

Too many threads. She did not know which held the greatest importance.

A thread: Nanuq.

Another thread: Yuki.

Another thread: the Raven's tattoo, the knowledge it bound in secret.

That was the missing piece: Nanuq's secret. A perceived weakness to his character. Apaay assumed that whatever secret the Raven knew of, it was in relation to Nanuq's time spent Across the Sea. But what would someone like Nanuq, a man, a bear, both and neither, whose only concern was his legacy, need to hide?

Quiet, and in a very un-Face Stealer-like voice, Numiak asked, "What are you thinking, wolfling?"

She was thinking it was nice to be here, warm from the fire, and safe, and not alone. And she was thinking that was a dangerous thought indeed.

Sparks scattered against the darkened walls. It reminded Apaay of the shadows she and Eska would shape with their hands against the glowing walls of their ice house during the long night. This memory, dear to her. Apaay curled one hand into a fist and turned her attention back to the question. "What is Nanuq like?" If she had a better understanding of his character, it might help them pinpoint his motivations, give insight into his past.

"His methods of torture are . . . gruesome."

Apaay's stomach turned. "To war refugees?"

"No." Numiak rubbed his eyes with his thumb and forefinger. "To his own men."

And so he told her. He explained Nanuq's methods of chaining a man in his bear form while his comrades took weapons to the bear's flesh. Whips, spears, it did not matter, so long as the man could not escape, so long as his white pelt bled. It was a reminder: men were animals at heart, and Nanuq would not fail to treat them as such.

The horror of Numiak's tale spread through her like paralysis. When he was done, Apaay didn't know what to say. She didn't understand the point of harming your own people, men who fought for your cause, even if she believed the cause to be unjust.

"Nanuq is horrible," Apaay croaked through a wad of sickness caught in her throat. "Horrible and cruel."

"He is," Numiak agreed. "Which is why I wonder what came of him during his time Across the Sea, and if the Raven's tattoo might shed light onto it. The tattoo contains a dark curse, which adds a layer of protection. It is my assumption that we will need to find the person who administered the tattoo for its removal."

Reaching forward, he stirred the dying fire. A flash of paler skin drew her eye to the inside of his wrist, the hardened knot of an old scar. It seemed familiar.

Numiak noticed where her attention had gone. She sensed something warring in him before he said, "Ten years ago I was traveling along the eastern coast toward a small Analak village in my wolf skins. I did not see the trap concealed beneath the snow." A short pause, though not without weight. "It snapped shut on my paw, crushing bone. I could not change back into my human form due to fatigue."

Apaay had seen these traps before—rigid, cruel, foreign. "How did you escape?"

The smallest of smiles graced his mouth. "A young girl freed me." Numiak's gaze locked steadily onto hers, drew out the realization like a thread pulled free.

The girl was her.

Apaay remembered that day clearly. How the wolf's hot blood melted the white snow beneath. And its pelt, colored like ink, its eyes yellow orbs, piercing with intelligence. She found this information to fit together a little too neatly.

"I would visit your village every so often to check on you," he explained. "I didn't see the trap."

"It wasn't us," Apaay said. Metal was a cold, impersonal material and came not from the North but from somewhere Across the Sea.

"Do you think I don't know that?" His eyes were so dark the fire

← 195 →

reflected in his pupils. "Your people are kind and generous. I would not expect them to use something so . . . dishonest."

"Why didn't you say anything?" She had noticed his scar when they'd exchanged the first blood oath in the labyrinth. Apaay recalled, too, his limp in the Nayinkai—her assumption that he had aggravated an old injury while fighting Umiq in their quest to ally with the Owl Clan.

"Would you have believed me, back then?"

No, she wouldn't have.

The fire devoured the young cut wood, sparks dying as they hit the air. When Numiak next spoke, his voice came low.

"I often think of how I found you in that cave." She sensed his desire to look at her, and the guilt holding him back. "You were starved. Skin and bones." Slowly, he set down the stick he'd used to stir the fire back to life. "I had done that to you."

So they were finally here. It was inevitable, after all, having not been previously discussed.

Apaay exhaled through her nose. "Yes."

He did not speak for a long time. "Some nights I lie awake and hate myself for it." Each word eked out, heavy with self-loathing. "I had treated you cruelly in the labyrinth. I was the demon you believed me to be, no better than my name. And when I found you, brought you to the Wood, I showed you no compassion. Again, I was cruel. But I thought, your hatred toward me, it was something. Better than apathy, better than the numbness you showcased.

"And still, after everything I had done to you, you came back for me in Talguk. Quite literally stabbed my brother in the back—" Numiak stopped. The uneven edge of his breathing sawed at the air, and at last, he lifted his eyes to hers. "Why did you do that?" he murmured, in a way that told her he had wondered this not once, but enough to carry it with him all the miles they'd traveled, and only now had he gathered the courage to ask.

It was simple. For the first time, it was simple between them.

"Because you were no longer my enemy," she said.

His lips flattened. His throat worked. That they must sit in this room and share all the mistakes they had made, the hurt they had caused one another, and those they cared for, was not the most comfortable situation, but it was important to acknowledge.

"For what it's worth," he said, "I'm sorry. I know I apologized to you at Sinika, and I thought that might be enough. But it's not enough. It will never be enough." Numiak stared into the fire. "You are not the only person I have hurt, but you are too important to me now to pretend I did no wrong. I am trying to make amends. I want you to know that whatever happens, wherever you are, you will always have a friend in me."

"Thank you," she whispered. "And for what it's worth . . . I forgive you."

Whatever lingering resentment Apaay had been clinging to, she let it go. Let it follow the river's current out to sea. Let it, finally, be free.

The forgiveness was for her, but she recognized how much Numiak needed it, too. With his shoulders relaxed, it eased from him a burden she hadn't realized he'd been bearing.

The fire provided a warm glow, and the inn slept. Beyond the window, distant waves peaked and died. The sound lulled her.

Numiak touched her hand, and Apaay snapped her eyes open. A door squealed.

Footsteps on the stairs.

"Window," he hissed.

She scrambled after him as he pushed open the shutters and peered up and down the deserted street. There was nothing to break their fall below, the drop too dangerous to attempt unless they wanted a broken leg.

The door handle jiggled softly.

Reaching up, the Face Stealer hauled himself onto the roof as the lock clicked and the door swung silently open. Two masculine forms filled the doorway, their faces smudged by shadow. Numiak's hand appeared. Apaay grabbed hold, and the strength of his arm heaved her upward.

"They're on the roof!"

It was a mad, wild, thrilling dash for their lives, across uneven terrain, the sloped, overlapping rooftops of Kunivik, and peril in one misstep, or a tripped landing leading to a fatal fall many levels below.

Boots slammed into metal, into wood, startling those in their homes awake. Another leap, a skid, and gasping breath, the coastal winds cold and punishing. The whale skeletons arched above like a labyrinth of interconnecting threads of bone.

Apaay did not know how far they ran, skidding down inclines and hiding behind jutting turrets. The seaside port city extended farther than she had imagined. Buildings littered the area as far as the eye could see. As they reached another break in the roofs, Numiak leaped across it effortlessly. Apaay halted at the sloped edge.

"Can you make it?" he panted, scanning the alleyways below. Shouts echoed in the distance. Reinforcements, most likely.

She calculated the stretch of open air, the likelihood that she could spring the gap. Apaay didn't have long legs, not like Numiak.

She said, "Probably."

A glance over her shoulder showed the two men a ways back, racing to close the expanse. Apaay gave herself room to perform a running jump and flung herself across the drop.

She'd miscalculated the distance. She knew as soon as her feet pushed off the ledge. By then, it was too late. Apaay was airborne. Falling. Her stomach lodged into her throat. Numiak's eyes widened, and only by some inhuman feat did he manage to grab her arm. Her shoulder seared in pain as she jerked to a halt, swinging in midair, and Numiak grunted, clinging to the roof's edge by his fingertips.

Apaay looked down. Broken, discarded crates cluttered the darkened street below, sharp and lethal. She laughed maniacally.

A curse and a heave, and Numiak dragged her single-handedly onto the roof. He sat back on his heels, gritting his teeth while Apaay tried to catch her breath. The metal sheets, slick with the sweat of her palms, buckled beneath their combined weight. He held his arm at an awkward angle against his body.

"Are you hurt?" she asked. "Did they get you?"

"Dislocated shoulder." Sweat sheened his brow. "Shit." Breath held, he jerked his arm to the side. Apaay heard the snap of his joint locking back into place.

They scrambled up a peaked roof, down its other side. The whale skeletons glowed white and pristine. Bones upon bones.

"Four on the roof," said Numiak, pulling her forward by the hand again. "More on the ground." Something whizzed by his ear.

The great undulating shape of the whale spine curved over the street, running parallel, and the ribs curled over the many structures. Apaay used one of the rib bones to swing herself over a gap, dropping with a roll. The shouts of pursuit were gaining on them.

At the next break in the rooftops, Numiak took a flying leap, landing easily. Apaay tossed her body over the gap, yet something popped in her ankle upon landing. She bit back a cry as her leg buckled.

Immediately, Numiak crouched by her side. "Where does it hurt?"

She hissed out a curse. "My ankle. I think it's twisted."

His eyes flicked from their pursuers, to Apaay, to the drop below, back to Apaay. One moment he was standing on the roof, and then he wasn't. "Down here."

She hobbled to the edge and spotted him in the narrow alley darkened by the surrounding buildings, peering up at her. "Jump," he said. "I'll catch you."

Apaay eyed the drop. It was two levels below. She didn't have that kind of faith.

"Hurry, Apaay."

"What if I break my leg?"

"What if you don't?"

Her nostrils flared. "Not helping."

"I said I'll catch you."

Apaay sat so her legs dangled, fingertips biting into the roof's rough, wooden texture. It was a long way down. "Numiak?"

"Let go."

She did, a small *oof* expelling as he caught her around the waist. Gently, he set her down with a look of concern.

"I'll be fine." They could worry about her ankle later, preferably when not on the run.

They stood in front of a nondescript building that smelled of sweet perfume, the door battered. Numiak turned to her, a question in his eyes. "Do you trust me?"

Apaay hesitated only a fraction of a second. "Yes."

He knocked. Their pursuers' footsteps faded momentarily before returning with increased urgency. They may have been on the next street over.

The door opened a crack, enough for a single eye to take in their rumpled appearances. It surveyed Apaay in distaste, but upon catching sight of the Face Stealer, the door opened wide to reveal a stunning, buxom woman draped across the doorframe, showcasing clothes made from colorful woven fabric and cut scandalously high. Apaay stared at the woman's bare thighs in shock.

"How much for entrance?" demanded Numiak. "And for my friend to borrow your dress?"

The woman's eyebrows hiked upward. She may have been seal Unua for the wet blacks of her eyes and their unusual roundness. "How much are you willing to pay?" she purred in a throaty voice.

Leaning forward, he whispered something into her ear. The woman smirked as she drew back, tucking the payment he passed her into the space between her breasts.

Apaay swallowed an unpleasant taste in her mouth.

The woman gestured them inside and slipped out of her dress. The space was shrouded in gray and gold, a fusing of smoke and weak lamplight, not unlike sunlight poking through fog.

"Put this on." Numiak tossed the garment in Apaay's direction.

She glared at him, already regretting the decision to trust him. "A little privacy would be nice." He was gazing openly at her, as if awaiting her nudeness.

He grinned wolfishly, yet turned his back. Apaay yanked on the slip of fabric, glanced down, and fought the urge to cover herself with her hands. The hem stopped at mid-thigh, and chilly air stroked her ankles. She looked ridiculous. "Now what?"

He turned, that smoky gaze caressing the areas of bared skin: shoulders, arms, collarbones, calves. Reaching out, he grabbed her hand. The roughness of his calluses felt deliciously abrasive, and heat ignited across the back of her neck.

"Now," he said, "we blend in."

Down the hall, through the curtained doorway, into a large, low-ceilinged room crammed wall-to-wall with people, enough smoke to clot her lungs for all eternity, and the sticky heat of sweet-smelling skin. Apaay, in scandalized shock, allowed the Face Stealer to lead her deeper into the madness.

Everyone was participating in some form of sexual act. Couples lounged on couches or sprawled in chairs, arms and fingers twining around necks or into hair, deep, open-mouthed kisses pressed to mouths and collarbones and naked chests. Apaay shuffled her feet, tried not to look, tried not to listen, tried to block out this reality. Clothes peeled away. Too much flesh. Fingers wandered, stroked, bit in.

She averted her gaze at the open intimacy, but there was always something more alarming to note. "What is this place?"

"A pleasure house." The hand not holding hers pressed against her lower back. On one of the couches, two women fondled each other's breasts, between their legs, until they stiffened and cried out.

Her blush reached an entirely new level of intensity. Her skin felt scorched.

"Can't they do this somewhere private?" People were watching.

Well, that wasn't true, exactly. Apaay was the only person watching. Everyone else was busy.

From the corner of her eye, she watched the Face Stealer's mouth quirk.

"This isn't funny," she whisper-hissed.

"Do you see me laughing?" His gaze lowered to rest on her face. In fact, he looked quite serious. She felt her blood pressure rising. A pulsing beneath her skin. "Say the word," he murmured, "and this ends. All right?"

He had asked for her trust, and she'd given it to him, but any moment now she would demand answers.

Before she could, Numiak tugged her down onto a vacated couch, positioning her across his lap. Apaay went rigid.

"Play along." His whisper coasted on warm breath against the shell of her ear.

Play along?

Play *along*?

Apaay felt as though her mind were splintering into pieces. Someone moaned, and her eyes flitted around the room, seeking the offender. No, she couldn't look. She must sit here and . . . Damn the man. What was she supposed to do with her hands? He was warm, too warm. With her shoulder pressed against his chest, the beat of his heart hammered through her.

Apaay was acutely alert, every piece of herself alive and singing. Numiak didn't appear to notice her awkwardness. He kept glancing at the door even as he held her close, stroking her back absently, the heat of his palm marking the line of her spine. Apaay imagined it was supposed to soothe, but with the forced intimacy, it had the opposite effect.

"Numiak."

"Shh." His hand slowed, and drew out the motion like an unraveling knot.

Movement over his shoulder drew her attention. The seal Unua soldiers had discovered their hiding place and now searched through the masses, weapons held high in threat.

She began to struggle. Numiak's arm banded around her waist, keeping her in place.

"Don't look at them." His low voice rumbled. "Look at me."

He may as well have asked her to stare into the sun without squinting. She couldn't. Couldn't move, couldn't think, could barely remember to breathe properly. His thighs, hard with muscle beneath her bottom, every point of contact like a molten vein splitting open. The spice of his breath teased.

Numiak's hand braced her thigh, searing through the flimsy fabric. Apaay startled so badly she clipped him with her elbow. His palm, the fingers fully spread, was wide enough to surround the entire upper curve.

Say the word, and this ends.

"Tell me, wolfling." His hand slid downward, keeping the dress as a barrier. It made little difference. Apaay felt its rough strength as he thumbed the bottom hem, where fabric ended and flesh began. "Has a man ever touched you like this before?"

Bumps pebbled across her skin even as the heat of the smoke gathered closer. Oh, hell. Was it possible to die from hyperventilation?

"Or here?" The tip of his nose brushed the lobe of her ear, and Apaay fought the urge to arch her neck. She was spinning, she was slipping into pure sensation, she was wavering, those defenses weakened and brought low. It was insanity.

Apaay had always considered his voice to be a weapon, words honed from the lash of his tongue. Out of cruelty came kindness, and now this: soft seduction. Things were different now. The Face Stealer wasn't dangerous because he was her enemy. He was dangerous because he *wasn't*.

Apaay squeezed her eyes shut. This was all for show. Of course it was. She needed a distraction. He was a distraction. He was—

Numiak's hand dipped under her dress and found the flesh of her thigh. Apaay locked up tighter, bowed her head toward his shoulder so he wouldn't see the pained expression contort her face. The sensation of his hot skin on hers, the friction—it was exquisite. A dull throb pulsed between her legs.

"Relax," he purred.

His voice soaked through her defenses, like rain seeping into earth. Apaay fought its hold. It was all she had left, this threadbare shred of restraint. If she relented control to the Face Stealer, Apaay did not know if she would remember herself.

"Maybe if you would stop touching me," she snapped as his fingers slid higher. Her hands fisted in her lap, so acute was her desire to touch him in turn.

"Tell me to stop and I will." Amusement in his tone. Bastard.

She almost did. Apaay had no doubt that he would. So why didn't she? Why suffer through this madness, this exquisite torture? Apaay thought of the beautiful woman at the door and wondered what Numiak had whispered in her ear. Maybe she didn't want him to stop. Maybe it was time to accept that truth.

"Or," he said in afterthought, "you could tell me what you like."

The breath stuttered in her lungs.

They had officially crossed a line. She could not respond. If she did . . . no. This was neither the time nor the place. Apaay closed her eyes and pretended she had not heard him. Only then might she escape this room unscathed.

Everything narrowed to touch. Her thoughts drifted with the

cloying perfume. The fractured moans of others finding release wound her tighter. Tension climbed and reached its crest. Her nerves felt as though they had been flayed open and singed at the ends.

"Did you know," Numiak murmured, "that I have never felt softer skin?"

"N-no."

"Mm. It's true."

A tortured sound squeezed out as his fingertips ran along the inside of her knee, lingering there, before drifting back up her thigh, curving inward to where the skin was finer and more sensitive. Her blood leaped beneath his touch, and Apaay swayed, the Face Stealer's other hand rooting around her waist.

It felt like she'd ingested an entire bowl of moonflower tea. Her bones melted, liquid and soft, and the low buzzing in her ears swelled with increasing presence. He continued to trace various patterns up her thigh, higher, higher, yet always eased back before reaching too far, as if sensing this was the boundary she had set.

Tucking her face into his neck, Apaay inhaled the scent of his skin, dizzy with the desire warming her blood. Faint heat bloomed against her neck and vanished as soon as she took notice of it. The press of his mouth? *More*, she might have demanded, might have shifted his hand higher beneath her dress where heat gathered.

When his hand coasted up her side, edging the curve of her breast, her fingers dug into his arm. He did it again, moving closer to its peaked center. Apaay began to tremble in earnest now. It was too much. It wasn't enough.

The moment before he would have brushed her nipple, Numiak brought his lips to her ear. "Wolfling."

Apaay shivered and licked her lips. "Yes?" Strained.

"They're gone."

← 25 →

Dawn arrived with bitter cold. Ila, peering through the bars of her cell, awaited the door at the end of the dark hallway to open, the guards appearing to drag them to another day of hard labor.

Today, she thought. After weeks of these endless black days, it would all end today.

Saniraq met Ila at their shared cell wall. Ila had grown used to the woman's observation, how she asked many questions, yet spoke little. *All right?* signed Saniraq.

She wanted to say yes. If only it were true. *No.*

Ila was sick with worry. Too many things could go wrong. These women, all of whom she was gradually coming to identify as her pack, understood their roles in this plan. They knew of Ila's deal with the guard. While she attempted to *escape*, they would create a distraction in the clearing.

Malina's leadership skills were invaluable. She knew how to rally these women better than Ila ever could.

She signed, *In case something goes wrong, I want you to make sure the women get out.*

Saniraq appraised her with a studious eye. *You think something will go wrong?*

I don't know. And that was the worst of it. *But in case something does, Malina will take you all to a safe place.*

You have spoken to her about this? Surprised.

Ila nodded. And she thought she had earned a bit more of the irritable woman's respect because of it. Ideally, they would all escape together, but Ila knew the issue was bigger than herself. The survival of the Wolf Kingdom didn't lie with her. It lay with the whole of them.

Currently, Malina spoke to Tipki across the walkway, hammering out last-minute details. Malina would use the distraction to slip away unseen. The guards wouldn't notice one missing captive, not at first. While Ila dealt with stealing Tulimaq's staff, Malina would focus her attention on freeing those in the cells, once the guard returned them to the cell block.

Saniraq said, *Malina may deny it, but we needed you, Ila. Many of us had lost hope we would ever be free again. You gave us that hope. So thank you.*

Ila, unused to the praise, blushed. *Thank me when we are free.*

As if on cue, the door opened at the end of the hall. Ila straightened. Cell doors—unlocked. A plodding in single file to the brightness beyond the walls.

The other prisoners were already at work. Shovels cut through dirt. Holes grew deeper, piles of earth grew higher, all surrounded by Nanuq's kirn, with their open-jawed hoods, theirs clubs, and the sharp-roofed buildings at their backs. Malina caught Ila's eye as she grabbed a shovel and situated herself near Tipki.

Around midday, the newest captives arrived, stumbling in messy lines from the woods to the west. Ila wondered where they had been hiding, how far they had traveled, how their refuge had been discovered.

From the corner of her eye, Ila watched Tipki knock Malina into the hole she'd been digging—purely by accident, of course. This led to a rather violent fist fight between two, six, twelve women, more. It was an uproar of tangled limbs and bloody noses. Guards attempted to break the women apart, but as a shovel smashed across a man's face, Ila understood they were now fighting for their lives.

Ila searched for Birthmark, spotting him nearby. At his signal, she bolted through the trees, running as fast as she could, knowing someone would give chase. The labor camp vanished behind the enclosed trees. A bird, startled by her flight, sought safety in the canopy above. It didn't take long for fatigue to set in, thin and malnourished as she was. The ground rose abruptly. Ila scrambled up the hill, slowing the higher she climbed. Escape—her adrenaline-filled limbs believed it, but her mind knew otherwise.

Someone crashed into her back. Though she'd expected it, the force of impact surprised her, as did the guard's aggression in his attempt to lash her hands behind her back from where they'd fallen. The obedient captive. She could play the part one last time.

The trek back to the labor camp passed too quickly. The guard didn't treat her kindly, but then again, they never did.

When the camp came into view, Ila began to struggle. The terror she experienced was real. But she must pretend, for Tulimaq's sake, that what awaited her was death, not a setup. The animal in her reared, and Ila thrashed, kicking out with her feet as they entered the clearing.

The blow was so forceful it ricocheted through her entire body. Ila was standing, and then she was on her knees. A man loomed over her. It was an act, she told herself. Just an act. But after today, no one would ever lay a hand on her again. She swore it.

The other captives stared wide-eyed at the commotion. The guards were so engaged with this unexpected spectacle they did not punish those who had stopped digging. Ila didn't see Malina anywhere. She hoped that meant the woman had managed to hide.

Someone pushed to the front of the crowd—Tulimaq. He began to speak with Birthmark in bursts of angry hand gestures. His mouth moved too quickly for Ila to catch any part of the conversation, but Birthmark shook his head. This seemed to enrage Tulimaq further. The older man smirked, then shrugged.

"Put her back in the cell," said Birthmark. "I'll deal with her later."

He gave her an almost imperceptible nod before the guards dragged her away. Soon, she was back behind bars, alone, the outer door swinging shut with finality. Almost as if she had never left.

Make it good.

Ila would shout and spit until they heard her.

Screaming, Ila slammed her fists against the iron bars. Her bruised hands, taking still more punishment. Her next scream came from a place so deeply buried it felt as if someone had lit a fire in her lungs. The skin of her knuckles broke open, hot blood smearing onto the chilled metal. *It's an act*, she thought again. But the stinging in her eyes was not.

On shaky legs, Ila fell back, turned, paced and paced, and itched for something to hold onto. Her thoughts fractured. They returned, as she had not wanted them to, to Tulimaq. The guard had been certain he would show. She did not want to think about what his absence meant. The former combat master had taught her to fight and fight hard, to strike and strike again without faltering. More importantly, he'd taught her never to trust him.

Dim, grainy light leaked through a small hole in the roof. From the corner of her eye, she caught sight of a figure staring at her through the bars. Ila's shock trickled through her slowly. Tulimaq unlocked the door and pulled it closed behind him, not bothering to lock it. He gripped his staff firmly. Her mother's talq hung from his waist.

"That was a foolish thing for you to do."

Of course he'd come to belittle her. Her lips curled into a sneer. *It was a perfectly rational decision.*

"They will kill you."

So they'll kill me, she answered with bravado.

He stepped closer, farther into the cell. Good. The jaws of this beast opened wide, hungry for vengeance.

"Why do you care so little for your life?" he demanded.

What does it matter? She gritted her teeth, her hands slapping out the words. *You don't care. You* never *cared*. It infuriated her even as it broke something in her, that this man had taken advantage of her naivety when she had only wanted to connect with others, like her, who did not always know their place. He'd once told her the world was cruel. She hadn't believed him then.

Tulimaq stepped into her space, forcing her nearer to the wall. He was so close she saw the fine hair follicles above his upper lip.

"No," he said. "That's the problem." The words vibrated between them. She smelled tea leaves on his breath. "I care too much."

Ila inhaled sharply as the air grew charged with awareness. The intensity of Tulimaq's gaze dragged at her like a dark undertow, the space between them disappearing mote by mote.

The boy cares for you. Use it to your advantage.

As if in a trance, Ila leaned forward and brushed a chaste, timid kiss across his mouth.

She jerked back, her lips tingling with heat. Tulimaq's eyes, wholly black, seemed to deepen with an unspeakable emotion. Ila tensed as he clamped strong fingers around her arms, the staff falling to the ground, and crushed his mouth to hers.

The force sent her back slamming into the wall. Ila's stomach swooped in a low dive. His teeth nipped at her mouth, demanding it open for him, and Ila, unable to protect herself against the onslaught, found her lips parting, a shudder running through her limbs.

They were body to body, hips aligned. Tulimaq slanted his mouth over hers, the kiss deepening further. She felt greed in the heat pouring off his skin, fury in the taut back muscles and bruising embrace, and above all, the helplessness of despising something, but true desire overriding it.

Ila had no idea what she was doing. Her skin felt singed where his long-fingered hands touched: arms, shoulders, hips, thighs. He coaxed desire from her mouth, and the blood throbbed hotly in her face and chest. This hadn't been the plan, not at all. The truth was, the kiss had been for her, had come about from her own selfish needs.

Ila made a small sound in her throat. His groan sparked along her tongue.

Breaking away, Ila turned her head to suck in air. The hot suction of his mouth explored the curve of her neck. Ila arched her back on a cry, clinging to his shoulders so her knees wouldn't give out. From the corner of her eye, she spotted the staff at his feet.

Tulimaq's mouth returned to hers. It felt like an apology, as much of one as she would receive from him. He was a child at heart, tossed away, yet it was a man standing before her, touching her, making his wants known. His hands curved around her neck, his thumbs tipping up her chin. Time slipped away. Ila forgot so many things.

But she had not forgotten her purpose. Abruptly, Ila shoved him back. Tulimaq, in his surprise, stumbled, allowing Ila to snatch up the staff and bolt for the door.

Two steps from freedom, Tulimaq snagged the back of her parka, and Ila whirled, fueled by her inner turmoil, a tremendous power crackling through the slender weapon. A beam of light shot from the shard of bone, hitting him square in the chest, hurling him against the bars. Tulimaq fell and did not move.

Ila snatched her mother's talq before fumbling in his pocket for the keys. The world tilted beneath her feet. She would remember this moment. A time when her loyalty had been tested, and Ila had chosen herself. Keys in hand, she locked Tulimaq inside the cell, his crumpled form visible through the slats.

Ila ran out the door and into the light.

26

Two steps out the door, and her way was blocked. Birthmark, the wretched man who had carved marks into her skin, who had relished every scream he'd wrung from her body, rose like the tallest of trees over her head, seven of his officers flanking him. Smoke billowed beyond their shoulders.

He smiled hungrily. "Very good. You have proven to be of some use, but your end of the deal is done." Holding out his hand, he waited for Ila to relinquish the staff.

She didn't move. Power. It was a slender piece of wood marked with carvings, and right now, Ila held it in her hands.

The man's smile slid into a sneer as the moments passed. "Don't be a fool."

He gestured to his right, to the line of women being led into the cell block. One of the guards, holding a burning torch, positioned himself at the door.

"Hand over the staff," he said, "or my man will set the building on fire, and everyone in it."

The torch wavered in the breeze. Could Ila risk it? She was outnumbered, but the staff's power equaled that of a tempest. Strong enough to fell multiple trees, as it had once done all those months ago in her escape attempt from Tulimaq. Strong enough to save her people.

Ila smiled.

In one liquid motion, she slashed in a downward curve, putting all her intention behind the blow.

The air shuddered, rupturing with white light. Power boomed and tossed the men across the clearing.

Ila sped toward the cell block. The dry wood had caught fire that climbed the walls and gnawed the door. The guard charged, and Ila planted her feet to await his arrival. He swung. Ila blocked. As their blades cracked, Ila kicked at the man's knee, which buckled. She drove the blade into his throat, killing him instantly.

By the time she reached the building, it was swallowed by a mass of flames, the sky bleeding red above. Tears streamed from her eyes and immediately evaporated on her skin, and it was pain and more pain, the smoke killing the air inside her lungs. She tore off a strip of her tattered parka, wrapped it around her lower face. Stay awake, stay aware, and all would be well.

The staff hummed with power. White light careened in the direction of the cell block, and she watched in horrified wonder as it blasted a hole straight through. Heat punched outward—close, compact air sending wood splintering in all directions. Smoke fled the darkened interior.

Ila plunged through the roiling black cloud. In seconds, the skin of her neck, face, and hands began to blister. The scar above her ear throbbed in strange memory, these charred walls exchanged for those of a larger, windowed structure.

She fumbled with the keys to unlock the first cell. The four collapsed women inside didn't stir, Tipki among them. Ila slapped her packmate on the cheek hard enough to leave an imprint.

Tipki came to, slow and disoriented. Ila pointed at her cellmates, then at the massive hole that had ripped open the side of the building. Tipki blinked, trying to rid her eyes of the smoke. Eventually, she nodded in understanding and began dragging the first woman toward safety while Ila unlocked the rest of the cells. One by one, they dragged the bodies from the burning building and into the cool forest as fire leaped across the structures, leaving charred ruin in its wake.

Twelve women did not wake at all.

Twelve out of twenty-two.

"What should we do with them?" Tipki asked. The whites of her eyes glowed from a face caked with the deepest, blackest soot.

Everyone turned to Pili, who touched each of her friends' faces in sadness. They lay side by side with their hands resting atop their stomachs. Ila wrapped a hand around her throat. This life had not been kind to them. She sincerely hoped their next life was better.

"We don't have time to bury them," she said with a haggard expression. A fit of coughing briefly stole her breath. "We'll need to leave them."

Emiat, one of the youngest in the group, stood from where she had been mourning her sibling. "I'm not leaving my sister here to rot."

"Do you think I wish to do so?" Pili said, anger pinching her cracked, bleeding lips. "These women deserve a proper burial in our homeland."

Ila pushed forward. They hadn't time to stand here and argue. *Stay, if you feel so inclined.* She looked each surviving woman square in the eye, then searched for Malina. Their time together had been rife with animosity, but even the former Pack commander knew they could not linger. They would travel south before turning west toward their homeland. Malina, who knew the terrain, would lead, leaving Ila at the rear with Saniraq, Tipki acting as a scout.

Except Malina wasn't here.

Has anyone seen Malina? she asked.

No one had. Malina would have noticed the smoke and returned to help. The only reason why she wouldn't was if she had been detained.

Ila grabbed Saniraq's arm. *You and Tipki lead the women south. I'm going to look for Malina.*

Tipki stepped forward. "Let me go. Please." She gripped her braid tightly in both hands, worrying the strands between her fingers.

No matter how often Tipki and Malina squabbled, they were family, their ties intertwined from the years spent serving side by side in the Pack, and further fortified by this camp. It was important for Tipki to go after Malina just as it was important for Ila to lead the others to safety.

Ila pointed through the trees. *We head south. Catch up to us when you can.* They'd follow their scent trail in their wolf skins. The injured women, unfortunately, hadn't the strength to shift. Ila hadn't yet mastered the ability either.

The smoke provided adequate cover, and they reached the mountain base without interference. Heat and light wavered the air around her. The buildings belched flaming embers, brittle bones of black char poking from the growing piles of ash. Ila skirted one of the larger structures that collapsed in a wave of unbearable heat. She nudged the woman in front of her, urging her to pick up the pace.

The smoke thinned with the increasing distance. The women, crawling hand over foot up the rocky mountainside, did so with quiet resolve. Every so often, Ila scanned the land at her back. The camp, consumed by furious red light. She hurried to close the gap with the others, tried to ignore the prickling down her spine, as though someone watched their harried flight.

At last, they crested the top and descended into the valley on the mountain's southern face, always at a clipped walk or occasional jog. The women were exhausted, their bodies depleted, and still Ila demanded they go on. The hair at her nape continued to twitch with the feeling of being watched. Someone was following them.

If caught, there would be no second chance at escape. They would be tortured, then killed. But if Ila could lead the guards in the wrong direction, grant the women additional time . . . It was easier to hide one person than ten.

Ila caught Pili's arm. *Keep moving south,* she said. *I'll be back.*

Once the women disappeared from view, she turned and raced in the opposite direction, back toward the labor camp, Tulimaq's staff, strange and crackling with power, in hand.

She traveled a safe enough distance from the group, but not

too far that the smoke choked her vision. Crouching behind a tree, she tried to separate the darker shapes in the foreground from the smoky, red-tinged background. It didn't take long to spot movement. A slim, dark figure picked its way through the woods, pausing every so often, as if searching the ground for signs of passage.

He moved like someone who was used to hiding, who did not know what it was like to stand out in the open.

Eventually, she lost sight of him. Stepping out from behind the tree, Ila followed in the direction he'd disappeared. She had no hope of outsmarting Tulimaq. His tracking skills were far superior. But even he couldn't navigate the veil of black smoke quickly. If she managed to take him by surprise—

Suddenly, the staff was ripped from her grip, the slivered blade speeding toward her neck.

Ila dove out of reach, pulling the talq from her waistband and pivoting to face the former combat master.

They had stood like this time and again, weapons raised. Tulimaq with his staff, and she with her mother's talq. Flames enveloped the area at his back.

This was her life, hanging by a thread, and Tulimaq holding the blade that might sever it. These were the lives of her friends, people the world had believed to be gone. This was her birthright, and she refused to let him take it from her.

Tulimaq swung. Ila met the blow head-on. The weapons locked above them, their arms straining with the force of pushing against the other's strength. Ila broke away and lunged for his right abdominal wall, putting her entire weight into the cut. Tulimaq redirected the blow with a wave of power. She flew into a tree, head slamming against the hard wood, and retched watery black fluid from the ash she had ingested.

Tulimaq approached slowly. To give her time to recover? To create the illusion of fair play? Or perhaps he wanted to draw out this torture until the very end, in which case, Ila was looking forward to making his task as difficult as possible. She picked up the talq from where it had fallen. After all, it belonged to her. When he was within striking distance, she feinted, then whipped the weapon toward the opening he'd unintentionally given her when attempting to block. The blade sliced through hide, into skin.

Then he was gone. She whirled, searching for any sign of him. There—in her periphery. Ila darted behind the tree. Chips of bark exploded from where the blade had sunk deep into the wood. Something had unbalanced the former combat master. He wasn't completely present. A subtle unhinging, leading to small, potentially lethal, mistakes. By the time he managed to yank the staff free, Ila had already ducked under his guard, the edge of her talq tucked beneath his chin. Tulimaq froze, his muscles locking into place.

"You forgot," he said, and Ila's focus unwillingly drew to his mouth.

Her first lesson—never take your eyes off your opponent—and one she had completely overlooked in the rush of power she'd felt at having bested Tulimaq. The butt of his staff slammed into her toes. The talq flew free as he knocked her arm aside, a shallow cut welling blood from where the blade had nicked him beneath the jaw.

Tulimaq blinked sweat from his eyes. Soot smeared the plane of his cheek. His chest heaved.

Ila's hands shook, but she stood tall. She held her ground. She refused to yield. For her name was Matilaqaa, and she was through running. If she was going to die, it would not be on her knees.

Step by step, Tulimaq closed the distance until the blade of his staff dimpled the skin above her heart.

Stinging ash pulled tears from the corners of her eyes. This blight that existed between Tulimaq and herself had to end. A blade to the heart was the only way.

Do it, she challenged. *Be the son your father always wanted you to be.*

His lips whitened. A foolish thing, to bait him, but she was so furious at him, at herself, at everything, that she didn't care. She hated him. No, that wasn't right. She was supposed to hate him, and if she did not, then there must be something wrong with her mind or mental state or . . .

"You do not know what you ask of me."

I know, she signed. *Just as I know you are too cowardly to see it through.*

Tulimaq's upper lip peeled back to reveal long, pointed, glistening canines. His eyes were wild, flickering. She had never felt the warring in him, this one finite thing: to choose.

Do it, she demanded. *Do it now!*

Suddenly, his head snapped to the side as if he had heard something. A long moment passed.

Lowering his weapon, he stepped away. "Go then."

Ila didn't move. She expected the guards to emerge from their smoke-veiled surroundings. A trap sprung.

"*Go*," he snarled.

She tripped backward in her haste to put distance between them. Tulimaq was Nanuq's son, he was a traitor, he was a liar, he was her enemy. He told her to go, and she snatched up her mother's talq and went, fast as the wind. She'd watched his mouth shape the words, yet his eyes . . .

His eyes had told her to stay.

27

Apaay didn't know how she made it back to Nigun the next morning. Never had her legs been so close to failing, as if she were a newborn calf learning its own gait. With their identities exposed, she and Numiak couldn't return to the inn. They'd traveled by cairn, and from there, trekked the descent leading to the grassland butting up against Nigun's gates.

Play along. The memory sat hot against her skin. It hadn't been pretend, not for her. The tension winding knots through her body had been all too real.

The gates loomed before them, the grassland at their backs. Numiak gave the signal to the men above, and slowly, the behemoth structures yawned wide, allowing them entrance.

As they entered the city, Apaay asked, "When we first arrived in Kunivik, did you notice the seal Unua's weapons?"

He didn't look at her as he responded, "No."

That was fine. Apaay wasn't too keen on meeting his eye either. But something nagged at her. Something she hadn't noticed until now, hundreds of miles separating them from the coast. "They were made by the Caribou Nomads."

Numiak's even stride faltered as they turned down the tunnel emptying into the central atrium. "Many people carry weapons from the Northern Territory," he said, and closed his eyes in understanding. "But those were Yuki's men."

She slowed. The image gained clarity, sharpening Apaay's understanding. She met his gaze squarely. "When I first snuck into Nigun, I hid inside a container filled with white powder, which fell into the water. The men were upset." Troubled, too. She saw that now. "I think they use that powder when forging their weapons."

There was a pause. "What of it?"

"One of the men was concerned about telling the commander they would be two hundred weapons short. I assumed he was talking about the caribou army." Apaay trailed her fingertips across the wall, reverting to that moment, submerged in the warm river, voices carrying through the dark tunnels. "But what if it wasn't the caribou army?" She wanted to reject this possibility, but the pieces fit together a little too neatly. "What if the commander is forcing his people to make weapons for Nanuq's army?"

The Face Stealer set his black gaze upon her in growing understanding.

She said, "Don't you think it's strange the caribou Unua weren't touched by the war *at all*? Considering Nanuq destroyed the Wolf Kingdom, took land from the Owl Clan, it's unusual, right?" While there remained the possibility that the Northern Territory had been too far out of reach, Nanuq seemed like someone who never left anything unfinished. Why spare the caribou Unua unless he had need of them?

"It is." Numiak frowned, his doubt giving way to concern.

"What if the commander made a deal with Nanuq—to supply him with weapons in exchange for amnesty? Think about it. The commander controls his people with the vine nectar. So long as they are compliant, they will continue to do his bidding." Unaware that they aided the very person who sought to control them, and all of the North.

"You make a valid point." Numiak pressed his thumb to his lower lip in thought. "And if it is true—if the commander works for Nanuq—I wonder who else has fallen to his rule, what other potential allies might already be corrupted."

As time went on, Apaay realized the people they could trust grew smaller every day. Soon, there would be none left. "What do you think happened to the Council of Nine? Is there a Council of Nine?" Or had the commander ended them, too?

"I don't think the commander killed them. I think he would want to control them. My thought is they would be close at hand, subdued, locked away in case he had need of them."

They had nearly reached the central chamber, though the tunnels were strangely absent of their usual guards. Apaay said, "His rooms?"

"That would be my assumption." He stopped her prior to them reaching the doors. "I'll go. You stay here. So long as the commander sees one of us, he'll assume the other is nearby."

It was noble of him to volunteer, but . . .

"No." Apaay rested a hand on his arm. "You're too conspicuous. I'll go. I'll change my face. He won't ever know it's me."

"It's not safe," he growled.

"It is the world." She would wear a face like armor. She would uncover whatever sinister plot the commander concocted. She would expose him for what he was: a traitor. "If I'm not back within the hour, then something has happened to me."

Judging by Numiak's furious expression, he did not approve of this plan, not one bit, but he said, "Show me the face first."

With Apaay's emotional barriers having been brought down, energy flowed through her body unimpeded. She changed her face to that of a caribou Unua woman. Eyes larger, nose broader. Though she could not hide all the ways she was not part of the Herd, at a passing glance, no one would suspect a thing.

He nodded. "Well done."

"I'll be back soon."

"Apaay." Numiak caught her arm. His touch made her remember so many things. "Be careful."

She searched his gaze. "You, too."

As soon as he passed into the chamber, Apaay retraced their steps as quickly as she dared, for she did not want the guards to grow suspicious. The commander frequently roamed the lower levels, which made her suspect that was where he slept.

Her footsteps echoed as she descended a set of stairs. The air cooled the deeper underground she went. It held the stale odor she had grown used to, of having been trapped between rock for decades.

A set of doors marked the end of the long tunnel, an immense pair of antlers shaped as elegant door handles. It certainly appeared to be a place of rank, save for the absence of guards. Strange. If these were the commander's rooms, why the lack of guards? Why not a fleet of them? Maybe she was overthinking.

The door opened with a push. No lock, no mechanism to prevent her entry. Apaay scoffed. The commander possessed no shortage of arrogance. What was there to hide when the Herd believed every lie from his mouth?

Thick shadows steeped the room. Rich furs and tapestries decorated the interior, the floors warmed by caribou pelts. A vast bed constructed of wood squatted dead center in the room.

Light from the tunnel streamed through the doorway, highlighting another door across the space. Apaay hurried toward it, turned the knob, and pushed inside.

A low-burning lamp illuminated eight stone tables arranged in two parallel rows. Lying atop them were eight men and women, their eyes closed and their hands folded across their chests, which lifted and fell steadily. They were alive, every councilmember, though seemingly trapped in sleep.

The sight pricked her senses. The air smelled sweet. Their faces, completely unlined, did not appear to be in pain. Rather, a sense of peace surrounded them.

These men and women, even with graying hair, appeared no older than herself. Was this part of the enchantment? Did the spring have something to do with it? Apaay touched the cheek of a man who, judging by his pure white hair, was an elder of this nation. Yet the skin, elastic and dewy with youth, belonged to someone many decades younger.

"Hello?" She patted his cheek. "Hello?" He didn't wake.

Slowly, Apaay backed away. There was dark power at work here. Was this sleep caused by some type of potion? If so, she'd need an antidote to reverse the effects, and Apaay didn't have time to look for one. This was evidence enough of the commander's corruption, but how to prove it to the Herd when they viewed this man as their savior?

A creak of wood alerted Apaay to another's presence.

The commander stepped into the room, shutting the door with a soft click. Head tilted, he studied Apaay curiously and said, "Something does not belong here."

She shifted to position the tables between them. A sword gleamed in his hand. A nigana hung from his hip. He did not appear surprised by her presence. Apaay wondered if he'd expected this. Wondered if he'd somehow manipulated everything to bring her here.

It happened in an instant. The commander struck out in a low arc toward her abdomen. The blade cut the air in perfect precision. She scrambled back, ducked under the table, and heard the thunk of a sword cleaving wood.

Apaay sprung for the door, but the commander was deadly quick, something she had not expected. He charged her from the side. She swerved to avoid his blade and cut right, keeping close to the wall, the tables between them.

"Leaving so soon?" he called joyfully. "Please, stay awhile."

A blade screamed past her ear. Apaay gasped and threw herself out of range, accidentally ramming her shoulder against the wall in the process. Metal scraped stone and blasted sparks from the sword point. Apaay lunged, grappling for the weapon. A vein bulged in the commander's otherwise smooth forehead. If she could draw him to the floor, she'd gain the upper hand. Unfortunately, the man had complete control over his balance. She tried to age his eyes with her newfound abilities, to cloud them, blind him, but his fist smashed into her jaw and fractured her concentration.

Through sheer willpower, Apaay held on to the sword. Her knee snapped upward into his groin. He evaded, and only quick thinking saved her from a beheading. With his arm extended, Apaay's punch landed in the muscle between arm and shoulder, dislodging his grip. The blade skittered out of reach across the floor. Apaay lunged for the hilt as the commander slammed into her from behind.

She managed to keep her footing, but one of his hands closed around her throat and squeezed, cutting off her air supply. "Not quick enough," he spat, his strength overpowering. Apaay bit the palm clamped over her mouth as hard as possible. Teeth severed flesh, sinking deep. Blood gushed down her throat, down her chin, hot and thick with salt. The commander released her with a furious curse, then slapped her across the face so hard her vision blackened and she hit the floor, wheezing.

Apaay attempted to crawl under one of the tables, but he snatched her ankle and dragged her out into the open, and she was suddenly airborne, flying toward the wall. The impact rattled every bone in her body. She crumpled.

The commander observed her feeble struggles with a lack of satisfaction. He said, "For some reason, I thought this would be entertaining. Where is your fight? Stand up."

She didn't think anything was broken, despite the pain in her shoulder. Her twisted ankle twinged from the rooftop chase. Her legs trembled as she pushed to her feet. The commander was mad, completely mad. He would kill her. She would not walk out of this place alive. This deep in the rock, would anyone hear her screams?

The commander charged. His five-tined nigana bore down. He expected her to flee. He wanted the chase. Apaay used her exceptional agility to lunge inside of his guard, rendering the weapon useless at short range. If she could trip him somehow, Apaay would gain the advantage, but he was always one step ahead. He tipped her balance too far. Apaay hit the ground a second time.

"I know a snitch when I see one," he said calmly, his slippers entering her line of sight. Apaay groaned and rolled onto her side.

Digging his fingers into her arm, the commander yanked her upright, exposing her to his malevolent gaze. "I know who you are, Apaay of the Analak." An insidious grin stretched his thick, cracked lips. "The demon thought changing your face would keep you safe from harm? I assumed he would be smarter."

He assumed Numiak had altered her appearance. Let him think that. Absolutely no one could know about her newfound identity, or her power. Those they could trust were few.

"You do not even defend him?"

Apaay would have spit in the commander's face if she didn't think he would break her nose for it.

"Do you think to out me to my own people? They will not follow you, and that is because they do not know you."

A few heartbeats passed before she drudged up the energy to respond. "They don't need to know me. Once they learn the truth, they'll see everything."

He yanked her so close Apaay could see every horrid pore in his skin. "You are not part of the Herd," he hissed. "The Herd follows where their leader goes. And you are not their leader—I am."

He dragged her all the way to the central chamber, a room of deafening quiet. The entire nomadic population had gathered. Apaay looked to the raised platform, to the group of masked men in white skins who she had never seen before. And kneeling at their feet, bound, gagged—Kirimat and the Face Stealer.

The commander carted her onto the platform. "Tell them," he said with a victorious flash of teeth. "Tell them everything."

The commander's hold loosened. He knew she wouldn't try to run, not with Kirimat and Numiak captured, so she turned to the Herd and spoke her piece. "People of the Herd," Apaay cried, her voice carrying to all corners of the chamber. "My name is Apaay of the Analak, and I bring you unfortunate news."

Blank stares behind too many masks. Were the people too far gone to bring back? She had to try.

"This man, your commander—" She pointed. "—has deceived you in his thirst for power."

Rumbling laughter lifted the hair on her arms. The commander smiled at her as if to say, *Silly girl.*

Indeed, not a flicker of suspicion or fear livened their glazed eyes. Was a carefully curated life, even a false one, worth it in the end?

"I can prove that he is lying." The statement buoyed her confidence. They wouldn't be able to dispute this evidence. "Inside his rooms, the other councilmembers lie trapped in a deep sleep. Outside these walls, war approaches. These men," she said, pointing to the soldiers wearing polar bear pelts, "are kirn of the Empire. Their leader, Nanuq, seeks to enslave the North and all who live here. The Northern Territory is not safe."

A nameless, faceless person said into the silence, "There are no territories."

"There weren't," she corrected. "The caribou Unua retreated underground prior to their formation. The commander kept you locked away as war raged, led by a tyrant ruler set on destroying everything, and now it is happening again. Nanuq seeks an incredible power. Nanuq, your enemy and the very man you have welcomed into your home."

The commander spoke his dissent. All attention locked onto him.

"Apaay of the Analak has betrayed our trust and spurned our hospitality." The Herd drew forward, a huddling, slavering mass, an ugly growth on skin. "She cannot be trusted. Even now, she poisons you with lies. She, who spoiled our sacred hot spring."

A collective intake of breath sucked the air from the room. The vines swung like dried innards overhead.

Apaay gaped. "That's not true. He gave us permission to use the water! Numiak was hurt—"

The commander's palm caught the side of her face. Apaay hit the ground with a cry, blood flooding her mouth.

Numiak lunged forward with a roar, the sound muffled by his gag. It took six men to hold him. Six men to drag him down, pin him like an animal.

The commander smiled down at her pityingly. *Poor girl*, his expression said. *Poor lost, confused girl.* "Are you aware that she has brought a demon into our home?"

At first, it was but a single gasp. Then the gasp echoed, became two, then three, then more. Apaay's teeth were chattering so hard her jaw ached. Her cheek throbbed, stinging and red.

"Yes," the commander whispered. "You may have heard of him."

Numiak bowed over his knees, back expanding and contracting fitfully.

"The Face Stealer."

The Herd shifted as the air drew taut with horrified fear. Some flinched. Numiak's eyes bled hot with fury.

"Face Stealer," they whispered.

"Demon," they hissed.

The commander was planting the seeds of her demise. All eyes on her, on Numiak. Thousands upon thousands of them. Who was she, where did she come from, why was she cavorting with those offenders, bound and gagged behind her? In their eyes, it was *she* who had done something wrong.

"Who will see these traitors punished?" the commander demanded.

The Herd pushed toward the platform as someone called from the back, "I will hear the girl's pleas."

The crowd parted, allowing a woman to push toward the front. The same woman who had mistaken Apaay's identity over a week ago.

"People of the Herd," she began, voice high and eyes clear. "The commander claims this woman is a thief and a threat, but for twenty years our eyes have been closed and our minds dulled."

A blanketing hush followed, thick as deep snow. The room was all eyes and anxious breath. Apaay sought a sign of lucidity in their enlarged pupils, some flickering uncertainty or slight head tilt.

"My name is Samut. My father," she said, "is Councilman Iriumatuq."

Thousands of eyes blinked dazedly. The woman nodded. "It is a name many of you do not remember. Even now, you struggle to place it. I, myself, have not seen my father since I was a child, and I wonder if he lives." She looked to the commander, a red, livid hatred igniting in her gaze.

"It is said the Council was created to maintain order in our society," she said. "But I ask you this: if the Council of Nine truly governs our people, why is there only one man on that dais?"

All was quiet, all was still.

She went on. "The nectar you drink makes you forget the horrors of the night before. Massacres of our own people. Have you asked yourself where the skins you wear come from?"

People shifted in confusion. "What is she saying?" someone asked among the crowd, but Apaay could not place the voice. The commander's head snapped in the direction the question had come from.

The woman, Samut, smiled in triumph. "The skins we wear are our brothers and mothers and children. In drinking the vine's nectar, we lose awareness of our actions, our surroundings. I fear the commander has led us astray."

The commander's fingers dug into Apaay's upper arm, though his expression remained composed. They did not see how a power-hungry predator lurked beneath his beguiling words.

"What Apaay says is true," the woman continued. "The world is not what it once was. I have heard things, seen things you could not even imagine. The Polar Bear Empire expands with dangerous haste. These men—" She gestured to the soldiers. "—are not our allies. They corrupt our lands, our people, our way of life. To them, we are disposable."

The commander's chuckle morphed into full-blown laughter that rang out, wild and sinister. "People of the Herd." His black eyes gleamed like polished stone. "Outside influences have corrupted this woman's mind. Are we not safe here? Do you not fall asleep each night with your bellies full and your children safe?"

The mass rippled like the disturbed surface of a lake. Then came shouts, voices of assent. Apaay wondered if the population was even aware that many of their children were gone, killed in one of the nightly gatherings, or if the nectar blocked those memories completely.

"Shall we make an example?" he roared to the crowd. "Shall we see what comes of those who do not follow the Herd?"

The caribou Unua cried out their agreement, tossing up their fists, jostling for a closer look.

The commander dragged his knife across Kirimat's throat.

28

Apaay screamed, lunging for Kirimat as her neck peeled apart and her eyes dulled. Numiak roared through his gag, his back bowed, arms and legs straining against the rope binding his hands. Kirimat's body thumped onto the floorboards. Tossed aside like it was nothing.

Apaay sagged in the commander's grip, too shocked by Kirimat's death to realize that chaos had erupted in the hall. In the short time she had come to know this woman, Apaay realized they had become friends.

The doors burst open. Men in white furs poured forth. It was a wave, a frenzy, a stampede. The Herd took to their caribou forms, long legs adapted for fleeing fast over flat terrain, and heavy, solid hooves. The men came: ten, fifty, four hundred, more. Their dense, stocky builds shoved aside the slender Caribou Nomads. They wore the pelts of their brethren atop their shoulders, massive paws resting against their barrel chests. Apaay watched, horrorstruck, as one swung its sword, eyes black beneath the open-jawed hood of its uniform, and severed a caribou's head clean off its shoulders.

Nanuq's men, the kirn of the Empire, were here.

The screams deafened, animal and man alike. Blood splashed the trampled grass. Water heaved onto the riverbanks from the

Herd's struggle to escape, and the vines, they slithered like tongues from the overhanging canopy, the fat white blossoms bulging from the ends, expelling a cloying sweetness. Apaay was frozen. Numb. It was one death after another, by nigana, by sword, by hidden daggers plunged into hearts. She watched the slow topple of caribou into the river, watched as they thrashed and did not resurface, dragged down by the impossible weight of their antlers. Nanuq's men cut a seamless path through the chaos, planting themselves in a protective circle around the commander, who stood calmly on the dais, looking out.

The lack of emotion, the dead pits of his eyes, chilled Apaay to the bone. The commander didn't care about his people. He likely never had. He cared only for power, and to bolster that power with a heavy, rolling fear. Apaay had done little to stop him. She'd done not one thing. Blood, then suffering, and now infiltration, the oozing of Nanuq's influence, deep into the sacred waters of Nigun.

It was too late.

Apaay lunged for the commander, clawing at his sickeningly detached expression. "You're mad!" she screamed.

He laughed, clamping rough hands on her upper arms, his mouth a sneering curve. Apaay struggled to free herself. "That is the way of the world, dear girl. When will you see that under Nanuq's guiding hand, our lives will be infinitely greater? Join him," he said, "and you will want for nothing."

It hit her then. If Nanuq's kirn were present, where was Nanuq? She scanned the disorder despite having no idea what the man looked like.

"He's not here," the commander said. "Don't fret, my dear."

The man was completely delusional. Supercilious beyond words. "Now that Nanuq has a foothold in Nigun, he will dispose of you."

The sneer returned, a baring of blunted, uniform teeth. "I am the commander of the Herd. He has entrusted me to continue leading my people. I give him weapons, he lends me a force strong enough to ensure our sister city will fall in line." He tossed her atop Kirimat's body. "Foolish girl."

Apaay caught Numiak's eye. His chest rose and fell harshly. They exchanged a look of understanding. He knew, as she did, that one of them had to escape. The Face Stealer was valuable. The commander would keep him alive. Apaay would go, and eventually, Numiak would follow once he managed to get away.

With the commander's attention fixated on the chaos he'd unleashed, Apaay scrambled off the platform and plunged into the fray.

She fought her way toward the edge of the room, dodging antlers and weapons, sharp elbows and clawing hands. Apaay could barely keep her head above the jostling limbs. Was nearly impaled by a caribou tossing its great head. Nanuq's kirn continued to propel their force into the hall, even as a few lucid caribou Unua struggled to shut the massive entrance doors against the enemy. Bodies fell and were crushed beneath stamping hooves. Her chest felt like strangulation. The blood-stench rose like a cloud, coating the back of her tongue and dragging tears from her eyes. If she reached the river, she could swim to safety, await Numiak in the Aatu.

Apaay let the crowd carry her to the edge of the room. Patches of white flashed against the dark rock. Body upon body hit the floor. The kirn swung clubs, bludgeoning faces, and swords as long as one's arm. Apaay watched a caribou's foreleg snap, its deep chest dip, its body crumple. Their legs were so slender. Like the stem of a leaf.

The horde surged, crushing her against the wall. She screamed as her bones groaned beneath the onslaught of pressure, and the rock scratched her cheek. Her spine cracked. Someone's knee dug into the soft flesh of her thigh. Blindly, Apaay snapped her elbow into whoever was plastered against her back. The pressure lifted momentarily, allowing her the chance to continue toward the exit. But there were children. So young. They couldn't fight this force.

A boy was sobbing in terror. He was looking around, screaming, "Mama!" as the rush carried him toward an area overrun by polar bear Unua. Apaay sprang, latching her fingers around his small wrist, and dragged him into one of the outlying tunnels.

"Listen to me," she croaked. "You need to be brave." Her hands clamped around his shoulders. He trembled. "If you head for the gates, you'll be crushed, do you understand?"

The boy hiccupped, his eyes swollen and red. "Mama," he said.

"See this tunnel? It will lead you to the river. Find as many children as you can and take them to the boats. Paddle upstream to the storage room. There's an opening in the wall that will lead you outside."

His quavering mouth parted in confusion. "Outside?" he whispered.

If she could save one life, it would be enough. "Go," she said. "Find your friends. Take them to the river." Then the crowd swarmed, and she lost sight of the boy.

The air was mist and blood, and the scent made the Herd's eyes roll wildly, their antlers clack in terror. Behind, a low bellow reverberated in the tunnel, then abruptly cut off. A wet slap followed.

As Apaay rounded a corner, someone jerked her into an alcove. It was the woman who had made the speech: Samut. Sweat streaked her skin and blood trickled down her temple. One of her antlers had snapped and now dangled from a piece of attached velvet.

"I remember," gasped the woman. "I remember now." Her grip on Apaay's arm bruised. "Help me help my people."

Someone knocked into Apaay's back. "How?" All life was sacred to the Analak, but if she could take down the commander to protect the innocent . . . it might be worth the risk.

"The forge contains barrels of blasting powder. If we set the barrels alight, it will drive the polar bear Unua from our home."

"Blasting powder?"

"It's a fuel, like wood. We use it to feed the forge, but when lit in mass quantities, it creates an explosion."

Apaay swiped her forearm across her sweaty forehead, trying to maintain focus on the conversation. To set the powder alight, all of Nigun would be at risk, every person inside its walls. Including Numiak.

She shook her head. No, he would escape. He was probably already free, on his way to their old campsite. "What about the Herd?"

Samut bared her square teeth. "I'll lead my people to the gates."

← →

The forge was located one level below the central chamber, obscured deeper in the rock. The stampede hadn't yet reached this far down, so she and Samut were alone. A few lamps still burned, and the smell of metal tinged the air they breathed. The cavernous space was dominated by an enormous forge. It could fit three ice houses comfortably inside. Weapons were strewn across the floor, a few crates upended. It had been abandoned in a hurry.

"Here." Samut hurried to a stack of unopened crates and pried off one of the lids. The same white powder the men had transported down the river on Apaay's very first day in Nigun filled the square-shaped interior. "Once it's lit," she said, tucking a length of rope into the top of the open crate, "we'll have a few minutes."

Apaay nodded. Samut struck the flint. A spark bloomed in the dark and set the rope alight.

There came the sound of thunder.

At first, it was but distant rumbling, like the eruption of a far-off avalanche. Apaay and Samut exchanged a look of confusion. Grit and dust puffed from the ceiling like a dry rain. The ground began to shake, faint tremors giving way to aftershocks that split rock and shook the mountain above.

"No," breathed Samut. "No, go back!" She ran to meet the wave of caribou Unua that appeared at the bottom of the stairs. "It's not safe! Turn around!"

The Herd shoved into the tunnel, forcing Apaay back against the wall. Samut disappeared in the confusion, though her voice carried, a pleading tone begging them to turn back, but fear had overridden all reason. Their eyes rolled and saliva dripped from their panting mouths.

That's when Apaay spotted a familiar face. Pilan was among them, shouting orders to flee, his staff lifted high into the air. Apaay caught his arm, cried, "You have to get out of here. The forge—" But someone crashed into her back, sending her forward.

Blood trickled from Pilan's hairline, plastering his dark curls to his forehead. "What about the forge?"

"Samut lit the blasting powder."

The man's sweaty face paled. "Numiak was ahead of me. He was looking for you."

Her stomach hollowed out. Apaay was already turning, wasting precious seconds trying to jostle her way to the front of the fleeing crowd. How much time had passed since Samut lit the fuse? "Numiak!" she screamed. The forge entrance was all darkness but for a single flame crawling up the length of rope. "Numiak!"

The tunnel erupted.

← 29 →

The force of the explosion hurled Apaay backward. There was a crack, body against stone, before cool darkness enfolded the overwhelming heat and light. She collapsed and did not move.

The air pulsated around her bent limbs. Her ears rang shrilly. Her vision had gone dark. The hardened earth felt cool beneath her, but the air was chokingly dense, to the point where each inhale wheezed, and dizziness swamped her. Apaay reached up to touch the side of her head, felt warm liquid trickle over her fingers.

Her surroundings returned in fragments of sight and sound. A world charred at the edges, blistered orange and red, and breaking, crumbling rock, and smoke. Complete and total decimation. The tunnel was gone. The walls had caved in, chunks missing in consequence of the blast. Beneath the crackling of hungry flames, tormented screams shattered the last of her calm, whimpers of those still alive. More smoke belched from the ruined forge, stealing the remainder of her sight.

Apaay's grasp on reality wavered. She fell unconscious for an indeterminate amount of time, awakening from a sharp crack that seemed to split the very air around her, followed by something far more frightening: a quaking in the walls.

Apaay had only seconds to move. Scrabbling toward a remaining portion of the wall, she managed to curl into the tightest ball possible, covering her head with her arms as the tunnel broke open above and rained shards of the sharpest rock. Cries of agony flooded the tunnel. Apaay didn't realize she was crying until she tasted salt, tear tracks cooling lines across her scorched skin.

"Help me!" someone called weakly. "Please, help!"

"I can't breathe."

"Papa, where are you?"

Apaay's teeth chattered, and she thought, *Numiak*.

Had he passed beyond the forge before the explosion? No one could have survived the blast so near. Without his power, he would not have been able to protect himself. And what of Samut?

"Apaay?"

She stiffened, her ears sharpening to pick up sound. "I'm here!" she screamed brokenly. "Samut!" Any movement shot pain through her lower body. The rocks were crushing her legs.

She heard the woman picking her way across the ruin. Then weight lifted from Apaay's body, the rocks tossed aside. Samut peered down at her. Ash caked her face, the whites of her eyes glowing in contrast. "Can you stand?"

Apaay wept. She couldn't stop shaking. The older woman said, "You're all right. Hush now. Let's get you to your feet. Good girl." Once Apaay was standing, Samut said, "I'm going to see if the staircase is clear. I'll be back for you. Stay here."

"But—"

"Stay."

The smoke swallowed Samut. The resulting cave-in had reduced the tunnel to mounds of rocks and bodies, or rather, pieces of bodies, the dark, stinging haze pressing on her lungs. A ring of fire glimmered from the forge entrance, or what remained of it.

Desperation sent her body into a stunted forward motion. Pile after pile, Apaay clambered through the rubble. She had to learn what had become of Numiak.

She stumbled onward, picking herself up when she went down,

which was often. Her throat tightened when she reached the forge. The antlered weapons had been blasted to slivers. Char blackened the wall faces. The crates had disintegrated in the boiling heat. Only devouring flame remained.

Her terror was an animal, a sucking black hole. If he had been here, surely there must be something left of him.

"Numiak." Her eyes stung so badly she had to clench them shut for a brief reprieve. "Numiak!" A frantic scream. Her throat was so dry the sound fractured.

When she spotted what appeared to be a body, the ringing in Apaay's ears returned at full force. Fire blazed all around, the heat so intense her skin felt like it was peeling apart.

Long legs, sprawled at unnatural angles. A torso, or what was left of it. Mats of long, dark, singed hair.

A hand clamped over her arm, yanking her backward. Apaay stumbled, was lifted and tossed over someone's shoulder, and they were running from the flames, leaping over piles of rubble. Moments later, she was set down, away from the worst of the heat.

"What the hell are you doing?" Numiak demanded, shoving his soot-streaked face into her line of vision. His eyes glowed the violet shade of fear. "Are you trying to get yourself killed?"

"I was looking for *you*," she croaked. Aside from rips in his maq, he didn't appear injured. It was a particular gift of his, she thought, to cheat death as many times as he had.

His nostrils flared as he checked her over for injury, yet his hands, when they tightened around her shoulders, were gentle. "Are you hurt?"

"No. Samut was with me, but she went to check for a way out."

"Both staircases are blocked by the cave-in."

The ground rumbled with aftershocks, which widened any crack that had formed in the rock, further destabilizing the area. "Is there another way out?"

He shook his head. Looked to the fire creeping toward them, the blasted wreck of the forge. Apaay felt woozy. Sick.

"Apaay." His voice snapped out. "Stay awake." He shook her until her eyelids lifted, and his expression softened. "Stay with me."

She must be truly delirious if she interpreted those words to mean anything but staying conscious. *Stay with me*, as if he desired her to remain by his side, always.

"I don't suppose you could create one of your special doorways," Apaay wheezed. She vaguely recalled him producing such a thing back in the labyrinth. Once, after they had exchanged the blood oath. Again, while disguised as Irnik, he'd sent Yuki elsewhere so they could escape the room that had stored the five faces, hers included. "That would be extremely convenient right now, your—" She wiggled her fingers. "Shadow power."

"No, wolfling. I can't."

Right. Numiak lacked his power. Apaay couldn't form something from nothing unless it was an identity, for her power was not an extension of Taggak. There must be another way. If only she could think. The smoke offered no clarity.

"Then use my power." He had done it before on the outskirts of Talguk.

"The city is protected by their god from such acts of power. A small amount wouldn't register, but creating a doorway requires a substantial sum. The protections in place prevent me from doing so. I'm unable to breach them."

But the shadow power made her think of something else: Taggak. The Face Stealer wasn't the only one with connections to the Shadow Realm.

"Call the Raven," she rasped, leaning heavily against his side. It felt like the surface of her tongue had been scraped raw. "The dark oath promised he would keep us safe."

"He said he would keep your people safe, and only because he agreed to uphold the protections I already had in place. Our lives were not part of that agreement. I do not think he will come."

A broken moan carried down the tunnel.

"He will," she said with the utmost conviction, coughing fitfully.

They had nothing to lose. "Ask." She and Numiak could not breach the city's god-touched protections, but since the Raven was a god himself, his power might be able to nullify the shields in place.

Numiak's mouth pulled into a frown. "Raven," he cried. "You agreed to protect Apaay's people at all costs. Does that not include Apaay herself? Help her. Save her. Do not turn from your oath."

They waited, sweating off their skin and hair, dying as they stood.

"Shit," he growled.

That about covered it.

Grabbing her arm, he half-dragged her toward one of the massive rock piles that had formed from the explosion. "Climb."

Heat and light licked at her skin, tightening it to excruciating agony. Her palms were open sores as she scrambled up the rock pile, Numiak bracing her lower back when she began to slip backward.

"See that ledge?" He pointed to the silhouette of an overhang through the screen of smoke—remnants of the walkway one level above. "Step onto my palms. I'm going to toss you up."

"What about Samut?" The woman hadn't returned.

"Who?"

"Samut. The woman who stood up to the commander."

"We don't have time."

"No!" She wiped the sweat pouring down her face with a shaky hand. "I can't leave her." Because of her inaction, Kirimat had died. She could not live with another death on her hands. "If you won't find her, I will."

Numiak scowled. As he well knew, when Apaay made up her mind, there was no changing it. "Stay here." He scrambled down the rock pile and returned minutes later with Samut by his side. He tossed the woman up to the ledge first before telling Apaay, "Step up."

Bracing herself on his shoulder, Apaay placed her foot into his cupped hands. One immense heave snapped her into the air.

She caught the ledge by the tips of her fingers, but the blood transferred from her palm onto the rock, slickening the surface. Her hand slipped, and she fell into Numiak's arms.

"Again," he said, tossing her up a second time. Her fingers dug into the pocked surface long enough that she could haul herself onto the cracked walkway. A fit of coughing stole her breath.

Apaay sensed the men before she saw them. The smoke shifted with their eerie silhouettes. She fumbled for a rock, her body thrumming with high tension. Metal sang as a sword cut through the smoke. Apaay dropped so the weapon cut above her head, and suddenly Samut appeared, kicking the man into the pit below. Apaay's chest felt like it was being ripped in two, there was so little breathable air.

"Thanks," she rasped feebly.

Samut nodded to Numiak as he appeared over the ledge. "I'm going after the commander. Stay safe."

When she was gone, Numiak nudged Apaay forward. "Crawl, wolfling." The fire billowed orange light, and grew, *grew*.

Unlike the lower level, this tunnel was mostly intact. When Nanuq's men appeared, Numiak cut them down, shifting his body so he produced a path through which Apaay could follow. If they stood between him and the exit, they died. Swiftly, efficiently, simply.

They didn't get far before the fighting completely overwhelmed them, blocking their means of escape. Wheezing heavily, Apaay sagged against the wall.

"It's not stopping," she said. There were too many of Nanuq's kirn and not enough allies.

"I know."

And still the men came. Numiak was tireless. He ensured no enemy came near. He severed limbs and split skulls. Imagine who he had been twenty years before, his fighting abilities honed daily. He would have been a terrifying force.

They could not stay here, but they had nowhere to go, and the smoke was slowly depleting the air they so desperately needed.

All at once, cool shade guttered the firelight, like a blanket dropped over one's head. The Raven materialized in front of them, scrutinizing their disheveled states with those eyes like wells of blood set in a face whose structure was more bone than skin, that wide mouth like a tear in fabric. He was far more discomfiting than

Apaay remembered. The blue-gray tattoo inked into his chin and jaw all but glowed. A long black cloak fluttered around his skeletal form, though there was no wind.

Numiak growled, "You're late."

The Raven blinked without a change in expression. "Are you dead?"

"No."

"Then I am early."

The dark god glanced at their surroundings with complete disregard. A sweep of his bony hand sent the nearest horde crashing into the wall.

Numiak's mouth flattened with grim resolve. "Raven, I need my power."

"You have forgotten the dark oath so soon? How convenient." He sounded as bored and unimpressed as Apaay remembered.

"Forget the damn oath!" Numiak roared. "This is something I ask of you to give freely. Without my power, I am severely limited in what I can accomplish. This includes removing that tattoo of yours."

Apaay gasped. "Behind—"

Without removing his attention from Numiak, the Raven clenched his hand around air. The polar bear Unua, sword raised to sever the dark god's neck from behind, imploded in a spray of night shade.

She blinked. "—you."

Those hooded red eyes rested on Numiak's grimy face. "How bold you have become, to ask this of me. You forget your place, demon."

"You can keep half of my power," he continued, pushing his agenda. "It will still allow you to come and go from Taggak at will, and you would be free of your obligation in keeping Apaay safe."

"Who said it was an obligation?"

Numiak hissed something under his breath. "What is it you want? Ask and it is yours. But be quick about it."

The god adjusted his flowing cloak. The scarlet of his eyes flared with rare impatience. "I forgot how irritatingly needy you were.

Very well." He cut into his palm, then Numiak's. For the second time in many months, they clasped hands, and the air pulsed from the raw power transferring between their bodies.

When they stepped away, the Raven's skin healed almost immediately. The Face Stealer's, however, did not.

A single blast of power from Numiak cleared the tunnel, creating a pathway that would lead them to safety.

"Do not forget your promise, demon," intoned the Raven. "One way or another, this tattoo will be removed, and my imprisonment along with it." With that, he was gone.

They made haste to the upper levels of Nigun. Death marked a trail all the way to the central chamber. The carnage they witnessed was only a fraction of the caribou Unua population, which existed in the tens of thousands. Those dead had to stretch into the thousands. Apaay could not comprehend the true number.

They had reached the chamber when Apaay spotted a figure slipping from the hall, vanishing down one of the tunnels. She froze. "The commander."

"Apaay, we don't have time."

She searched the ground. A discarded spear lay near a pile of bodies. She snatched it up, and a second spear as well, and sprinted after the man who had killed Kirimat, Numiak's voice lost to its echo. His capture would allow the Herd to dole out justice for the pain he had caused so many.

Down one tunnel, and another, delving into darker rock, deeper shadows, thicker smoke. Footsteps pounded behind her—Numiak's, she assumed. She pushed on, leaping over bodies and splashing through scarlet puddles, which shone opaque in the shuttered light. Apaay knew the feel of a spear in her hand, the path of its release. Her aim was true.

The spear head buried itself in the commander's thigh. He screamed as he fell.

With a great cry, Apaay brought the base of the second spear down in a short, snapping motion toward the man's leg. It would have cracked bone had it made contact. But the commander was slippery. He rolled and kicked out, catching her in the knee. Apaay struck the ground hard. He managed to put a few yards of distance between them when a second spear plunged into his side. The commander gasped and hit the ground, skidding to a stop on his back.

Apaay's head swung around. Samut approached calmly, her mouth set, eyes glittering with insurmountable rage. In one hand, she held a talq, its blade already crusted with blood.

The commander's eyes widened.

"Hello, commander." The woman halted at his side, studying him as if he were no better than a grub in the ground.

"I—"

"Save your lies," Samut spat. "They are worthless to me." She flipped her weapon in a smooth motion, hilt over blade, again, and again. The commander tracked the movement. "We're going to play a game. It's called, *Is it true?* Your part is simple. All you have to do," she said, voice lowering, "is answer *yes* or *no*. Do you understand?"

His upper lip twitched. That a woman dared challenge him, Apaay imagined the commander found himself in an unfamiliar position.

Samut tucked her talq blade beneath his chin. "I said, *Do you understand?*"

"Yes," he hissed.

"Good. My question is this: are you responsible for incapacitating the Council of Nine, brainwashing the citizens of Nigun, and committing treason by opening our gates to Nanuq's men?"

The commander's sneer deepened. "Yes, but you already knew that."

"I did," Samut agreed. "I just wanted to make sure you knew it, too. I'll be sure to tell my father you said hello," she said, and drove her talq into the commander's still-beating heart.

30

It took three weeks to bury the dead. In total, over seven thousand of the Caribou Nomads had fallen the day Nanuq's kirn infiltrated Nigun, countless more taken by the brainwashed gatherings that had occurred nightly. In the years that followed, the massacre would be known as the Red Death.

The earth was soft. There would be no rocks piled atop bodies, as Analak custom dictated. They dug graves down into the rich dark soil, shaping out hollows, and laid the bodies with their heads facing east to greet the sun. After putting any and all surviving kirn to death, the newly restored Council of Nine held vigils for the fallen. The commander had not received that honor. His disgraceful and treasonous actions forever marked him as a traitor.

When the last of the Herd had been buried, Apaay and Numiak laid Kirimat to rest beneath one of the old forest trees. It's what her family would have done back in Unana, had they still been alive. But Apaay knew it would never be enough.

It took the evening. The sky shone the blue-gray of a pearl. Numiak transformed into his wolf skins while Apaay stood off to the side. Kirimat's grave was a simple construct—a slate of stone bearing the inscription of her name. It said nothing of how she had died, or of her bravery, her place of birth. The truth was, no one from Nigun would remember her. No one would remember a lot of things.

It was not the first time she and Numiak had stood before a grave. The parallel of this situation with one of Apaay's most painful memories, the inversion of who mourned, could not be overlooked. Apaay would never forget the feel of a shovel in her hand, nor of the permafrost breaking beneath the blunt tool. Nakaluq had left this life too soon.

Numiak set Kirimat's spirit free with one last song. Its mournful, welling tone made Apaay's heart ache so that she, too, felt the depth of Numiak's loss. It poured out across the Aatu, flowed down the River Pak, the River Iniak, all the way out to sea, until the sound died. Until there was only the wind.

"May I?" Apaay asked.

Yellow eyes stark against his black fur, Numiak dipped his snout and allowed her to kneel before the marker. She thought of Nakaluq as she spoke the words to aid Kirimat's spirit in passing on, dear Nakaluq, whose body lay cold in a distant garden somewhere in the in-between, and her eyes stung. These tears were for Kirimat, but they were for him, too.

"May you wander the land free of pain," Apaay murmured. "May you drink from the clear mountain stream, and run through the green summer grasses, and dream beneath the stars. May you reap the bounties of this beautiful earth." The wind sighed as though for one last goodbye. "Until we meet again. Farewell, my friend."

When it was done, Numiak shifted back to his human form and knelt at the marker, head bowed.

"I failed her."

If there was one thing Apaay understood, it was this. "It wasn't your fault."

"Yes," he said. "It was."

Apaay moved to stand at his back. She hesitated, then touched his shoulder with the tips of her fingers. A moment later, his hand reached up to engulf hers.

Though he did not speak of it, she knew Numiak was thinking of the war, the day of the invasion. He was thinking of how he had arrived at Unana too late. He was thinking of pain in his chest as Yuki stole his heart. He was thinking of how so many had died, but he, miraculously, had survived.

Apaay squeezed his hand. "You could not have known what would happen."

"But you always wonder, don't you? You wonder if, had you done one thing differently . . ." There was a pause. "This is only the beginning. Many more will die before this war ends."

With the commander dead and the Council revived, they had discussed how to move forward. The Caribou Nomads were fractured. That was to be expected. An estimated half of the surviving Herd had decided to migrate to Nalwa, having not taken well to the knowledge that war was upon them. They would travel far in hopes of outrunning the storm, and Apaay didn't have the heart to tell them there was nowhere they could hide. Nanuq would find them. The only question was when.

Those who remained in Nigun had elected Samut to fill the ninth seat on the Council. As well, the Council had voted unanimously to ally with Numiak in the war effort. It was a step.

"What now?" Apaay asked, kneeling at his side. She took comfort in the brush of his shoulder against hers, his heat and solidity.

Numiak peered through the breaks in the trees to the grassland beyond, where a waning sun colored the stalks violet and orange, the last colors before the snows arrived. "Now," he said, "we return to Sinika to discuss the next steps with the Avi. I sent a message to Ro, informing him that the Council has sided with us. It's time we begin acting as a unified force. That means making difficult decisions."

Alarm fluttered like a pulse through her. As if decisions had not already been difficult enough. "Do we have to go there right away? Could we stop to visit my family?"

She knew the answer before he opened his mouth, the regret plain in his expression. "I'm sorry, wolfling. It's not safe. I would hate to draw attention to the village, no matter how protected it might be."

Her throat swelled with the stone that lodged there. She understood, even if it was difficult to accept. Four months was long enough to be without one's family. She had hoped to visit Chena and her daughter, whose name-soul she did not know.

"I imagine I'm not going to like this," she muttered.

"Probably not. Someone needs to infiltrate the Southern Territory."

She'd anticipated it would come to this, or something like it. Lack of knowledge surrounding Nanuq's movements put them at a severe disadvantage. Of course someone would eventually take the place Kimmir had once filled as Numiak's spy.

"Do you know who you'll send?"

"I have someone in mind." His steady gaze came to rest upon her. "You."

Apaay went still. "You're joking. That's—" She would die, simple as that. "It's not safe."

"I believed the same as well, but I've been thinking, and I'm convinced the Southern Territory would be the safest place for you."

She gaped at him. He was utterly serious. "We are talking about the Polar Bear Empire, right?"

"Think about it. Nanuq believes the object of power to be, firstly, an object, and secondly, located in the Western Territory. The Southern Territory is the last place he would look. The closer you are to him, the safer you will be."

It was at that moment Apaay decided the Face Stealer was, in fact, insane.

"Numiak." The serenity with which she spoke was impressive. "You understand I'm not a trained soldier, right? I don't know the first thing about being a spy."

"I'm aware. Which is why you wouldn't travel to the Southern Territory alone."

That startled a laugh from her. "You're saying you would come with me?"

"Of course." His expression said she was absurd to think otherwise. "There are hundreds of servants, cooks, messengers in Nanuq's service. New ones come and go from the palace all the time. With your abilities, you would be in an ideal position to gather information. But it's your choice, Apaay. Make no mistake, this mission will be dangerous. If you decide you'd rather not risk it, we'll find another way."

Nanuq's influence stretched far wider than they had thought possible. He was closing in. They needed to learn whatever secret Nanuq protected, kept hidden away from the rest of the world. They needed to learn of his intentions.

Yet Apaay's thoughts inevitably returned to Kirimat, the freshly dug grave. She and Numiak had buried a friend today, and it would not be the last occurrence.

"It's really happening, isn't it?" she asked wearily. "War."

"Yes," he said. "And this is not even the worst of it."

How much worse could things get? "Tell me about it," she said. "Tell me about . . . about war." That word, *war*, died before it ever truly formed. Apaay wanted to prepare herself. She could be brave, so long as she knew what she would face.

"It's an ugly thing." Numiak turned toward her in concern. The shade beneath the trees limned his eyes in silver. "I don't want to frighten you."

Considerate of him, but unhelpful. Look at how easily one man had corrupted the entire caribou Unua nation by taking advantage of their ignorance. Apaay was no longer that village girl. She had seen the world. "I need to know."

He scrubbed a hand across his jaw, the dark, prickling bristles scraping the pads of his fingers. He took a very long, very deep breath before releasing it slowly. "War," he said, "is waiting. It is waiting for your commander to give you an order. It is waiting for a correspondence to arrive. It is waiting to see if your wounded comrade will last the night. It is waiting, crouched behind rocks or brush, or in trenches, or tree canopies, for a counterattack. It is the highest highs and the lowest lows experienced in mere hours of separation."

There was a silence before he went on. "When you are nearing victory, there is nothing like it. You feel like a god, like a king, like nothing can touch you with an army amassed at your back.

"But when you are on the losing side . . ." His throat bobbed, and Apaay fought the overwhelming need to touch him: his hand, the slope of his back.

"When you are on the losing side," Numiak repeated in a more subdued tone, "war is the stink of death on your clothes, your body so caked in mud and shit and blood that you no longer feel like a person. There is no sense of time on the battlefield. You swing and swing and watch men fall, and as you swing, a feeling comes over you. You know—not believe, not hope—*know*, that your strike will land true.

"And then it does and there is only flesh cleaving beneath your blade and the sound of bones snapping in your ears, and the stench of carnage is so thick you can't breathe without retching." Another swallow. His lips thinned to pale lines. "And at the end—if there is, in fact, an end—you no longer remember the reason for fighting. There is so much death, you ask yourself if it's worth it."

Apaay's breath trembled like an autumn leaf. There had been a time when she would have sat in the woods near her home as summer deepened, thinking of simple things. It felt like ages ago.

So much had changed. Most evidently, a new, greater purpose. Apaay had something to fight for. Her life, but more than that, her way of life. A way of life that might be lost if she stood idle. If she did not have family, if she did not have community, if she did not have the traditions of her people, their stories, she had nothing. The Analak deserved their place in the North, too.

This was her path now, so she would walk it. What lay at the end of it, well, she would soon learn.

"I will do it." The words lay heavy in her mouth. "I will go into Nanuq's territory." And do what needed to be done.

Numiak said, "As will I."

"Together?"

He covered her hand with his, and squeezed. "Together."

31

The arena was packed from wall to wall, the stench of unwashed bodies overwhelming. The place was practically straining at the seams. Bystanders spilled out from the stairs. The hot air curled in on itself, and sweat dripped onto the dirt floor, imbedding its foul odor. The press of bodies turned the room dark and warm, womb-like.

Tonight, blood would be spilled.

The mud-packed floor cooled the soles of Kenai's tired feet. He stood in the center of the arena, as he had done yesterday, and the day before, on and on, each fight smearing into the next. Above, lost somewhere among the audience congregating around the driftwood fence that encircled the pit, the announcer called out, "And who will face this opponent?"

Inhaling deeply through his nose, he scanned the crowd for a potential adversary. Yesterday's leg injury—a pulled muscle—darted pain up the back of his right thigh. He maintained his centered, even-footed stance, for the moment he showcased weakness, the fight would end before it had even begun.

No one stepped forward. Was that it then? No one desired to fight? Or did they pity him, that he had won few matches, and far between? Last week, he'd sustained injuries so sever they'd had to drag him from the arena. But he had returned. Because if he could not win, then maybe he deserved this punishment.

"I will face this man."

His eye snapped to the right, in the direction the voice had come from. If he didn't know any better, Kenai would swear it sounded like—

A small gap in the fence allowed someone to squeeze through and drop down into the arena. A hush passed over the crammed space.

With a lazy, fluid gait, his opponent crossed into the center of the pit. The audience revived itself with a few murmurs. Bets were made. Currency passed from hand to hand. And then his opponent lifted her hand in acknowledgement, and the air rang with the force of the crowd's roar.

Kenai studied the woman with keen focus, wariness prickling over his body. She was small and slender, one side of her head shaved. He remembered her. He didn't remember a lot of things these days, but he remembered her. It had been weeks since he'd watched this woman pummel a larger man into the ground. An impressive display of agility, skill, control.

"Take your mark."

They faced one another, and Kenai's pulse rose to meet that of the surrounding energy. The woman's upper lip curled briefly as she took him in. An expression that communicated she did not believe him to be worthy.

"Begin."

He blinked, and she was gone. Kenai half-turned when a kick to his lower back sent him flying forward.

He hit the ground and rolled. The ache hardened in his bones, and he leaped to his feet. The woman kicked out low. She struck out for his face. His forearm whipped up. Block. She was already moving for his stomach. Blocked again.

She hit hard and without mercy. She hit to break bones. Her fist rammed against his bearded jaw, and blood spewed outward from a split lip. At her next kick, something flared to life inside him. Recognition. He leaped sideways and twisted, making sure he kept his back to the wall. That kick-strike combination was a distinctly wolf Unua style of hand-to-hand combat. Except—no, now she was performing some complicated pattern of evasive blows he'd never witnessed before. Was he searching for proof that didn't exist? He was almost certain she was wolf Unua.

The woman's face locked into rigidity. She had come to win, and Kenai stood in her way. Her hands blurred, yet he managed to land a blow to her gut, one lightning jab, before sliding out of reach. She took advantage of her impressive agility and hurled her fists upon him. They pelted down like hail. He could not block them fast enough.

His nose broke beneath the heel of her palm. His teeth sang from a clip to the chin. Blindly, Kenai swung. He hit something—her shoulder, maybe. Another strike landed against his temple and snapped his head sideways.

With a roar, Kenai charged. His opponent waited until he was within reach to sidestep and strike his kidneys from behind, pounding them into pulped meat. The blows made contact with brutal precision. Pain roared through the back of his skull as he stumbled.

He went to one knee, dropped, and managed to pivot back onto his feet quickly enough to thwart an open-palmed strike to his face. The woman was strong, agile, strategic in her movements—all qualities he had once possessed. Before he'd grown weak.

The bell rang, signaling a break in the match.

Dizzily, Kenai stumbled to a chair on one side of the arena. The woman bent over her knees, panting, blood dripping from her mouth. Then she lifted her head. Gazed at him in curiosity, and a harder emotion he couldn't identify.

It was highly unlikely that anyone from his past would recognize him, what with the extent of his facial scarring, the swelling from all the beatings he'd received in this arena. Still, Kenai didn't need the attention. He turned away from her. He was here for a bit of coin to buy a hot meal, that's all. Even if, or when, he lost, someone always took pity on him.

Yuki was due to arrive any day now, but he'd failed to recruit a single person to Nanuq's cause. The Banished Lands represented a lawless place, the worst of poverty, but at least the people here were free. They weren't willing to sacrifice that for Nanuq's collar around their necks. If she arrived to find him empty-handed, then she would leave, and Kenai would have no one. The thought was eroding his mind.

She would come for him. He had to believe it.

The bell rang, signaling the end of the break.

Kenai and his opponent returned to the center of the arena. He cleared his mind of all that uncertainty, or attempted to, rather. The ground may have been cold and hard, but it was steady. He could count on it to hold his weight.

"Begin."

The woman's fist exploded toward his face, and he ducked, lunging forward to catch her around the waist.

They hit the ground. The woman rolled to her feet, impossibly quick, her fists snapping out to hit various pressure points on his body. Her heel slammed into his inner thigh, hitting a nerve. His muscle seized, spasming in agony. Her blows rained down in unending punishment as though to mete out vengeance. That was when Kenai began to forget.

With every blow to the head, a piece of his past was erased.

With every knee to the gut, he slipped further down into the dark.

He began to forget why he had come here.

Why had he come to the Banished Lands? To rally men to Nanuq's side? To prove his worth to Yuki? To make something of himself?

Who was he, exactly? What did he want? Why was he still alone after all this time? Why did Numiak hate him so? Maybe he had come to the Banished Lands to answer these questions, which plagued him. Maybe it was what he needed, deep down.

He needed to remember.

PART TWO

PREY

32

They stopped at dusk, when the sky had cooled to the color of shallow water. Their group of ten had dwindled to eight, then six, and now five. Mile after mile, Ila and those who had escaped the labor camp fled across the alpine range. South, then west, then south again. They slept and ate little, focusing only on putting as much distance between them and that wretched hellhole as they could.

The first to fall had been Imina, taken by smoke inhalation two days following their escape. Her cousin had befallen the same fate. They'd buried both women in a hole in the ground, markerless. Five days later, Emiat's body had given up. Two decades of back-breaking work and she could not go on. Ila had cried, though she hardly knew the woman.

Now Pili had taken ill. Ila didn't know how much more loss she could take.

Malina stalked the camp like a caged animal, barking orders at those who remained of their original group. Gather firewood. Scout the area for signs of passage. Collect water. Search for shelter. Ila focused on ensuring Pili was settled and comfortable, happy to leave Malina well enough alone. Over the weeks, she had learned to anticipate the rise and fall of the woman's temper. Best to give her space when she was in a mood.

And Malina was *always* in a mood.

Ila offered Pili a waterskin made from the hide of a caribou her pack had felled. The old woman drank deeply before returning it with a shaky hand. The gray skin of her face clung to her old bones.

How are you feeling? Ila signed.

The old woman's head lolled against the pine tree. Though she looked at her, Ila sensed that her attention was elsewhere. As the days passed, Pili drifted.

Are you hungry?

Pili shivered. Ila tucked a blanket around her shoulders. She had no idea how near Lun they were, though they had descended into the Atakana's western valley days before. An arduous, brutal climb, full of icy winds that hadn't warmed despite the summer sun.

Saniraq used to live in the small mountain village, named after its local river. There, they would rest and recuperate and, if possible, seek out any wolf Unua who had gone into hiding. They had yet to figure out a way to disseminate the information of Ila's return. If Nanuq was gathering an army, then so, too, would they.

"I did not think I would experience freedom in this lifetime again."

Ila stared into the older woman's clouded eyes. She wondered how much of Pili's world had grown dark.

You're safe now, she said. *I won't let anything happen to you.*

A fit of coughing wracked her companion's body. Ila hurriedly passed her a piece of cloth, which Pili used to cover her mouth. Flecks of blood stained the fabric when she pulled it away.

Ila's stomach clamped at the sight.

Pili sighed. "Your mother would be proud."

Hush now. You must save your strength.

Deep folds cushioned her eyes. Her mouth curved with melancholy. "Matilaqaa. No matter what happens, I am glad to have met you."

Alarm spiked at this direction of conversation. Pili began to cough heavily, fighting for air. Malina ran toward them across the clearing.

"Get away from her," she snarled, flashing her impressive

canines. Shoving Ila to the side, she pulled Pili's frail hands to her chest.

Picking herself off the ground with a hostile glare at Malina, Ila retreated to another tree, settling against it. Her hands and feet ached from the long trek in her wolf form, which she had finally managed to attain days before. Saniraq explained that the high levels of adrenaline had most likely unlocked the instinct. Worry, the need to constantly be on the move, resulted in poor sleep. But she felt alive in her wolf skins. Felt like her true self.

Sometime later, Malina dropped into a crouch beside her. Ila stiffened. She hadn't the energy to guess when it was safe to speak to Malina or not. All her energy went toward keeping their group together.

"She's gotten worse since yesterday." Malina's eyes were red-rimmed, smudges giving hollows to her already too-thin face. Ila had never seen the woman this close to breaking before. She was nothing if not resolute. "I had hoped the infection would clear from her lungs by now."

Ila asked, her hands moving stiffly, *What would you have us do?*

"She needs a healer."

There was no healer.

"She needs rest."

They could not rest.

"She needs time."

Didn't they all? But there was none to be had.

"Are you listening to me?"

When was she not?

The fatigue of the last few days seemed to hit her all at once. Ila sagged against the tree. *Yes, Malina. I'm listening.*

"But you're angry. Because I pushed you." Before Ila could respond, she said, "I'm under a lot of stress, we all are, and I'm worried about Pili."

Ila considered how to navigate the issue. An apology would be nice, but she did not expect one. Malina would rather tear off her own limbs than admit a wrongdoing.

She signed, *If you admit you pushed me, why not apologize?*

"I just did."

You made excuses for your behavior. It's not the same thing.

The woman's jaw shifted back and forth. Grinding her teeth together, no doubt. "What do you want from me?"

Ila went to that tranquil place inside herself, the one that harbored calm when the world was a storm. Her fingers twinged in pain. *I want nothing from you. All I want is to reach Lun safely.*

In typical Malina fashion, she grabbed a branch at their feet and hurled it as far as possible. Her mouth opened, then shut. "Sorry," she said.

It would have to be enough.

Ila felt the vibrations seconds before Malina tensed. Moments later, two wolves crashed through the brush before shifting to their human forms. "There's a group of men heading this way," Saniraq panted, swiping strands of hair from her sweaty forehead. The two braids curving down the sides of her scalp had loosened, caught with leaves and twigs. "Fifteen at least. They smell of bear."

Ila looked to Malina in alarm. They exchanged a swift nod before Ila went to help Pili to her feet. Except the old woman shook her head, batting Ila's hands away. Confusion took hold. *Pili?*

"You will need to move swiftly and cover much ground. I will only slow you down."

Surely she was not suggesting . . . no.

We stay together. She was firm in this. They suffered, they escaped, they survived—never to be parted. They were her pack.

Pili shook her head in remorse. "Matilaqaa."

Oh, she knew the look of one who had made a decision, whose mind would not change.

No one gets left behind, she signed with resolve. If that meant fighting, standing their ground, then so be it.

"What is it? What's wrong?" Malina had appeared, frowning at Pili's seated position. "Get up, Pili. We're leaving." She tugged on the old woman's arm.

"You won't be able to outrun the men with me in your group. It is imperative you reach Lun safely."

But Malina wasn't listening. "Get up, or I will carry you." Her upper lip twitched, and she pressed it against its lower counterpart as it quivered. "I will drag you all the way to Lun if I have to."

"Think," said Pili. "What will those men do when they catch up? What was the point of escape if we are to return to captivity?" There was a pause, during which she coughed forcefully.

Saniraq stared into the trees on high alert. Ila felt the men's footsteps through the hard earth in the distance. They were moving quickly.

Malina said, "If we leave now, we will outrun them."

"Malina." Kind eyes. "If I do not die this day, it will be the next, or the next. My lungs are too weak."

"No." It was all she said. "No." Her lips pulled back, revealing a mouth full of fearsome points. "It's not true." Then everything broke all at once.

Her expression crumpled, and her mouth, and her eyes, filling swiftly, a sight Ila had never before witnessed as Malina dropped to her knees. "I'm not leaving you."

"My beautiful daughter." Pili cupped Malina's cheek with a withered hand. "You must."

Ila startled in complete shock.

Daughter?

Malina clung to the old woman, quaking like a leaf in the wind. "You can't ask that of me. You can't."

"I can, and I will. Listen."

"No, you listen."

"Malina."

Tipki paced in the background, tapping her fingertips together nervously. She looked to Saniraq, then to Ila, and stepped forward. "Malina, the men—"

"Can't you give us one damn minute?" she cried, head snapping toward Tipki. "Can't you see that I'm . . . that we're . . ." One of her hands curled into the dirt. "If we can't return home together, then what does it matter?"

Ila wondered how it felt to leave those you loved behind, not once, but again and again in an undying cycle, as Malina must feel reliving the invasion, those Packmates who hadn't survived.

"This is my mother," Malina said. "I can't leave my mother," she said. "I can't leave her to those men. You don't understand. You can't."

Tipki looked to Ila with round, tear-filled, pleading eyes.

She found it difficult to swallow. Pili had welcomed her into their harsh, mistrustful world when no one else had. She knew what would follow. They would leave: she, Malina, Saniraq, and Tipki. Pili would not.

Wooden footsteps brought Ila to Malina's side. Tentatively, she touched the woman's shoulder. Malina looked up at her, distraught.

She signed, *It's time.*

Pili grabbed her daughter's quivering chin, holding it stable. "Any hope of our people returning lies with Matilaqaa. She must live. And you must live as well. Promise me you will look after one another."

"Ma—"

"Promise me."

Her expression tightened. Something was breaking inside Malina. It was grinding into dust, it was turning to rubble, turning to ruin, it was wrenching open a hole in her chest where her heart had once beat. Ila knew, because that was how it felt to leave those you loved, knowing it would be long before you were ever reunited. "Yes, all right, *all right.*" Her body heaved, and she collapsed into her mother's arms. "I . . . I promise."

"My daughter." Pili brushed a tender kiss to Malina's damp cheek. Radiating from her expression was the pure, white light of peace. "I will see you on the other side."

← →

They ran.

Four wolves, crashing through the alpine range: two gray, one cream, and tawny Ila with her pale underbelly. A steep descent led into the foothills. The creeks merged with larger streams, veins of clear, frigid water glimmering in what sunlight managed to squeeze through the dense canopy overhead.

We should be close, Malina said in the mind-speak that allowed them to communicate in their wolf forms. In single file, they trotted through a deciduous part of the forest, trees of maple and birch, their coniferous cousins few and far between. Ila inhaled. She scented the men trailing them on the wind, and a darker scent beneath, old and faint, rain and snow having stripped it of strength.

Blood.

Her hackles rose, and they slowed. Tipki sniffed the ground, along with Saniraq. Ila assessed the surrounding area with caution. A rustle in the canopy drew her eye. Merely a bird.

Malina's large, triangular ears swiveled this way and that. *I think we passed the safehouse a few miles back.*

Wind tousled the fur of Ila's ruff. *Which way?* The wind changed direction, and the scent of man intensified.

It should be—

Birds startled into flight as the clearing was shot full of arrows.

They scattered. Ila darted through low, compact foliage, an arrow grazing the fur on her back and thudding into a tree, quivering.

This way! Malina cried.

They splashed through streams and leaped over fallen trees. *Slow down.* This from Tipki, her mind-speak voice spiking in panic. Ila sensed Saniraq bringing up the rear.

A group of men burst from the bushes. Tipki and Saniraq cut one way, Ila and Malina another. Malina managed to slip past them, but a fresh wave of arrows cut off Ila's escape. Before her stood a man with a blade, mud coating his face, his expression hungry for violence.

She backed away slowly, growling low in her throat.

Dirt and leaves scattered around her legs as Ila skidded to avoid the swinging blade. With a burst of speed, she plunged into the undergrowth, winding her way downhill. They had discussed what to do if something like this were to happen. Find the last water source they had crossed and wait for the others.

It took some time. Progress was slow due to Ila giving their pursuers a wide berth, but eventually she reached the last creek they had crossed. Luckily, she didn't have to wait long. Malina arrived, coated in mud, but unharmed.

The others? Malina asked.

I lost sight of them a while back. And they had traveled out of range, hindering communication via the mind-speak.

Malina lifted her nose to the air. *It's not safe out in the open.* Ila sensed the warring in her. To go? To stay? *This way.*

She followed her packmate at a steady lope. Less than a mile later, they ducked into a burrow concealed by a fallen tree that smelled strongly of muskrat. The low tunnel opened into a space large enough for a human to stand in. The walls were smooth dirt, packed down at the floor.

Saniraq arrived soon after, also unharmed.

Where's Tipki? Malina demanded.

We were separated, said Saniraq in uncertainty. *I thought she would have come here.*

A moment passed.

Saniraq's ears flattened against her skull.

Malina paced the room, shaggy head bent low. *I'm going to find her.*

I'm going with you, Ila said.

No. I can't protect you if you're putting yourself in dangerous situations. You will stay with Saniraq.

Her hackles rose. *Is your life worth so much less than mine?*

The gold flecks in Malina's eyes glowed in the dim of the burrow. Perhaps she, too, was remembering Pili's final request. *Yes.* She stalked to the entrance. *Stay.*

Then she was gone.

← →

Shouldn't they be back by now? Ila asked sometime later.

Saniraq gnawed at a spot on one of her forelegs, the cream-colored fur coated in mud. *Patience, Ila.*

Ila laid her head atop her paws and sighed. The world was nearer to her in the skin of a predator. The ground was not something to stand on. It was a home for those that dwelled below.

I should have gone after Tipki.

Saniraq lifted her head, nose twitching. *Malina told you to stay behind to keep you safe, not because she thought you were incapable of fending for yourself.*

She didn't want anyone to carry her. It was no one's responsibility but her own. Her life wasn't worth more than anyone else's, despite what Malina believed.

Saniraq suddenly pushed to her feet, tail curled and erect over her back.

Malina entered the den first, followed closely by Tipki, one of her hind legs tucked against her gray belly. She hobbled into the enclosed space, and Ila greeted her with a lick to her snout.

A sprain, Tipki said, a whine in her mind-speak voice.

Saniraq crawled to her friend's side, licking the injured leg. Malina sat back on her haunches, keeping her distance from everyone.

Sadness trickled down the threads connecting each of the pack members. Ila was only able to sense these emotions in her wolf form, and she knew this one flowed like an unhindered river from Malina. This woman was not the most affectionate person, nor the most welcoming, but Ila had never doubted the love she had for their pack members, or for Pili.

Padding over to Malina, she sat and leaned into her packmate's body. Malina stiffened, clearly uncomfortable by the attempt at comfort. A warning growl vibrated through Ila's skin. She pretended not to notice and said, *Were you followed?*

We used a stream for cover.

That didn't exactly answer her question.

Tipki nosed Saniraq's ear in affection. *I don't think the bear men picked up my trail, but I overheard them talking.* She pulled away, her ears folding flat against her head. *Nanuq's army occupies Unana.*

All around, similar expressions of shock—or as shocked as a pack of wolves could look.

They had hoped to return to an abandoned capital city. There, they would access Lun via the tunnels that ran beneath Unana and extended into the mountains, possibly beyond, which Malina had used occasionally during her time in the military. Now it sounded foolish and naive. It was land, resources. Why wouldn't Nanuq take it for himself, a symbol of his prowess and might?

If they could not access the tunnels, they would have to take the longer, more treacherous route to Lun, overground via the Atakana's starkest peaks. It would add weeks to their journey.

Malina assessed each of them meticulously, eyebrows pushing inward, snout twitching. Even as a wolf, she looked to be scowling. *Do you remember the Horn of Amaroq?*

A few gasps through the mind-speak. Ila glanced at them curiously. *What is the Horn of Amaroq?*

An instrument of war, created by our god himself, said Tipki with excitement. *Our stories claim it was fashioned from the bones of his ancestors, those that came before the gods. When blown, it can be heard from all corners of the North.*

Our stories, as in Ila's stories, too. She supposed they were now.

Malina closed her eyes. *It was my unit that blew the horn when Nanuq's forces came from the west. But by then, it was too late. If we blow the horn, our allies will heed its call. Our people will rally to you.*

Wouldn't it have been destroyed in the invasion? Ila asked.

The horn is god-touched. It cannot be destroyed except by Amaroq himself. It's located in one of the den's towers, and I believe it was spared the worst of the fire, or so I've heard.

What about drawing attention to ourselves? That's why they had decided to shelter in Lun. Blowing the horn would absolutely alert Nanuq's army to their presence. She understood the need for allies, but at an enormous risk to their lives?

This changes things. Malina shifted her attention to Ila. *Nanuq's occupation of Unana changes things. I thought we'd have months to find allies, other wolf Unua in hiding, but we don't. We have weeks, if that. Whatever it is Nanuq intends to do, he will leave ruin in his wake. Blowing the horn is the quickest way to alerting those who might join us—the Owl Clan, maybe even the Caribou Nomads.*

And what happens after the horn is blown? Because as far as she knew, that army would destroy them. They'd never make it out of the city alive.

Malina was quiet. Eventually, Saniraq spoke in her calm, steady manner. *There is a way out of the tower, right?*

Tipki jumped in. *Yes. One of the tunnels connects the tower to the mountains. We could use the safehouses along the way.*

You both served with Numiak in the Pack, said Ila. *If he heard the horn, would he know where to find us? What if he doesn't know the city is occupied?*

It has been a long time. Malina touched her snout to Ila's paw. *There is a rendezvous point in case Unana was ever breached, which all Packmates know of. I do not know if he remembers it.*

Leading was no easy task. How could Ila possibly choose? They could blow the Horn of Amaroq and rally a great force, or they could just as easily—and more likely—die.

Tipki lifted her snout with spirit. *I say we rain war on those men. I say we tell the entire North we're through hiding. We stake a claim.*

Pup, Malina muttered, though affectionately.

Three pairs of eyes settled on Ila. They awaited her decision, she realized. As the Vaal of their broken nation, she had the final say.

Ila thought it was past time the North knew of the Wolf Kingdom's return.

If something goes wrong, she said, *we abandon the plan. We find another way to spread word.* She spoke to all, yet her gaze never moved from Malina, for she was the most headstrong.

Tipki lowered her muzzle in a sign of deference, followed by Saniraq. Malina was the last to do so, and ferocity burned like fire in her eyes.

They were women, they were wolves, and they were taking back their city.

← 33 →

The last time Apaay had visited Sinika, the sky had been dark, her heart weary. Now, the sun shone fully. She let the light pour in.

Gone was the glowing, snow-blanketed, ice-dusted city. Gone were the small glass orbs flickering with blue flame lining the pathways and labyrinthine platforms and ramps and stairs, or hanging from the great curved boughs overhead. Green grass spread like a flood across the hills and valleys of the Aatu, sprouting cheerful wildflowers of palest violet and yellow in its wake. The North's brief summer welcomed migratory birds from lands farther south, small chittering things. When the nesting season ended in a few short weeks, they would return south with their fledglings, escaping before autumn's colder weather set in. Apaay loved the North exactly like this: growing.

"Tell me again why we can't walk in as ourselves," Apaay muttered as she and Numiak moved among the owl Unua, crossing one of the arched bridges to a multi-level platform built around one of the massive conifers. Their hair was as white as those around them. No one suspected a thing.

"Because," said Numiak cheerily, his long gait forcing her to quicken her pace, "this is more fun."

After many weeks of travel, their journey from Nigun had reached its end. Once they met with the Avi, they'd discuss Nanuq and what had befallen the Caribou Nomads, their next step as a larger, unified force. It was all slightly overwhelming, in truth. Things were beginning to unfold with increasing urgency.

Apaay climbed a set of stairs to a higher platform, where a group of men with top knots had congregated to restring their glossy wooden bows. She had only explored a small portion of Sinika during her first visit. In actuality, the capital city spanned all the miles nestled between the River Pak and the River Iniak, the rushing white water acting as northern and southern boundaries. In this new, unexplored section of the city, the trees lacked many of the large, glass globes that offered shelter from the wind, thus providing additional space for the narrow, winding staircases, the platforms stacked atop one another with no need for bridges.

The Owl Clan was gathering. For what, she did not know. Humans and owls alike perched on branches, their faces decorated with white paint. The air shimmered with the undeniable pull of anticipation. Raucous noise, crowing cheers. Numiak touched her arm, gesturing her to follow. "This way."

They took the stairs, up and up and up, emerging onto the highest platform of the tallest tree—a dizzying height. Apaay stood on the very crest, the wind fighting to pull her hair free from its braid, and the spreading canopy rippled like the curling waves of the sea. This was the world, and she saw everything. No matter how much the North took, it always gave things back.

"What are we doing up here?" Apaay asked.

"It's the best location to watch the race." He settled on the edge of the platform, and Apaay sat beside him, her feet dangling, their shoulders touching. In the understory, the owl Unua milled about as dark specks.

On a platform many levels below, six boys on the cusp of manhood stood shoulder to shoulder, arms loose at their sides.

Numiak spoke into her ear so she could hear him above the wind. "It's a rite of passage among their men. In their twelfth year, the boys fly the course to showcase their agility and speed."

Analak boys went through a similar ritual: the summer hunt. It was but one example of how boys were raised differently from girls. Growing up, Chena's brother, Muktuk, had woken each morning, forced to go outside no matter the weather so as to acclimate to the cold.

Numiak pointed into the trees. The topknot men with their beige arm and leg wrappings stood at the ready, arrows nocked against taut bowstrings.

Apaay gaped in horror. "They try to kill them?"

"The arrows lack pointed ends. If they killed every boy who attempted the course, they would have no men to protect the cities. They coat the blunted tips in paint. If a boy is hit, the paint will transfer onto his feathers, and he will be disqualified. I attended Ro's rite when we were boys. He still holds the record for the fastest completed time."

Apaay scanned the platforms for signs of Ro, Kaan, or Ila, as she suspected they would be present, but there were so many people she couldn't begin to distinguish them. "Can I ask you something?"

Numiak watched the boys ready themselves. Sunlight warmed the tawny shade of his skin, the prickly shadow that had formed on his jaw the last few days without having shaved. He dipped his chin in affirmation.

"How did Ro end up in a wheelchair?"

A long moment of silence passed. Apaay didn't push him. He'd heard her. She knew he had. It wasn't the first time she had wondered, but it was the first time she had asked. She still didn't know if it was her place to do so.

Bumps sprouted up her arms as a raptor cry poured across the land like water after the thaw. As one, the boys leaped from the platform and shifted mid-fall. Their wings snapped out to catch the air in soundless motion, a sight of ferocious beauty, yet harmony, too.

The first arrow cut the air. The boys scattered, swerving to avoid the paint that, should it stain their feathers, would deem them unworthy. One boy managed to escape, only to be hit in the back a moment later, blue paint darkening the white plumes. He dropped.

Apaay gasped, and Numiak stiffened. She turned toward him, but he wasn't looking at her. His gaze was locked on her hand, which now curled over the top of his thigh, fingers digging in.

When he lifted his head, her stomach bottomed out as something feral flickered in his eyes.

Apaay snatched her hand back. "Sorry."

A single black brow arched high. "Are you? Sorry?"

"Yes," she whispered. Why was she whispering? She had no idea.

Numiak's fingers curled around her nape, a firm and heavy heat. "I do love it when you lie."

Apaay swallowed. Perhaps she was not sorry then. She liked touching him. Liked it when he touched her.

Numiak refocused his attention on the course, though he didn't remove his hand. Eventually, the boys vanished around a corner.

"It was before I learned of the invasion," he began, "but after the distress signal had called me to Nannek from the eastern coast. The Owl Clan was overrun by Nanuq's army. Ro and the Flock fought on the front lines, combating the brunt of Nanuq's force. I went to give them aid." His tone spoke of regrets, even now, two decades later. "Nanuq's force was too great, but still we fought. I didn't see the archer through the trees. Ro took an arrow meant for me. It hit his spine, paralyzing him from the waist down."

Apaay clapped a hand over her mouth. She felt ill. "That's awful."

Numiak said, "He has experienced a loss I will never comprehend. That he risked his life to save mine, it is not something I will ever be able to repay."

Cheers erupted as the owls approached the start again. One, two, three birds darted past, swerving and diving around the deadly arrows. A fourth lagged behind. No sign of the fifth one. It must have been hit.

Numiak squinted into the distance, as if he could see the battle that had taken place so many decades before at a city that had fallen to the Polar Bear Empire. "During his recovery, Ro turned to tinkering with inventions, which, as it turns out, he's very good at. Following the war, a disease wiped out a huge number of trees, causing many of the owl Unua to die from exposure. Ro designed the domes to protect his people from the elements."

"I'm sure the Avi was pleased."

"Not as pleased as you would think," he said vaguely.

Shortly after, the race ended. Three of the six boys completed the course without injury. The other three would have a chance to compete again next year. A short ceremony took place to acknowledge the boys who would make that transition to manhood. Their long hair was pulled into topknots, then cut. Apaay watched the white strands fall to the platform in shock, but Numiak explained the symbolism—the shedding of an old life to allow a new one to flourish.

When the crowd began to disperse, she and Numiak descended the stairs to a platform filled with more birds than people. That's when Apaay heard a high-pitched, "Numi!"

The smile that broke across Numiak's face was like sunlight. He spun, catching the child that flew toward him in his arms.

His niece, Mika, screamed in delight and climbed up his body, and she was laughing, as was he, as was Apaay as she witnessed the joyful reunion. Arms wrapped tightly, Numiak squeezed Mika against his chest and buried his face in her flyaway black hair.

Kaan and Ro appeared behind Mika, staring at Numiak in momentary confusion. They made quite the pair. The tall, slender woman with cunning features, and the burly, handsome man in a wheelchair at her side. Siblings, yet their personalities couldn't be more different.

Kaan said, unimpressed, "The hair could be a shade whiter."

Ro shook his head at his sister's comment and moved forward in his chair, clasping hands with Numiak. "It's good to see you again. You're well?"

He grinned. "Completely healed, thanks to Apaay."

The relief was plain on Ro's face.

"Aren't you forgetting something?" Kaan, gold eyes flashing, chin-length hair swaying, sauntered up to them. "A reminder that you would have died were it not for me."

"How should I repay you?" Droll. "Is it a shrine you're looking for? I'm happy to build one. Just say the word."

"Hmph." But her eyes crinkled like veins in a leaf. "Where is Apaay anyway? I thought she was with you."

Apaay stepped forward. "I'm here."

Kaan gasped. Ro stared. Mika blinked owlishly.

Apaay did not wear her old face, and she did not wear her new one. She wore a different one entirely, with large eyes and a square jaw, and unadorned white hair the Face Stealer had lightened with his powers.

"You stole her face?" Kaan all but screeched.

Apaay and Numiak shared a look. "Not exactly," she replied.

Wolf Unua had an excellent sense of smell. The owl Unua, less so. It explained why Mika had recognized her uncle despite his change in appearance, while Ro and Kaan had not.

Numiak hefted Mika higher into his arms, planting a smacking kiss onto her cheek that made his niece giggle. "We should talk. Preferably somewhere private."

Kaan glanced between them suspiciously. "This way." She led them over a number of elaborately carved bridges, up one of the spiral staircases, and into the largest glass dome Apaay had seen yet. This one contained low-seated couches, cushioned chairs, an abundance of colorful pillows, and worn rugs. Mika ran off to play with her doll while everyone gathered. They were all here—except Ila, she noted with disappointment. Maybe she and Tulimaq were training somewhere. They would have reached Sinika weeks ago.

"So." Kaan pursed her lips, tapping a finger against the arm of her chair. "Heard you infiltrated the Northern Territory." She sniffed. "And I wasn't even invited."

Numiak chuckled. "I missed you, Kaan. I really did."

"Of course you did. Who wouldn't?" She shot her brother a warning look.

Ro lifted a hand in a gesture of goodwill. "I wasn't going to say anything."

"I'm sure."

He muttered something into his fist that caused Numiak to chuckle.

"What's that?" Kaan asked her brother sweetly, leaning forward.

"Nothing."

"That's what I thought." She bared her teeth, and Apaay remembered all too well Kaan's skill in combat, this fierce and implacable woman, and was glad that smile was not directed at her. "Are you going to tell us what happened or what?"

Numiak, who sat beside Apaay on one of the couches, lifted an eyebrow in her direction. "Wolfling?"

Apaay started from the beginning. She told Kaan and Ro of the weeks-long trek to Nigun, as well as the corruption that had plagued the underground city. She spoke of the nectar that cleansed the Caribou Nomads of their awareness, the hot spring's healing properties, the commander's downfall and subsequent reinstatement of the Council of Nine. In a few weeks, Samut would travel to Sinika as a Council representative so that the Caribou Nomads and Owl Clan could begin assembling their defense against Nanuq, whose forces amassed beyond the Central Territory.

Afterward, Kaan and Ro revealed their own troubles, what had transpired in the last few months. They spoke of felled trees, great swaths of the Aatu cut and cleared by Nanuq's men for reasons unknown, a continuation of the Dead Plains' destruction, of great change creeping northward. Daily, word arrived of the smaller, southern towns fleeing north to take refuge in Sinika, the most fortified city in the Central Territory. However, there was concern that their resources would not sustain the influx of people.

"Six hundred refugees last week," Ro said wearily. "That number is expected to double before tomorrow."

"How long will your stores last?" asked Numiak.

Kaan answered, "At this rate, not beyond autumn. Come winter, our people will starve."

Apaay was well acquainted with starvation. Her village suffered when the hunts were not successful. That slow, quiet death. "What is your father doing about it?" she asked.

"As much as he can," said Ro. "He's sent our people far and

wide to gather food, but it is not enough. And that's the least of our troubles."

Ro claimed a unit of the Flock had gone missing near Nannek. After weeks of searching, they had finally recovered the bodies, ripped to shreds and sloppily buried. Days later, a second unit had vanished. Their bodies had yet to be recovered.

"We believe Nanuq is using Nannek as a base," Ro said, his voice stable despite the difficult topic of conversation, "though we do not know what for."

"That's what we hope to find out," said Numiak, "once Apaay and I infiltrate the Southern Territory."

Kaan blinked. "What?"

The door opened, and a boy stuck his head into the room. He looked around nervously before his attention settled on Ro. "Sir, the Avi requests your presence."

Ro gripped the wheels of his chair. His voice went flat. "Tell him I'm busy at the moment."

The boy blanched. Apaay couldn't blame him. She wouldn't want to say such a thing to the Avi either. "But—"

"You're dismissed," he barked.

The boy fled, the slam of the door overly loud in the quiet.

As Apaay knew, there was no single form of quiet. There was the quiet of snowfall. There was the quiet of sleep. There was the quiet of one's thoughts.

This was the quiet of seething anger.

Kaan leveled a cold glare at her brother. "The poor boy is wetting his pants because you refuse to speak to Father."

"We're not discussing Father. We're discussing Apaay."

Perhaps, Apaay thought, they should discuss Ro's father. Or rather, his relationship—or lack thereof—with him.

"I don't understand." Kaan inspected Apaay with no small amount of doubt. "Not that I don't think Apaay isn't capable, but Kimmir was trained for his mission. He understood the risks."

She heard what the woman did not say. Apaay was incompetent. Apaay was too soft.

Apaay had thought it before: a person was not their face.

A person was their heart. And hers, she had come to learn, was stronger than she had ever believed.

Numiak's large hand engulfed her shoulder. "Do you want to tell them, or should I?"

Softness was not the same as weakness.

"No," she said. "I'll tell them." This was her story, after all. Apaay was someone who tried a thousand times and would try a thousand times more.

"If we're going to have an excruciatingly lengthy discussion about war," said Kaan, "can you at least change your faces back? I've nearly forgotten what you both look like."

Apaay and Numiak had discussed who they would reveal the truth to about her role as the Creator. Only Ro, Kaan, and Ila would know.

They switched their faces back. Numiak, of course, looked the same, whereas Apaay did not. Kaan and Ro frowned at her. Mika wandered over, clutching her doll, blinking big eyes up at Apaay in wonder. "Pretty," she whispered.

Numiak tugged Mika to his side, pressing a kiss to the top of her head. She giggled and ran off to play in the area of potted plants near the glass.

"I'm confused," said Kaan.

Folding her hands in her lap, Apaay began. "As you know, Nanuq seeks an object of power that he believes is somewhere in the Western Territory. But what he doesn't know is that the object is right here, in this very room."

"So you know what the object is?" Her hands curled into fists. The weapons master didn't appreciate waiting. Or being left in the dark.

"The object of power isn't an object. It's a person. And that person," Apaay said, "is me."

Ro examined Apaay as one would a complex puzzle. Kaan choked out a sound, which soon devolved into laughter, gasps of disbelief.

The laughter cut off as Kaan realized no one else shared in her humor. "You're serious?"

"A long time ago, Numiak gave me another girl's face so that Nanuq would not learn my true identity. I am the Creator. I have the ability to create new identities at will."

Kaan's face paled. Ro said nothing, only took everything in, leaving no detail overlooked. Mika, unaware of the emotional shift, began to hum beneath her breath.

Ro pulled at his lower lip in thought. "So Nanuq wants . . . a new identity?"

Apaay was still exploring the facets of her power. She could create new identities. She could change ones already in existence. But Nanuq sought to change his very *being*. He wished to rid himself of his polar bear half, the part that made him Unua. He wished to be man, through and through. "He seeks to replace his face with one that is completely human. That is how he will become fully man."

There was a long—a very long—silence.

"You knew about this?" Ro asked Numiak. If he was shocked, he didn't outwardly show it. "Why didn't you tell us?"

"The mission, remember? I was sworn to secrecy and couldn't discuss it with anyone, not even my Packmates. And anyway, I couldn't risk this information finding its way back to Nanuq."

Ro, a man who spoke little, but who knew much about war, nodded in understanding.

"That's—" Kaan's voice petered out.

Numiak snorted. "You're speechless. Never thought I'd see the day."

She tossed a pillow at his head, which he caught deftly, grinning.

"I can't believe you kept this from us all these years!" she cried. "And she—" Again, her mouth worked. "Why the *hell* are you sending Apaay into Nanuq's territory? As soon as he finds out what she is to him, he'll end her."

Apaay did not know what the future held, but she felt stronger and more sure of herself than she had in months. "I understand the risks. I may not have the training, but we need someone on the inside that can blend in. I can do that. We could use Tulimaq's help as well. If I make him a face, he could be another set of eyes in the capital." The combat master knew how to hold his own.

"Unfortunately, that will be impossible." Ro sighed, rubbing at the lines of tension that had gathered across his forehead. "Tulimaq has betrayed us."

A stark silence rang, lingering like a bad odor.

"Care to explain?" Numiak spoke in the tone of voice that lifted the hair on Apaay's arms, the one that warned her to keep her distance. And then the first coil of shadow drifted across his chest, down his legs to puddle on the ground. Apaay tensed at his side.

In a rare gesture of frustration, Ro snapped his wheelchair to the side and moved to stare out the glass. Numiak leaned forward, elbows on his knees. His eyes, a pale leaf-green, glittered like water on metal. Kaan looked grim. Apaay was still reeling from the statement.

"When Tulimaq and Ila did not arrive at Sinika, I sent out scouts to search for them. What I discovered was . . . not good." His sigh was the heaviest sound she had heard in a long while. He circled to face them. "Tulimaq was found at the labor camp where your people are being held, Numiak, but not as a prisoner. He is one of their superiors."

"What?" Numiak hissed. His lips barely moved.

"My scouts were given reason to believe Tulimaq is actually one of Nanuq's sons."

The dome shuddered ominously.

"Numiak!" Kaan snapped. She had jumped onto her chair to avoid the shadows writhing on the ground.

This couldn't be. Tulimaq was good. He was on their side. He had fought to protect the Wood from Yuki's army. He had trained Ila.

Ila.

Apaay lurched to her feet. There was pain in her heart, and the pain was called *Ila.* "Is she—?" Apaay couldn't say it.

The raw torment on Ro's face made her heart contract.

"I don't know," he said. "Something . . . happened. A fire broke out at the labor camp. It was mostly ash when my scouts arrived."

"Survivors?" asked Numiak tightly.

"If there were, they were nowhere to be found."

Cold horror trickled through her bloodstream. She was out the door, hardly aware that she had moved, Numiak's voice calling after her.

The end of the platform stopped her forward motion, the toes of her boots kissing the air where the wood fell away. Her eyes stung, and the tears fell, and Apaay knew that if Ila was gone, she would break. Didn't Ila know Apaay needed her? Apaay, who had made so many mistakes, was the furthest thing from perfect, but that was her largest regret: that Ila might think Apaay didn't care for her, and that she had died thinking such a thing.

"Apaay."

Her name, spoken with so much tenderness, cracked something in her chest. She expelled a lungful of air. "She can't— She—"

Grasping her shoulders, Numiak turned her to face him. "Look at me," he said, but gently.

Reluctantly, she did. The warmth of his touch seeped through her clothes, and Apaay had to stop herself from slumping forward into his chest.

He studied her for a long while before he spoke. "Ila is a fighter. If she was held captive, my guess is she would do whatever it took to escape. There's still a chance she's alive."

Ila wasn't any threat to Tulimaq. What reason would he have to hurt her, kill her? "And if she's not?"

He looked torn. As if he wanted nothing more than to console her, but that could not be done if they were to face the truth.

"What exactly is Tulimaq capable of?" If she knew, might she guard her heart against future hurts related to Ila's well-being?

He released a short, pained breath. "I don't want to scare you. Tulimaq fooled us. Plenty of polar bear Unua fled the Southern Territory when Nanuq rose to power, so it was never out of the realm of possibility that Tulimaq was a refugee. I had assumed as much, but if he is Nanuq's son . . ." Numiak shook his head, his features lined with severity. "Then he is capable of anything."

← 34 →

"I've always wondered what I'd look like with a different nose," Kaan said from where she sat with her back against a tree. "Care to give it a go?"

Apaay had spent the morning transforming Kaan's face upon the woman's request. Three days had passed since her arrival, and she'd spent the majority of that time sharpening her skills. The domed structures provided an ideal practice space due to their relative isolation. This one contained copious amounts of flowering plants, a small pond, and even fully-grown trees.

"What do you have in mind?" Apaay asked, mentally tracing the shape of Kaan's sharp cheekbones and pointed chin.

"Make it the most hideous nose you can think of. Give me a wart or something."

She snorted, but did as instructed.

The woman held up a small mirror and shrieked, laughing herself hoarse. "I'm hideous!" She flapped her hands. "Another. Give me another!"

This nose more closely resembled a bird's beak. Mouth pursed, Kaan tilted her face from side to side, studying herself from all angles. "What do you think? Too much? Or just large enough to attract attention?"

Nothing was ever too much for Kaan. "Honestly? It works for you."

"Hm." She lowered the mirror. "How about a unibrow?"

Seconds later, Kaan poked at the bushy, worm-like creature crawling across her forehead. They laughed and laughed, and it was good.

It was good.

Once their laughter subsided and Apaay returned Kaan's face to its normal state, a companionable silence fell between them. The insects buzzed pleasantly among the sweet-smelling blooms, and water lapped at the pond's edge. Kaan accepted Apaay's new face without issue, but would her family? Would they recognize her in a crowd?

"I was wondering," said Apaay, "if there's a way to send a message to my family." She bit her wobbly lip, caught Kaan's panicked expression in her periphery. "Sorry," she whispered.

"Oh, no. It's not that." She embraced Apaay, shushing her softly. "Don't tell the others, but I'm an idiot. I should have offered. It must be hard for you."

It seemed as if she had only gotten her family back before they had been forced into separation again. Being here, laughing with Kaan, it was healing, yet painful, too. She thought of all the terrible jokes she and Eska once shared. It had been long since she had told a joke simply for the pleasure of it being terrible.

"Actually—" Pulling back, Kaan dug into her pocket and produced a folded piece of parchment and a piece of charcoal. "I can write it now, if you want. I'll pass it on to the messenger later today. One of the Flock stationed at the village will be able to translate it to your family."

Apaay licked the salt from her lips and wiped her stinging eyes. "Tell them I love them," she managed through an aching throat. "And that I promise I will see them soon." Kaan sketched out various symbols. "And tell Chena I expect to learn of her daughter's name-soul as soon as we're reunited."

Kaan paused in her notating and glanced up. "Name-soul?"

"It's one of the ways the Analak strengthen the ties with people in their community. Newborns are named after those who have already passed. This ensures the deceased's—the namesake's—spirit lives on." Although, sometimes people bestowed their namesake onto a newborn when they were still alive. Those instances were much less common. "People can also impart endearment names onto others. Like I used to call my sister *tiny whale* when we were children, because her cheeks were so round. But our father called her *little bird*, because her laugh sounded like a bird call."

Kaan chuckled. "Tiny whale." She then asked, "Who are you named after?"

"My maternal grandmother. I call my mother naajaluk—daughter."

Kaan's intrigue deepened. "And she calls you . . . mother?"

Apaay smiled. "It can be confusing for those who aren't Analak." Her focus returned to the message. "Thank you for this." She touched a corner of the parchment. "I appreciate it more than you know." Nothing else mattered except telling those she loved that she was thinking of them.

"Of course. I'll make sure they receive it. With Ila missing, I can't imagine how you've been feeling."

As if she needed reminding. "Any news?"

Kaan shook her head. Ro had sent scouts. North and south and east and west, they caught the thermals and searched for Ila, but—nothing.

"I pushed her away," she whispered. "I trusted the wrong person. It's my fault."

"No." The older woman grabbed her hand. "You could not have known this would happen. Tulimaq fooled us all."

"Then I've been fooled twice, because Kenai fooled me as well."

Kaan sighed, picked off another flower from the bush. "Kenai has always struggled with doing the right thing. I'm not surprised he chose to be at Yuki's side. However twisted her affection toward him, it's still more than he received as a child."

Apaay considered this. She felt braver, concealed among the leaves. "You knew Kenai growing up."

"Yes. Kenai was older, of course, and had his own life in the

military. He didn't spend a lot of time with Numiak. Or anyone, for
that matter. He tended to isolate himself."

Apaay, remembering her last conversation with him, said, "I
think he's confused."

"Aren't we all? It's no excuse for everything he's done. He got
what he deserved the day Numiak captured him." She shredded the
petals into tiny fragments, watching them float onto the grass.

"What happened?"

"They fought. It was gruesome and bloody. Numiak took his
brother's eye. Me, I would have stabbed him through the heart. I
would not be able to stand by while someone destroyed my home."

"You really love your people."

"They are everything to me. My father—" She stopped, as if
gathering herself. "He didn't spend much time with me or Umiq,
growing up. Because he was so focused on Ro, I got free rein of the
city. So I spent time with my people. They cared for me, laughed
with me, shared food with me, told stories about their lives. Even if
I wasn't the heir, I could lead in different ways. I could connect with
our people and strengthen our nation through other means."

And Kaan, in Apaay's opinion, was exactly the person who
would ensure her vision came to fruition. "If Ro isn't interested in
taking your father's place, who would be next in line?"

"Umiq. The first-born son is heir. After, it goes in order of age
with daughters. Ro can avoid his duties all he wants, but one day,
he'll have to lead our people, whether he's ready or not." She clapped
her hands. "Quick. Change my face."

Apaay gifted her friend with a pair of large, fleshy lips.

Numiak chose to appear at that moment, his black hair
unbound, shining like polished stone. He took one look at Kaan's
transformation and said, "Definitely an improvement."

Kaan flashed her teeth. "Make him look like an eyesore," she
demanded of Apaay. "Really, it's unfair how pretty he is."

He turned to Apaay with a look of knowing. "Do you agree?
Am I too pretty?"

Pretty suggested delicacy, fragility, softness. A more apt
description would be *arresting*.

"Hm," was her only response.

Cunning glinted in his enlarged pupils, as if he knew what she did not say.

The truth was, Apaay wouldn't change a thing about him. It was maddening how attractive she found him. Most days, Apaay pretended these feelings did not exist. Most days, it worked.

Numiak vanished and reappeared sitting between them, startling a bird into flight from a nearby bush. The warm air buzzed pleasantly with insects. It was impossible to tell that beyond the thick glass, the air cooled with the approaching long night. "Not all women," he crooned, voice rippling against Apaay's ear, "are blind to my allure."

Her pulse leaped. A deep inhale brought the scent of his skin to her nostrils, that smoky, woodsy flavor, both a comfort and a delight.

Kaan snorted with a softly muttered, "Gag."

"If you're so certain of your allure," Apaay tossed back, "why not try your luck with one of them?" She flapped a hand toward the multitude of women milling about the pond, as perfect and pretty as the garden blooms, their children splashing in the water.

"Yes," he said. "Why don't I?"

He materialized near a little footbridge shaded by fruit trees and approached one of the women with a frustrating lack of self-consciousness. There it was, his easy, devilish grin. Apaay felt something clench in the pit of her stomach.

She crushed the flower in her hand.

Kaan nudged her in the ribs. "Don't let him get to you. Playing the game is half the fun for him."

To which Apaay had to wonder: what game?

Shortly after, Kaan left to help the archers stockpile more arrows. Apaay watched the conversation play out between Numiak and his new friend glumly. Eventually, the woman wandered off, and he returned to her side.

"Well?" Flippant.

"Well what?"

"Did she fall for your charm?"

He smiled crookedly. Apaay was about three seconds away from punching him in his too-perfect face. "I guess you'll never know."

The moment she actually considered hitting him, he unexpectedly reached for her hand, uncurling her fingers from around the flower she'd ruined. The smashed petals dropped to the soft grass underfoot. "I want to show you something. Will you come with me?"

Honestly. "Why don't you ask your new friend?"

The tenderness in his gaze melted her heart's hard exterior. He had yet to let go of her hand. "I'm asking you. The woman who saved me—twice now, I might add—and whose trust I value more than anything."

Eyes narrowing, Apaay snatched her hand away and stood, a bit breathless. She couldn't defend herself against him when he said things like that. "Laying the charm on thick, are you?"

"No charm." He reached for her hand again. "Just truth."

← →

They met Ro at a cave entrance on the city outskirts. Gesturing them to follow, he led them deep underground, their footsteps and the squeak of his wheelchair the only sounds. After perhaps a mile of steady descent, the ground leveled, the dark, narrow tunnel opening up to an enormous cavern, a shaft of sunlight spearing through a hole at the top, and a massive blue fire raging in the center of the room.

The air was so oppressively hot Apaay found it difficult to breathe. The flames crackled loudly, licking at the empty space above. She had never seen a fire this large. It was at least ten times the size of the meeting hall in her village. "What is this place?"

"This is the forge," said Ro. He waved to a few workers who busily shoveled piles of rocks into the fire or pushed carts full of mineral down the many tunnels branching from the main room. "It's where we extract the metals needed for our blue flame."

The overwhelming heat of the fire pinched Apaay's skin uncomfortably. "How is it extracted?" she wondered.

Ro maneuvered his chair over an uneven strip of ground, leading them deeper into the forge. "The rock is collected as mineral deposits from the rivers. Heat from the fire breaks down the rock, yet leaves the metal, which we use as fuel to light the city."

"The forge also acts as a line of defense," Numiak explained. "Lines of metal run throughout the underground tunnels. In the case of an invasion, the metal is lit, and the ground becomes too hot to walk on. It prevented Nanuq from crossing the River Iniak into Sinika."

Apaay processed this information as she noted the massive metal containers lining one of the cave walls.

Ro said, "We're tunneling farther south. I want to secure the towns close to Nannek and the Dead Plains. It shouldn't take more than a few months."

The question was, did they have a few months?

Ro showed her the smaller forges tucked away down alternate tunnels. She learned the importance of these fires, how it allowed the owl Unua to build their domed city, how it was heat and light and protection. A blue substance bubbled in one of the vats, steam rising to cloud the space.

These tunnels, along with the stockpiled weapons, would go a long way in reinforcing their defenses. The Avi had even sent some of his Flock northward—additional protection for the caribou Unua while Nigun was being rebuilt. Nanuq's kirn may have failed to conquer the city, but it remained highly unstable, the ideal target for a stronger force.

Near the end of their tour, two archers from the Flock arrived, their hair in disarray as if they had covered a lot of ground in a short amount of time. Apaay recognized them by the topknots and the beige armbands they wore.

"Sir." The shorter of the two men addressed Ro. His eyes flicked to Numiak, then away.

Ro said, "Is there news?"

The men exchanged a glance. Neither seemed inclined to speak first.

"Well?" Ro snapped. "Speak."

The taller of the two glanced at Numiak, then said, "Sir, the information is sensitive."

Numiak stiffened, and Apaay realized what the man implied.

Understanding crossed Ro's expression. "I see." He did not look at Numiak when he said, "I need to address this. I'll return shortly." And he followed his men back up the tunnel.

Apaay hesitated in speaking. She recognized his hurt, for she knew how vulnerable the heart could be. "Numiak—"

"Don't."

She flinched at the ice in his tone. Even if it wasn't directed at her, it still stung. "I'm sure there are protocols he has to follow."

"You and I both know that's not the case." He turned away from her. "Let's not pretend it is."

They spent time exploring the forge until Ro returned, alone. Whatever he had been called away for, it seemed to have aged him.

Numiak strode to his side. "What happened?" Low, urgent.

Ro's reluctance felt palpable, like dust caked on one's tongue. He gestured them away from the forge workers so they could not be overheard. "We came across a refugee camp, about one hundred miles north of here. Or rather, it used to be a refugee camp. Everyone had been killed, even the children."

"What?" Numiak whisper-hissed. "By whom? Nanuq?"

Apaay bit the inside of her cheek as the horror bubbled and spewed inside her. The enemy, growing bolder. What were the odds it was the same camp Kenai had devastated?

Ro hesitated. "Signs point toward Nanuq, yes, or Yuki's army." He was trying to communicate something without actually saying it. Apaay saw the moment it hit.

"Ah," said Numiak bitterly. "Of course. It's the only explanation, right? It has to be." He strode off, but not too far that he was lost to shadow.

"What's wrong?" Apaay asked Ro in concern.

Briefly, he closed his eyes. One of the workers dumped a tub of metal into the fire. It flared high and bright. "My men—and in extension, many of my people—believe this massacre to be Numiak's doing."

Apaay gaped. "That's not true. He was with me the entire time. And Ke—" She shut her mouth. Bad idea to discuss Kenai with Numiak nearby. "It's not true," she repeated.

"I know it's not true, but they don't." He indicated the gathering workers at his back, the hissed accusations under their breath. "The alliance doesn't stop people from living in the past."

"Well, maybe you should talk some sense into them," she growled, tossing up a hand. "You're the heir. They'll follow you."

"You're mistaken, Apaay. I am not my father."

Apaay would probably regret saying this. It wasn't her place. But she didn't care. "Perhaps you do not give them a reason to follow you." Budding anger pushed her forward. "Numiak is your friend. You know his heart. You know he would never . . ." It sickened her. "If he's your friend, don't you think it's your job to defend him?"

"My job," he enunciated flatly, "is to keep my people safe."

"And how does the spread of false information accomplish that?"

He didn't answer.

"Numiak explained why he left Nannek in the middle of battle. That the city fell to Nanuq is unfortunate, but he had his own nation to protect." People always wanted something or someone to blame. "Or did your people forget the Wolf Kingdom fell, too?"

It wasn't her place. She told herself this again. Ro was the most level-headed person she knew, but he had done Numiak a disservice. After her own failures with Ila, she did not want Ro making the same mistake she had—inaction and avoidance. "Don't you think you should stand up for what is right, even if your people believe you to be wrong?"

Ro sat straight-backed in his chair. Quietly, he said, "It is not so easy."

Through it all, Numiak had remained silent. He studied them with black, mistrustful eyes. This had gone wrong so quickly. Apaay remembered waking in an unfamiliar healing room months ago, learning the villagers—her own people—believed she had killed those she loved most. It had shaken something inside her.

"Numiak, this—" She stopped, went on. "It will be all right."

"Will it now?" The chill of his voice crawled along Apaay's skin. He moved to the shadowed area against the wall, as if drawn to it. "Ro's people expect this of me. I wonder if you do, too."

Her heart twinged, and she swallowed. "You know I don't think that."

"Then tell me what I should do," he snarled. "I see the way his people look at me. Does my reputation now extend to murder as well? What about rape?" Green eyes blazed from his brown face. "I haven't stolen a single face since I left the labyrinth, but even if I had, I wouldn't kill an innocent person, especially one trying to defend their livelihood. And I—" He broke off with a strangled sound.

Cautiously, Apaay took a step toward him. His hands were fisted so tightly the knuckles pushed white against his skin. "We can fix this."

"No, Apaay. This isn't something that can be *fixed*. Who I am cannot be *fixed*." He touched a trembling hand to his temple, staring at the ground. "Ro, please see that Apaay returns to Sinika safely."

He vanished in a ripple of shade.

← 35 →

The following night, they were called to dinner with the Avi. Numiak, however, was not present.

Apaay hadn't seen him since yesterday. She'd spent the day exploring the city with Mika. The girl had dragged Apaay to all her favorite spots, including what she lovingly titled *the bubble house*—a dome stuffed with the softest pillows and blankets. The hours had passed, the sun barely lifting high enough to breach the canopy, and still Numiak hadn't shown.

Apaay picked at her plate of food, paying no attention to the dinner conversation. She remembered the suspicion plain on those men's faces. She remembered, too, the coldness in Numiak's voice.

Ro should have spoken against his men.

The cool air coaxed the forest sounds from hiding. The Avi occupied the head of the table, his white hair pulled back into a tail. Ro sat on his right. To the Avi's left: Kaan; his eldest daughter, Umiq; archers from the Flock; the clan leaders, those who oversaw trade, law, health, and development, among other things. Everyone talked and talked and talked and no one, not one person, mentioned Numiak's absence. Apaay glanced at the empty plate on her left. It wasn't right. He should be here.

Apaay's chair scraped against the floorboards as she abruptly stood, and the chatter ceased.

Kaan glanced over from where she'd been conversing with an elderly man. Her grandfather? "Everything all right?" she asked, gold eyes flashing in concern.

"No," she said, voice carrying across the deepening dusk. "No, it's not all right." She turned to Ro, who avoided eye contact.

"You should have fought for him," she growled. "After all he's done for you . . ." Oh, she was angrier than she'd been in a long time. "Yet you sit here as if you do not know the reason for his absence. Numiak is the one who brought us together. You forget he lost his home too, his people. I thought you were better than this."

The clan leaders stared at her blankly. Kaan's gaze darted from Ro to Apaay and back again, brow furrowed. The Avi appraised his son with lukewarm interest. Only Umiq reacted distastefully. It seemed she still hadn't forgiven Numiak for abandoning her people in the war—despite him having spared her life when they'd fought the Nayinkai.

A man to Ro's left stood, glaring haughtily. He was the clan leader of Unua relations, she believed. "You forget your place. Do you know who you're speaking to?"

Ro lifted a hand. "It's all right, Urlag." He sounded tired.

The man sat and attacked his whale meat as though it were the enemy, glowering at her over his fork every few bites. Ro, however, still couldn't meet her eye. And wasn't that a shame.

"I'm going to look for Numiak," Apaay whispered, leaving the dinner table to bewildered silence.

Crossing one of the eastern bridges, she headed toward a winding staircase spiraling around one of the trees. Level after level, she climbed, the air growing thin with cold. Back home, when Apaay had felt too small for the world, she would find the tallest point—a hill, a tree—and she would climb. Being nearer to the sky always soothed the jagged edges of her soul, the harm she inflicted on herself by believing she wasn't enough.

Apaay discovered Numiak perched on the edge of the same

platform where they'd watched the rite last week. His dark outline merged with the shadowed needles, etched deeper against the gray twilight. It was an image of isolation. There he was, singular, the whole of the North stretched before him. She had not previously understood how lonely a life Numiak must lead.

Apaay strode forward, then stopped, unsure if she was welcome. "You weren't at dinner."

He spoke without turning around. "I'm poor company at the moment."

"Only at the moment?"

A tense silence passed. His voice darkened, laced with the pain he tried so hard to hide. "Go away, wolfling. You don't want to be around me right now."

I see you, she thought. *I see you and I hear you and you are not alone and I am here.*

I am here.

This was what he needed: to strike and strike hard, to fall into feeling without fear of judgment. Apaay would be that person for him.

"There you go again, putting words into my mouth. You have no idea what I want." And the truth was as cruel as the wind, because Apaay hadn't any idea either. She took another step closer, wondered if it was a mistake. "But maybe you're right. A demon birthed from the darkness of Taggak? It seems you're the last person anyone would trust."

Apaay watched the blow make impact. She did not take pleasure in it. She bared these uncomfortable thoughts for him, knowing he wouldn't be able to do it himself. "People say there is no good in you."

He stayed quiet.

She said, "They fear you."

She said, "They do not understand you."

She said, "They have no desire to."

"And why shouldn't they fear me?" he bellowed, head snapping around to face her. The pits of his eyes showed little white. Strands of black hair hung untethered around his face. "I am who they say," he hissed, pressing a hand to his chest. "A nightmare who comes for them when the sun goes down, who snatches the faces of their children and mothers and fathers, who reaps and sows ruin in my wake. That is my burden. That is who I've always been. What reason have they to trust me?"

His self-loathing was all too familiar. That destructive force chewing on your insides. Over time, it exacerbated. A drop became a pool, a lake, a sea. But even when she'd been at her lowest point, he hadn't let the darkness win. Hadn't let it consume her completely.

Numiak was a demon, but he was also a man, someone who few knew deeper than his skin, and now she was within the walls he'd built around himself, near as a heartbeat. It did not seem so terrible a place to be.

Steeling herself, Apaay curled a hand over the hard ridge of his shoulder. He froze at her touch. "Do you honestly believe that?"

She could feel his heart through the soft hide of his clothes, a heavy, punishing strike.

"What compels you to steal faces?" she asked.

Numiak sighed, one long expulsion of sound. He didn't speak right away. Apaay didn't push. Either he would tell her or he wouldn't.

"My ability to steal faces came about because of Taggak's darkness rooting inside me, but it wasn't until Yuki stole my heart and forced me into her service that the extent of my powers became apparent.

"At first, she used me to punish those who had wronged her. Then she began targeting communities that had stopped following the old rules, gifting her offerings. I admit, the night I arrived at your village, I did not realize it was your sister's face I had stolen. It's sometimes hard to distinguish people's features beneath their parka hoods. A terrible mistake that led you into the labyrinth, into this mess." He shook his head.

"Yuki may have controlled my power, but sometimes I stole faces to remind myself of what I was. My true nature. Yesterday proved that. Even Ro—"

"No," Apaay snapped. "Ro was caught between the duty to a

friend and the duty to his people. He doesn't think anything of the sort."

The wind picked up. She shivered and said, "Do you want to know what I see?"

"Why argue? You're going to tell me what you think regardless." He sounded tired. The words held no edge.

"You're right. I am." But her tone softened. "I see someone who was forced to choose between two evils, so he chose the lesser one. I see someone who sacrificed everything to save his brother from a similar, if not worse, fate. I see a boy who only wanted his brother's love, but gained his resentment instead. Your feelings are justified. I don't know how anyone overcomes that."

Numiak looked out. The air was tinged with melancholy. "Do you know what it was like, being made? Everything and everyone I loved had suddenly turned against me. You can imagine what that does to a person." For a time, he was quiet. "We see the end product but never ask ourselves what led to the shaping of someone, what came before, as if there couldn't *be* a before."

She settled beside him, unconsciously sitting closer so his body blocked the wind. "Yes." She was guilty of that, and said as much.

"Well, I gave you enough reasons to think the worst of me."

"Who says I still don't think the worst of you?" Apaay teased, hoping to pull him from his poor mood, but eventually her smile fell at his unresponsiveness, and she acknowledged this wasn't the time for jokes, not when he was hurting. "Can I ask you something?"

Looking down at his hands, he clenched and unclenched them atop his thighs. "You may."

"Why did you take the fall for your brother?" Numiak had to have weighed the likelihood that Kenai would turn on him after learning of their father's supposed murder, so why had he chosen the dark? Where did one draw the line between living for yourself and living for someone else?

He said, "I guess I still hoped there was some way we could overcome the divide between us. I was afraid that, had the decision been given to him, Kenai would have chosen death, and then I'd have no one. If Kenai had discovered he'd killed our father, it would have broken him. The way Kenai loves is . . . too much. It's a need, like water or air. An obsession."

She had glimpsed this torment in Kenai. But he had released her from capture in the end. Whether he acknowledged it or not, a part of Kenai cared for his brother.

"Yesterday in the forge," Numiak said, "I started thinking maybe Ro's men were right. Maybe I am a terrifying, corrupt, immoral, power-hungry demon, and I should get used to it because it will never change. Ro is a good man. One day he'll be Avi, a fine leader to his people. They deserve someone like him."

"They deserve someone like you, too."

"They deserve to be rid of me."

"Don't say things like that. They're not true."

"Aren't they?" Slowly, he turned his head, that black gaze crawling over her.

Apaay swallowed. Whispered, "We have to hope things will turn out for the better."

"Hope." He faced forward again. "It feels like I've been battling that word for the better part of my life." He sounded bitter, which in turn made Apaay's eyes sting.

"There is a saying my people say. *The night is long, but the sun will soon greet you.*" The sentiment fell against her ears like the sun against her face. "I thought of those words when Chena's daughter was born."

And there she was, again bound in that close, hot air of the birthing chamber, terrified for her friend as she took that first step into motherhood. The memory rose as a lump in her throat. "I was thinking, I have spent the last four months in absolute despair, trying to keep my head above water, and yet I was honored with the gift of witnessing new life." The lump thickened. Apaay's breath turned ragged. "That moment," she said, voice lowering to a whisper, "it changed me."

Apaay had understood then, as that wrinkled child entered the world with a gusty cry, that she would never be able to return to the person she had been. She'd had to let that part of herself go in order to make room for what could be, her healing.

"Sometimes," she said, "we feel like we don't deserve hope. But it's what we need, what we all need. Do you know how many times I wanted to give up in the labyrinth, and after? I had to believe there was something better on the other side. Our hardships aren't for naught." Apaay covered his hand with hers. "They shape our lives. They give us proof that we can overcome."

Frowning, Numiak glanced at their hands locked together like threads. Her face warmed the longer he stared, but she did not let go.

She moved to stand behind him. His hair hung untethered down his back. Tentatively, Apaay touched the bottom fringe.

For the second time in so many minutes, he froze.

"May I?" she asked, aware that her request was an intimate affair, should he agree.

A comb appeared in hand, which he passed back to her wordlessly.

Apaay began combing through the tangles, starting at the bottom and working her way to the top. Once free of the knots, the strands of his hair slipped through her fingers like water. "So tell me more about this role I'll need to play in Nur." They were bound for the Southern Territory capital in only a few days.

"Well." His voice roughened. "You will be accompanying me as my servant."

"Your servant. I see." According to Numiak, the Polar Bear Empire followed a strict hierarchy regulated by status, or lack thereof. "And what does the role of a servant entail?"

Relief washed over her when he decided to play along, leaving his black mood somewhere among the pine trees. "Cooking, cleaning, various chores." A pause. "Among other things."

She should have stopped there.

"Like what?" Apaay asked, grateful for the steadiness of her response.

Low laughter reached her ears. "I guess that depends."

The words sent a thrill through her blood. "On what?"

"On what you have in mind."

The comb snagged on a knot near his scalp. Her hands shook

as she gently loosened it with one of the comb's teeth. Numiak's nearness, the heat of his back through the soft hide, the span of his shoulders, and smooth, shifting muscle beneath, all contributed to a general feeling of lightheadedness. The gods were laughing at how Apaay had antagonized a predator who had cornered her.

What did she remember? Sitting on his lap with her legs spread. Pleasure so acute it felt like it was gouging her from the inside.

"Do you want to know what I have in mind?" Numiak asked.

"What is it," she croaked, "that you have in mind?" At last, Apaay worked the final tangle free. She dropped her hand as he turned to face her. His eyes were very dark.

"In the Southern Territory," he said, "a master may require help dressing and undressing. As well, the master may request assistance while he bathes."

Apaay did not think her mouth could get any drier. Her tongue felt like tree bark.

"And I s-suppose, bearing that I am to play a part—" She swallowed. "You might, um, require such assistance?"

The barest curve shaped his lips. "Perhaps."

Her face and chest warmed. She finally gathered the courage, or the insanity, to say, "And what kind of master are you?"

The points of Numiak's canines glinted. "Wolfling," he said, shifting imperceptibly closer. "You are playing a dangerous game."

She was. They both were.

As he reached for her, Apaay took a startled step backward and found her heels at the edge of the platform, the wind buffeting her back. He caught her hand in his, their skin pressed palm to palm, yet without a knife or blood or power at stake, and he took that palm, achingly slow, and drew it to rest over his heart. It beat steady and strong, at an increased tempo.

Apaay licked her lips. Whispered, "I'm going to fall."

Light pooled on his face, as though he held two suns in his eyes. "Do you think I won't catch you?"

Apaay searched his gaze and found a tenderness she had never before seen. "I didn't think I mattered to you that much."

His hand tightened over hers. The blanket of his power draped across her shoulders, and its hum lulled her into a feeling of safety and peace. "You matter to me. Too much, if I'm being honest."

Apaay hadn't known he felt this way. It frightened her even as it warmed her. But he needed to know that he mattered, too.

"Do you know why I returned to the forge to look for you, back in Nigun?" she whispered.

Numiak's gaze remained fixated on her mouth. "Why?"

"Because you are someone worth saving." The statement rang the way only truth could, pure and without artifice. "I believed it then, and I believe it now. You are good, Numiak. You are." Here, now, all walls had come down, all masks ripped away, all defenses gone. In every man, woman, person, was there not a child wanting love?

His throat worked. Fatigue dug grooves around his eyes, but he no longer looked so alone. "Thank you," Numiak whispered hoarsely.

Then Apaay did something she never thought she would do, not even under pain of death. But the past had been forgiven, and she was compelled beyond all reason. And so, drawn in by the scent of woodsmoke against his skin, she brushed a kiss to his bristled cheek, lingering. "Think of me," she said, pulling back and moving toward the stairs.

Apaay was too far away to hear his murmured, "I already do."

36

"Get up." Someone jerked on his arm.

Kenai groaned. His body screamed at the abrupt movement. He wasn't dead. It wouldn't hurt this much if he were. Kenai wondered if that was a good thing.

He cracked open his one eye. The skin around it had swelled, reducing his vision to a murky slit. The fog cleared, lines sharpening, and he stared into the face of the woman he'd fought six, seven days ago? Petite, with one side of her head shaved. He didn't remember much of that night. Or the night after.

Gingerly, Kenai sat up, using the wall at his back for support. He'd spent his nights holed up in the back corner of this alley for weeks now.

The woman examined him with surprising disdain. Her upper lip curled. "Pathetic."

His head ached. His lungs wheezed on the inhale. "Who are you?"

"Someone who is about to make your life infinitely better. Come with me."

In the end, he didn't have much of a choice. She single-handedly dragged his body through the lower slums. Fifteen minutes later, she kicked open a door and dumped him in a single-roomed shack with little else. The place was deserted. It smelled like old piss.

In another life, Kenai would have never allowed this woman to drag him, quite literally, through mud and filth and his own humiliation. He'd once served as a high-ranking member of the Pack, a leader among his people. He'd never suffered such disrespect. But days and weeks stuck on this hunk of floating rock had pummeled the fight right out of him. He'd finally accepted a hard truth.

Yuki was not coming for him. She had never planned on meeting him here. She had sent him away. Again. She did not think he was worthy enough to stand by her side.

"I've been keeping tabs on you," said the woman, standing with the wall at her back and her legs braced shoulder-width apart. "And I'm getting tired of watching your ass get beaten into the dirt every night."

Funny. So was he.

He studied her in much the same way she did him: sizing up an opponent. "Why do you care?"

"I don't, actually." She shrugged. "But I think we can be of some use to one another."

Kenai put a hand to his pounding head. Pressure throbbed behind his eye. He was definitely dehydrated, but the nearest clean stream was a five-mile walk westward.

"What's your name?" she asked.

Only years of military experience wiped the panic from his expression. If this woman was indeed wolf Unua, as he suspected, she would recognize his given name. Kenai of the Wolf Kingdom. Traitor.

"Masuk," he said. The name Apaay had gifted him in the labyrinth, the name of a man from her village who had shown great resilience in life. At the time, Kenai had accepted that name because he wanted to see himself the way she saw him: strong. It was laughable how weak he truly was, how weak he had always been. The truth was, Numiak had always been stronger than him. He'd endured their father's hatred his entire life, and he never once broke.

The woman quirked an eyebrow. "Well, Masuk. I've asked around about you. No one knows where you came from. I suppose you could have been dropped with the mainland shipment, but that only occurs every three months, and it's still another month away. You're clearly wolf Unua, but I smell polar bear Unua on your clothes. That's unusual." Her suspicion morphed into something he couldn't quite read. A flicker of recognition? But no, that was impossible. "Are you in league with Nanuq?"

His head snapped up. "What do you know of Nanuq?"

Another shrug. "That he's starting a war—or finishing it, rather." Her scraggly eyebrows snapped together. "I hear you're looking for recruits. I can find you some. Of course, I'd need a favor in return."

Kenai considered the offer. Now that he could study the woman without risk of a fist crushing his cheek, he wondered. Could she have been sentenced to the Banished Lands—by him? What were the odds? "That depends on the favor."

She nodded, as if she'd expected this. "My partner and I are looking for someone who can disappear easily. Our last man found his unfortunate end face-down in the surf. We're one man short for an upcoming raid, and we need an incentive."

The pieces began to lock together as the larger image became clear. "You need me as bait."

The woman smiled. Once, she may have been pretty, had the island not taken its toll on her. "If that's what you want to call it, then sure."

It was exactly the sort of bad decision that would end with him dead in a ditch. In fact, it was practically guaranteed in a place like this. "No, thank you." He stood, albeit wobbly. He hadn't come all this way to be used and discarded. He'd had enough of that treatment from Yuki. But he wouldn't dwell on that now. Anyway, if she'd abandoned him here, what was the point of finding recruits? It's not like he could escape this island anyway. Maybe it's what he deserved, in the end.

"Where will you go?" The question reached him as his hand curved over the doorknob. "You can't leave the island. Will you return to the fights? What will that solve? What are you running from?"

His knuckles tightened. All this time, he thought he'd been running to something: a life with the one he loved. But if Yuki didn't care for him as he feared, what else had he misjudged in his past? Was it possible he had misjudged Numiak, too?

He winced. Too painful to think about. Numiak, their father's murder, the invasion, Kenai's betrayal of their people—it was one snarling knot, and Kenai could not think of one thread without his fingers touching upon another. He was confused. He had believed the world's forces to act against him, when in reality he had built the environment he now found himself in, one betrayal, one lie, at a time. The turmoil lived inside him, his organs, his breath, his skin. Who was he, truly? And was it not too late to learn the truth?

The woman was right. He had nothing and no one. He was caged here, wasting his days prowling the shore.

At last, Kenai turned around. "I don't need recruits. I need a way off this island."

Her lips pursed. "I can make that happen."

"You didn't tell me your name."

"Oh." The woman laughed. "You'll get that when you've proven your worth."

37

"I want to thank you all for your presence. As you know, war will soon be upon us, so time is of the essence."

On the morning of Apaay and Numiak's departure, everyone gathered in the war chamber: the Avi, Ro, Kaan, Umiq, the clan leaders, and, Apaay noted with surprise, Kimmir, who sat on Ro's left. The last she'd seen of the spy, he'd been near death. That he had survived was a miracle, but she was glad to see him well.

The white plumage framing the Avi's collar shifted like grass in the wind. Although his face was unmarred by lines, Apaay knew he was many centuries old. "There has been a change in plans. Ro and I have agreed it's too dangerous to communicate via messages. The skies are being watched."

Everyone looked to Ro for confirmation. He, in turn, looked to Apaay out of reluctance to make eye contact with Numiak. The past few days had been rife with tension. Ro had not apologized for his behavior. Numiak, consequently, ignored him.

Ro said, "As an alternative, I've set you up with a contact in the lower city, a weaver who goes by the name of Desna."

"Is this woman polar bear Unua?" the clan leader of Unua relations, Urlag, demanded.

"She is," Ro said in a tone that demanded no argument. "She

was Kimmir's contact during his years in Nanuq's army. She is trustworthy."

Urlag grunted. "It's not right."

Ro continued on as if the man hadn't spoken.

"If I need to touch base," he said to Apaay, "I'll send a message through Desna. Likewise, you should use her if you need to send a message to me."

"Did you hear that?" she asked Numiak.

He nodded vaguely. Still ignoring Ro. Apaay rolled her eyes.

"If anything goes wrong prior to your departure date, anything at all, you get out," said the Avi, who looked to Numiak before fixing that golden gaze on Apaay for a much longer interval.

The Avi had received a summons. Nanuq requested his presence—and the presence of his children—at Nur, the Southern Territory capital. He wished for the North's leaders to gather and discuss the future of their land. It was a trap, no doubt, but it offered the perfect cover for their mission.

During their week-long stay, the Face Stealer would pose as Ro. Apaay would pose as his servant. With their disguises, they would infiltrate the palace that was Nanuq's home. They would find any and all information related to Nanuq's movements. They would not stop until it was done.

Her stomach twisted uncomfortably. If someone had told her a year ago she would purposefully place herself in grave peril, Apaay would have laughed. But the fear was too great. She hadn't room for laughter, only dread.

Another hour of discussion, and the meeting reached its close. Once the Avi and his clan leaders filed out of the room, only Apaay, Numiak, Ro, and Kaan remained.

Apaay thought, *What if this is the last time I see my friends?*

She thought, *What if I do not come back?*

Silence encompassed the room. Ro folded his hands across his lap. He said roughly, "Take the cairn east of the city. It will drop you a few miles north of Nur, near the main road." His attention flitted to Numiak, then away.

Numiak nodded stiffly. "Noted."

"This is ridiculous," Kaan snapped, tossing up a hand. "We are preparing for war, and you two are acting like a bunch of emotionally stunted children." She huffed. "Ro, do you apologize for not standing up for Numiak when the time called for it, and for acting like a spineless coward in the face of it all?"

Ro, frowning, looked from Kaan, to Numiak, back to Kaan. "Yes? I mean—" He nodded. "Yes." Assured.

"Numiak, do you forgive my brother for his oversight, and for his aversion to conflict, even though you acted like an emotionless prick because you lack the capacity to talk about your feelings?"

He blinked, eyes wide. "Yes."

"Then it's settled." Kaan clapped her hands once. "Now say your goodbyes. Preferably while I'm still young."

Apaay was impressed. Never underestimate Kaan in her ability to cut to the heart of an issue.

"I'm sorry," Ro said. He looked far too grave, as if this might be the most important apology he would ever make.

"I know." Numiak's throat bobbed. "I'm sorry, too." There was a silence, then: "Spineless coward."

Ro's lips twitched. "Emotionless prick. Don't do anything I wouldn't do."

"Which is to say," said Kaan, "don't do anything stupid." Her smile, close-mouthed and strained, belied her carefree tone.

"Now when have I done anything stupid?" He attempted a grin. It faded as quickly as it appeared.

"Are you asking me to count the ways? Because I will."

Something softened in his expression. "I know."

Kaan bit her lip and glanced away, blinking rapidly.

Ro and Numiak clasped hands, then pulled each other close. It was a gesture of deep friendship, one that had spanned centuries and bloodshed and war. Apaay couldn't help but feel it was also a goodbye.

Next, Kaan caught Numiak in a tight embrace, her head tucked under his chin, the black of his hair mixing with the white of hers.

"Stay safe," the weapons master whispered.

Apaay expected him to reply with, *I am very hard to kill*, but that was no longer true now that his heart had been returned to him. He only said, "I will," and pulled away.

Kaan then turned to Apaay. She hugged with her entire body, and Apaay thought of how lucky she was to know this strong, passionate, courageous woman, and to call her a friend.

"Be safe," Kaan whispered into her ear. "Promise me."

She hooked her chin over the taller woman's shoulder. This was Numiak's family. And it was her family, too. "I promise."

"Look after each other," Ro said as he drew her into an embrace. "Numi?"

The four of them turned toward the small, frightened voice. Mika stood in the doorway, eyes huge with confusion, her doll clutched in one hand. "You're going away again?"

Numiak knelt before his niece, cradling her small face in his hands. "Not for long."

Her mouth trembled. "I don't want you to go."

"I know, sweetheart."

He pulled Mika into his arms, one hand cupping the back of her head. The girl stared at Apaay over his shoulder. She didn't cry though. Didn't make a sound.

"Remember what I told you?" he asked gently.

Mika nodded. "I'll be strong. I'll be a warrior—like you."

"I'll come back for you," he whispered against her cheek. "I promise."

← →

They arrived by cairn a few miles north of Nur, as Ro had promised. They'd spent the last few days outlining every component of this plan, from the layout of the capital, to the names of Nanuq's closest advisors, to a list of those they could trust. A simple enough answer: no one. They could trust absolutely no one.

"What if we're unable to meet Desna during the week?" Apaay asked as they picked their way through the shrubbery bordering the wide dirt road leading south. "Wouldn't it be better to meet her prior to entering the palace?" Ro had instructed them to enter the palace first, then contact Desna later in the week, but if anything went wrong during their mission, she was their way out of the city.

"We stick to Ro's instructions."

"But—"

"Apaay." He pulled her to a halt. "Ro has acted as the Avi's general for decades. He knows what he's doing. Kimmir would have never survived long in Nanuq's army otherwise. If he says we wait, then we wait. We have no idea who lives in the city, what faces Nanuq's scouts might wear. We follow the orders we've been given."

After a long moment, she nodded. "As soon as possible, we meet with Desna."

"Agreed." He glanced over his shoulder. Gaps in the brush revealed movement beyond—travelers on the road. "We should probably change. We'll reach Nur soon."

They already wore the necessary clothes, and Numiak had colored their hair white prior to departure. Apaay wore nondescript arm and leg wrappings, whereas Numiak wore black, a color that distinguished him as heir. He had exchanged his summer maq for a parka to combat the approaching winter chill. It was of high quality, the seams stitched in patterns that drew the eye, the front slit allowing air to move about his legs. Apaay's parka was noticeably shoddy, but that was to be expected of a lowly servant, as Numiak had explained. All that remained were their faces.

Closing her eyes, Apaay drew the thread of glowing white power from the pit of her stomach. Bones shifted beneath her skin—a painless, if uncomfortable—process. She widened the narrow shape of her face, softened the jaw, and gave her skin a patchy coloring, as if chafed from the cold. Young, bland, forgettable. It would work.

Next, she turned her attention to Numiak. Resting her fingertips against his chin, she brought to mind Ro's facial features. It wasn't necessary, to touch, but it quickened the process. Large, rounded eyes. A mouth that spoke of kindness and soft things.

Apaay stepped back, satisfied with her work. No one would ever be able to tell the difference, save the lack of wheelchair. Numiak had assured her Nanuq did not know the permanence of Ro's injury.

"Remember what we spoke of."

Apaay nodded. "We stick to the plan."

"We stick together."

"Together," she agreed.

They followed the road south, merging with a large group of people that included Nanuq's kirn and a variety of merchants. The Southern Territory was bare of trees, but not in the way of the tundra. The multitude of dead stumps littering the pocked soil told a story of what had once been. Where were the migratory birds? Where were the hare and lemmings? And why, *why* had the ancient whitewoods been felled? Did Nanuq not understand the harm that stemmed from this drastic of a change?

The Raven had informed them the wildlife were fleeing north. Here lay the evidence.

The Polar Bear Empire possessed the largest army of the Unua nations, with Nur home to the largest military base. The kirn had a deadened look to them, like a fire gone cold. They were built with heavy shoulders, squat thighs. Their booted feet slapped the ground like thunder.

Sun-darkened skin and narrow black eyes glowed beneath the open-jawed polar bear heads enveloping their skulls. White pelts curved around their necks and shoulders, cascaded down their backs.

They were amassing.

They were readying themselves for war.

Numiak squeezed the back of Apaay's neck in comfort. "Steady," he murmured.

Eventually, the road grew so crowded Apaay could not take two steps without bumping into someone else. Carts laden with piles of stone trundled forward. Women bearing a child on each hip followed their husbands, who carried furs or meats or weapons for trade. Only she and Numiak bore the white hair of the Owl Clan.

A canyon loomed ahead, with two vast gates set at the base of the divide, open to the flood of travelers. Apaay and Numiak slipped through without notice, carrying on as the road squeezed into a thread of a path. The canyon walls rose so high they could not be scaled. The path sloped deeper.

At last, the walls opened up. Apaay hadn't known what to expect of Nur. She thought it might be a dull, soulless place. In truth, it sparkled, as if the sprawl of buildings had been sculpted from the glittering quartz veins trapped in the rock. If she squinted hard enough, she could make out a blue sliver in the distance: the place where canyon met sea, waves beating against coastal walls.

"There it is," Numiak said.

Built atop a plateau in the city's center, Nanuq's palace sprouted from the surrounding city like an overgrown weed. Curved walls of pale gray stone encompassed a vast area. Sunlight pierced its deeply slanted rooftops, which were hewn from metal. The majority of Nur's roofs were, actually. Apaay couldn't fully appreciate the vista due to the distracting nature of the glinting backdrop.

They rejoined the surge of people. Aside from the roofs, the city itself was all rock, with tiny square windows made of colored glass. It smelled like a forge: metal and fire. Everyone carried a weapon, whether it be a sword or dagger or club, the occasional nigana or talq. The city was full of eyes. How many were Nanuq's kirn?

They traveled initially through the lower city, a place where people eked out a living through craft or trade, before reaching the upper city, a sanctuary of clear, tidy rows of homes, the reek of unwashed bodies exchanged for fragrant perfume.

It took them nearly an hour to reach the palace gates. Ten men guarded the entrance, with additional forces detected atop the wall. Apaay lowered her eyes as she'd been instructed to beforehand. She, a servant, was of the lowest status in polar bear Unua society. She could not speak unless given permission to. She was to remain unnoticed unless someone had need of her. The idea of controlling someone else's life in this respect made her stomach pitch uncomfortably. She understood then how truly isolated the Analak were compared to the rest of the world.

One of the ten armed men flanking the gates stepped forward. A heavy sword of black metal hung at his hip. White fur sprouted from his shoulders. "State your purpose."

"I am Ro of the Owl Clan, and this is my servant. We have been invited to meet with Nanuq." He passed over the invitation.

The man examined the seal closely. With a nod, he returned the summons. "In order to pass beyond the gates, we must ensure your intentions are true. As such, all guests are required to consume ilumi."

Numiak tensed, though it was a subtle thing. Apaay didn't know what ilumi meant. Something unwanted.

The guard passed a small vial to Numiak, who said, "Of course." He poured it into his mouth.

The guard said, "Are you Ro of the Owl Clan, heir to the Avi?"

"Yes."

"Do you wish to harm the Great Bear, his kingdom, or his subjects?"

"No."

The man turned to Apaay. He passed her a vial as well. She hesitated and looked to Numiak, who nodded.

Apaay downed the contents, expecting a foreign taste in her mouth, but it was only water. She suspected Numiak had tampered with it.

The guard repeated the questions. "Are you servant to Ro of the Owl Clan?"

"Yes."

"Do you wish to harm the Great Bear, his kingdom, or his subjects?"

"No."

The guard waved to someone atop the wall. The gates groaned open, the mechanisms of the interlocking teeth screeching harshly. Once she and Numiak had passed through, they slammed shut with finality behind them.

Accompanied by one of the guards, they crossed a large courtyard, climbed the steps leading to the entrance doors, and stepped inside. Apaay had seen much on her travels, but Nanuq's palace was something else entirely. The floor, a shiny, reflective black, captured the illumination of those lamps interspersed throughout the room. Everything was polished to a high shine. The space, vast and echoing. Cold. Her entire village could fit into this hall.

The entrance transitioned into a larger space—"The throne

room," announced the guard—with two parallel rows of columns running the length of the rectangular room. At the end awaited an empty dais crowned by a stone chair of spectacular proportions—eerily similar to Yuki's throne in the labyrinth.

A side door led them to additional quarters dripping with opulence. Yet as shiny and glittering and dazzling as the palace looked, Apaay couldn't help but notice its flaws. How disjointed everything seemed. There was furniture, ornately carved and plenty of it, but it lacked purpose. What need did Nanuq have for so many chairs if no one utilized them? How did the staff warm the space if it was so inefficiently large, the ceiling too far away to see clearly? This was a place from beyond the North.

As they rounded a corner, something hanging on the wall caught Apaay's eye. "What is that?" She leaned in for a closer inspection. Slender, tube-like in shape. It gleamed like a metal trap.

"It's called a firearm," Numiak said. "It's a weapon. Do you remember the white powder that blew up Nigun's forge? It's used in firearms." He pointed to the circular opening at the end of the tube-like structure. "The force of the ignition projects objects called bullets from the opening."

Apaay couldn't help but stare. She had never heard of something so vile. That it was hanging on Nanuq's palace wall reaffirmed his idealization of man, his desire to shed his polar bear skins permanently.

The guard led them up three flights of stairs, down a hall with deep red walls. "These are your quarters," he said, pushing open a set of wooden double doors. The bedroom consisted of an absurdly massive bed, a divider that shielded a small bathing area, and a handful of cushioned chairs. "Your servant will arrive momentarily."

"That won't be necessary," Numiak said. "My servant is more than capable of attending to me."

The guard inclined his head. "I understand. However, Nanuq insists that his own staff serves guests."

Numiak didn't respond. Perhaps as an heir might do when unsatisfied with the answer he has received.

When the guard had gone, Numiak locked the door. Apaay's

attention caught on a small bedding pallet in the corner, a blanket folded atop. Numiak noticed it as well.

"You can have the bed," he told her. "I'll take the floor."

"I'll take the floor. It will be too suspicious if I take the bed." The pallet was too small for him anyway.

"Then we'll both take the floor," he said unhelpfully.

The sound of a lock giving way halted their conversation.

A woman dressed in a filthy, sac-like garment entered. She smiled at Numiak, a pretty, albeit bland, smile. Long, tangled hair was pulled back from her face. Once, she might have been beautiful. Her eyes were old though, her posture sloped and uneven. "Apologies. The Great Bear requests the doors remain unlocked."

"Then why have a lock in the first place?" Numiak countered.

The woman's smile dimmed. Apaay widened her eyes at him from behind the woman's back, a silent, *What are you doing?* If their objective was to avoid attention, these combative questions weren't helping. Luckily, the woman brushed aside his inquiry. "My name is Aniirlit. I will be overseeing your comfort for the duration of your stay."

He lifted his chin. "I am Ro, and this is Apaay."

She took in his dusty appearance with a complete lack of concern. "Dinner will convene within the hour. I'll collect hot water for your bath while your servant undresses you." She left, yet kept the door ajar upon her exit.

At the word *undress*, Apaay glanced at Numiak to find him baring his teeth in a wolfish grin.

With a sound of disgust, she tossed a pillow at him, which he caught before it hit his face. "I'm not undressing you," she hissed, "so if you want to bathe, do so yourself."

"Ah, but if I wait, Aniirlit will return. Then you'll have to undress me. You wouldn't want to expose our cover, would you?"

Apaay squared herself against the lashing panic in her breast. A restless thing it was, unable to be quieted in his presence. "If you want to expose our cover, that is not my problem."

He sobered, tossing the pillow back onto the bed. "We'll do it your way then."

Aniirlit returned with two other servants, each carrying large buckets full of steaming water, and fresh towels. They filled the wooden basin, then left Numiak to wash as Apaay rifled through his pack for clean clothes.

"What outfit should you wear?" she asked, spreading his clothes out on the bed. The blanket—cloth, not fur—had been woven into an interesting pattern of blue and white shapes. She ran a finger across it curiously.

Water splashed as he shifted in the tub. "Find the parka with the ceremonial collar. I'll wear it with the black arm wrappings."

Apaay set his clothes aside. She tried not to think of how thin a line they toed. There was so little room for error in their plan. One misstep, and it would all go up in smoke.

When Numiak had finished washing, he grabbed the towel she'd hung over the divider and emerged with it wrapped around his waist. Water beaded on his arms and chest, and dripped from the ends of his hair. He stalked toward the bed on soundless feet. Apaay couldn't stop staring at his legs. They had always been concealed by his trousers. Now she noted their well-muscled forms, the defined calves, dark hair plastered to his skin. The sight of his bare feet sent an illicit shock through her.

They studied one another from opposite sides of the bed. Apaay's traitorous gaze drifted to his chest. His nipples had hardened in the cooler air. The towel hugged his solid waist. Water coursed in rivulets across the musculature of his abdomen and clung to the trail of dark hair running down his stomach.

When her attention returned to his face, it felt as if all the air had been sucked from her lungs.

"So you will stare at me half-naked—" His attention latched onto where she'd caught her lower lip between her teeth. "—but you will not undress me."

She swallowed to bring moisture to her mouth. "No harm in looking."

"And when a look becomes a touch?" His voice deepened and slowed, pouring over her. "What then?"

Apaay loosed a constricted breath. Her heart pitched forward, tripping over its own rhythm, for he was coming around the bed. He was moving like a fox slipping through underbrush, without haste. Numiak's torso, the expanse of flawless brown skin, filled her vision, his chest almost touching her nose. His skin smelled like rain on hot stone.

What then?

Apaay didn't know. But she thought she was ready to find out.

He dropped something into her hand. "Your turn."

Apaay glanced down in confusion. It was a towel. Right. Her turn to bathe.

"Unless you'd like me to join you?" he suggested, grinning.

Apaay darted behind the barrier and out of sight.

She discovered that Numiak had replenished the wooden tub with fresh, clean water. Steam rolled across its surface.

Apaay undressed and sank into the bath with a grateful sigh, all that grit and dirt and sweat disintegrating in the heat. She couldn't remember when she'd last had the luxury of a hot bath, and thus took her sweet time scrubbing herself clean.

After, she rested her head against the lip of the tub. This was nice. Peaceful, if only for a moment. A brief reprieve before reality intruded.

"Wolfling."

Apaay jerked, sloshing water over the sides of the tub. How long had she been out? "Yes?"

There was a pause. "Just making sure you're still awake." He sounded close, as if he were leaning against the other side of the divide.

"I am," she gritted out.

"Mm." Another pause. "Let me know if you need help bathing."

Apaay slipped beneath the water and blocked him out.

38

They were perhaps twenty miles southeast of the capital. With the dusk of waning summer heavy on her tongue, Ila crouched beside Malina in the darkened forest, bracken tangled thickly around their legs. It was cold enough to snap bone. Soon, they would need to find warmer clothing.

"There he is," Malina said, pointing through the trees to a heavyset man sharpening his sword near the fire. The commanders of Nanuq's army wore fanged necklaces pulled tight around their throats—the teeth of their slain enemies. And this man's necklace was crowded with teeth of every imaginable size and shape.

Easily two thousand kirn occupied the wooded clearing. Tents of pale hide rustled, and the many fires glowed like eyes. The open jaws of their slain brothers curved over the tops of the men's skulls, just as bone masks concealed the upper potions of their faces. For the past two days, Ila and her pack sisters had closely monitored this camp and its occupants. It was almost time to move.

On one side of the camp, men practiced sparring in a heavily shaded area. Their motions lacked grace. Rather, they dealt strikes of substance, brutalized swings that contained the raw power to remove one's head with the stone clubs they wielded. Their wide-legged trousers flapped, and strips of fur hung from their belts. Ila watched a pair move through a pattern of exercises and tucked this information into the back of her mind for later analysis. No detail was too unimportant. No element overlooked.

Malina squeezed Ila's arm, signaling that Tipki and Saniraq had howled their song from their location deep in the forest.

The camp snapped to alertness in an instant. Men on their feet, clubs and metal weapons raised. Men stumbling from their tents, half-dressed, shivering. And wolfsong, pouring into every crack and crevasse.

At last, their commander stood, scanning the area, gripping the hilt of his sword.

He dipped his chin at two men. "Go."

They dashed into the darkening forest, in the direction of the howling. Malina remained tense at her side. This next stage in the plan must unfold in proper order. When Malina signaled the second howl, they transformed into wolves themselves.

The first shift came from within. The mind of a human switched with that of an animal. Something popped in Ila's legs. Her skin throbbed with odd pulsations, the bones stretching, the muscles and tendons rearranging themselves. Her teeth lengthened. Her eyes adjusted with sharp clarity. Four legs, two triangular ears, and a tail.

Be safe, Ila said through the mind-speak. Malina touched her snout to her ear and was off, leaping west, leaving her companion to crouch low in the thicket, watching the commander stalk the camp.

Minutes later, Malina's wolfsong poured through the connection. The commander sent an additional two men into the woods. Perfect. Ila watched them race into the trees before she followed.

As a single unit, the pack spread out, tracking the men. Their long, lupine legs ate up the distance, aiding them in slipping under high brush. Using the mind-speak, images rose in their minds of each pack member's location. Located farther west, Tipki and Saniraq waited to ambush the first two soldiers near a stream. Malina, a mile ahead, had already taken down one of the men. That left Ila with the slowest kirn, a large, robust man with an uneven gait.

She stalked him from a distance. Blood flowed through this body of instinct, for she was the earth and the earth was her, fatted off what the land grew. The soldier stomped a winding path through the old-growth forest, lifting his nose every so often to catch the scent of what he believed to be his prey. Then the wind changed direction, alerting him to Ila's location, and he froze.

With a burst of speed, she closed the distance. The man glanced over his shoulder, tripped, but caught himself. Between one step and the next, his skin split and sprouted white fur. His shoulders stretched. His limbs thickened, and he lumbered to a halt, turning.

Ila sprung. The bear lunged, swiping one massive paw, and the force of its blow could be felt in the rush of air as it passed, the immense strength in those powerful haunches. Teeth snapped near her shoulder. Ila dove between its legs, using her superior agility to avoid its crushing bite.

But she was still growing accustomed to her wolf skins, tuning into her other senses to compensate for her lack of hearing, and so she didn't sense the bear shifting position.

A blow sent Ila crashing against a tree. Agony blasted through her body, and she whined. The bear charged. She stumbled in an attempt to stand, yet went down again, one paw buckling beneath her weight.

Malina darted from the brush and launched herself onto the bear's back. Her snout dug into the back of its neck, and she tossed her head left and right, tearing into flesh. In one sliver of an instant, Ila took its throat.

The bear shook its head in an attempt to dislodge her. Ila sank her teeth deeper into its gullet, hot blood spilling over her tongue. It roared, but it was a feeble thing. Its front paws hit the earth. Its legs buckled, the great white mass crashing down like a snowdrift from above.

In death, the man returned to his human state. In life, Ila and Malina remained as they were. They had survived, and they would do so again.

An hour later, Ila and her pack buried their enemies. They dug a pit many miles from camp and dumped the bodies. After, they washed in the stream. The icy mountain runoff ran red with kirn blood. Ila scrubbed her hands thoroughly, her mind stinging with brutal clarity. If she had killed a man, enemy though he might have been, what else would she do in pursuit of restoring her broken nation?

Fingers snapped near her face. Ila startled, focusing on Malina. *What?*

"I asked if you were ready," the older woman said.

Ila wondered if there was such a thing as ready. In her mind, there was *then*, and there was *now*. The only difference was how far she had gone, and how far she might go.

Come, said Ila. And, reaching down to the pile of polar bear furs, she slipped into the skins of her enemy.

← →

They coated their skin in mud and dung. The wettest, thickest, foulest substance they could find, smearing it under their clothes, in the crooks of their elbows, behind their ears, overlaying every patch of skin save their eyes. It was not the most pleasant disguise, but it would help mask their scents from Nanuq's soldiers, just as the bulk of these uniforms helped mask their figures. Polar bear Unua, while sturdy, were not particularly tall.

Animal musk permeated the camp, and man, always man. Their stink and their sweat, the ground pounded hard from their boots. Ila's heart beat erratically. She held herself with high tension.

Tipki and Saniraq strode into camp first and headed straight for the commander. They would inform him the wolves had been wounded, yet had unfortunately managed to escape—cause for the scent of wolf Unua blood on their clothes. Ila and Malina settled around one of the fires, joining a few men who sharpened their weapons in the orange glow. No one spared them a glance, which meant the mud-dung substance was doing a well-enough job of concealing their true scents. So long as they didn't draw attention to themselves, they would live to see the morrow.

If only their plan had worked.

One of the soldiers lifted his head. Ila was thankful the masks only covered the eyes and nose, otherwise she wouldn't have been able to read lips. "What's that smell?"

The men began to sniff the air curiously. Eventually, all eyes fell to Malina.

The woman froze.

"You smell like shit," said one man.

Ila's eyes flared behind her mask in warning. She was well aware of her pack sister's short temper. And it wasn't as if the man was wrong. Malina did smell awful, as did she, as did all of them.

Ila glanced around for Tipki and Saniraq. They busied themselves with erecting a tent, and thus did not notice the disaster waiting to explode in their faces. It was probably better that way. She couldn't imagine these men standing up for one another in light of a harmless insult.

A skinny man with an ugly scar running the length of his jaw sneered in repulsion. "Haven't you heard of bathing, Kil? Do us all a favor and go wash." The man went so far as to kick Malina off the log. He laughed, as did the others. Their repulsive, fanged teeth on display, bits of old meat stuck between. Their breath was rank as a corpse.

Slowly, Malina stood. Always, they must act with intention. There was no reason for uncertainty as a kirn of the Empire. These were their friends, their fellow men of combat. Should Malina do anything but what these men expected of her, should she question them in any way, they would grow suspicious. Although surely the man Malina posed as would talk back? Wouldn't it be more suspicious if she didn't?

Obviously, Malina couldn't wash. The men watched her closely as she trotted off, disappearing into the woods. Most likely, she'd keep a low profile, allow the men to forget about this incident, before reentering the camp.

Unfortunately, that left Ila alone. She leaned closer to the fire, ignoring the men, keeping her talq near at hand. They had not been here for five minutes and already Ila wondered if this had been a mistake. They still had to survive dinner—and the night.

When the soldiers lined up for their meal, Ila waited until the majority had received their food before joining the line herself. As soon as she received her bowl, she returned to the fire. Across camp, Tipki had become entangled in what appeared to be a heated conversation with a younger man. His fist shot out. Tipki managed to avoid the first punch, but the second knocked her in the jaw, threatening to tear off her mask.

Someone shoved the offender to the side—Malina. He swung at her in retaliation. She sidestepped, tripped him, and laughed with the rest of the kirn as the man fell face-first into a mud puddle. Ila stared with growing horror. What was Malina doing? And Tipki, for that matter?

It was the strangest thing she'd ever seen. A miracle, really. Malina offered the man a hand, which he took, and she hauled him out of the mud with a laugh, slapping him on the back. Then the man received his food, and Malina received hers, and they went their separate ways.

"That was too damn close," Malina said, plopping down onto the log across from Ila. She smelled as wretched as ever. "I'm getting too old for this."

The shadows lengthened as the fires burned low. The men, after consuming their meals, retreated to their tents and bedrolls. Then: encroaching darkness, and wavering air above hot coals.

Wake up, Ila thought, but this was no dream.

There was so much left to lose.

39

The kitchen housed one of the largest hearths Apaay had ever seen, and as such, the air was stifling. Long tables piled high with fruits and vegetables extended from end to end in the room of mud-packed walls. Clay pots holding various sauces, meats, roots, and other foods Apaay had never heard of sat in the coals, simmering in the low heat. They were the constant. Everything else was chaos.

Apaay had managed to wedge herself into a corner of the room, away from the thickest of the activity. Servants chopped meat, poured drinks, carried dishes, scrubbed pots, all to a constant chatter of laughter, complaints, and palace gossip. It was so different from what Apaay was used to. One seal, butchered, her family encircling the carcass, blood coating her hands, salt heavy in her nostrils.

Aniirlit thrust a pitcher of water in her direction. Strands of hair curled away from the woman's face due to the humidity. "We need another pair of hands to refill drinks. Can you do that?"

Apaay stared down at the pitcher as her heart began to pound. Keeping out of sight ensured she would not attract unwanted attention, and she had hoped to eavesdrop on the staff. "Well—"

"Let me rephrase that. Go out into the hall. Stand against the wall and watch their glasses. When the water gets low, refill them. All right?" She began pushing Apaay toward a narrow staircase that led to the dining room one level above, which was currently filled with guests from various corners of the North, all brought here at Nanuq's behest.

Apaay quickly turned toward her. "But—"

"Go," Aniirlit snapped.

Apaay climbed the stairs grudgingly. The dining room—what the guard had called the throne room during her initial tour of the palace—had been transformed for guest arrival and now housed an enormous table built to sit at least sixty. Ivory cloth swathed the walls and columns, giving the illusion of moonlight pooling from the ceiling, along the towering, rounded windows, though the sun would not disappear completely for another month. Apaay planted herself in one corner next to a life-sized statue in the shape of a caribou. Others dotted the space as well, foxes and wolverines and, hidden in the rafters, owls and geese. The black, reflective floor had been covered entirely in polar bear pelts.

As directed, she stood against the wall. Watched the glasses. She did not give people reason to seek her out, yet Apaay sensed the guests' curiosity. Her white hair attracted attention. Her skin grew damp the longer she stood there, frozen, completely out of her element.

Someone touched her arm. Apaay jumped, sloshing water onto her feet.

It was a young man, a servant with kind eyes. He gestured to his own pitcher of water. *Move*, he mouthed.

Apaay nodded, her throat tightening. She followed him to the table and began refilling glasses, watching him from the corner of her eye to ensure she completed the task correctly. The stone walls gave life to whispers. Maybe that explained why no one spoke. Their eyes continually flitted to the shut doors at the end of the room, the vacant dais, the statues. Nanuq had yet to arrive.

The white of Numiak's hair drew her attention. He sat in the middle of the table between two kirn, who were discernable by their open-jawed hoods. When Numiak sought her gaze, a smile ghosted across his mouth and was gone.

The number of guests that did not identify as polar bear Unua was actually quite small. Numiak, of course, acted as the supposed Owl Clan representative. A trio of women from the Seal Colonies, their heads shaved, occupied one end of the table. Apaay stared in shock. She'd met these women before. They'd tracked her into Talguk. One of them had plunged a blade into Apaay's gut. *May your death come slowly.* Were they here on Yuki's behest?

The only nations not present were the Caribou Nomads— Apaay wondered if Nanuq knew they were no longer supplying him weapons—and the Wolf Kingdom, for obvious reasons, though no one would suspect a wolf Unua sat right under their noses, wearing the face of another man. The Analak weren't present either, thankfully. She assumed Nanuq did not see them as a threat, considering their neutral standpoint in the war prior. The remaining guests were polar bear Unua, merchants and tradesmen, and Nanuq's kirn, whose numbers dwarfed the rest by an uncomfortable amount.

A horn blew high and clear from the palace interior. Apaay hurried back to her station against the wall as everyone's attention turned toward the doors. She prepared herself. She breathed.

The great slabs of wood opened with an animal's squeal. A man and a woman glided through side by side, their footsteps in sync. They were slight things, with deep brown skin and oily, glowing eyes. White pelts rested heavy on their shoulders.

Everyone rose to their feet. The man wore a necklace of teeth that cut into his neck, all canines. The woman, although lovely, appeared to be no warmer than a block of ice. They sat flanking the empty chair at the head of the table.

At last, a third person entered the hall. The image Apaay had constructed in her mind—a terror, a beast—loomed forth, but it was for naught. For Nanuq was a man, no less and no more.

He wasn't exactly tall, nor was he imposing or well-muscled. In actuality, he was rather pretty despite his middle age, especially his eyes, which were ringed by dark eyelashes, and eyelids that had a hooded, dreamy look about them. If she had not been aware of his entrance, he would have certainly been overlooked. He walked with one shoulder hitched higher than the other, as if from an old injury. His black hair, untouched by gray, fell free around his face.

When Nanuq reached the table, there was a collective intake of breath. Apaay tightened her hold on the pitcher and waited for him to speak.

"Friends." Another surprise. His voice reminded her of music, lovely and coaxing. "Welcome. It is an honor to share your company, and to open my home to you. These are my children, the ikov and ikovna, and they, too, welcome you." He gestured to the man and woman sitting on either side of him, having used the titles that signified the male and female heirs of the Polar Bear Empire, which Ro had informed Apaay of prior to departure from Sinika. "I imagine you are hungry, for most of you have traveled far. There will be plenty of time for introductions later. I look forward to your company this week as we discuss the future of the North, and how our ties to one another might strengthen it. Now please, eat."

On cue, staff members filed out bearing plates heaped with food. They served the first course and took their leave. Silence steeped the room, but eventually, low conversation sprung from the table. The guests may have smiled, they may have laughed, but their mouths did not match what their eyes so plainly said: they would rather be anywhere but inside these high walls.

For the first twenty minutes, Nanuq observed the conversation. His children picked at their food without speaking or looking at anyone, though his daughter, Apaay noticed, kept sneaking glances at Numiak. Apaay refilled water glasses, lingering as long as she dared, trying to pluck various points of information from people's mouths. No one mentioned the war. They stuck to safer topics. Trade. The difficult winter ahead.

After the third course was served, Nanuq directed his attention to Numiak. "And how is your family, Ro?"

"They are well, thank you."

"And your father? How is he?"

"I believe I said he is well." He set down his knife, met the man's direct gaze, and smiled.

Nanuq leaned back in his seat, head tilted at a studious angle. His ridiculously long eyelashes added a degree of femininity to his appearance. "I see. I thought perhaps he had taken ill and that was the reason for his absence." A moment of silence passed. "I've received some disappointing news of late."

"Oh?" Numiak sipped his wine seemingly without a care.

"Yes. I heard your father made an alliance with the Face Stealer. It was why I had invited him here, you see. I was looking forward to discussing this alliance. That he has chosen to align himself with a demon, there must be some incentive for him, no?"

Numiak neither confirmed nor denied this statement. "The Avi's first obligation is to his people. The Central Territory has witnessed increasing unrest the last few months. As a leader yourself, surely you understand why he could not be present."

Nanuq sliced the seal meat on his plate. The knife parted the red flesh like water. Apaay hovered near a guest's elbow a few seats down, refilling a glass of water as slowly as possible. "Yes," he replied quietly. "I suppose."

"I hope you're not too disappointed that I came in his stead."

"Of course not." The king brought the piece of meat to his mouth, closing his eyes as he chewed, as if savoring the flavor. "One day, your father will no longer be around. Perhaps it is better this way. There is much you can learn here."

Apaay found Nanuq's choice of words telling. *No longer around*, as though the Avi's death would force Ro into his position, rather than permitting a peaceful transfer of power, a father stepping down to allow his son to rise.

"I am curious," said Numiak, "how you learned of this alliance."

Nanuq's eyes brightened with a certain fondness. All around, his guests continued to eat, unaware of the temperature in the room dropping to a chill. Apaay moved to refill the next glass, squeezing herself between Nanuq's son and one of the kirn. "As heir, surely you understand the importance of eyes and ears in other territories?"

Numiak considered his glass of wine. Apaay knew that look. Pondering multiple replies, discarding those that did not serve his purpose. "The territories exist for a reason." And who could overlook the irony that they had been put into place following a war of Nanuq's choosing?

He hummed in satisfaction. "I often wonder what the world would be like with no territories. It's a shame, keeping separate from each other when there is so much to learn."

"The territories ensure peace."

"Is it peace they give us," Nanuq countered, "or merely the illusion of peace?" He pushed forward in his agenda. "The Polar Bear Empire has experienced an era of immense prosperity. Imagine if I were to share that prosperity with the other nations?"

"Your prosperity," Numiak growled, fingers tightening on his wine glass, "is a result of stealing land from the—from my people. Nannek was our city. The Dead Plains were once rich with forest, resources. You dishonor me in presuming to share this prosperity, when it is naught but a stolen good."

Nanuq studied him over the rim of his glass in subtle delight. He said, "You are a much more engaging conversationalist than your father. I think I prefer your company to his. Honesty is always greatly appreciated. A rare trait to find in others."

As Apaay stepped back, the kirn to her right accidentally elbowed her in the arm. Water slopped from the pitcher and onto the ikov's lap. He jumped upright with a curse.

The conversation abruptly died.

Apaay stood frozen. The panic was rising. She didn't know where to look.

"Sorry," she whispered, then wondered if that, too, was a mistake.

The man offered her a stiff smile. "It's all right." He looked to his father, who observed Apaay with the piqued interest of one who has suddenly noticed something that had previously been hidden to him.

A hand closed around Apaay's arm. Someone hauled her backward, down the staircase, back to the kitchen, tossing her against one of the tables.

"Fool," Aniirlit hissed. "Are you trying to get yourself killed?"

HUNT

Apaay thought she might be sick.

"I don't know what it's like where you're from," the older woman said, "but in Nur, you avoid drawing attention to yourself unless you want to face Nanuq's wrath. And only a fool would want that. Here." She tossed a rag at Apaay's face. "Make yourself useful and scrub the pots. I don't want to see a speck of food on them."

← →

Hours later, the door to her room opened. Apaay sat up on her pallet, squinting through the dark. Numiak. He moved through the shadows so effortlessly it was difficult to pin him down.

"How bad was it?" she whispered, clutching the blankets in her lap.

She sensed, rather than saw, his shape. Broad in the shoulder, a fluid gait that brought him to the edge of his bed, where he sat. "Nothing we can't handle."

"You're lying. Tell me the truth."

He sighed, scrubbed a hand over his face. "You've attracted Nanuq's attention. He will question the blunder. He will ask himself *why.*"

Her muscles tensed with the need to flee. They could leave. Right now. It was not too late.

Even as she thought this, Apaay knew they could not. Their success hinged on this information. The very information that might weaken Nanuq, maybe cripple his plans if they were fortunate. They must stay and see this task through.

"Do you think he knows?" If Nanuq suspected anything, he would keep a close eye on her, thus hindering Apaay's ability to wander the palace freely.

"No, wolfling. He doesn't know. The protections I placed on our identities are stronger than his ability to sniff them out."

That mollified her, and she settled back into the blankets. Apaay drifted for a time when Numiak announced, "I said I would take the floor."

"And I said that wasn't necessary."

He loosed a soft laugh, turning over to face her. His eyes glittered like dark stars.

Apaay whispered, with sudden inspiration, "What do you call an evil caribou?"

She sensed his amusement. "The commander?"

"No, besides that."

"Hm." The light in his eyes winked out momentarily—he had blinked. "I don't know."

"A teribou."

Numiak chuckled. "Probably your worst one yet."

She bit her lip, feeling comforted by this interaction. Eska would have said something similar, she was sure. "Let's hope there's more to come."

"I'm sure there will be. Goodnight, wolfling."

Apaay smiled into the dark. "Goodnight."

40

Tonight, a deal would be struck.

Water lapped at the old pier, stinking of rotten things. With summer at its end, the days grew short and the sky slipped from perpetual twilight into a shade that bordered on darkness, without prelude. Crouched inside a decrepit, waterlogged building propped on stilts above the shoreline, Kenai watched for movement near the harbor. The midnight hour had come and gone, but their marks hadn't shown.

"Anything?" came a muted voice from behind.

He turned, slumping beneath the open window. "No." Leaning against an equally rotten wall across from him, Ukasna—the woman had finally given her name—sat beside another figure Kenai was still coming to understand.

The Pale One was more phantom than human. A slender figure encased in caribou hide trousers and a close-fitting maq, and soft-soled boots. Kenai had never seen the thief's face. It was always covered by a bone mask, the only revealing trait a pair of blue-gray eyes, pallid and eerie.

He'd been working with Ukasna and the Pale One for nearly two weeks now. In exchange for his services, they fed him, clothed him, and offered him a roof over his head, albeit a leaky one, but at least he didn't have to worry about waking up with a knife at his throat. As such, he no longer partook in the underground fighting ring.

With his arms crossed, Kenai watched the Pale One dump the contents of a small pouch onto the warped floorboards. "Aren't you concerned? It's half past the hour."

The Pale One rolled some of the herbs into a wooden pipe, then lit the bowled end. A coil of smoke wound up, partially veiling the thief's thin, raw-boned face. "No." Faded blue eyes considered him. "This is a power play. All the slumlords partake. So long as I get my cut, I could care less if they're late."

Kenai inhaled the smoke deep into his lungs. It smelled sweet and earthy. The herb was called lun-lun, named after the city near which it grew and, when smoked, slowed the heart and head with numbness and leached one's irises of color. Kenai had partaken in it during his time in the Pack, and remembered with fondness a night of howling laughter with his Packmates.

Lun-lun addiction drove the majority of these deals. Money to purchase the herb in bulk. Seemed a waste of one's life, but Kenai couldn't judge when he had his own demons to contend with.

Ukasna, who flipped her dagger lazily and somehow managed to catch the hilt rather than the blade without looking at it, said, "Only the weak-minded fall prey to timeliness."

Kenai fought a smile, the first in a long time. The Pale One hadn't trusted Kenai, not at first, despite Ukasna's insistence. Over time, he'd proven his usefulness. His military background provided he knew how to follow instructions. He knew how to disappear, should the need arise. And punctuality had been ingrained in him from a young age, weak-minded or not.

They were a study in contrasts, Ukasna and the thief. The Pale One spoke little. Ukasna at times didn't know when to shut her mouth. Her strength came from physicality. The Pale One used their words, the shadows, and their unusual mimicry skills to outwit others. While Kenai was almost certain Ukasna was wolf Unua, he had no idea where the Pale One's origins lay.

"I wonder, Masuk. Do you run from the person who gave you that scar?" The Pale One gestured with their pipe.

Kenai dropped his hand, having not realized he'd been tracing the uneven puckering of his left cheek, the remains of his eye socket. "The Face Stealer gave me this scar," he said flatly.

"The Face Stealer." The Pale One rolled the carved wood between their fingers. The shift in the thief's jaw suggested an impression of curving lips, though it wasn't enough to be considered a smile.

Kenai said, "You know the Face Stealer." It was not a question.

"He has hired me for services in the past."

"What kind of services?"

"That information is for those who pay." The Pale One's perusal of Kenai in his grimy state was of the opinion that he couldn't afford the cost. Kenai must have fallen far if he agreed with the observation. He had only planned on keeping the company of these two for a week at most, but he wondered if he might stay here permanently. He could build a new life for himself, one free of the approaching war. Out here, where no one knew of his past, he was freer than he had been in a long time.

"They're here," Ukasna said.

Immediately, the Pale One extinguished their pipe, pocketed the still-smoking object, and slipped out the door. Ukasna and Kenai peeked over the windowsill, watching the thief's dark, slender shape wind down the beach to the jutting dock. A larger silhouette waited to greet the thief.

The black sea wavered, hissing as it hit sand.

A sack of lun-lun passed from one hand to another. Payment was counted, or it would have been if a second silhouette hadn't suddenly appeared on the dock.

"Something's wrong." Ukasna jumped to her feet, and then the Pale One dropped, hitting the wooden planks. The second shadow hefted the now-limp body across wide shoulders and leaped from the dock, hurrying toward the main road, the second figure not far behind.

Ukasna was already sprinting for the door, Kenai at her heels. The woman was fast. Mud and shit squelched beneath their boots. At the late hour, the streets were mostly deserted. Kenai had learned quickly not to wander out after dark.

"Keep heading straight," she called to him, before darting down a darkened side street. Kenai followed her instructions, though he wasn't familiar enough with the terrain to know which streets intersected, for they were a network of labyrinthine veins, clogged with sludge. The sea breeze, choked by the refuse of the slums, faded into memory.

A feeling of being watched came over him. Kenai was no stranger to it. He looked to the roofs and slowed, ears pricked for the sound of footsteps behind him. The structures fell into further dilapidation. Homes sinking into the squelch, listing to the side from lack of foundation. He felt the passing time like a wound leaking out.

Someone grabbed his arm. He whirled, his dagger a blur of dull silver.

It was Ukasna.

Strands of hair had pulled free of her side braid to cling to her sweat-sheened neck. "Any luck?"

"What do you think?"

She leaned against the side of a building, palms against the rough wood, and closed her eyes with an uttered oath. "A set-up. I should have known. There's bad blood between the Pale One and the Black Sands. A few months ago the Pale One shorted the slumlords payment. And they came to collect." With explosive fury, she spewed out a string of curses and kicked the wall of the building. Her foot went straight through the rotten beams.

Kenai watched her calmly.

She said, "Help me rescue the Pale One, and I'll get you on a ship back to the mainland. You have my word."

After a pause of consideration, he gave a slow nod. "So what's the plan?"

"I'm not really the planning type. The Pale One always organized things. I'm the woman who wields sharp objects and my fists with deadly intent." It sounded as though she mocked herself.

Kenai had been involved with a few hostage situations during his years in the Pack. He knew how to carry out a rescue mission. What he lacked was information. "Do you know where the Black Sands camp?"

"Yes, but I don't have a death wish. You can't just walk in and ask for our thief back."

Not a problem. "Do you know anyone who might be willing to help?"

Ukasna toed the pile of crumbly wood. "No one would do it out of the goodness of their hearts."

"Then someone who owes you a favor." It was the next best thing. Better, because they'd have leverage. The last thing Kenai wanted was to barge into a house of dangerous criminals, but without this mission, he'd never get off this forsaken island.

She grinned. "Favors, I can do. Come on."

Their destination: a stilted establishment that appeared to be one cough away from collapse. The leaky roof sagged inward, soft like an animal's hot innards. A set of precarious stairs built of driftwood and what Kenai suspected were human bones led to a squat entrance door one level above. Its many windows allowed access to the sea breeze. A wise choice, for the amount of sweet-smelling lun-lun smoke pouring from the building's open orifices was enough to permanently blind him.

"Let me do the talking. You stand there and look pretty."

He knew her well enough to know it wasn't an insult to his appearance. That's just who Ukasna was.

The walls bowed outward from the amount of bodies shoved inside. Ukasna moved through the crowd like she belonged. And she did, Kenai realized. It was he who did not.

She slammed her palm on a table shared by four men, toppling drinks and drawing their attention with admirable efficiency. "Hello, Pim."

A man with teeth of pure gold bared the glimmering display in an aggressive smile. His eyes were colorless, evidence of his lun-lun addiction. "Ukasna." He blew a stream of smoke into her face as though it were his own personal greeting. "What brings you to my abode?"

The woman slapped aside his pipe from where it hung between his lips. It clattered across the table. "Manners, Pim." Her voice was insultingly droll.

Pim's companions bristled, but the older man held up a hand, his gaze trained on Ukasna with acute interest. "I take it your visit isn't coincidental."

"I always knew you were smart. The fact is, you owe the Pale One a favor. I've come to collect."

"Oh?" Calmly, he lifted a filthy glass containing an equally filthy liquid to his mouth. It had the exact shade and consistency of excrement. "My favor is to the Pale One, not you. Where is the thief?"

"Taken by the Black Sands. Double-crossed. I need help getting them out alive. I'm sure the Pale One would consider your debt repaid, were we to succeed."

Pim shifted his attention to Kenai. "Who's this?"

"That's Masuk, but don't you worry about him."

Kenai touched his dagger, relieved to note it hadn't been lifted off his person. These were the sort of people who always had at least five knives on them at all times.

As if deciding he wasn't impressed with Kenai, he refocused on Ukasna. "Let's say, theoretically of course, I do help you. What's in it for me? Seems a bit much, helping save the thief when the debt I owe is so small in comparison."

Ukasna smiled. "Well for starters, I won't dump your body someplace where it won't ever be found. How does that sound?"

41

The click of the lock startled Apaay awake. It took seconds for her awareness to sharpen, the room to crystallize into focus. The curtains had been drawn hours before, and the darkness was nearly complete.

A figure bled into the shadows: hunched and thin, moving with purpose. It skirted around a chair, pressed against the wall, shuffling closer to where Numiak slept unaware. Apaay hadn't the time to think. She launched herself off the pallet, bringing down the intruder.

A lamp flared.

Numiak sat up in bed, taking in the scene: Apaay sprawled in a heap, Aniirlit trapped beneath her.

With Apaay's arm wrapped around the woman's neck, her knee digging into the small of her back, Aniirlit could not break free. The years spent wrestling with Eska had not been a complete waste after all.

Numiak said, deathly quiet, "Is this how you welcome all of Nanuq's guests?" He was bare from the waist up, the blankets pooled around his hips, his white hair unkempt. Apaay was glad she had decided to sleep on the floor.

She rolled off Aniirlit, who stood with a baleful glare, brushing herself off and adjusting her clothes. "I apologize, sir. I needed—"

"I do not care about your needs." His voice was so low so as to sound inaudible. "I care about why you have broken into my room at this hour of the morning."

Aniirlit paled. Her fingers twitched against her slim thighs. "It is the same for every guest, sir. Nanuq requires it."

There was the quiet of sleep, and then there was the quiet of interrupted sleep, and they were two very different things.

"What do you mean he *requires* it?"

The woman licked her lips. "We are given orders. To check on the guests nightly."

"Why?"

Irritation flashed across her expression, but she tamped it down. "To keep Nanuq safe. You must understand, it is difficult for him to trust that others' intentions are good."

Apaay didn't believe this woman for a second. Aniirlit had been searching for something, likely on Nanuq's behalf, but what?

Clearing her throat, Apaay said to Numiak, "Sir."

Only she noticed the twitch of his mouth. They had roles to play, after all. "Yes?"

"Perhaps it might be wise to bring this matter to Nanuq's attention. Shed some light on the circumstances." They could shift this situation in their favor, hammer out its use to their benefit. Present to Nanuq an image of false weakness. They were unsure. They did not know who to trust. But Nanuq, the Great Bear . . . well. If they gave him reason to believe he had earned their trust, Nanuq might shift his attention elsewhere.

"I would have to agree," Numiak drawled with considerable satisfaction. He then said to Aniirlit, "I would like to speak with Nanuq."

The woman grew more flustered. "Sir, the Great Bear is sleeping—"

"As was I." The gold of his irises darkened to the low-burning shade of a cooling fire. "Fetch him, or I will."

Faster than Apaay could blink, Aniirlit fled the room, not even bothering to shut the door behind her.

"Well," said Apaay.

"I can't say I wasn't expecting something like that to happen."

"Did you hear her unlock the door, or did you wake up when I tackled her?"

He unlocked the trunk shoved against the foot of the bed and pulled out his maq, shrugging on the thin, sleeveless garment. "I heard the lock."

"What do you think she was looking for?"

"Good evening."

Nanuq occupied the doorway, dressed in his bedding clothes. Truly, he was a small man, only slightly taller than Apaay. The fabric swamped his body. "May I come in?" Underneath the muted question lurked a streak of ice.

Averting her eyes, Apaay moved aside to let him pass, a male servant trailing him. Aniirlit entered the room last, head ducked, fingers laced together. It could not have been possible for Nanuq to arrive so quickly, considering his rooms were located somewhere on the opposite side of the palace. The fine hairs lifted on her body. Had he been anticipating this meeting?

"It has come to my attention," Nanuq said, "that one of my staff has overstepped her bounds."

Numiak walked a fine line. To appear concerned with the situation, but to not accuse Nanuq of the offense outright. "I have concerns. The safety and well-being of my party has been put into question, as well as the lack of privacy. I came here under the impression that we might work toward mutual trust."

"I understand your concerns, and I apologize. The keys are a safety precaution. I'm not sure if you're aware, but a number of months ago I discovered that one of my high-ranking kirn was a spy, had been for nearly a decade. Rest assured, your life is not in danger, nor the life of your servant, but I could not take any chances. It is difficult to know who to trust these days." His pretty eyes were soft, his voice soft, his posture soft. One might even assume him to be weak. "However, my staff know not to disturb sleeping guests. This slight will not go unpunished."

The male servant—the one who had helped her refill drinks last night, Apaay realized—presented his master a long wooden box. She believed his name to be Pama.

Pushing open the lid, Nanuq removed whatever lay inside the box. A black, serpentine object uncoiled from his slender hand, curling onto the ground. Apaay did not know what she was looking at.

Nanuq offered the object to Numiak with an avid, hungry expression. Aniirlit was noticeably paler. "You understand this cannot go unpunished. My servants are, above all else, obedient. Ten lashes to the back. She will not make this mistake again."

It was a weapon. Something to break open skin.

Numiak had gone absolutely still. "She is not my charge."

"Ah, but it was you she had wronged, so it must be you to serve out justice." When Numiak didn't immediately accept the weapon, Nanuq placed the handle gently, almost reverently, in his hand, like a most-beloved toy.

Apaay fought revulsion. How much of this punishment was for Aniirlit and how much was for Numiak, a back-handed slap to the muzzle of a dog that did not come to heel, the way Numiak had challenged their host at the previous night's dinner? A way to put someone neatly in their place.

Numiak tightened his fingers around the handle, and Apaay recognized what this would do to him. "I understand," he murmured.

"Very good." Nanuq smiled.

Aniirlit, as if having received this punishment before, knelt and presented her back to them.

Nanuq clasped his fingers in front of him. "You may begin at your leisure."

The worst part was not the sight of the woman's blood blooming in scarlet petals across her back. It was not even Nanuq's ravenous expression as he watched the scene unfold.

The worst part was how quietly Aniirlit accepted the punishment. The whip whistled, cracking like bone, and the woman made not a sound. Apaay flinched as the coiling snake made contact with Aniirlit's skin. Eventually, she had to look away.

By the time Numiak was done, he gripped the whip so tightly the wooden handle creaked. Sliding free of his sweaty fingers, it thunked onto the blood-soaked floor.

"Is that satisfactory?" asked Nanuq calmly.

Numiak didn't respond. He stared at the opposite wall, expressionless, while Nanuq took his leave. His servant, Pama, grabbed the bloody whip. They left, shutting the door behind them.

Shakily, Apaay hurried to the basin in the corner and grabbed one of the cloths, wetting it. She returned to wipe the sweat from Aniirlit's blotchy face, but the woman jerked away, her eyes hot with fury and humiliation. "What are you doing?"

Apaay blinked, her hand hovering in the air awkwardly. "I was . . . I thought—"

Aniirlit snatched the cloth from Apaay's fingers and tossed it across the room. She stood. Blood coursed down the tattered ruin of her back. "If you're finished." She spared them no mind as she strode to the door.

"What about your back?" Apaay called after her.

The words hissed out, brittle and chilled. "What about it?"

← →

The week passed fleetingly. By the fifth day, Apaay had learned the majority of the servants' names. She'd learned the location of Nanuq's quarters, his office, his war chamber. She'd learned the location of his children's chambers as well. Not that she believed them to hold any pertinent information, but it didn't hurt to be thorough. Apaay hadn't seen much of Numiak throughout the morning. He, along with the rest of the guests, had joined Nanuq for a tour of the capital. Following the midday meal, however, Apaay suggested seeking out Desna, their contact in the lower city, and Numiak agreed. No one would miss her, since she was allowed an hour break after clean-up.

"We'll use the tunnel," he said. "Better to know ahead of time where it empties out."

Right. Because if things made a turn for the worst, it would be their only way out of the palace.

They waited until the staff departed, many wandering into the gardens to eat, before descending one of the servant's staircases down into a food storage room. According to their map of the palace, the tunnel should be located on the north wall. Apaay and Numiak shoved aside stacks of crates. Then sacks of root vegetables. Then more crates.

"Are we sure this is the right place?" Apaay asked.

"Here it is." A final shove revealed a small, dark opening near the corner. Numiak went first. Apaay followed, crouching down until the opening widened, allowing her to stand.

"Cozy," she said.

The tunnel slithered deep into cold earth, but with their brisk pace, the chill never went deeper than her skin. Sooner than she had anticipated, they reached a battered, wooden door. Numiak tried the handle. Stuck. He rammed his shoulder against it, and the door burst open, sending him careening forward. Apaay, meanwhile, stepped neatly across the threshold into a narrow street that was so crowded, no one noticed their sudden appearance.

Nur had been hammered and carved out, a place of utility. The lower city teemed. The noises reminded her of Kunivik, conversation and laughter and creaking wood and clattering in the distance and the occasional whine of a starving dog.

Glimpses inside Nur's sweltering forges revealed stacks of newly hammered swords. Apaay also noticed enormous carts laden with felled whitewood trees being hauled into the city, their rickety wheels squealing from the weight.

At one point, Apaay caught sight of a man in the distance. He turned, and for a moment, light illuminated his face in profile. She stared at him in confusion until he merged with a group of people crossing the road.

"What is it?" Numiak's hand went to her elbow, helping veer her around an abandoned cart.

"I thought—" She could have sworn she'd seen that man before. The scarring on his face, and the bone structure, reminded her of Kenai, though it was not a complete likeness. "Never mind."

They turned down the narrowest street yet, barely wide enough for two people to walk abreast. Numiak stopped at a wooden door located at the street's end and knocked. A slot pulled away from the center of the door, revealing a pair of narrowed eyes that flitted between him and Apaay. "Were you followed?"

"Lost two men a while back."

Apaay startled. She hadn't realized Nanuq's men were trailing them.

The slot snapped shut, a lock tumbled free, and the door creaked open on squeaky hinges.

Numiak stepped into the building first. It was spacious and smelled of rotting plants, the walls lined with long tables piled high with cloth. The windows had been shuttered. Lamplight provided pale, glowing pockets amidst the dark.

The woman who'd opened the door was sturdy in the thigh, with wide shoulders and hair cropped short at the ears, a thin strand decorated with a trio of blue beads. She equaled Numiak in height.

"I am Desna," said the woman. "You must be Apaay."

"Yes." She watched the weaver shut and lock the door. "This is—"

"The Face Stealer," Desna supplied, appraising him with suspicion.

He bowed his head graciously. "To my friends, I am called Numiak."

"We're not friends." Curt. "This way."

He smiled after the woman. "I like her."

"You would."

His hand came to rest against her nape as though it belonged there. She was coming to anticipate his touches far too readily. "I admire a woman who speaks her mind. I would even consider it a weakness of mine." Numiak's warm gaze roved her face with twinkling affection, an ease to this companionship they'd developed. It felt much earned.

"Now you," he added.

"Now me what?"

"What's a weakness of yours?" The corners of his mouth tugged wider. "Let me guess. Alluring charm. Physical prowess. Big hands . . . among other things."

Her face flamed at the insinuation. But who would she be if she couldn't strike back? "Then I suppose it's a shame you fall *short* in those other areas." With a bland smile, she fluttered her eyelashes and pulled free to follow Desna to a back room, feeling positively victorious about the spluttering sounds behind her.

The small interior room smelled strongly of smelted metal. Desna plopped herself into a vacant chair, arms crossed, legs crossed, glowering. The sight was eerily reminiscent of Kaan, though the women looked nothing alike.

Apaay took an empty seat across from Desna, who said, "You found the tunnel?"

"Well enough," said Numiak.

The weaver's eyes went flat and cold. "I wasn't speaking to you."

"That is obvious."

Desna held his gaze. "Ro warned me you were full of shit. And now I know he's right."

"Full of shit," said Numiak, holding up a finger, "but an excellent spy."

Apaay wondered if this woman would toss them out before they could pass on their information. She kicked Numiak in the shin, and he went quiet.

"Nanuq may be a tyrant," Desna said scathingly, "but he's no fool. He knows enemies have infiltrated his city. It's only a matter of time before he learns of my treason."

Which made Apaay wonder why Desna had risked her life.

"What news?" the weaver asked. Following this meeting, she would send Ro their updates, which he would receive from the safety of Sinika.

Apaay exchanged a glance with Numiak before responding. "I haven't heard or found anything worth noting. The servants talk, but not about the war." They were more concerned about who bedded who, and had weekly wagers on which woman would get pregnant first. Needless to say, Apaay didn't take part in them. "I haven't had an opportunity to explore Nanuq's quarters. Most days I'm in the kitchen." Pama cleaned Nanuq's rooms daily, but she didn't know how to broach the topic of tagging along on his task without drawing suspicion to herself. As for Aniirlit, Apaay hadn't earned nearly enough of the woman's favor to talk with her about the war. In fact, she was quite certain the woman despised her.

"I've had very little luck as well," Numiak said. "Despite Nanuq's attempts to sway the Owl Clan to his side, he keeps his intentions close. Although he said if I was willing to kill the Avi, he guaranteed I would retain a place of power in this so-called improved North." He shook his head in disgust. "Nanuq glorifies man. It's all he can talk about—taking that next step toward greatness."

Apaay clenched and unclenched her hands. She wondered yet again what had driven Nanuq to this obsession.

"His army grows," said Desna. "I've another contact in the palace who informed me of his latest roster. His kirn now stand at seventy thousand strong."

Her stomach dropped. "Seventy thousand?" she whispered. She couldn't fathom such a number.

Numiak's face drained of color. "Even combining the Flock with the caribou Unua, we have maybe half that."

What were they to do? What was the point of coming here if Nanuq would crush them with his insurmountable army?

"Who is your contact?" Numiak demanded.

Desna lifted her chin. "I will not divulge that information, for their own protection." She paused and, as if sensing there would be no more intrusive questions, continued with her previous thought. "The majority of his army is based in Nur at the moment, with overflow into his base at Kaal. I suspect he will use that force to strike into the Central Territory."

Apaay was inclined to agree. She knew little of military tactics, but Nanuq planned to invade Sinika sooner or later. As it was, smaller units of kirn had crossed the border, ransacking the smaller towns, before disappearing without a trace. Apaay recalled Ro informing them of missing Flock members, whose bodies were never recovered.

Numiak said, one fist resting atop his thigh, "Ro will need to be informed of those updated numbers."

"He already knows. He also told me to remind you to not do anything stupid." Her lazy perusal made it quite clear Desna agreed with the sentiment.

With a muttered oath, he bent forward, scrubbing his face roughly with his hands. The weaver studied him with a curious lack of interest, then said, "There's no need to lose hope just yet."

Hope. The word caught Apaay's attention. "What do you mean?"

Desna lifted her chin. Beyond the creaking wooden walls, what sounded like a large gathering of people wandered past. "There is talk in the lower city of a woman who runs with wolves. Last I heard, she was moving west, toward Unana."

Numiak's lambent gaze locked onto Desna. It held all the intensity of the sun.

"What's so special about this woman?" Apaay asked, at the same moment Numiak cut in, "We don't have time for that. We need to find out when and where Nanuq will strike first."

Apaay shot him a glare, but he was too busy studying Desna to notice.

The woman said, "Then you're in luck. Nanuq has called a meeting with his Assembly tomorrow. I suspect they will be discussing the information you need."

Information they had yet to gather. But Apaay had an idea. They would act like water. They would carve out a new path in the rock.

She said, "By chance, are there any women on the Assembly?"

42

The sun attempted its futile climb from below the horizon when Kenai, Ukasna, and Pim hammered out the last details of the Pale One's rescue. And not a moment too soon.

They, along with four of Pim's men, exited the questionable establishment separately so they would not draw the crowd's suspicion—not that anyone was clearheaded enough to pay them attention. Over the course of the deepening night, the patrons had grown increasingly lethargic as the amount of lun-lun consumption doubled, then tripled. People dropped into slumber and did not move.

Kenai was the last to leave, and he picked his way around the collapsed individuals. He followed Ukasna's lead down the street, then right, heading farther inland. The soft ground squelched beneath his boots. Low clouds rolled in from the east with gilded edges, the innards softly bruised. According to Ukasna, the Black Sands claimed most of the western slums as their territory, with their safehouse located on its outskirts. The slumlords wanted their money and would keep the Pale One alive long enough to receive it. Beyond the moment when money exchanged hands, the thief's life was forfeit.

Ahead, she gestured him down a path that squeezed between

two rows of narrow, sagging homes. Every so often, the sea breeze managed to penetrate the wretched stench, offering a brief reprieve of salt and wild freedom.

Ukasna tucked herself against the side of one of the buildings. "The Black Sands are beyond that fence," she whispered, motioning to the driftwood construct spotted in the sliver of space at the end of the alley. Pim and his men would provide a distraction while Kenai and Ukasna focused on saving the Pale One.

A northern tern's cry pierced the night: Pim's signal. Ukasna hopped the fence, Kenai close behind, utterly silent as they slunk nearer to their target. In his periphery, four shadowed shapes blurred near the back of the ramshackle home. Ukasna ducked beneath one of the boarded-up windows. Kenai slotted himself beside her.

There came a shout from inside. A door banged open. More startled cries, and clanging metal. Ukasna entered first, kicking down the door. It was so decayed it crumbled to paste beneath her heel. She barged inside with her weapons already swinging, one of her daggers hitting its mark before she finished crossing the threshold. Kenai protected her back and killed anyone in sight. Together, they rained down on the Black Sands like demons sent from Taggak.

Within minutes, over half the men in the building were dead. Pim's men, having dealt with the slumlords outside, entered through the front doorway, moving like a death storm, spiraling outward and drawing their victims into the violent eye. Kenai had never seen anything like it. Four men died by his blade, then two more. The violence crept through his blood, and that fire carried him into the next room where the Pale One was bound, unconscious, yet alive, their chest rising and falling in fits.

Three men stood guard around the Pale One, gaunt and lean like the rest of the island's inhabitants. Kenai's first knife thunked into a man's throat. The second flew wide, narrowly missing the thief. He lunged, catching the man around the middle and sending them crashing to the ground. He snapped his neck. Neat, efficient. Too easy. It had been too damn easy. He stood. Only one man remained, legs braced, sword at the ready. His flushed, sweaty skin revealed his terror. Kenai took no satisfaction from it. The man should be afraid.

"Papa?"

Kenai froze as a young boy peered out from the second room. A child, messy brown hair and bloodless features, the beginnings of tears gathering in the corners of his eyes. Had Kenai ever been that young?

The older man froze. His skin took on a sickly pallor, the color of a fear so intense it made one ill. The man, who must be this boy's father, was located on the other side of the room. Kenai could throw a knife faster than the man could cross the space.

They stared at one another, and as the moments passed, the tension thickened, a question of who would move first. The man understood that to attack was to doom his son to die, and his grip on the weapon slackened. "Please," he rasped. His throat worked. "Don't hurt him."

Before Kenai could respond, a memory snapped through him.

Years and years ago, during a particularly dark night, his father had returned home, swimming with drink. Kenai couldn't remember how old he'd been. Eleven, maybe. He'd yet to join the Pack.

The door had banged open, startling him. His father lurched inside. Spotted Numiak sitting in a corner, a rock clutched to his scrawny chest. At the sight of his youngest son, whose face was in the exact image of his late wife's, he tripped forward, growling like a feral animal.

Kenai reached for their father. "Papa, wait."

Their father hadn't been kind then. He'd shoved Kenai so hard the back of his skull slammed against the wall. Numiak screamed and rushed to Kenai's crumpled form, flinging himself across his older brother's body, a shield. Somewhere amidst the darker memories of the years leading up to their father's murder, Kenai had forgotten this one.

His surroundings returned to the abandoned home, the dead men in the adjacent room. From his hunched position in the doorway, the boy had begun to cry. The father's attention kept flitting between his son and Kenai.

Something compelled Kenai to turn away. His chest ached. "Go." His voice rasped out, low and furious. "Take your son, and don't come back."

The man didn't question the order as he hauled his son into his arms and fled. The door banged shut, then listed on the frame, its hinges bent and useless.

The skirmish had lasted no more than a handful of minutes, a blood-spattered whirl of activity. The house was quiet. The Black Sands, at least those who had been present, were dead. With a shaking hand, Kenai tucked his blade against the small of his back. He had done his part, kept his end of the bargain. It was done.

He left.

← 43 →

The war chamber reminded Apaay of a cave: windowless, walls of dark stone, the air frigid. It housed a single wooden table. One chair at the head. Five on either side. Eleven chairs total.

Apaay sat in one of the cushioned seats and fought the spike of nausea in her gut. She was a woman among men, she was a spy, she was severely out of her element, fighting every instinct to flee like a deer through the brush.

She must lie as if her life depended on it, for it did.

The Assembly spoke amongst themselves. They wore thick white pelts draped across the backs of their necks, parkas stitched with impressive designs, and necklaces of glinting teeth. Apaay was the only one who did not participate in conversation. She wore the face and clothes of Assemblywoman Urum, while the real Assemblywoman Urum suffered from a sudden, agonizing battle between her stomach and a meal of spoiled whale meat. Numiak had not revealed the details as to how he'd managed the feat. It was probably for the best.

The door opened. Apaay's heart leaped and plummeted in a single breath. The Assembly stood, Apaay the last to scramble upright, as Nanuq entered, closing the door behind him. Although he was a small man, the change in atmosphere when he entered the room made it clear there was no lack of respect. Or fear.

"Thank you for your timeliness," said Nanuq by way of greeting. Once he took his seat at the head of the table, everyone followed suit.

He smiled. His teeth were small and orderly, save the elongated canines. "There has been news."

Apaay sucked in a slow, inaudible breath, exhaled through her nose.

Focus.

Interlacing his fingers, Nanuq rested his hands atop the table. Thin white scars crisscrossed the backs of his hands. One of his thumb nails was missing, having healed to a knob of paler skin. Apaay didn't realize she was staring until she lifted her head and met Nanuq's direct gaze.

He said, without moving those piercing eyes from hers, "It has recently come to my attention that one of the Wolf Kingdom heirs is alive."

A collective intake of breath sliced through the tension that had clouded the air. Even Apaay failed to conceal her shock.

This was news. Big news. Numiak thought his people were dead, captured. He thought his kingdom wiped out, no one to lead them. Yet Nanuq claimed one of the heirs was alive. What could this mean for the future?

One of the assemblymen asked, "How did you learn of this, Great One?"

Nanuq smiled. It was almost paternal. "It seems my son has somehow found himself entangled with the heir. Apparently she was captured and taken to one of the labor camps, yet managed to escape with some of the other captives. She has eluded capture since then, but my scouts believe she is heading west, toward Unana."

Nanuq couldn't be speaking of the ikov, could he? As far as she knew, his heir spent most of his days not doing much of anything. Did this mean he had another son? Then—oh.

Tulimaq.

"How long ago?"

Those pretty hazel eyes slipped briefly out of focus. "Six weeks. Her name is Matilaqaa. The guards say she is deaf."

Apaay internalized that word like a heartbeat.

Deaf.

It was as if Apaay had found herself caught in the middle of flurry. She at the center, unmoving, and the men's voices flinging high and low, because something else had captured her attention, snapped on it like a metal trap.

Matilaqaa.

Ila.

Mat*ila*qaa.

Then Ila was alive. She was alive and—

It couldn't be.

Her hands curled into fists atop her thighs, and Apaay asked herself a question she had pondered since the very beginning. Why had Ila been locked away in the labyrinth?

Back then, she'd only known as much as Ila had told her: that the young woman had never known a life outside of the labyrinth. But what if Numiak had put her there for her own protection, away from Nanuq? Numiak did nothing without intent. Why should this be any different? Why go through the trouble of keeping Ila safe unless she was important?

What was it Desna had said? A woman moving west toward Unana.

A woman who runs with wolves.

Because as heir to the Wolf Kingdom, she was, in part, a wolf.

Oh, it was neat. Very neat. Apaay had grown complacent. She had stopped asking questions, or rather, she had been asking the wrong ones. Ila was alive. She was wolf Unua, heir to the Wolf Kingdom. And Numiak had always known, just as he knew everything else, and hadn't bothered to tell her. Bastard.

Apaay refocused on the conversation.

"Once she is found," Nanuq continued, "I will have half of what I need to complete my liberation. Which brings me to my next question: what of the Northern Territory?"

A man with a deeply receding hairline fiddled with something in his hand. Sweat beaded on his brow and dripped from the tip of his nose. "I received word, Great One. About your northern unit." It wasn't Apaay's imagination—the man grew paler.

"Go on," Nanuq said.

The man licked his lips. Apaay found the sight disconcerting. "There has been a massacre, Great One. We believe the Caribou Nomads mutinied against their commander. Our attempt at a coup failed. They have reinstated the Council of Nine." He broke off, wheezing.

"I see." In a painfully slow motion, Nanuq turned his head, resting his gaze on Apaay. "Assemblywoman Urum, I believe you have been in touch with the Caribou Nomad commander. You assured me he had his people under control. Were you aware of this change?"

Sweat prickled Apaay's palms. She thought of home. Wrestling with Eska in the snow. Kaan's shrieking laughter. The heat of Numiak's shoulder against hers, their feet dangling over a tree platform. These memories did not cause her fear. If her heart did not remain steady, Nanuq would know.

What was worse: the truth, a lie, or to say nothing?

Apaay cleared her throat and said, with forced confidence, "Yes, Great One."

"And you did not think to inform me of this matter?" It was a subtle thing, the sweetening of his tone. Apaay felt a droplet of sweat roll down the back of her neck. She thought, *This is how a prey animal must feel before jaws clamp around its gullet.* Rolling eyes and wild fright.

"I thought it better to wait."

"Why?"

"Because . . ." The word rasped against her dry throat. Nanuq's eyes were like sharp points, pinning her to the back of the chair. "Because," she said, regaining some composure, "I wasn't sure if I could trust anyone's word, what with Nigun's instability. You understand my dilemma. I did not want to provide false information. I did not want to endanger your life."

Nanuq seemed surprised, though mostly appeased. He nodded in a distracted manner. "Yes. I understand. Do we have proof the Caribou Nomads have turned on us?"

The man from earlier said, "I believe so."

"I will need confirmation. Without access to the hot spring, I will be unable to complete the transformation. If that's the case . . ." He shook his head. "Send a message to Tulimaq. Tell him he is to prepare for an invasion of the Northern Territory. Come winter, Nigun will be mine."

← →

Since Apaay couldn't return to her room as Assemblywoman Urum, she left the palace, crossing into the upper city, before ducking down a deserted ally. She changed into the servants clothes she had stashed there hours before, replacing the assemblywoman's face with that of a bland serving girl, and removed the fabric that had covered her white hair. Apaay then fled back to the palace as if the world were burning at her feet, up the stairs to the third level, down the hall, bursting into her quarters with every intention of spilling Nanuq's horrible plans to Numiak, to demand why he had kept Ila's identity a secret from her.

But the room was empty.

"Apaay."

Whirling, she took in Aniirlit standing in the doorway.

"You're supposed to be in the kitchen."

"Sorry." She wondered where Numiak could have gone. "I must have lost track of time."

"I'm sure." Offering her a toothy grin, she hauled Apaay down three flights of stairs to the steamy dampness of the kitchen. Once again, Apaay was to refill water glasses—her least favorite task.

Frail sunlight dribbled through the windows, coloring the white pelts warming the floor to gold. The entire table was a splendor of heaping meats and vegetables. A glimpse of white hair loosened her nerves, but when she peered closer, Apaay felt volatile once more.

Tonight, Numiak sat next to the ikovna, whose dark hair shone deeply black, a pure shine of opaqueness. The elegant furs encasing her slender limbs befitted her station. The sight of their heads bent close sent a tremor through Apaay's chest. Shock, yet deeper, crueler, more abrasive. Her hand trembled. Apaay locked her wrist so she wouldn't drop the pitcher.

She was overreacting. Right? Right. Numiak could converse with whoever he wanted. In fact, it was expected. Ignoring the ikovna would be rude, considering their proximity. Meanwhile, Apaay's duty was to refill water glasses.

And that's exactly what she did. She completed her task without anyone noticing her presence. The duty of a servant. Still, Numiak had never failed to catch her eye during previous meals, a reassurance, the smallest of gestures to remind her they were a team. Tonight, it seemed as if he didn't notice her at all. His deep laughter resonated in the echoing space before giving way to low, murmured words. Words meant for the ikovna, a beautiful woman with dark eyes and dark hair, and whose father sat at the end of the table, seeing all. A woman, Apaay realized uncomfortably, who was not her.

It was fine. All part of the plan. Numiak acted as Ro, who was a guest. Lies, which the Face Stealer was so very good at. A ruse.

Yet when the ikovna's fingers alighted on his, Numiak didn't pull away.

Apaay went cold—the true, crushing absence of the sun—right down to her bones. It was a game, that's all. Nanuq's daughter was the manipulator, and Numiak played the role of the amicable, approachable heir.

Someone nudged her shoulder. She snapped her head to the side. Pama lifted his pitcher and mouthed, "Water."

She scanned the table and discovered multiple glasses empty, Nanuq's displeasure clear.

With an apologetic look toward Nanuq, Apaay hurried to fill the glasses. Meanwhile, Numiak leaned into the ikovna's personal space, and that long-fingered hand, the one that had curved possessively around her thigh in the pleasure house, found its way to the young woman's knee.

Her heart lurched like a drunkard. *It's not real. It doesn't mean anything.* Blindly, she returned to her spot against the wall, her face hot with humiliation. Not once during the meal did Numiak glance her way. She felt violently betrayed by that.

Four hours—that's how long dinner lasted, and how long Apaay was forced to watch the amorous spectacle unfold. The ikovna was practically sprawled across Numiak's lap, her mouth lush temptation, one hand having tangled in the long white strands of his hair. Had she looked like this, Apaay wondered, in the pleasure house? Had her eyes been that deep, her mouth that soft, the desire so acute it was as if she could feel it peeling back her flesh?

I'm right here, she wanted to scream at him. *Look at me.*

He did not.

Steeling her spine, Apaay willed the heat to dissipate from her cheeks. It did, with no small amount of willpower. She wiped the distress from her features, banished the tension crawling up her neck. Then she returned to pouring water and did not look at Numiak for the rest of the evening. Easy.

After the final course had been served, Nanuq stood to address his guests. "Friends." The word drifted out, amiable, pleasing to the ear. If she hadn't known what this man was capable of, she might have trusted him. "I want to thank you for your presence, your willingness to discuss the future of our beloved North. I have learned much from you all. I understand your fears and insecurities. I know many of you are far from home."

Apaay thought of the high canyon walls, blocking sight from the rest of the world.

"Rest well tonight. Tomorrow, the feast will begin at sundown. I look forward to building a future together, one where we will *all* be seen." He gave a shallow bow, low enough to showcase his appreciation, but nothing beyond that. "Enjoy the rest of your evening."

Once Nanuq took his leave, many of the guests followed suit, stuffed full of wine and warm food. Despite the prickling heat against her back, Apaay ignored Numiak's insistent gaze, kept her back to him, laughed at something Pama said. It was petty, but so what. Let him see how it felt to be ignored.

With the throne room vacated, Apaay began clearing the table with the rest of the staff. She took her time. She didn't want to return to her room for fear of it being empty, Numiak having chosen to spend the night elsewhere.

It was late. Only a few servants remained in the kitchen as Apaay finished scrubbing the last pot of the evening. Pama had settled in front of the low-burning fire, followed by Aniirlit. Apaay hesitated in approaching, but the older woman, who studied her with a surprising lack of animosity, said, "You did well tonight. You did not spill the water once. Sit."

Apaay sat.

"Wine?"

Pama offered her the skin with a look of knowing. He had a kindness to him, something she desperately needed at the moment.

Apaay accepted the skin readily. She knew of wine. It was a tart liquid that made her head spin when consumed in large quantities. Every few years, Papa would return with a skin or two, having acquired them on the Island of Kir.

Apaay took an experimental sip and grimaced. It was as sour as she remembered.

Firelight tossed flickering shadows onto their forms. Apaay passed the wine, but eventually, it made its way back to her, and she took another swallow. Better than returning to an empty room.

Surprisingly, Aniirlit spoke first. "What's it like," she murmured to Apaay, "out there?"

Apaay thought for a moment. If she were wearing a different face, her true face, she would speak of the land. She would say the tundra was endless, that one could look forever and not see a horizon. She would say the long night turned the sea smooth, the ice hard, the stars so plentiful they dusted the sky in their snowy glow. She would speak of her people. She would say family was more than blood. She would say the most powerful thing she'd ever known was the singularity of the Analak. If her people were the sea, then she was but a drop, yet all moved to the same ancient flow. But her eyes were gold and her hair was white, and she could not speak of it. So she said, "Where I'm from, the land—and its people—are free."

Aniirlit stared into the flames, her face illuminated. "It sounds lovely."

And that was how Apaay spent the remainder of her evening, saying absolutely nothing in the presence of people like her, a dying fire as their company. Aniirlit stoked the fire despite this. After a moment, the wood caught, and the flames rose high and bright. It seemed there was still something left to burn.

Eventually, the fire died, and the wine surrendered its last drop. After saying her goodbyes, Apaay navigated her way back upstairs, swaying only a little. The numbness helped dampen her nerves as she hesitated outside the door. It was completely ridiculous that she must knock to enter her own room, so Apaay decided she would not. If Numiak was occupied, that wasn't her problem.

Hardening her heart against what awaited her inside, Apaay entered the room.

It was empty, the bed untouched, the lamps having burned low. He hadn't returned.

An ugly emotion wedged itself between her heart and ribs. They'd made no promises to one another, after all.

"Where the hell were you?"

Apaay jerked in fright, ramming her hip against a side table. Numiak emerged from behind the divider, torso bare, trousers sitting low on his hips. Apaay didn't acknowledge him as she turned to rummage through her pack. He was here. So what? He had an obligation to the mission, yes, but that didn't mean the ikovna wasn't awaiting him in her room this very moment. The thought made her ill.

Apaay yanked out her sleepwear. "I was in the kitchen."

He propped one shoulder against the wall, studying her. "Dinner ended hours ago."

"Let me remind you that someone needed to clean." Her voice held a chill. "I stayed afterward to talk with the staff." She moved to the other side of the divider to change.

"Not to divulge information, I hope."

The accusation stuck a poker in her anger. "I'm not a fool." Not about that, at least.

"You could have let me know," he growled. "I thought something had happened to you."

Apaay nearly laughed. The only reason she didn't was because it would have sounded crumbly, in pieces, and she didn't want him knowing how hurt she was over this. "I'm surprised you even noticed," she snapped, tossing aside her servant's garb and slipping on the more comfortable sleepwear, "considering you and the ikovna looked seconds away from coupling at the dinner table."

Shocked silence fell.

Apaay waited for an explanation, but he didn't offer one. Somehow, that made it worse.

Pushing aside her hair with a shaky hand, she snatched her clothes off the ground. The air in the room prickled with encroaching darkness, a sign of Numiak's mounting fury.

Lifting her chin, Apaay stepped around the barrier to face him. He stood with his feet planted, his arms crossed. A muscle pulsed in his jaw. "Perhaps our definitions of coupling are different. As far as I knew, Runa and I were just talking."

Of course they were on a first-name basis with one another. "Talking? As she sat on your lap?"

"It wasn't like that."

"Don't tell me what I saw." Nanuq's daughter was lovely. Naturally, Numiak would look at her with desire in his eyes. That made Apaay an even bigger fool, because sometimes *she* had thought to be the object of his desires.

He stepped forward, his lips dangerously thin. Apaay held her ground. "So I cannot use the ikovna to obtain information on Nanuq, but you can flirt and ply that servant boy with pretty smiles?"

Apaay's mouth dropped. In her shock, she completely forgot to mention Nanuq's plan, Ila's identity, Numiak's precarious mountain of lies. "Pama? There's nothing between us."

"Don't tell me what I saw."

That he used her own words against her made Apaay want to smash something. Preferably his face.

"What you *saw*," she spat, closing the distance with a single step, "was a figment of your imagination."

"I see him watching you during dinner. Does he know how easily you lie?"

"Do you think I like lying to Pama? He's a good person."

His upper lip curled. "He's a servant."

The accusation stilled something inside her. Cruelty came easily to him. She'd nearly forgotten. "I can't believe you'd say something like that." Anger on Pama's behalf tore through her, twining with the deep-seeded hurt she felt, the shame in her inability to control her emotions. "But I suppose I shouldn't be surprised. If I remember correctly, you never had a problem watching those in captivity suffer." It was a low blow, but she watched him flinch with deep satisfaction.

His answering growl sounded more animal than human. "We agreed to gather information by whatever means necessary. You knew this."

"I wasn't aware that included taking others to bed."

He smiled. "Jealous, wolfling?" His pupils enlarged to dark pools.

"Jealous?" Apaay had learned a thing or two from the Face Stealer. She had learned how to play his game. "Of what? A demon who will stop at nothing to get what he wants and doesn't give a damn about anyone else? Or perhaps the ikovna, whose father single-handedly eradicated your nation?" Another step forward brought them toe to toe. He was no longer smiling.

"Yes," she said. "Did you forget that the woman you were trying to woo is your enemy? Have you forgotten the tens of thousands of wolf Unua dead in the ground?" Every black, bitter emotion surged upon her tongue. "Maybe your people were right in judging you when you turned. Maybe you deserve this face, this skin, this darkness." Her voice grew coarse as she brought the last of her words down on him like a blade to the neck. "Taggak didn't make you into this person," Apaay hissed. "It just revealed what you've always been."

Numiak's eyes all but glowed, livid with the pain he didn't try to hide. In that moment, Apaay hated herself.

"My apologies," he said stiffly. "If I had known I was that unappealing to you, I would have saved myself the trouble a long time ago."

Before she could speak, he blotted into shadow.

The ensuing silence crashed onto her chest, and her knees gave out. Then came the tears. Furious, shameful tears that squeezed every shred of air from her lungs, and guilt hardening as a pit in her stomach. What kind of person had she become that she would spew such insensitivity? No matter what Numiak had flung at her, she had been so much worse.

Apaay had gone to a place she couldn't come back from. He had spoken of his vulnerabilities in confidence, trusting that she would not abuse the information. But tonight, Apaay had wielded his past as a weapon, something hard-edged. Fear had made her lash out. Fear that he would not choose her.

That was it, wasn't it? Deep down, Apaay was *terrified* of how she felt.

What cruel irony, that she would fall for the man who had uprooted her life, who had caused her suffering, who had helped her heal, who teased her endlessly, who made her yearn for something precious despite the tumult of war.

She'd let those emotions blind her to their mission. Together. They would see this through together, yet Apaay had forgotten, overreacted, and done the unthinkable.

But he was so frustrating at times, and how did Numiak not see that he'd hurt her, too? Did he even care?

Apaay scrubbed her hands down her tear-streaked face. No, he cared, of course he did. She hadn't any doubt of that. She reminded herself of who, exactly, Numiak was. Her friend. He was her friend.

She needed to fix this.

Apaay was up and out the door, descending the stairs two at a time. Upon reaching the first level, she turned a corner and slammed into a body.

She reared back. "I'm so sor—" The apology wilted on her tongue, and she immediately dropped into a bow, not daring to speak.

Two slender fingers lifted her chin, forcing Apaay to look up. "Rise," said Nanuq.

She did, a shiver running through her body at his touch. Then she noticed the books scattered on the ground. Her pulse surged in panic. Apaay knelt and began gathering the material, accidentally cutting herself on one of the book corners in the process. In normal circumstances, she would have apologized profusely for her behavior, but she was not allowed to speak unless instructed to.

She held the stacked books out to him. Except Nanuq wasn't looking at the books. He was studying her finger, the place where a drop of blood had pushed through the split skin.

Apaay tensed as he reached for something in his pocket.

It was only a square of cloth.

"May I?"

At her nod, he pressed the fabric to the cut, soaking up the blood.

"I am sorry you had to witness Aniirlit's punishment the other day," said Nanuq. "She doesn't seem to learn."

Apaay didn't know how to respond, so she kept quiet. It was safer that way.

With a frown, he folded the cloth and slipped it into his pocket. "I wonder though. Do you understand why she had to receive the lash?"

The delicate hairs on the back of her neck twitched. The truth was, she did not. Apaay didn't think she ever would. "No, sir."

"To undermine a leader is to weaken the foundation of a society."

And yet, it seemed that Nanuq's staff was the foundation of this society, or at least a part of it. Without them, his palace would cease to run. Without those working in the lower city, there would be no industry. Nanuq viewed his world from the position of a man in power. His decisions ensured his view remained unchanged.

"I do not think Ro appreciated the lesson I tried to teach him," Nanuq went on in a regretful tone. "A leader must understand what it means to build, and to rule, and sometimes that means reminding others of their place, no matter how unpleasant the task might be." He took in Apaay's blank expression and sighed. "I trust the preparations for tomorrow night's dinner are underway?"

"Yes, sir."

"I'm glad." True appreciation lit the depths of his eyes. "I have a feeling it's going to be simply unforgettable."

44

The night rested, tranquil and unruffled, yet for Ila, sleep would not come. Curled on her side near the long-dead fire, she considered what this day would bring. Had her decision to seek the Horn of Amaroq been rational? Or would she inadvertently lead them into a mouth full of teeth? Even if they blew the horn, it didn't guarantee their call for aid would be answered. A leader was selfless. A leader was decisive. Her pack sisters would follow her into grave peril, though she had never asked this of them. If they died, it would be her burden to bear.

When dawn burgeoned, pink and new, lightening the eternal twilight of late summer, Ila prepared for the day. A storm-like agitation gathered as the army broke down camp and packed supplies. The days grew short. The growing season had reached its end, and snow would soon sweep in to deaden the woods.

"Attention!" the commander barked.

As one, the soldiers snapped their spines straight, legs together, heels in perfect alignment. Ila and her pack followed a hairs-breath behind.

The man strode the length of the clearing, studying each of them in turn. Ila did not think she imagined the way his gaze lingered on her. "Today, we make haste for Unana. Our brethren have been called to arms, and we will join them. Do not delay."

Ila looked to Tipki, Saniraq, Malina. They would make it through, so long as they had each other.

Their unit marched west through tangled undergrowth. Jostled among the army, Ila wasn't aware of how far they traveled, only that the distance passed with alarming speed. Each step, carrying her nearer to Nanuq's killing force. The current ebbed and flowed but always pushed onward. The available space diminished, forcing the bodies into closer proximity. Squeezed as tightly as children in a womb. Malina had been here before, and Tipki: surrounded by enemies on all sides.

It was midday when a second unit joined with theirs. The newest addition had to be close to two thousand strong, and still more flowed from the wood's interior. The mass strengthened— weapons, armor, flesh—and rolled with slow deliberation so that no fragment of earth was spared the strike of their boots. Ila, panting behind her mask, was sweating so heavily the mud covering her skin began sloughing off.

The trees broke ahead. The canopy peeled back to reveal a ripple of blue softened by white clouds. The army surged around Ila, who had stopped in the shadow of the tree line.

It was a city of two parts. Here, the forest had begun taking back the land piece by piece, the tired structures of toppled roofs and scorched walls, open doorways that led to ruined interiors. A road of broken stones crumbled under massive roots that surged like waves. Trees sprouted from rooftops or shoved their solid bodies in the spaces where buildings once stood. In some areas, the vines were so thick Ila could not see what they covered. This, she realized, was Unana's derelict edge.

The terrain sloped toward the city's center. Unana had been built in a shallow valley, with the River Mitka flowing to the west. It offered the perfect vantage point. The flood of kirn into the city, emerging from the green fringe, the streets swelling with bodies, the white uniforms bright against the stone constructs, the surge oozing into the streets that squeezed into narrower veins in the distance.

Malina's face paled at the sight before them.

The sheer size of Nanuq's force was incomprehensible. It was a sea with no horizon.

How many? Ila signed.

The former Pack commander scanned the growing mass. Saniraq pulled Tipki's hand from her mouth, as she'd begun to chew on the ends of her already ragged fingernails. Tipki had once mentioned her aversion to crowds in passing. Yet one of the reasons she preferred acting as a scout. "Upward of thirty thousand."

They were only four.

As if sensing Ila's mounting distress, Saniraq squeezed her hand. "We're close."

The second section of Unana rose in the distance. An impressive stone structure, built into the mountainside at its back: the den, where her family had once dwelled. The heart of this great city.

"I remember this street," Malina said. "There's a lookout two miles west." She pointed. "I was stationed there when Nanuq invaded. They took this quarter first." Ila imagined the woman picking apart her memories, trying to fit the Unana she remembered with the Unana that was now. "Too many died that day."

Malina never sought comfort in others, nor did she expect it. Maybe that's why Ila curved her arm around the woman's back and rested her head on her shoulder.

Her packmate tensed. "What are you doing?"

Tipki plastered herself to Malina's other side before the woman could peel away, snuggling close. Malina sighed. "Pup." Ila smiled despite the peril surrounding them.

"It's group hug time, and you're participating whether you like it or not. Saniraq, get over here."

If Tipki announced it was time for a group hug, they hugged. Saniraq joined, and they all did their best to smother Malina because they knew how much she disliked it, even if her sadness over Pili's death sometimes bled through the barriers she'd erected around her heart. Ila loved her pack sisters. She didn't know what she would do without them.

The influx of soldiers forced them down one of the streets. Vibrations quaked the stone. At the first intersection, Malina examined a corner of one of the buildings, running her fingers over the interlocking stones. She shook her head. Not this street. The underground tunnels leading to the den were close though.

The current carried them farther and farther from the city's edge, deeper into the capital's heart. The ruin spread through every narrow crack: walls reduced to rubble, piles of rock and wood, the ground having buckled in places. It told the tragic tale of a people who had fought but, in the end, had fallen. At some point, the street merged into a large, open square where the majority of the army had gathered. In the distance, the den appeared small and shrunken.

Suddenly, the earth trembled with what could only be the combined voices of thirty thousand men crying out at once. It was so powerful that Ila felt her eardrums vibrate from the pressure, the ghost of a monstrous sound.

She stood on tiptoe to peer over the heads of the men surrounding her. They were gathering, but for what? The mass began to shift eastward. Ila grasped for Saniraq's hand so they wouldn't be separated. Malina and Tipki scanned the area, baring their teeth at anyone who got too close as, gradually, the kirn pushed their way toward a platform raised in the city square.

A silhouette backlit by the meager sunlight stepped onto the platform. The earth trembled again, and the crowd undulated like a breaking wave. Ila pressed close to Tipki, Saniraq and Malina guarding her back. Then the figure turned, and light caught the side of his face. A man of average height, slender, a bladed staff in hand.

Tulimaq.

The blood drained from Ila's face so quickly it chilled her skin.

Her hand latched onto Malina's arm. She had last seen Tulimaq through a veil of smoke, a sky tinged orange at his back, and a wind turned dark with burning, the blade of his staff pressed to her heart.

Go then.

Ila had told no one of those final moments in the labor camp. Worse than the memory was how his face had lingered with her. She had carried it miles through the Atakana. She had slept with it tucked away like the dirty secret it was. Now he was here, alive, in the flesh.

Tulimaq appraised the army that had congregated at his feet. He looked inhumanly cold, like what she imagined Nanuq's son to be: a future conqueror.

What's he saying? Though Ila could not read his lips from this distance, she knew he must be speaking, for the buzzing quality in the air died. The light fell across his skin in strange shapes, and she realized it reflected against the burns he had sustained, the patches pale and shiny with healing.

"Isn't that . . .?" Saniraq looked to Ila in question, but Ila couldn't meet her friend's eye, so ashamed was she of her feelings.

Malina, Ila said. *Please.*

The woman hesitated in a rare moment of uncertainty, likely wondering what she and Saniraq were communicating, but she repeated the words that came from his mouth. "My fellow kirn. You do not know me, but I know you. When I was a boy, I heard stories of the war, and of the great kirn of the Empire. The best of the polar bear Unua."

A man jostled Ila in his enthusiasm. She felt woozy with all that Tulimaq said.

"Never did I believe I would one day stand before the greatest army the North has ever known, and guide you into what awaits us. But my father has placed his trust in me. I swear on my life I will not let you down. My name is Tulimaq of the Polar Bear Empire, and it is an honor to serve you."

This next scream felt like the air was rupturing against Ila's skin. She couldn't believe this was the same Tulimaq who had needed darkness to mask the pain of confession, agony over a lost mother, years forced to grow up alone.

"The Polar Bear Empire has always prided itself on its ambitious and enduring nature. Like many of you, my father grew up sickly and poor. But an opportunity arose, one that eventually changed the face of our great nation."

What Ila didn't understand was how Tulimaq had been given a station of high rank. As far as she knew, Nanuq hadn't acknowledged him since childhood. Had that changed since their last encounter?

"As a boy, my father traveled to Across the Sea. It was there he learned of man's greatness. Order in the unique hierarchy of their society, one where those with the means to lead do, and those that don't, follow. And so Nanuq brought that order back with him to the Southern Territory, bringing an end to our civil war. Much has changed since the old king's death, but here we are. To begin anew."

Tipki gaped, her lips thin and cracked with dehydration. "He's mad."

Mad, Ila wondered, or desperate? This didn't sound like Tulimaq at all. They were Nanuq's words, forced into Tulimaq's mouth.

"My father has a vision for our world. A desire to balance that which has been unbalanced. For too long, animal and man have lived separate lives, but the Great Bear seeks to eliminate that divide. Under his direction, there will be one mind, one heart. A North that is shared, that is made for all."

The air erupted with a crackling, storm-like quality. Pure, untapped energy as the army roared its agreement, thirty thousand hearts beating as one, gathered atop the ruins of a conquered city.

"In two months' time, we march on Nigun. Help spread our nation's prosperity. Walk with me into this new world. Fight with me, with my father, your king. Nanuq, who is almost a man."

Another round of cheers.

"This," he said, "is evolution!"

In horror, Ila turned to her pack, at a complete loss for words. Did the Caribou Nomads know they were being targeted? Was the Owl Clan next? Where were Apaay, Kaan, Ro, and Numiak in all this? They hadn't been in contact since the Wood's abandonment. That had been months ago.

We need to warn them.

"No." Malina was firm in this. "We focus on our task. When that's done, then we can think about how to help your friends."

"Malina's right." Saniraq observed their surroundings warily. "We can't allow ourselves to get distracted. Not now."

Ila bit the inside of her cheek in frustration. She'd told her pack about her friends, but she had not told them she would be nothing without them, especially Apaay. Enough time had passed for Ila to recognize their painful parting as a good thing. Without it, she wouldn't have grown into her own person, able to stand on two feet. Able to lead.

Still, they were right. She knew this. But that did not lessen her worry.

Tulimaq acknowledged the crowd with his serious countenance. Ila kept hoping to glimpse the person she had known in the Wood. Though quiet and severe, there had always been an undercurrent of honor to him.

Ila didn't notice the shifting air current until it was too late. It blew from the north. She and her pack stood upwind.

Tulimaq tensed, straightening in a swift motion that was almost painful to the eye. He scanned the square, scouring the thousands and thousands of bodies that were identical in appearance: bone masks, pelts cloaking their heads and shoulders.

His gaze drifted over her mask, the same mask as that of the thirty thousand surrounding soldiers. And yet his eyes locked onto hers, and though Ila glanced away, her stomach bottoming out, she feared the damage had already been done.

He knows I'm here. She jerked Malina in the direction of the street they had emerged from, the others trailing. A bead of sweat slithered down her neck as she fought the urge to turn around, to *see.* In the end, that urge won out.

Tulimaq stared at her retreat, one foot already off the platform, as if he might jump into the crowd and follow.

Hurry.

Malina took the lead, shoving against the jostling crowd. They managed to carve out a path, with some effort.

"Here." She tugged them down a less crowded street. They took a left at the first intersection, Ila's hand on Malina's lower back, Tipki's hand in hers, with Saniraq trailing closely, keeping a watchful eye behind. Malina examined the corner of a large, toppled building, then shook her head, gestured them to keep moving.

As one, they entered a darkened alley formed by the nonexistent space between two buildings. Ila was nothing but a shape in darkness. They all were. The buildings were too high and the path too narrow to allow anything more than fractured light to squeeze through.

Ila slowed, the back of her neck prickling, and gripped the hilt of her talq. Tulimaq could not have rooted them out so quickly. Too many kirn to sift through. As she turned, she spotted a shadow peeling away from the wall near the crowded street. Ila whipped around. Hurled her weapon, hilt over antler blade, at the figure's chest.

It dove out of range, dodging a strike from Tipki in the process. Two blades filled Tipki's hands, and she slashed the air, slender wrists crisscrossing, driving the shadow back.

Malina appeared from behind. The phantom dropped and rolled, kicking Malina's leg out from under her. Saniraq leaped over her packmate's body. A foot to the phantom's chest, and Ila thought they had it, but the shadow grasped Saniraq's foot and twisted it in mid-air, causing the woman to flip. A shape materialized through the darkness. Metal, gleaming and cold.

Ila shoved Malina onto the ground seconds before a knife sliced the air where she'd been standing.

Tipki lunged, pummeling the phantom's upper torso, but a blow to the chest sent the woman tumbling backward, flipping over her back. Saniraq took her place, legs planted on either side of her packmate so Tipki wouldn't be trampled. Malina and Ila lunged, striking toward the phantom's head and stomach. It sprang, kicking off the wall. Ila missed. Malina overbalanced and received a kick that sent her crashing headfirst into the stone wall.

But Ila was turning, and fury landed like a blow upon her chest, because after weeks fleeing the labor camp, burying their pack members' bodies, having no time to think much less mourn, they had reached Unana, and no one, *no one*, would stand in her way. Teeth bared, her arm snapped out, a clean, cutting motion, her fist smashing into the phantom's nose.

The figure dropped and curled on the ground in pain.

Ila winced at her throbbing knuckles. *Watch the entrance*, she signed to Tipki. *Malina, Saniraq, you're with me.*

Together, they moved to investigate. Malina took it upon herself to press her foot to the assailant's throat. A trickle of weak sunlight brightened the side of the man's face not hidden by the mask. Ila felt the uncertainty creep among her group as they recognized him as one of the soldiers from their unit. He must have followed them from camp.

"What do we do?" Saniraq asked.

"We kill him." Malina's eyes were two hollows in her raw-boned face. "One less polar bear Unua won't make a difference."

As she tugged her knife free, Ila stayed her arm. The older woman looked to her in question, features twisted with hatred.

Killing wasn't always the answer, though Malina would argue otherwise. There were consequences this near Nanuq's forces. A death among the polar bear Unua was cause for investigation. They would never make it out of here alive.

Let him up, Ila signed.

Malina and Saniraq hauled the kirn to his feet. He was slighter than she expected. Blood gushed from his broken nose and smeared his chin and neck. He smelled of wet earth.

You come alone, she signed, looking to Saniraq expectantly. Judging by his confusion, she had been correct in assuming he could not understand sign language. Saniraq relayed to him what Ila had communicated since, as far as she knew, Malina didn't understand signing. Or rather, she had never made an attempt to converse with Ila in that manner.

He nodded to Saniraq, though his gaze remained on Ila. "I do." Shadows dripped into the mask's eyeholes, leaving only the white sclera visible.

Why?

"I seek the same thing you do."

And that is?

"Access to the den."

Ila, normally so free in her expressions, kept her reaction neutral. *Why do you want access to the den?* She worried that whatever he wanted would directly interfere with their mission.

His posture was loose, strangely so. "I don't ask of your needs. There should be no concern with mine."

"Do you want to die?" Malina demanded, pushing closer in threat. Saniraq calmed her with a touch on the arm.

Ila's hands twitched with nerves, and not because of Malina's volatile temper. The man had multiple blades pointed at his throat. So why did it feel as if he held the knife, with Ila's throat bared to its point?

The pack awaited her instruction. To kill this man or let him live. To let him speak or silence him forever. He knew of their plan. How? They'd been careful.

Pushing through the circle of protection, Ila studied the soldier more closely. *Tell us why we should not kill you.* She didn't want to end someone's life. She found death so unnecessary. But that did not mean she wouldn't, if her hand was forced.

"One scream," said the man, "and every kirn in Nanuq's army will know a pack of wolves has slipped right under their noses."

45

Kenai sat on the edge of the dock, his toes dipped into the sea, when he heard approaching footsteps marked by the squeal of the warped wooden planks underfoot. He ignored them. The wind caressed his face and salt droplets clung coolly to his skin. He had spent years away from Tor, but it seemed fitting that he had returned. The undulating motion of the water never failed to soothe him. No matter how many times it retreated from the coast, it always returned, again and again and again.

Whoever walked the dock stopped behind him. If it were the Pale One, he wouldn't have heard the thief's footsteps at all. Ukasna, then.

She didn't speak, and neither did he. The waves said everything he could not. Kenai had been running all this time, but this was where the shore ended, and he could run no farther. So now he must ask himself of the next step. He must ask himself what kind of life he desired, and whether or not he deserved it.

The wood groaned as she closed the remaining distance and settled beside him. Ukasna inhaled a deep, burning lungful of air. "See that ship?" She gestured to a sleek vessel bobbing in the current near one of the far docks. "It sails within the hour. I spoke with its captain, and I've booked you passage back to the mainland."

The water sloshed around his submerged feet. "Thank you," he murmured. Ukasna had kept her promise, yet he wondered why his chest felt heavy at the thought of leaving this wild, unruly place.

"You are unhappy."

"I am preoccupied," he lied. "There's a difference."

Kenai studied the ship before his gaze returned to the darkening horizon. Soon, the sun would disappear, the last rays of light blocked by the curved earth. Darkness and cold awaited him. Winter. It wouldn't be long now.

Ukasna sighed a sound of complete disappointment, and he hated how his gut clenched in response. "I thought you might have learned something here. It turns out you've learned absolutely nothing."

His attention snapped to the woman beside him. "And what could I possibly learn from this place?" He gestured to the dilapidated buildings perched on the rock, sinking lower over time as saltwater intrusion softened the ground.

"Not from this place," she clarified. "From yourself. You came here telling lies. I had hoped when it was time for you to leave, you might have learned to tell the truth."

It felt like he'd taken a plunge into icy water. *Truth.* He hated that word. It was the beast that forever stalked his heels, and it was terrifying. If everything he had believed to be true was, in fact, a lie, where did that leave him?

He scoffed. "I tell lies? You're a thief, you and the Pale One both."

She shrugged. "At least I'm honest about it."

The disappointment cut into his insides, and he wondered if somehow, all these years, he'd been the one holding the knife.

"You don't know me," he growled. "You know nothing about me. You used me to obtain your precious lun-lun—"

"I know who you are, Kenai."

He went completely still. It had been so long since he'd heard that name. His name, nearly forgotten.

"I've known since the moment I saw you."

He almost said, *Even with the scarring?* But he bore marks in other ways, ones not imprinted on his skin.

At this, he turned. Ukasna blocked the collection of buildings clumped at her back as she studied him. "You're wolf Unua," he said. It didn't come as a surprise, despite having questioned Ukasna's heritage. Perhaps he had always known.

"I am."

"And the Pale One?" For he had wondered about the thief's heritage as well.

Ukasna shook her head. "I'm not sure." There was a silence. "I used to serve under your brother's command. Yours, too, in a way. A commander is nothing without his second."

Kenai focused on controlling his breathing. Slow, level. Inhale, exhale. He'd known the risks of coming here. For whatever reason, he thought he'd managed to avoid notice. "I—" What could he say? Nothing. Absolutely nothing.

He studied her in careful scrutiny, but he sensed no recognition. He remembered every name of every Packmate in his unit. There had never been an Ukasna. "What's your given name?"

"My name is no longer relevant. After our kingdom fell, I became Ukasna, and that is who I am."

The wind hissed between them. It felt as though Ukasna were gathering her words, preparing to strike, each blow cast with intent. Kenai braced himself for more difficult truths, which he had not been able to face fully. The Banished Lands had revealed every glossed-over imperfection of himself, a false perception, a layer that, when pulled back, revealed something decrepit and cratered with cavities.

"I always wondered what had happened that day," she continued, an edge of sadness to the words. "You brought us to Kesikan Pass. You claimed there was no risk of an avalanche, yet snow roared down the mountainside, tearing our unit apart."

His hands clamped over the edge of the dock. At the time, only Kenai had known of Nanuq's plan to invade Unana via the coast, though he'd sent a smaller force as a distraction through the Atakana. As a result, Numiak had ordered them to Kesikan Pass to block the kirn's progress. They were to remain at its entrance due to recent snowfall, a high risk of avalanches. Kenai had ordered them deep into the valley instead. With his unit wiped out, it allowed Nanuq's army passage through the Atakana. He'd barely made it out of the pass alive himself. "What do you want from me?"

"The truth, to start."

No matter how far he traveled, his past always managed to find him. It seemed, at long last, that he had reached the end of the road. "Did I betray you, the Pack, my nation? Yes, I did. It is done. It cannot be undone." He had wanted a different life. He had wanted to start over, start fresh. Flowers grown from a ruinous earth. He had made a choice long ago, and now he no longer knew if it had been the right one, or made for the right reasons.

"But you regret it," said Ukasna.

He had buried these thoughts time and again. He was tired of rehashing old news.

He was tired.

Dropping his head, he said, "I wanted to be with the woman I loved. My father was gone. My brother was . . ." He couldn't say it. *Demon.* Because it pained him whenever he gave recognition to Numiak.

"The Face Stealer," Ukasna whispered, for she would know. It was no secret. Everyone in the Western Territory had known the day Numiak, beloved Pack commander, had been sentenced to Taggak as punishment for his crime.

"I was selfish, all right? All my life, those I loved were taken from me." His voice died on a croak. "In my mind, there was but one person I might still save, and together, we might build a life."

The waves lapped gently.

"She'll never love you," said Ukasna quietly.

You're wrong, he wanted to say. But the words wouldn't come. He had spoken of Yuki to Ukasna and the thief, in snippets, and then at length, and then in sporadic moments that had faded over the passing weeks as he'd reached his lowest point, lower even than the days following his father's murder. Something compelled him to return to her side, though he could no longer say for certain what.

He had loved the Sea Mother as a young man, whole and unbroken, and he had loved her in the two decades caged by his brother. Why did he love Yuki when she had abandoned him? He could not answer this question, for he no longer recognized his own heart. She would do whatever it took to make Nanuq's vision a reality. She would never stop seeking her father's approval.

Kenai took a deep breath. "Why did you help me if you knew who I was?"

"Curiosity." She shrugged. "And I admit, a part of me took satisfaction in seeing how far you had fallen." Ukasna flipped one of her blades, caught it without looking. "You once served as my superior. You were honorable. You saved lives. You protected the citizens of our great nation. The way I see it, it's never too late to be who you might have been."

Kenai fought to control his emotions, which thrashed through him. His throat tightened. The person Ukasna spoke of no longer existed. He was a murderer, a traitor, an outcast.

"Who might I have been?" he wondered, suddenly desperate to know.

She turned to face him. "I don't know." A stream of dying light punctured through the cloud cover, illuminating a portion of the woman's face. A young face, yet the eyes were old. "We made a vow once, as Packmates, to protect and fight for one another." The accusatory tone made Kenai feel utterly bare, the skin flayed open and the nerves exposed, all parts of himself he had attempted to bury, dragged to the surface, somehow, during his time spent on this broken island. "Who says you can't do it again?"

With those parting words, she rose to her feet and picked her way down the dock, leaving Kenai to watch the ship that would take him away. His fingers dug into the wood, pressing indentations into its soft, rotten planks.

The truth was this: Kenai wanted the truth. But he didn't know if he was ready for it.

He whipped around. "It's too late for me," he cried out to Ukasna's back, hating the way his voice fractured. It had been so long since he'd felt something other than anger that he didn't dare hope.

Ukasna stopped and turned. "Kenai." Her voice floated back to him with none of the hatred he had expected, only gentleness and compassion. "It's never too late to be who you might have been. Never."

← 46 →

When Apaay woke the next morning, she found Numiak's bed as tidy as when he had left the night before. He hadn't returned.

She flopped back into the fur blankets as alarm lashed through her. Without Numiak's presence, their room was a large, swallowing place. What did his absence mean? Where would he have gone? To the ikovna? Surely not. He wouldn't leave her in Nanuq's palace, vulnerable and alone, though she wondered if she deserved it after the cruelty she had shown him.

Now more than ever, they needed to work as a team. They should return to Sinika as soon as possible, send word to the Council of Nine. It couldn't wait.

Once Apaay dressed, she went in search of Numiak. He was not in the gardens. He was not in the throne room, or anywhere on the grounds, for that matter. She considered going into the city to speak with Desna, because maybe there had been a change in plans? Unfortunately, she didn't have the time.

Apaay climbed the stairs to the third level. The quiet, deserted corridor branched off. She could continue straight, but Apaay glanced right, sensing a chill to the air. At the very end of the corridor, Numiak—disguised as Ro—spoke to a guard of similar build. She couldn't hear their conversation, but the tonality suggested a certain amount of tension. And though Apaay swore she hadn't made a sound, Numiak lifted his head and caught her eye, his surprise swiftly veiled. Another short exchange with the guard. He then gestured her down a nearby passage for privacy.

"What were you talking to that guard about?" Suspicion shaved her words to slender points.

"That," he said coldly, "is none of your business."

Apaay flinched. She had spent the morning garnering her courage, yet it deflated in an instant. Six words was all it took.

"I've been looking for you," she said.

"I'm sure."

Her skin stung with a shameful, creeping flush. "Will you look at me?"

He did, eventually. The lack of emotion told her nothing of what he felt. But Apaay knew. How could she not? Even a demon needed compassion. She had realized that too late.

And now she was looking at this man, this demon, who was her friend, who had carried her through the darkest days of her life, even when she had fought him with every step, and there was nothing Apaay did not feel for him.

"I'm sorry," she whispered. "I am so, so sorry about what I said to you last night. I didn't mean it." She stepped forward, though judging by his aloofness, she was not welcome any nearer to him.

The smile he graced her with was like the very first of his smiles she had witnessed in the labyrinth, sleek as the sea ice, without warmth. "Wolfling," he said. "Let's not say things we don't mean."

It had the desired effect, puncturing like an arrow to the heart, and Apaay could not even be angry at him for it. So she nodded and said, "I wanted to talk to you about the meeting. It's . . . not good."

"Tell me."

Apaay reiterated everything that had been said, every detail, no matter how small, save one. When she was done, Numiak had abandoned his attempts to rid himself of her company. "I was afraid this would happen." He'd covered his eyes with one hand, shielding them from the bright, golden glow of the lamps on the wall. War always moved to slake its hunger. If it did not eat, it would die. "I'll have Desna send a message to Ro. Samut should have arrived at

Sinika by now. She will need to warn her people of the invasion. I am loathe to think of how vast an army Tulimaq commands."

"Yes," Apaay responded curtly, letting the last detail snap free, "especially when Ila, the Wolf Kingdom heir, is supposedly on her way to Unana."

His head snapped around. "What did you say?"

So it was true. His surprise, a reaction to her discovery of this knowledge, not of the information itself.

Apaay vibrated with restrained fury. "Nanuq knows Ila is alive. Why didn't you tell me? You've known from the very beginning and you've had all this time. For that matter, did you even bother to tell Ila?" While she assumed he hadn't, considering Ila had never mentioned it to Apaay, their friendship had been strained prior to going their separate ways, so it wasn't out of the realm of possibility. "If you stopped keeping secrets from everyone, maybe Ila's capture could have been prevented!"

He grinded his molars together so viciously she heard the squeak of saliva between his teeth. "What's done is done. Now you know. And if Ila is on her way to Unana, then I suspect she knows as well."

It was too much. As if Apaay didn't have enough to worry about, now she would agonize over Ila's safety.

"I think we should leave. Today. Now. We have the information we came here for." The dread she'd felt since fleeing that meeting had only intensified in the passing hours.

He said, with obvious reluctance, "I do not disagree, but it's only one more night. Were we to leave now, I fear Nanuq would not react reasonably to our departure. He'd interpret it as a slight to his hospitality, and an indirect statement of our allegiance against him."

"But we are against him," she hissed. "He can't seriously think the Owl Clan would join him after everything he's done?"

"I think that's exactly what he believes—that his vision for order, a clear hierarchy, will be of service to the other nations."

That wasn't the point. "Yesterday, he told me he had a feeling tonight's dinner would be *simply unforgettable*. What do you think he meant by that?"

His eyes narrowed with newfound interest. "Those were his exact words?"

"Yes." She wet her lips. "Should I pack our things? To be safe?"

They stood quite close. If Apaay had thought her touch was welcome, she would have reached for his hand.

"That would be wise, I think." Numiak stepped back. The heat from his body was sorely missed. "Tonight, I will be in disguise. I'm not sure what face I'll take—a polar bear Unua's, maybe. Do what you can to prevent the wine from being served. Spill it if you have to. I wouldn't put it past Nanuq to poison his guests."

The urge to ask him to stay hit her so forcefully Apaay had to bite the inside of her cheek to stop herself. She'd hoped this conversation would smooth the edges between them, but it had only served to remind her that she was alone.

"Fine. I'll see you at dinner, I guess."

They parted ways, and Apaay returned to their chambers. Once safely behind a locked door, she scrambled to shove their clothes into their packs. Numiak insisted on attending dinner—fine. But at least they'd be prepared if things went wrong. Nanuq had something planned. Why else would he invite so many people from the city unless he wanted them to witness some spectacle?

The lock tumbled. The door creaked open at her back. Apaay whirled, her heart pounding. It was Aniirlit, bearing a bundle of fabric.

The woman's attention fell to the stuffed packs. "Master Ro is out?"

Apaay knew how this must look. The harried, frightful look about her. Her shaking hands.

Not for the first time, she wondered why the door had a lock if someone else had the key.

"Yes," Apaay said, shoving the last of the clothes away and straightening. Aniirlit had seen proof of their early departure. There was little she could do about that now.

"Here." She passed some clothes to Apaay. "You will need to change for tonight."

The garments imitated the style of those that Aniirlit wore, with a strip of white fur cleaving vertically down the front: the mark of Nanuq's rule.

"I'm not Nanuq's charge," Apaay said slowly, the back of her neck prickling with foreboding.

"But you serve in the house of the Great Bear," Aniirlit replied. "So tonight, you will bear his mark."

← →

The kitchen was, to put it lightly, chaos. The boiling air clouded so densely it felt as if Apaay were breathing underwater. At one end of the room, a hearty stew bubbled in the coals. At the other sat the skins of wine, which were currently being organized by Pama, awaiting pouring. A wine whose taste could possibly mask a killing poison.

A decision had to be made.

Making a show of tripping over a table leg, Apaay slammed into Pama's back. He fumbled with the skin, spilling a few droplets, but was able to regain his balance, much to Apaay's dismay. He glanced at her in a panic. "Careful!"

"Sorry." She ducked her head sheepishly.

Well, that hadn't worked out the way she'd hoped.

The staff began carrying the wine upstairs. What if Nanuq poisoned not only the wine, but the rest of the food as well? What if he didn't poison anything and she drew attention to herself for no reason?

"Apaay!" Aniirlit's snapping voice rang out. "What are you doing standing around? Make yourself useful!"

Apaay shuffled closer to the wall, picking up a stack of plates at random. Two men currently hauled the enormous vat of stew across the kitchen to await dishing into bowls. They would have to pass Pama in the process. With the vat so unwieldy, it wouldn't take much to tip the balance.

No one was paying any attention to her. The men grunted, heaving the soup closer. And Apaay sort of . . . stuck out her foot. Not too far, but far enough.

One of the men's feet caught on her ankle. The cauldron lurched from the imbalance. The soup slopped and the vat tipped, and it was a flood, spattering all over the floor. And Pama, poor Pama with the wine skins, slipped, his hands flying out to catch himself. Dark red wine mixed with the pale stew, like blood in snow.

Apaay stared at the mess. The clatter and din slowed, and softened, and died. Every staff member in the kitchen gaped at her in horror.

A hand latched onto her upper arm. Aniirlit dragged her into a corner, shoved her against the wall. Then her palm cracked against Apaay's cheek.

She gasped in pain.

"You listen to me," the woman spat. "Nothing, and I mean *nothing*, will ruin this evening. You might not think this is of any importance to you, but for the staff, our success is protection from Nanuq. Disrupt this night, and I will personally toss your hide to the bears. Do I make myself clear?"

Her back scraped against the rough stone as she tried putting space between them. "It was an honest mistake."

"Honest?" Aniirlit's upper lip curled the barest fraction. "I don't know who you are Apaay, but I do know you haven't been honest with me." She narrowed her eyes. "I wonder: how is it that both the soup *and* the wine spilled? You were the only person in the vicinity at the time."

Apaay thought her stomach might have dropped somewhere on the ground.

"Is that your plan?" she whisper-hissed, pressing closer. "Sabotage? I saw the packs. When are you and Master Ro planning on leaving?"

Yes, her stomach was definitely on the ground.

After a long moment of assessment, Aniirlit stepped back, glaring. "Fortunately for you, I haven't the time to unravel this mystery. Go out into the hall and make sure the guests have what they need. Give me another reason to suspect you, and I won't hesitate to inform the Great Bear of your questionable allegiance."

Apaay fled by way of the servant's staircase. Aniirlit's threat chased her to the top of the stairs, where she stopped, catching her breath. It wasn't as suffocating up here. The air cooled the redness that had pressed into her skin.

If Aniirlit knew she and Numiak planned to escape, would the woman put a stop to it? Should she risk telling Numiak?

She groaned, closing her eyes.

Someone began climbing the stairs. Apaay pushed through the doors into the hall in case it was Aniirlit and stationed herself in a corner. Beyond the windows, the last remnants of late summer lingered red and violet in the coiling dusk. Inside, the décor was reminiscent of the long night, of frost and first snow. White drapes gave the illusion of moonlight. Lamplight tossed shadow and gold over every curved and sharpened surface. It was lovely and cold and Apaay trusted none of it.

She scanned the room with a critical eye. The table was set, Nanuq's chair empty at the head. Servants had already begun pouring the wine, a red liquid of deep opaqueness that made the skin on her arms prickle. One of the guests lifted a glass to his lips and sipped. She watched him dab the red droplets from his mouth with a white napkin.

And speaking of white. She noticed the absence of Numiak's pale hair immediately. Tonight, he wore another man's face, but whose? How would he make it known to her?

"You forgot something."

She startled at Pama's appearance. He pressed a pitcher of water into her hand.

Right. Water. She smiled gratefully. "Thank you. And I apologize for my clumsiness earlier."

"It's all right. Just . . . be careful."

As he moved toward one end of the table, Apaay filled glasses, though her mind was elsewhere.

With that done, she returned to her station. She spotted Nanuq's daughter speaking with a handsome man with dark, rounded eyes. Polar bear Unua, but he wasn't a soldier. Perhaps he was an esteemed member of high society. Apaay examined him for any noticeable sign that it was Numiak. His hand gestures. The arrogance of his posture.

At one point in the conversation, he caught her eye, and they stared at one another across the room. Apaay's cheeks warmed.

He dipped his chin in acknowledgement before refocusing his attention on the ikovna.

At least she now knew what face Numiak wore.

"I am curious if you've seen Master Ro around."

Apaay turned her head slowly.

With one slender shoulder propped against the wall, Nanuq sipped from a glass, eyes on the room. His arrival had not been announced, for whatever reason.

It took two attempts before she could find her voice. "No, sir. I have not."

He made a sound of vague interest. "How odd." There it was again, that uncomfortably pacifying tone. The kindness that was not kindness at all. "I do expect my guests to show, if only for appearance's sake."

Numiak hadn't mentioned what excuse he would use to explain his absence. Apaay chose her words with care. "My master doesn't generally inform me of his intentions, sir."

"Of course not." He spoke with obvious amusement. She found nothing humorous in the situation.

As he scanned the room again, Apaay took a closer study of the man beside her. Long, curling lashes framed hazel eyes that were both wistful and keen. His parka was incredibly detailed in its design, accented by dark gray fur—a fox that had molted its winter pelt, most likely—circling the ends of the sleeves and a good portion of the bottom hem. It was far more intricate than anything he had worn before. Indeed, Apaay had always found his modest dress confusing, given his station.

"Do you recall our previous conversation?" he asked curiously.

Apaay looked to see if Numiak had noticed them speaking, but he still conversed with the ikovna. Of all the people in the room, why had Nanuq sought her out? "Yes, sir."

He seemed pleased by her answer. "Then let me ask you this. What do you think would happen, were a nation's leader to fall?"

"To be honest, I'm not sure." There was no designated leader, no governing official, in her culture. People looked to the elders in times of conflict, and the shamans were of course spiritual guides, but as a whole, the community worked together to ensure its survival.

"My dear, without a strong sense of leadership, a nation could devolve."

She startled. "Devolve?"

"Yes. Imagine what would happen if there were no guides. Why, people would become animals!" He laughed.

As Nanuq lifted his glass for another sip, the collar of his parka gaped, revealing a strip of naked skin. Thin, pale, crisscrossing lines wrapped around the curve of his shoulder. Apaay recognized them for what they were: scars.

His gaze snagged on hers. She straightened and shifted her attention elsewhere, her face hot, even as she wondered who or what had put those marks on his skin.

He studied her in profile. She focused on not letting her hands shake around the water pitcher.

Nanuq leaned closer, his eyes brightening with a dull light. "Please inform Master Ro that I expect his presence within the hour. I would hate to return his servant to him with the skin split open on her back." With that, he straightened and took his leave.

Apaay, feeling suddenly ill, hurried back to the servant's passage. Away from Nanuq's prying eyes, she could breathe. She and Numiak should have left this morning. It was too late for that now.

Or was it? They could leave, theoretically. They had an hour. And if Apaay disappeared for that length of time, no one would think twice, assuming she was busy in the kitchen. They'd grab their packs and flee to Desna's workshop, take the tunnel hidden beneath the floorboards to where it supposedly emptied out beyond the city gates.

Travel north.

Find the cairn.

Return to Sinika.

Dinner had not yet been served, but Apaay didn't think she could wait any longer. If Numiak didn't show, it was her skin on the line. Aniirlit had threatened to expose them. She would do the woman a favor and leave and never step foot in this shining palace again.

After returning the water pitcher to the kitchen, she reentered the hall, looking for Nanuq. He was nowhere to be seen. Good. A servant interacting with a guest would draw his suspicion.

The ikovna had turned her attention elsewhere. Numiak sat alone, studying his water glass. Apaay came to his side. He lifted his head, appraising her with no small amount of curiosity. This face, while handsome, was not the one she desired to see.

"I need to speak with you," she whispered into his ear. "In private."

Numiak's eyebrows lifted in surprise, but he didn't question her request. With a nod, he excused himself from the table and led her down one of the corridors, where silence sank deep in the stone. A shadowed doorway led them to an empty room with a couch, a few chairs, and one lamp burning. Apaay shut the door and turned to face him.

Numiak studied her with odd detachment. That hurt. The distance between them had to end. Someone had to cross it. Whether the attempt ended in failure, well, at least she had tried.

"I know we already discussed this, but I really think we should reconsider staying through the rest of the meal. It's not safe. Nanuq is looking for Ro and if you don't show up he threatened to hurt me and—" She couldn't take the tension. No more lies. They hurt too much.

She swallowed. "I want you to know I'm sorry for what I said. It was completely out of line and . . ." And she was absolutely out of her mind to think of these things now, but if Numiak wouldn't accept her apology, perhaps he would accept a gift instead.

Apaay's heart pounded out an uneven rhythm, but she did not falter as she placed her hands on Numiak's chest, rose onto her toes, and pressed her mouth to his.

Desire rose to the very edges of her skin. Numiak's breath was warm, a spill of heat into her throat as the anticipation of kissing him rose to a head.

Then it died, wholly and completely. His breath was warm, but his lips were cold and stiff with reluctance. He did not want her kiss. He did not want *her*.

Humiliation washed through Apaay as she pulled away.

"I don't know if I should be flattered or offended," a voice drawled.

Apaay spun around. The Face Stealer stood in the open doorway, wearing his mien of lovely cruelty, shadows blotting out his form. Without taking his eyes off her, he shut the door with a soft click and flipped the lock. A wash of cold air hit her back.

She looked over her shoulder, but the other man had disappeared.

Apaay gaped at where he had been standing. "Where did you send him?"

Numiak continued his measured approach. "Somewhere far away from here."

She stumbled back, rounding the couch, and he followed, a predator unwilling to let its prey out of sight. "You thought that man was me." They halted at opposite ends of the couch, Apaay watching his movements warily.

"I thought no such thing."

A slow smile stretched the length of his vicious mouth. It was positively carnal. "Oh, how sweetly you lie."

Her pulse thrummed and thrummed. Apaay feigned disinterest. "Maybe I kissed him because I wanted to." It was humiliating to think he had witnessed her attempts at seduction to a man she had believed to be him.

"Was he an adequate kisser?"

She lifted her chin. Of course he would use the word *adequate*. "As a matter of fact, he was far better than adequate. It was a perfectly lovely kiss."

"Lovely, was it?" He closed the distance between them with that long, leisurely stride. "But did he make you *feel*?" The last word rumbled against her ear, and the heat of his breath along its outer shell made Apaay unconsciously arch her neck toward him. The pull to take one step nearer, body to body, was so fierce she dug her fingernails into her palms, the pain helping clear her mind.

"What if he did?" she challenged. "What if I choose him?"

"You have the freedom to choose whoever you want," he said calmly, "but it would not stop me from ripping out his tongue."

The idea of Numiak being driven to violence in the name of desire made her heart skip a beat. Her reaction probably wasn't healthy, for obvious reasons. "If you hate the thought of him being a better kisser than you," she managed, voice wavering, "then prove him wrong."

His voice softened dangerously. "Is that a command?"

Was it? Heat, sweat, desire—she smelled them all, a perfume on his skin. Apaay realized she could command him, if she desired to. She could wield power, same as him.

"I call in the blood oath."

Abruptly, the desire in his eyes extinguished. The shape of his mouth compressed as the oath pulled taut between them, demanding it be fulfilled.

Apaay had misstepped. She knew as soon as the words left her mouth. But she could not take them back. It was too late.

Numiak moved to stare out the window overlooking the gardens. After what seemed like an eternity, he faced her. Darkness bled like a stain across his bone structure, and strips of moonlight cut across his forehead, shadow snaking down into the collar of his parka. "Why do you have to use the blood oath? Why not just ask me?"

"Isn't that your preference? Deals and trades and debts?" She wielded fear like a weapon, holding it in front of her heart so that it might always be protected. "You want people to owe you."

"Not you," he said roughly. "Not between us."

"It's always been that way between us."

"No, it hasn't. Not for months now."

Her mouth opened, then closed. It was true. The girl whose reflection she viewed in the glass knew it to be true as well.

The truth was this: a blanket of pale fox fur tucked around her weary, wasted body during the darkest days of her life, a soft cushioned chair beneath her, and the air smelling of parchment, a lamp left on to banish the darkness.

The truth was this: his heart, warm and fluttering, passed safely back into his hands.

The truth was this: the black threads of his hair sliding through her fingers, the open sky at her back and Sinika at her feet, her palm pressed to his chest, and peace settling over her.

The truth was this: *You save her, Kaan.*

Numiak touched his fingertips to the frosted glass. "Why did you say those things about me yesterday, about my past?" Ache tinged his voice, which in turn hurt *her.* She hadn't the means to defend herself against it. "I told you those things in confidence. I trusted you to listen without judgment."

"I know, I *know.*" She'd known exactly what she was saying, yet she'd said it anyway.

There was a pause. His breathing, and hers, combating for space, yet attempting to reach some elusive harmony. "You really hurt me, Apaay."

The confession stomped its wretched boots all over her heart. The twinge sprouted into a throb, which morphed into deep anguish, shame tightening her throat. "I'm sorry." It was a croak.

"You didn't answer the question."

Apaay hated seeing him like this. When his eyes were no color at all, for the pupils had bled to the outer rings. When he was unkind to himself, and punishing. Why had she said those things? *Confess.* Then there would be no part of her he did not see.

The tears rose up, stinging. "I was hurt, and angry—"

"Why? Why were you angry?" Moonlight flamed across his face, and Apaay saw everything. His eyes, they were beautiful. "Were you . . ." His voice softened in uncertainty. "Did you feel something? For me?"

She had no words. How did one describe the marvel of the sun emerging after six months of darkness? How did she put into words the significance and necessity of Numiak's presence in her life, an attachment that had grown deeper roots than she had ever expected, and that, against all odds, had been nurtured, had grown?

Apaay wanted to tell him so many things, each one a confession, but they clogged her throat, effectively cutting off her ability to speak.

The silence of anticipated response had stretched for too long. Numiak's expression shuttered. "I see."

"Wait!" Apaay lunged, capturing his arm before he could vanish again. Tears streamed from her eyes. "Please don't leave. I'm sorry. I'm so deeply sorry for hurting you. I lashed out because, well, because when I saw the ikovna sitting in your lap, I was jealous." Apaay's legs felt seconds away from collapse. "I was jealous and I was scared. Is that what you want to hear? I was terrified of what those feelings meant because you are a demon, the person who destroyed my life and the life of my people. I'm supposed to hate you." She was crying with such force that her throat ached. "But every time I needed you, you were there, and I hated that, too."

Her lips trembled. Fear rose like gorge in her throat. Apaay was learning how to hold to life fiercely, to never settle, to never apologize for who she was or where she had come from, to live a life that was true, a hard, bright, sharp thing, and that meant honesty in all its facets. "And now I look at you—" Her breath hitched. "I look at you and see my dear friend, someone who I trust with my life, someone who I would *die* for, and who I think would die for me, and I don't know what to do." There it was: sharp and too jagged to touch. "Tell me what to do."

The sight of Numiak's own tear-filled gaze shocked her to the core. This openness, something tender and new and fearful blooming—Apaay had never seen that look from him before.

"Apaay." With quiet reverence, his hands lifted to frame her face, thumbs resting against her cheekbones, warm and sure. "If you don't know how I feel about you by now, then I must be doing something wrong."

She moistened her dry lips. "Wh-what do you mean?"

A bit of laughter slipped into his tone. "Wolfling." He sighed, a fond, happy sound. "You have been driving me out of my *mind*."

That was good, right?

"These past three months have been the happiest and most frustrating of my life. You have managed to push me to the very brink of insanity, and there were days when I wondered what would happen were I to step off that ledge." He studied her with such careful intimacy, as though taking into account each detail, tucking them away for later scrutiny. "I told myself that being your friend was enough. That's what you needed after the labyrinth. But the truth is, it's not enough. Not for me."

Apaay shied from his gaze, because she was a coward when it came to him. Always had been. His admission tugged her nearer to a truth she was too afraid to acknowledge. "Then what do you want?"

"You vexing woman." His voice deepened with a new richness that puckered the skin of her arms. "Look at me."

She did. Eyes the color of moist soil stared back. Strangely enough, it felt as if she were looking into Numiak's true eye color for the first time, as if only now was he allowing her to see it.

"I want every part of you that you're willing to give me," he said. "I want your mind. I want your body. I want your trust." His large hands curved around her neck, settling like a warm collar. "But more than anything, I want your heart."

The object of his desire thudded against her sternum with new fervor. His confession dizzied her. It was the most perfect, the most terrifying, of revelations. Apaay didn't know what to do with it. "What else?" she croaked.

The corners of his eyes crinkled like soft, worn hide. "I'm a selfish man, Apaay, especially when it comes to you. I want smiles that are just for me. I want to hear the sound of your laughter every day so that I might never forget it. I want to know of your fears intimately so that I might fight with you against them, and your dreams, so that I might help make them a reality. I want to lend you strength when you have none. I want the smell of your skin, the rhythm of your heartbeat, the sweet lies you tell me, the banter that makes me feel alive. I want you to always be on my mind." He drew her closer. "Apaay."

Her heart had long ago stopped beating with any form of steadiness. Apaay didn't know how she hadn't seen him before. The deep tenderness and affection, the yearning, and the fear, because there was always fear when it came to him. "You were always better with words than I," she whispered.

Leaning down, Numiak aligned his mouth with hers. "Ask me to kiss you, wolfling. Don't use the blood oath. Just ask."

The thought of his mouth on hers pulsed through her. Apaay was not strong enough to deny herself this one thing, even with Nanuq's dinner taking place down the hall. If that made her a fool, then so be it. "Kiss me," she said.

And oh, how he *smiled* at her.

Warm breath smelling of spice dampened her lips. Then Numiak angled his head and, with slow precision, gained entrance into her mouth.

Apaay didn't know how she thought the other man had ever been Numiak, because he was taking her apart so effortlessly it wiped her mind clean. The kiss, which began as the barest pressure of lips, deepened, until at last their mouths locked together, breath upon breath. Apaay made a soft sound of need.

Slipping one hand through her hair, Numiak cupped the back of her skull, his other palm pressing against her lower back, fingers splayed. She was dizzy. Spinning. *Hungry*. The musk of his skin, the coarseness of his cheeks, the hard parts of him pressing into the soft parts of her.

His clever tongue teased, licking at the inside of her cheek, coaxing her tongue out of hiding. Apaay reciprocated the tease tentatively. She had been kissed before, but never like this. A slow eating at each other's mouths. Pleasure of exploration. Pure desire manifested in the physical.

Soon the kiss descended into one of darkness, of madness, of insanity. Apaay suckled on Numiak's tongue, and his answering growl sent heat crawling up her chest. The fingers on her skull tightened. He nipped at her lips, suckled the bruised flesh, crushed her mouth beneath his in a ravenous, open-mouthed assault that demanded her surrender. It empowered her that she could reduce this man to baseless need with her mouth, her hands. Apaay went one step further and slotted one thigh between his legs, driving upward, curious as to how far she could push him.

Without breaking contact, Numiak hitched her legs around his waist. It felt completely natural to lock her ankles at the small of his back as he shoved her against the nearest wall with leashed aggression, like a dog snapping at its tether. The world was tilting and yet she wanted more, she wanted to drain every last drop of desire from his tongue, she wanted to crawl inside his skin, she wanted to never stop kissing him.

Then Numiak's length nestled against her core, and Apaay groaned.

His fingers dug into the undersides of her thighs. "All right?" he panted into her mouth.

"Yes." She pulled him closer, increasing the friction. Apaay knew enough about the male anatomy to understand what was happening, and she welcomed it, welcomed him.

Dragging his mouth from hers, Numiak trailed heated kisses to her ear and down her neck. "You're beautiful," he murmured.

She felt beautiful.

"And frustrating."

That gave her pause. "Frustrating?"

He grazed his teeth along a tendon, causing her to buck against him. Dark laughter feathered the air. Apaay hadn't enough breath in her lungs to curse him for it.

"When we were in that pleasure house," he continued in a gravelly tone, the wells of his pupils drawing her in, "I wanted to spirit you away to someplace private, where I could touch you the way I wanted to, with no distractions." A flush had stained his cheeks a deep red. Apaay felt the sweat cooling in the hollow of her throat, and it seemed Numiak noticed, too, for he leaned forward and licked it from her skin. She hissed out an exhale as his touch drifted behind her knees, down her calves, kneading the muscle there.

"How—" She gripped his broad shoulders to steady herself. "How would you have touched me?"

The scorched look he gave her threatened to singe every strand of hair on her head.

"Like this," he whispered, brushing a kiss to her sweaty temple. "Just like this."

Gripping her thighs, Numiak spread her legs wider and ground against her heat, drawing pleasure up her spine. It was glorious. It was agony. Apaay didn't realize she had started moving against him until he groaned, his face tucked into her neck.

Trapped between the wall and his body, Apaay was effectively pinned in place, which allowed those warm, long-fingered hands of his to wander. They were strong, able to wield weapons with ferocity. Arrogant, in the tapping of a single finger against a hard surface. Clever, too, as they had stroked her body in the pleasure house. As they were doing now.

"What do you want, wolfling?" Numiak caressed the sensitive skin of her inner thighs, skirting around the area that throbbed. He drew away and returned, nearer to the source of her pleasure, which was so acute it bordered on pain.

He knew what she wanted. He wasn't giving it to her.

Apaay shifted toward his fingers and cursed in frustration when they slipped away. "Higher," she whispered. The throbbing between her legs was insistent.

"Here?"

It was so close, but not close enough. Her face flamed as she repeated, "Higher."

"And now?"

She caught sight of his provocative smile. "Damn you, touch me already!"

He did, and the back of her head hit the wall as fire licked up her body, chewing on her nerve endings. Apaay bit her lip to suppress a moan, but at the next firm touch, it flew out. Whatever he was doing between her legs, it felt exquisite. Her facial muscles twitched. The pads of her fingers pressed into his hot skin. Through it all, Numiak's attention never strayed from her face, his own lips parted, flushed with rich color, and the bright, sharp edge of desire so near.

The ached flared, and the moment she reached that threshold, he removed his hand.

Cupping her backside, Numiak strode to the couch, where he laid her down gently before undressing her. First, her parka, tossed to the floor. Then her slippers. The trousers came next. Apaay, dressed in only her undergarments, stared up into Numiak's devouring gaze. She reached out in curiosity to touch the dark tendrils cloaking his arms and shoulders, felt their cool kiss against her fevered skin.

"Second thoughts?" Though his voice was light, his eyes were serious.

Apaay smiled with breathless elation. "No." She unwound her breastband and dropped it to the floor, fighting the urge to cover herself. It was like a touch, his gaze. A slow, delicious touch that brought a heaviness to her breasts, the cool air drawing her nipples to points.

Lowering himself on top of her, Numiak trailed sweet kisses from her shoulder to her cheek, his arousal nestled between her legs. The fingertips of one hand teased the top of her underwear. "May I?"

Apaay nodded, trembling. She wanted this. Of that, she had no doubts.

His hand slipped beneath her underwear and found the heat at the juncture of her thighs. Apaay cried out. It was too good. She arched into his probing touch, but he pinned her down by the hip.

"Patience." Numiak's smile was pure male satisfaction. "Now." In a conversational tone, he went on. "Tell me again what you want. This?" He skimmed a finger across her center, the touch featherlight.

Apaay lunged, catching his mouth with hers. A low keening rose in her throat as she moved against his hand, trying to angle her hips exactly right. Her leg and stomach muscles contracted. The toes of one foot pressed into the back of his calf. She tried to leverage herself nearer toward the intensity as her veins singed and smoked and her pulse careened and her legs twitched and a fog dampened all thought, nothing but the craze of wanting to climb higher, nearer to the fire that suffused her skin. Another twitch. Apaay whimpered from the stroke of his fingers. Clutching his back, she whispered brokenly, "Numiak."

He increased the pressure against her core. Slid his fingers through the dampness in a smooth, unbroken motion. Apaay felt her insides clench instinctively. She began to shake.

"I need you to do one more thing for me, wolfling."

"Yes," she panted, delirious, on the crest of a wave that would soon break.

It was barely breath, his words. Barely a ripple of sound. "Let go."

Release ripped through her, and Apaay muffled her cry against his shoulder as her body bowed and she moved through the throes of the greatest pleasure she had ever known. And he stayed with her. His voice in her ear, saying how lovely she was, and how strong, and fierce, and Apaay, Apaay, *Apaay*. And still the pleasure went on, wave after wave, its current sending her to a place of pure light.

The world returned to her in pieces. Numiak was stretched out on the couch beside her, his nose buried in her hair. His fingertips drifted across her collarbones, the touch drawing sparks along her skin. The window glass was so clear it looked like an open door, the spread of what appeared to be a burning earth in the growing garden beyond, red and yellow and orange, all the colors of flame.

"How do you feel?" he asked.

Apaay curled against him drowsily. "Your head is big enough. I see no reason to inflate it."

He chuckled, hugging her to his chest so her ear rested against his beating heart. It was a robust, sonorous sound. "It's all right. It'll be our secret."

Their legs slotted together like interlocking threads. Nothing would compare to the feeling of home, but Numiak's presence comforted her as nothing else did.

"I didn't think you felt the same way," she blurted.

He was quiet for a time. Dinner conversation drifted through the walls, a reminder that they would need to return soon. Apaay hadn't been gone for long. No one would come looking for her yet. "I did, but I had only just earned your trust. I didn't want to give you a reason to take it back."

She fiddled with the blue beads hanging from his single skinny braid. "When did you know?"

"Know what?"

Apaay punched him in the arm, and he howled with laughter. "You know what, bastard."

"I'm growing rather fond of that word. It's practically a term of endearment."

"Tell me."

"Bossy." He skimmed a hand over the swell of her hip, nosing her ear. "Oh, sometime between you beating me to a pulp and drugging my tea."

He'd found her starved and wounded like an animal, and she had wanted to kill him in that cave. Now here they were.

"And you?" he said.

She sighed in contentment, wondering how long they had before the dream dissipated. He was warm, wonderfully warm. "It was a gradual thing." And toward the beginning, a reluctant one, too. Apaay had been in denial for far too long. "But when I gave you back your heart," she whispered, watching her fingers spread across the slope of his chest, "that was when I began to trust you."

"Wolfling." Covering her hand with his, Numiak smiled into her eyes with complete adoration. "You may have returned my heart to me in Taggak, but I assure you it was yours long before that."

Apaay didn't know what to say except, "Oh."

He was still smiling at her when the door splintered open.

← 48 →

Apaay tensed as four shadows slanted across the back of the couch, the broken door swaying on bent hinges. Numiak dipped his mouth to her ear. "Get dressed. When I say run, you run."

She nodded, dropping to the floor quietly and slipping back into her clothes as he rose to face the intruders, his true mien on display. Ro's gold eyes had been exchanged for slate rimmed in scarlet.

Someone gasped. Apaay's hands trembled as she struggled to tug on her trousers. Crouched at the front of the couch, its high, arched back prevented whoever stood at the door from spotting her. There was nothing worse than a predator you could not see.

"The Face Stealer."

Aniirlit's voice.

Now dressed, Apaay waited for Numiak's signal. He stood with his legs braced, a few tendrils of his power curling reassuringly around her back. A second gasp cut off, followed by a scream. A chill dashed over Apaay's skin. She remained crouched, fingers digging into the cushion.

Numiak leaped over the back of the couch in one fluid motion. In his hand, a shadow blade. "Run," he said, and caught the first soldier's club on the downward swing.

Apaay sprinted across the room and burst out into the hall. She cut right, heading away from the sounds of laughter and clinking glasses. Once the soldiers alerted Nanuq to their deception, he'd lock down the city, close the gates. Her only option was to take the underground tunnel into the lower city. Desna would hide her until Numiak arrived.

Slapping footsteps warned her of another's approach. Apaay glanced over her shoulder. Aniirlit. She cursed and descended the stairs, but bypassed the kitchen and storerooms. She couldn't risk anyone learning of her escape route.

She reached the first level and tore down an unfamiliar hallway. The air rang with each gasping breath, and she turned left, left again, charging through a closed door. She reached a second corridor when someone rammed into her from behind.

Apaay hit the ground, but she was already moving, shifting her weight and rising up, flipping their positions, the motion as familiar as her name. Hands locked around wrists. Aniirlit countered, twisting Apaay's arm behind her back. She gritted her teeth and fought the hold. Aniirlit weighed more, was studier in the shoulders, but Apaay had everything to lose.

"Listen to me," Aniirlit hissed.

Apaay's elbow struck the woman in the mouth, and she cried out. Her grip loosened, allowing Apaay to struggle free. Another strike to the face sent the older woman crashing against the wall.

Untangling herself, Apaay fled, adrenaline burning holes through her veins. One of the guards turned a corner up ahead and charged. She rammed into him straight on, catching him by the ankle in the process so he went down. Then she was past him.

At the very end of the hall, a door sat ajar. Apaay ducked inside the darkened room, needing a moment to regroup. The room was stuffed with furniture, everything draped in shadow, the drapes closed. She stumbled to the farthest corner and crouched behind a stack of chairs.

It wasn't long before footsteps thundered down the corridor. Apaay tensed, breath held.

"She went this way," one man said.

"Search the kitchen again."

"We'll head her off at the north wing."

The footsteps gradually faded, and then, nothing.

Apaay exhaled.

The hall was dead. No guards in sight. If she moved with haste, if she did not stop, if she focused on what needed to be done, then all would be well.

All would be well.

Steeling herself, she dashed on silent feet around the corner. Nanuq would have been informed by now of the Face Stealer's deceit. She descended a servant's staircase to the storage room. After shoving aside the crates, she ducked into the cramped tunnel, which eventually broadened, allowing her to stand.

The cool, underground air felt most welcome against her overheated body. For a moment, she had to lean against the wall, so shaky were her legs, her body alight with pure adrenaline. Apaay suspected she could run the length of this city, all the way to the gates if needed. But she paced herself in navigating the miles-long tunnel to its eventual exit. From there, it was another half-mile to Desna's workshop.

"Desna?" She knocked, glancing over her shoulder at the shadowy street. A few tradesmen glanced at her in curiosity as they passed. No sign of Nanuq's kirn. "Hello, Desna?" Again, no response. Apaay tried the handle. The door swung open at her touch.

Shadows draped the workroom's interior. The dry, musty air contained a familiar sharp odor underneath.

The hair rose on the back of Apaay's neck.

"Desna?" She stepped inside. The lamps had been extinguished. No fire burned from the hearth. A feeling of absence lingered.

Another step brought her to the edge of the weaver's workstation. A few tools littered the planked floor, discarded strips of cloth, and a sword.

A lumpy, misshapen figure caught her eye.

Apaay moved closer, the dread already seizing her limbs with sudden cold. "Desna?"

The shape was a body. Or rather, pieces of a body, sitting stagnant in a pool of blood.

She stumbled backward, ramming into the edge of the table. The repulsive, iron scent clotted the back of her throat.

"I'm afraid your friend cannot help you now."

A hand locked around her neck. Apaay turned, striking out, but one of Nanuq's men tackled her, putting an end to her struggles by pressing down her legs while a second kirn bound her hands behind her back.

That didn't stop her from kicking and screaming as they dragged her back to the palace. Terror—it was the crumpling of her lungs. It was the scrape of her feet dragging along the sleek black floor. It was ten fingers wrapped around her upper arms. And it was the sight that greeted her beyond the throne room's heavy wooden doors.

Nanuq had invited one hundred of the city's most prominent tradesmen, merchants, artisans, and members of high society to his table this evening. And every single one of them was dead.

Pale, bloated faces stared vacuously from where the guests had collapsed, either on the floor, in their chairs, or onto the table, heads and arms covered in half-eaten food. The air reeked of spilled wine. Apaay's struggles began anew as her lungs contracted with the beginnings of a scream. They were dead, they were dead, everyone was dead.

Everyone, that is, except Nanuq. Comfortably seated on his throne at the end of the room, he watched the guards drag her down the column-lined walkway, watched them deposit her at the base of the dais. She stared at the ground, trembling.

"Hello, Apaay," Nanuq said. "I've been looking for you."

Her nostrils flared. She thought she would sick herself.

"Did you hear me, my dear?"

She could not stop shaking. His voice, his *voice*. How was it this soft-spoken man had massacred an entire nation? He wanted her to play along. Apaay would not.

Nanuq tutted. "Oh, this will not do."

Abruptly, she was yanked forward, dragged within a foot of Nanuq's face. She could not escape his gaze unless she closed her eyes, and Apaay feared that would only anger him further.

"That's better." A faint, albeit sad, smile tipped his mouth. "I am sorry things had to come to this, truly. I want you to know I do not blame you. You have been led astray. It is not your fault."

Led astray?

He frowned at seeing the confusion on her face. "How to explain?" Apaay believed his perplexity, the frustration at trying to convey his thoughts, was genuine. "It is not your fault you have been caught in this war. You could not have changed your circumstances. You were only a child at the time. Which is why I don't blame you for what you did. Not at all. To come into my home, a liar and a thief. To take what was mine. Why, had I been in your position, I might have done the same."

Not a sound broke the quiet. Then again, all the guests were dead.

The guards lowered Apaay to her knees. Nanuq rested a hand on her shoulder as if to comfort her, his fingers light as insect wings. She shied away from his touch. He knew something she didn't. That terrified her. "My daughter told me early on about you. She believed you to be hiding something."

His daughter? She hadn't said one word to the ikovna. Though she supposed she had glared at the woman a time or two.

"I must admit, I didn't believe her at first. My daughter, as much as she is valuable, has made mistakes in the past. Mistakes that have brought harm to our people. But she was insistent. And tonight, she came to me, told me of your packed bags. You were leaving, you and Master Ro. Or who I had believed to be Master Ro."

Apaay's confusion morphed into something ugly and wild, something she could not hold down, for it grew beyond her grasp. Only one person had seen her packed bags, and it had not been the ikovna.

A single pair of footsteps echoed in the cavernous space. Apaay didn't want to look, but she couldn't *not* look.

It was Aniirlit.

The woman stood straight-backed at Nanuq's side, studying Apaay with her head cocked, the right side of her face puffy and blood-darkened from where Apaay's elbow had made impact during their tussle. This couldn't be Nanuq's daughter. Aniirlit was a servant. She wore rags. She ate scraps for meals. Nanuq had punished her, brutally, for sneaking into Numiak's room. No father would take a whip to his daughter.

But the capital city of Nur was not her village, and these were not her people. Had that been Aniirlit's intention all along? Had she in actuality entered their chambers on Nanuq's orders, knowing she would be caught, knowing what punishment awaited her? Oh, Apaay had been a fool.

Nanuq seemed pleased by her shock. "My daughter, Aniirlit. She is nothing if not obedient. She plays her part well."

"You lied to me," Apaay whispered hoarsely.

The woman lifted an eyebrow. "And you did not?"

Nanuq hooted with quiet laughter. "Oh, I love this. How I love this." He rested a hand on his daughter's shoulder, and Aniirlit did not flinch.

The pit in Apaay's stomach yawned wider, deeper. They had shared wine, she and Pama and Aniirlit. Another falsity, for the woman had been a spy this whole time. She tugged against the rope uselessly. Her hands might have been bound, but they hadn't tied her legs. If she could make it to the servant's passage, there might be a chance. She'd reach the door . . . and the guards would cut her down.

"Aniirlit warned me you could not be trusted. There was something about you, something she could not put her finger on." With his elbows resting on the arms of his chair, he pressed his fingertips together and studied her from above. "Imagine my surprise when I discovered that, though your scent portrayed you as owl Unua, your blood told a different story entirely."

Nanuq pulled something from his pocket: a white cloth dotted with blood.

Apaay went colder than cold.

May I?

"Blood, you see—" He lifted the cloth. "—holds the true scent of one's heritage."

The shamans understood blood's unique properties. Apaay imagined the kitska would, too, in order to create their healing remedies. Apaay hadn't known, but then again, why would she? It was not as if her people could sense the difference, so poor was their sense of smell compared to the polar bear Unua.

He looked at her, head tilted. "You seem confused. You do know who you are, don't you?"

Apaay swallowed. She was afraid another lie might kill her. "I am Analak."

Nanuq's stare grew puzzled. "Oh dear." He shook his head pityingly. "Tell me it's not true. The Face Stealer did not inform you of your heritage?"

Her heart stuttered. She searched for a kind face, anyone at all. She needed her family. She needed Ila and Chena. She wanted to be far away from this room, warm and cozy in her ice house. But it was not meant to be.

Nanuq tsked his disappointment. "That is not acceptable. Not acceptable at all." He waved a hand. "Bring him in, please."

The doors opened, and five guards dragged Numiak into the room.

Apaay's cry of distress rang out. They had beaten him so thoroughly that the inflamed bruising extended across his entire face, swelling one eye completely shut, and even portions of his neck. His legs scraped against the floor. His parka had been ripped down the front. Blood painted his mouth scarlet. Numiak's remaining eye flashed white as it rolled.

Like her, they'd bound his wrists behind his back. His long black hair hung in ragged strands around his face. It took five men to hold him. He bucked and writhed, and spat the foulest of threats until one man struck him in the jaw. They dropped him at the bottom of the dais.

Nanuq studied the demon at his feet with trace amounts of fascination. "How like an animal you are."

Numiak bared his teeth. Admittedly, there was something untamed about him. He was normally so poised, even in the face of grave peril. That he was not revealed how dire of a situation they had found themselves in. Apaay swallowed down the sour taste in her mouth.

Pushing off his back foot, he lunged toward Nanuq, who smiled pleasantly as though he had anticipated this, and motioned to one of the guards.

There was a sound of splitting air and tearing flesh.

Numiak grunted, falling forward against the stairs as the horrible serpentine coil slithered to the floor, pulling the blood pouring from his back with it. It struck again with a high whine. The kirn doled out the punishment with the same detachment as someone performing surgery.

"If you insist on acting like an animal," said Nanuq mildly, "then I will treat you like one. Prove to me that you have the faculties to contain yourself, and this will end."

"Numiak," Apaay whispered, the word pained. "Stop. You'll only make it worse."

His arms trembled with the strain of trying to free himself. But he did calm, somewhat, and retreated to the bottom of the stairs. The lash fell quiet.

"Much better." Though Nanuq kept his focus on Numiak, it was Apaay he addressed. "He has been given a tonic that nullifies his powers. I do not anticipate he will be escaping this."

"Are you all right?" Numiak asked her.

Apaay nodded, unable to speak around the lump in her throat. They would figure a way out of this. They always had.

Nanuq said, "I wish we could have had this conversation under more civilized circumstances, but we cannot have all that we ask for." Aniirlit stood on his left. There was no sign of the woman who had posed as the ikovna. If she had done her job well, Apaay supposed Nanuq would have little reason to keep her around.

"First," he said, linking his fingers together, "I would like to express my disappointment in your behavior. I welcomed you into my home with open arms, yet you spurned my generosity. Masquerading as Ro of the Owl Clan, of all people." He shook his head, looked beyond them to a far-off place, one Apaay and Numiak were not privy to. "And yet, you were clever." His attention returned to them. The curling mouth quirked, on the verge of a smile. "I admire ingenuity."

Something had addled Nanuq's perspective of the world. Something that had driven him to steal a child from its home. What was he so desperate to hide, that he would bind the Raven in secrecy and trap him in Taggak? What had transpired to change him, assuming Nanuq had once been a different man?

"I have heard of you, Face Stealer."

Numiak spat onto the ground in defiance. Nanuq frowned slightly. Apaay didn't understand how Nanuq, a man so small, could radiate power as punishing as the sun. It was he who sat high on his chair, who looked down at them, bound like animals, power infused in his words. Nanuq, who was almost a man.

Their captor inclined his head, then rose to his feet. "You may assume I am deliberating your punishment. I must say, that is not true. Rather, I am wondering if I should punish you at all. You see—" His long, curled eyelashes lowered to shield his eyes. "Despite the general nuisance of this evening, you have brought me something incredibly valuable. Two things, actually. It has been a complex business, finding something that does not want to be found."

Numiak went rigid. "Don't." It was more grunt than speech.

"Don't?" The question was delicately phrased, as if he was not certain of the answer. "You are afraid of what you might lose. I understand. So let me reassure you." One by one, he descended the stairs until the tips of his slippers kissed one of Numiak's knees. "There is no need to panic, because you have already lost. What was yours is now mine. And you will not live to see the consequences of your actions."

He knew Apaay was the Creator. Somehow, he'd discovered her identity. But how?

"Speak," Numiak growled, "and I swear you will regret it."

Nanuq's wide grin sent a colder wave of fear through her. Apaay began to tremble as he skirted Numiak, the way one might with a puddle on the ground.

"Look at me, my dear. Let me see you."

As if she had a choice. He tilted up her chin, forcing her to look into his face.

"It was cleverly done." A vague nod. "Yes. Even as my skin touches yours, I sense nothing but a human woman. Had you not cut your finger on my book, why, I would have never known."

Numiak had stopped struggling.

He tucked a strand of hair behind her ear in a gesture reminiscent of her own father. "How lucky of me that in searching for the oldest daughter of the Wolf Kingdom, I stumbled across the younger."

Everything in Apaay stilled. She had the strangest notion that Nanuq was speaking of *her*.

Except that was impossible. She had a family—Mama, Papa, and Eska. She wasn't wolf Unua. She was Analak. To claim otherwise was absurd.

If not her, then who?

Numiak said, "Apaay—"

One of the guards kicked him in the face. An explosive exhalation followed, and he curled protectively over his knees, breathing harshly. Blood dripped from his open mouth.

Nanuq studied her with an uncomfortable amount of pity. He said, almost gently, "My dear, I'm referring to *you*."

She shook her head. Glanced at Numiak as though he alone could disprove it. "You're mistaken."

"Oh?" He folded his slender hands across his front. "How so?"

"I'm Analak."

"You *believe* you are Analak. They are two very different things."

Her uncertainty over the situation squeezed with increasing pressure, like a hand curling around her throat. He was right. They were two completely different things. But what he told her . . . it could not be.

Numiak wouldn't keep this from her. They had promised one another no more secrets, and this was the greatest and most terrible secret of all.

"Tell him it's not true," she whispered.

He stared resolutely at the floor. Why wouldn't he look at her?

Why, if not to avoid the weight of regret, of a choice he had made every day since they had met, to smile and lie until eventually she believed it, because Apaay hadn't known any better.

"Tell her the truth," Nanuq said. "She deserves that much, don't you think?"

"Not like this." The words were coarse, as though they'd been dragged across the ground and what remained were tattered edges. "Not when she has no choice in the matter."

"Choice?" Nanuq laughed. His eyelashes fluttered, partially shielding his gaze. "My boy, you never gave her a choice. You kept her in this cage. I am the one setting her free." He lifted a hand.

A piercing whistle, an abrupt crack. Numiak jerked from the whip landing true.

"Stop it!" Apaay cried.

But the air split and screamed, and the black serpent uncoiled and struck, lashing its tongue against the breadth of his shoulders, the curve of his spine. He grunted at the next blow. His facial muscles twitched in pain. His pale face glimmered with sweat.

When it was done, his back was in shreds. He hadn't the strength to hold himself up, and one of the kirn wrenched back Numiak's head, pried open his mouth, and dumped a clear liquid down his throat. He thrashed, but the man pinched his nostrils closed, his jaw shut, until Numiak was forced to swallow or suffocate. A word rose into her mind. *Ilumi.*

"Now." Nanuq returned to his seat and leaned forward. "Tell the girl the truth of her heritage."

She stared into Numiak's hollowed eyes, at the pain there, and the acceptance that resolved itself, hardening like a shell around soft innards. Whatever truth the ilumi forced out, Apaay knew things would never again be the same.

"Do you remember," he said, "when I spoke of a mission that sent me to Naga's coast?"

Half-heartedly, Apaay nodded. He could not possibly know, but she remembered everything he had ever told her. His first word to her: *Hello.* She had feared him then.

She did not want to hear these lies. They *were* lies. She would accept nothing else. Because if they were not . . .

He's lying to you.

He always lies.

Even when he promised he would not.

"It was a few days prior to the invasion," said Numiak. "Your parents feared for your life—"

"Those people are not my parents," she spat.

He paused. "The Vaal and Narg," he corrected softly, "feared for your life, and for your sister's. Your best chance at survival was to go into hiding."

Apaay clung to what she knew. Apaay, Analak, sister, daughter, friend. Apaay, Analak, sister, daughter, friend. This must be Numiak's plan. A way to divert Nanuq's attention. Provide false information and allow them time to untangle themselves from this mess. Maybe Numiak had managed to dispatch a message to Ro, and the Flock was on its way.

He said, "You were only a few weeks old. My mission was to take you far away—"

"Stop," she said in a broken whisper.

He did.

The whip came down again.

Numiak sucked in a ragged breath. He closed his eyes, as if that might help him endure *her* pain. "Far away," he continued, "to a place where Nanuq would never think to search for you. I was not to speak of it with anyone."

A tear slipped down the curve of her nose. Apaay bit her lip, trying to swallow back the ache that spread through her chest and burrowed into her heart. If she believed him to lie, why did this confession ring with truth?

"I took you to a village situated on Naga's coast. An Analak woman had recently given birth to a stillborn daughter. You were given the face of a human child so that your identity would not be discovered, and I left you in their ice house so that they could raise you. They didn't know of the switch. I altered their memories. Another Packmate had been assigned to relocate your sister, Matilaqaa, but he was killed in the invasion. I went back for her, hid her in the labyrinth."

Apaay sobbed freely now, bowing over her knees with the

weight of a life lost, a life she thought she'd known. He was wrong. Eska was her sister, not Ila. Mama and Papa were her parents. She came from a small village perched on Naga's edge. She was human. If she wasn't, if she was something else, she would know, wouldn't she?

"Apaay." Numiak's voice pitched in agony. "I'm sorry. I'm so sorry."

"If you were truly sorry," said Nanuq, "you would never have lied to her." It was horrible, but Apaay agreed with him.

Someone grabbed the back of her skull, forcing it backward. Fingers invaded her mouth and pried open her teeth. She thrashed as Numiak roared his fury. Sweet liquid trickled down her throat. And everything changed.

The objects in the foreground seemed to stretch, as if no longer bound by their shapes. A whooshing sound flitted like birdwings in her ears. The world softened, and the sounds rolled pleasantly, and where and how had she gotten here? Why was there a man bound beside her? Why were her hands bound, for that matter?

"Perhaps I am too cynical for this world," Nanuq murmured, "but since I cannot trust you to tell me the truth, I have given you ilumi. Do you know what that is?"

He spoke in reassuring tones, and warmth spread through her chest—the need of wanting to please him. The word did sound familiar, but she couldn't recall where she'd heard it from. She shook her head.

"It is a truth serum that is obtained by boiling polar bear liver. When mixed with salt water and grayroot, the toxicity is diminished. It will not kill you if taken in small doses."

A small, far-away piece of Apaay's mind understood. Polar bear liver was highly toxic when ingested. It was the only organ that wasn't harvested from a kill. That would make ilumi a form of weak poison, but she forgot this thought as soon as it passed.

"I brought your blood to my shaman," said Nanuq. "He confirmed that you are the second daughter of the Vaal and Narg. And then he told me something else."

Apaay thought she would very much like to know. While she did not know who the Vaal and Narg were, she knew of shamans. The spiritual leaders of her community. If a shaman could be trusted, then so, perhaps, could Nanuq. And anyway, his voice soothed her. Really, it was too musical for ears.

"He said there was a strange power to your blood. Tell me, Apaay. Do you know of this power the shaman spoke of?"

"Apaay, listen to me—" Another crack of the whip. It sounded far away. "Don't tell him anything."

"Pay no attention to the demon," Nanuq said mildly.

Her focus returned to the bound stranger. Unease flitted through her before it vanished. Demon? He didn't look like one. Even if this man was a demon, did he deserve this brutality, brought about by the curling end of a whip?

"My dear," Nanuq cooed. "Answer the question, please."

The man's kindness eased the tension she felt at seeing so much blood, this stranger bound, on his knees. He looked frightened, the demon. She wanted to tell him there was no need for fear. All would be well.

"Yes," she whispered.

"And what is this power?"

Apaay licked her lips. The man sounded intrigued, and why shouldn't he? It was a fascinating concept.

A voice deep in her mind demanded she say nothing, or lie, but the need to reveal the truth was too great. Such was the way of burdens. "I am what they call the Creator. I have the ability to create new identities at will."

"And?"

She did not desire to speak of it. Somewhere behind thick, muffled cloth, a voice screamed, *No*, but her mouth was already moving. "And to change existing ones."

His reaction wasn't what she expected. Nanuq's smile trembled. His eyes swam with rising tears, and he looked quite young in this moment. She wondered if it was a trick of the light.

"Good," he said roughly. "That is . . . most excellent, Apaay. Thank you."

Like the sun rising, the fog shrouding her mind lifted. Apaay blinked in confusion, for though she knew she'd been speaking, she could not remember what she had said. "Unfortunately," said Nanuq, "with your sister out of reach, I cannot give you the gift of reunion. But you, Face Stealer—" He turned to address the hunched, bloodied figure of Numiak below him. "Perhaps you would be interested in such a thing?"

The doors at the end of the hall yawned, allowing two figures to enter. Yuki, wearing a skirt of kelp touched by ropy hanks of damp, sea-slickened hair, glided across the column-lined hall. And trailing her: Kenai.

49

They hadn't a choice, in the end. They wanted to live, so the soldier came with them.

The entrance to the tunnel was located in one of the abandoned buildings, its south-facing wall nonexistent. The dwelling was minimal. A dirt floor, a low ceiling tall enough to accommodate a human standing upright, but better suited for the height of a wolf. Few windows. Similar to a burrow, a darkened space embraced by cool earth.

Saniraq guarded the kirn while they cleared away the rubble and pulled back the trapdoor. Ila peered into the dark cavity. Her every sense was heightened, tangled with the impossible notion that at the end of this tunnel, Ila would glimpse the place of her birth, which she did not remember. Her heartbeat slowed with some effort.

"Try anything," Malina said to the soldier, "and I'll gut you where you stand. Understood?"

He nodded. They had checked him for weapons earlier. Considering the man had very little body fat, it would be easy to feel any hidden object. The man was clean. Ila was certain they'd been thorough.

Malina descended the ladder first.

"You next," Saniraq said, poking the man's lower back with her dagger.

Wordlessly, he climbed down. Since the initial threat, he had been oddly compliant, but Ila supposed that was preferred to outright struggle. Saniraq went next, followed by Ila. Lastly, Tipki, closing the trapdoor upon her descent and shutting them in darkness. Ila's vision adjusted by the time she reached the bottom of the ladder where the group had gathered.

The hike felt like a lifetime. Now that Tulimaq had caught her scent, it was only a matter of time before he cornered them. Ila was suddenly supremely grateful for Saniraq, Malina, and Tipki's presence. She had never believed her deafness to be a disadvantage, but in a situation like this, she recognized the importance of being able to hear an enemy's approach.

After a time, Malina lifted a hand, slowing. The tunnel had risen steadily over the past mile, and the surface air cut the staleness of belowground from an unseen opening above. The tunnel curved abruptly. Malina went ahead, then returned and signaled them forward. They'd reached a door. A large pile of dirt partially blocked the passage where the ceiling had collapsed. From the invasion? Or the combined tread of thirty thousand men?

Malina tried the door. Dust rained around its frame, but otherwise it didn't budge. "A little help."

Tipki offered assistance while Saniraq guarded the soldier. A strip of light pushed through a crack in the wood, falling across the man's mask where the bottom edge met his smooth jaw. He watched this all unfold with a particular keenness.

With some effort, they managed to pry open the door. Malina peered through the crack. In order to reach the tower where the Horn of Amaroq was located, they would need to take a separate tunnel located on the second level, in the west wing.

"Do anything to draw attention to us," Malina said, stepping into the man's personal space, "and I will kill you."

"Of that," said the man, "I have no doubt."

They emerged into a room with wooden shelves hammered into the mud-packed walls. It smelled of roots and green things.

Food storage? The low ceiling forced them to crouch. Dark, cool, windowless. Malina managed to find another door, which opened easily.

She stuck out her head to check the area, signaled the all-clear, and slipped out. The soldier went next. Then Saniraq and Ila, three knives in her boots and her mother's beloved talq at the small of her back. Tipki followed, hefting one of the kirn's favored clubs.

Their internal connection was not as strong in their human forms compared to their wolf skins, but Ila was able to sense the differing energies to their movements nonetheless. Saniraq, in particular, was on high alert. Out of the four, she and Ila had the least amount of combat experience.

The storage room opened into a large space with an enormous hearth. This must have been the kitchen, Ila thought. A sizeable space to serve however many hundreds of people living in the den, staff or otherwise.

They were moving quickly now, up a set of stairs. They entered a wide, spacious hallway that seemed to run the length of the fortress. This area was decidedly more damaged, scorch marks blackening the square gray stones used for the flooring, the ground broken in places as though the earth had heaved, its internal organs spilling out. The northern wall, gone. It brought Ila back to the Face Stealer's memory, a secondhand account of the night she had received her scar. The world awash in orange, a heap of tangled blankets, the bed of her sister empty. It had all taken place right here. And she remembered none of it.

More stairs. Malina guided them over the heaps of rubble, fearless in how she pushed forward. They never would have made it this far without her. That was a truth no one questioned.

The next corridor they reached was completely blocked by wreckage. There was no way through.

Malina turned, the first sign of panic in her eyes.

Is there another way? asked Ila.

"It's possible one of the other tunnels merges with the one leading to the tower. It's been so long." She rubbed the puckered skin of her forehead in frustration. "Doesn't matter. There's no time.

The only other way to reach the horn is to physically climb the tower from the outside. I need an eastern-facing window. I'm not sure how far away we are from it."

Saniraq, who still guarded the soldier, said, "You're saying we need to leave the den to reach the tower." She didn't look enthused about it.

"Here." Tipki gestured to an opening in the wall that offered a panoramic view of the land surrounding the fortress, including the infiltrated city. The tower in question squatted at the base of a sheer cliff face, the gray stone mountain at its back. "See the path?"

"You mean the one that goes right over the heads of the army below?" No, Saniraq definitely wasn't happy.

"It looks exposed," said Tipki, "but that's because we're at a higher vantage point. The men won't be able to see us from their positions on the ground."

Perhaps a half-mile of distance separated them from the tower, the slender path rolling over the barren, undulating landscape full of protruding crags, before the rocks rose on either side to create a narrow gorge midway. Beyond the gorge, the land spread to hills, leading all the way to the tower's base. The high ground, with Nanuq's army a spillage of white in the lower city. Ila hadn't thought they'd have to literally climb the tower, but that's what they'd have to do. There was no door among the interlocking stones that constructed the rectangular structure.

Saniraq began to ask something when Ila, sensing the vibrations of approaching footsteps, held up a hand for silence and herded everyone around the corner, hidden from sight of whoever approached.

Two guards emerged from the stairwell at the end of the hall.

Then eight.

Then seven more.

The last to appear was a man. Tulimaq, calm as could be.

Ila flinched as Saniraq's hand slipped into hers. The woman studied her with raised eyebrows. She was too observant for her own good.

Malina gestured them back the way they'd come, toward the stairs. They took the staircase to the lower level, nudging their captive forward, and found another staircase. Dust sprang from the walls. A glance over her shoulder revealed Tipki exploding around the corner, blood oozing from a cut above her eye. Ila shoved Saniraq into the stairwell and waited for Tipki's arrival before following.

Nanuq's men infiltrated the stairwell soon after. Ila braced for impact as fear and memory guided her talq. One of the kirn struck with his club, but her aim was true, the talq hooking him under the chin. The man grabbed for his neck, blood spurting from between his fingers, and fell, tumbling down the treacherous staircase. Ila faced her next opponent. She cut toward the man's shoulder. As he slipped out of range, her blade hit the wall, sparks flaring from where the antler skittered across the rough stone. She lunged, striking the man in the throat, nose, and groin. A kick to his chest sent him falling into the men at his back. They used the opportunity to scramble down the staircase, which emptied into the hallway below.

Furious heat slammed into them, an explosion of sudden sun. The floor lurched. Tipki knocked into Malina's back. Ila managed to put an end to one of the soldiers before a second wave quaked the building, sending her crashing into the wall. The kirn flooded out into the corridor like a dam breaking free.

Tulimaq emerged from the stairwell.

Every curve, every pointed facet of his face, the shape of the bones beneath his skin, was inhumanly cold. This was not the man who had professed a tormented childhood through the bars of her cell, his truths handed to her in the dark unaware. Ila's throat squeezed at how completely detached he looked. Why could he not move forward? Why did he insist on pulling pain into himself? Ila had not killed his mother. She was not responsible for his broken upbringing.

But the most maddening part? A small, very small, voice whispered for Ila to lay down her weapon. To a man who had been granted little kindness in life, imagine what that gesture could do. Yet he held his staff, and she held her talq, and they faced one another as enemies.

Ila pushed to the front of her pack, despite their protests. He had come for her and her alone.

You don't want them, she signed, taking another step forward to draw his attention away from those she loved. *Let them go. Take me instead.* It would buy them time. Malina could lead them to the horn. Ila did not think Tulimaq would kill her. Not yet, anyway. He'd let her escape the labor camp. It meant something despite his denial.

He canted his head. Tulimaq was not easily read, but there—the skin around his eyes pinched.

He was angry.

"You always had too soft of a heart," he said. "It is perhaps your greatest weakness."

Not a weakness. Never a weakness. The love Ila shared for her packmates was stone-strong.

It was Tulimaq who was weak and alone.

He signaled to the kirn at his back, and they moved forward, fanning out. Ila's pack tucked themselves against her sides for protection. Their only leverage was the mysterious kirn who had accompanied them.

Ila yanked the soldier close, digging the point of her talq into the man's neck.

"One more step," warned Malina, "and he dies."

Tulimaq considered the masked soldier for a moment. "So kill him." There was a pause. "On second thought, allow me."

As he lifted his staff, the blade radiating with budding power, the soldier lunged. Tulimaq sent him backward with a wave of dark energy, and he crashed against the wall. The mask slipped off, but it was not a man's face underneath. The features were distinctly feminine.

Tulimaq's face leeched of color. "Mother."

50

"Nanuq." With a look of intimacy, the Sea Mother climbed the dais and brushed a kiss across the Great Bear's cheek.

Time and space had changed Yuki from their last encounter. She was the sea and the sea was her. It was her blood and her breath, her scent and her skin. Water clung to her eyelashes in clear droplets and reflected the swallowing wells of her eyes.

But Apaay's attention, inevitably, fell to Kenai. She hardly recognized the man standing at Yuki's side. His face was gaunt and touched by shadow, his clothes ragged and thin, the weight he had put on in the Wood having vanished. Long, black, scraggly hair fell around his face. He was the same man she'd found caged in the labyrinth, lost and alone.

It seemed Kenai had caught Nanuq's attention as well. "Who is this?"

"You mean you don't see the family resemblance?" Yuki all but purred, one hand resting atop Nanuq's. He didn't seem to mind. Kenai stared at the place where their fingers touched. Sweat glimmered on his brow. "This is the Face Stealer's brother."

"Brother." His mouth pinched. "I had a brother, once."

A shudder ripped down Apaay's spine, for Nanuq's eyes had

emptied. He looked out over the hall. The silence was his to take, his to bend. "Would you be surprised to know that he was human?"

Apaay heard what his expression lacked. Resentment intertwined with some complex, layered emotion that was both soft in the interior, yet rigid at the edges. She thought Nanuq looked the way a man did when he has lost something that cannot be returned to him.

"Yes," said Nanuq. "He was human, a boy from Across the Sea. When I arrived on the shores of his home, I knew no one. I was searching for something, though I did not know it at the time. He told me his name was Bjorn. He was proud of that name. *Bear*, in the language of his people. A strong name. Out of every villager I could have met, he was the first, and I asked myself why. I believed fate had brought us together. Perhaps the will of the gods."

Nanuq drew his hand from Yuki's. The Sea Mother, who seemed unconcerned with the sudden distance, perched on the arm of his chair.

"Bjorn and his father took me in. They lived in a coastal village and spent their days fishing. I learned quickly of their way of life. The years passed. I grew older. So, too, did the boy. War came to their borders. I learned how to wield a sword, among other things."

Numiak's ragged breathing cut the silence. Kenai stared straight ahead, stone-faced, his eye like a darkened window, the lamplight having long ago been extinguished. Apaay yanked at her bound wrists uselessly.

"I came from nothing. I had no family. My parents were dead." His voice rushed forward with a newfound, terrifying urgency. "Bjorn was my brother. He taught me the ways of his people. He revealed to me the secrets of forging metal. He led his people into battle, he and his father, and showed me the greatness of man."

He stopped. His chest rose and fell fitfully. When he continued, his voice lacked its previous uniformity.

"I was a part of it, that potential. I was accepted into their world, as violent as it was. I was made to believe I had a place at Bjorn's side. I slept beneath his roof, ate food from his table. For the first time in my life, I had a family."

There was the most terrible silence. "And when he learned of what I was," Nanuq whispered, a hoarse sound, "he put a chain around my neck." Lifting his eyes from where they had fallen to the shining black object in the hand of the kirn who had doled out Numiak's punishment, he locked Apaay in his sights. "He, too, favored the whip."

The air temperature plunged, frost hardening around Apaay's nostrils. If she had not been certain Numiak's powers had been nullified, she would have assumed he was responsible for the change.

"I had not realized that my brother had become a man. It was in his nature to chain me. *Animal*, he called me. *Beast*." He spat the words as if they were blood. Then, equally swift, the fury calmed, replaced with cool pragmatism. "It has taken many years of healing, but I realized I couldn't fault him for it. That is the hierarchy. That is his nature. If our positions had been switched, why, I imagine I would have done the same."

Apaay wondered what had happened to Bjorn, but she thought she knew. She only wondered if his death had been swift, or if Nanuq had drawn it out by the days, weeks, months. She thought maybe she knew that answer, too. The boy's father was almost certainly the man they'd found frozen to death, nothing but a crumpled note in his hand. He'd never learned what had become of his son.

Nanuq's gaze returned to Kenai. "Can you feel it? How deeply the resentment cuts? What is your story, I wonder?"

Kenai's back swelled. Apaay expected his voice to reflect his expression—flat, cold—but it reminded her of tumbled rocks, or grit. Something abrasive. "My brother killed the only people who ever truly cared for me."

That simply wasn't true. Why didn't Numiak correct him? Their father's death had been Kenai's fault.

Curled over his knees, eyes closed, Numiak whispered, "Kenai."

His brother stiffened.

Nanuq watched this all with an unusual amount of absorption. "Pama," he called.

The male servant appeared at once, that familiar lacquered box in hand. He offered it to Kenai, the lid lifted to reveal the weapon nestled inside. No matter how Apaay tried to catch Pama's eye, he avoided her gaze. She wondered if he'd known how this evening would end.

"This is the price I paid," Nanuq told Kenai, "for revealing to my brother my true form. He chained me for many months in my bear skins, left me out in the elements, denied me food. I grew hungry. Weak. As time went on and I began to lose weight, my mind splintered, the hunger was so acute. I ate dirt. My own feces. Snow. The snow made everything worse. I would have done anything for food. That is how Bjorn controlled me—through my body's natural urges.

"The first time he put a collar around my neck, I believed my punishment to be over. Prior to his discovery of my nature, Bjorn had only ever showed me kindness. Fool that I was, I thought maybe he had changed his mind." Nanuq's tone descended into one of disgust. "He led me to a pit filled with other bears—animals, not Unua—which he lowered me into. My mind was so far gone at that point I could not remember how to shift back to my human form. It would not have helped me, regardless.

"The men gathered and bet on which of the bears would live. I survived. The others did not. As a reward, my brother took a lash to my skin. The next day, it occurred again—the collar, the pits, the fights, the hunger, the lash. On and on, until I realized that if I did not change my situation myself, nothing would." He looked from Kenai to the awaiting whip. "There is something heady about power. I imagine you might find it therapeutic."

Kenai wet his lips nervously. His shaking fingers curled around the handle. Its long black coil twisted at his feet.

"Go on," said Nanuq, settling back to watch.

The man was sick. Apaay spat out a wad of phlegm. "Kenai, you don't know the whole story."

"What else is there to know?" He watched the tip of the serpentine weapon slither over the ground as though mesmerized by the motion. "Numiak hates me."

"No. He loves you."

With ragged breaths, he shifted to face her. Cracks ran through his frayed expression. He looked to be near his breaking point. What had Kenai experienced since their parting? "If he loved me, why did he take the people *I* loved away? Why did he take our father and our mother and Sita?"

Numiak lifted his head, his skin tinged gray from blood loss. The whip cracked like breaking glass. A cry followed, wrenched from behind his clenched teeth, his body heaving from the lash.

"Kenai, stop!" Apaay cried.

The whip hurled down again with unstoppable force. Kenai did not flinch.

"Kenai. *Kenai!*" She screamed until her voice grew hoarse.

He wouldn't stop. The black serpent coiled and struck, coiled and struck.

"Numiak." Apaay writhed in the guard's hold, screaming in fury as the man pushed her face into the floor. "I'm here." It was all she had, these words, yet they meant little, for she was powerless in all things.

"I see how much pain this man has brought you," said Nanuq to Kenai. The whip halted momentarily. "You could make it go away. With your brother gone, you need not suffer. Your father's death, your mother's death, your sister's death—all would be avenged."

Tears of frustration gathered in the creases of her eyes. "Things don't have to end this way. You can choose to forgive. I know you. I know you're lost. I know you're hurting. You don't know who to trust—"

"So then why should I trust you?" he ground out.

"Because it's time you accepted the truth. Numiak didn't kill your father. I told you this."

The fingers around the whip handle clenched and unclenched sporadically. Apaay knew how it felt to unravel, the paralysis that prevented you from acting. Too many threads and not enough hands to manage them.

Nanuq laughed from his deep recline and shook his head in absurdity. "My dear, he already knows the truth." Rising to his very average height, he descended the stairs and offered Kenai an object colored gold by the lamplight: a dagger of slender bone. "We are two men who were both betrayed by our brothers. In the end, only justice will bring peace."

And as that dagger passed into Kenai's hand, Apaay recognized that something was about to be forever changed.

"Kenai, please." Her voice broke. She understood him, or pieces of him, at least. How to reach him? How to make him believe? There had always been this struggle in him. As such, he looked for love in places where it did not exist. "If you kill Numiak, you will regret it for the rest of your life."

"Will he?" This from Nanuq. A man who, for the first time this evening, spoke with insecurity. "Shouldn't we want to end his suffering?"

"Is it his suffering you wish to end," she countered, "or your own?"

Nanuq said nothing.

Heat alighted in her shoulder joints as she strained to break free. "If he dies, you won't be able to remove your face."

"My dear." Faint amusement creased Nanuq's smooth brow. "I have no need of the demon. The hot spring has the power to remove my face. You have the power to forge me a new one, completely human. So you see, the Face Stealer is disposable. He always has been."

Her gaze snapped to Numiak, whose eyes were downcast. She would not think of what he meant—*disposable*. There was no such thing as the North without the Face Stealer in it.

"I will die before ever helping you," she hissed in growing alarm. Why wasn't Numiak fighting back? "Kill him, and I will not grant you the human face you need."

Nanuq's sigh drifted across the room. "Honorable, but unnecessary. I don't need you alive. I just need your blood. Your sacrifice will not be in vain, I assure you."

Apaay's chest squeezed with unbearable pressure as Kenai returned to his brother's side, dagger in hand. "Numiak didn't kill your father," she said. "You did. I'm sorry you lost people you loved, but I lost, too, and—"

"I killed him?" He laughed humorlessly. "I lost so much more than you could ever imagine." He studied the dagger in a detached manner, turning it this way and that. "I was a boy who became a man too soon."

Clawing a handful of Numiak's hair, Kenai drew back his brother's head. Numiak didn't fight it.

Silence fell like a slap.

"Do you know what I wish, Brother?" whispered Numiak.

Kenai's single eye grew wet, and shone, bright as a star. He growled out, as if the very word tore open his heart, "What?"

Three heartbeats passed before he spoke. "I wish we'd had more time."

Kenai's hand trembled as he lifted the dagger to Numiak's chest, and Apaay screamed at him to stop, please, we can fix this, you can fix this and he's your brother, he's your brother don't you see what you're doing, don't you care, Kenai, *Kenai!*

She thrashed, kicked at the guard's knee, which buckled. Apaay fought free before another guard tackled her. Her chin struck the stone, and she saw stars. The world was reeling. Yuki turned away. Aniirlit, who she had almost forgotten about, did as well. Apaay whispered brokenly, "Please."

"So do I, Brother." Kenai's nostrils flared. "So do I."

And as the first tear slipped down his scarred cheek, Kenai plunged the blade into his brother's heart.

There was a scream.

It was a sound of piercing, cutting cold. The sound of wind over ice, of true, land-locked winter. It shattered and reformed into a rise and fall of breaking emotion that spilled out, and cracked against the high ceiling. It went on, and on, and still on, a sound of the blackest anguish, a howl of pure emotion.

It was Apaay. *She* was screaming. The pressure gathered in her gut, surging upward, and it was as if she had become this sound, this agony in her limbs and chest and it felt like it was breaking open her skull, smashing it into pieces and her chest, oh, her chest felt like it was on *fire*, her lungs on *fire*, her heart on *fire*. The kirn struggled to contain her as she bit and scratched and flailed, desperate to free herself.

Numiak stared mutely at the weapon protruding from his chest. It was a somber sight. Like watching a tree fall. That initial crack that seemed to shake the world, and its slow topple toward the earth as Kenai yanked the dagger free and, with a choked sound, slid the blade across his brother's neck.

Her scream ended on a gasp as blood spilled onto the white pelts covering the floor.

Apaay watched the light leave Numiak's eyes. As if a cloud had drifted across the sun, and shaded it momentarily. Except the light grew dim, hazing into confusion. His pupils, once clear as water, darkened with murk. His brown-gold irises, a color she had never seen before, dulled. Not once did Apaay stop looking at him, as if that might reverse the consequences of Kenai's actions. His mouth worked soundlessly. His hair hung around his slackened face like dead vines. Blood seeped from his open mouth, wet and choking as his body at last fell still.

Then there was no light at all.

Apaay's breath hitched. Her lungs emptied out. She didn't understand what she was looking at. Numiak was here, but he wasn't *here*. Blood covered his body and it was everywhere and why wasn't he looking at her, why wasn't he fighting back?

"Numiak," she croaked.

He didn't answer.

"Numiak, get up—"

"I'm afraid he can no longer hear you, my dear," said Nanuq.

She felt empty. Swiftly and completely empty.

Numiak didn't move. And Apaay knew, with certainty, that he was dead.

A wave of grief crashed through her with such force that if she had not already been on the ground, her legs would have collapsed. It wasn't true. It couldn't be true. She fought the guards' hold with renewed vigor, screaming her rage and anguish, the encroaching darkness pressing chilled hands upon her. She suddenly understood what drove men to violence. "Let me go." Another tormented howl tore from her throat. An animal sound. "Let me *go*."

Nanuq lifted a hand, signaling his men to release her. Apaay stumbled to Numiak's side, her knees splashing in the scarlet pool. His arms were still bound, forcing his body into an awkward angle. She fought to untie the knot, but her hands were shaking harder than ever and the blood slickened her grip. Eventually, she freed his bindings. His neck was a mess, and his chest. His expression had sagged into one of hollowness.

A high keening filled her throat, and a great pressure pushed against the bones of her face, her temples, her forehead. "Numiak, please, please." Gently, Apaay brushed the long, tangled strands from his open eyes. She had always thought he saw too much. Now he would never see again.

Apaay dissolved into another fit of broken, garbled weeping, pressing her cheek against his and trying to ignore the blood seeping into his collar, its iron odor repulsive. The woodsmoke scent of his skin had gone.

"No," she whimpered, and felt the memory of Nakaluq's passing here in this room. Her dear friend. Gone. "No, no, no—"

She had not told him what he meant to her. How dear he was, every piece of him: the dark and the light, the sharp and the smooth. How, without him, she would not understand the depth of her own character. How she needed him. How, sometimes, she thought he needed her, too. This elusive, devilish, enigmatic demon. This frustrating man.

"Don't leave me," Apaay whispered against his temple, one hand fisted into his parka. She didn't know if she could face this war alone.

His body was already beginning to lose its warmth. The Face Stealer would never again terrorize innocents, never strike fear into people's hearts, never descend with the long night's arrival and slip away unseen. And he would never love her again either.

Apaay held him as tightly as possible, as if that might bring him back. Her throat strained, because she remembered that this was war, and it took what it believed to be owed. It was the Face Stealer's lack of heart that had kept him alive all these years. And it was the return of his heart that had killed him, in the end.

Through blurred vision, her gaze locked onto the one who held the knife. "You." Apaay stared at Kenai as if she had never seen him before. He was alive. Numiak was not.

She lunged. A guard caught her around the middle, hauling her back, but still she fought. "You killed him! He was your brother and you killed him!"

Kenai inspected Numiak's body. He didn't seem to notice her, though he said unsteadily, "My father's murder has been avenged."

"Numiak didn't kill your father," she cried. It hurt saying his name. "You did."

Kenai growled, "I would never—"

"Shut up," Apaay screamed. "Just *shut up*, you coward." Spittle flung from her lips. She rammed the back of her skull against the guard's nose, heard a satisfying crunch. Yuki watched the scene with bright, hungry eyes. Nanuq appeared faintly pleased, entertained with the unanticipated spectacle.

"I told you. I told you the truth. Your brother," she panted, "did everything for you. He would have died for you. All he ever wanted was for you to not see him as a burden."

The skin around Kenai's lips stretched across his teeth. His chin quivered.

Apaay tried to slow her breathing so she could organize her thoughts, but it was impossible. There was no stopping this unraveling. Maybe it was better this way. Truth, in all its ugly, misshapen glory. "Your father's death was a set-up."

The first hint of doubt ruffled his wounded expression. "What are you talking about?" Kenai bit out.

"That night, your Packmates took Numiak away. But he arranged it that way. The truth is, you killed your father. You, who loved and despised him, who begged for his affection, killed him in a moment of rage."

Kenai bared his teeth. "That's—"

"Numiak," she choked out, "discovered what you had done. He knew the truth would destroy you. So he wiped your memory and took the fall, made it look like he'd been responsible. You already hated him anyway. What was one more reason?"

Kenai's bloodless face flushed anew. "No."

"He accepted his punishment," she said. "The life of a pariah. All to protect you."

Kenai curled his hands into fists. He said, in a voice of pure despair, "I don't believe you!"

Yuki's tittering laughter floated over to them. She sighed, and her round, wet, black eyes gleamed. "As much as I hate to admit it, Kenai, she's right."

He turned to Yuki, whose hand rested on Nanuq's shoulder. He stared at that gloved hand before his attention shifted to her face. "Did you know?"

"Of course I knew. But whether by your hand or Numiak's, your father was dead. There was little I could do. It would not have made a difference."

The dazed shock of Kenai's expression told Apaay it would have made a difference. It would have made a sizeable difference.

A life was no small thing.

Yuki studied Numiak's lifeless form. "As much as I loathe a waste of power," she said, and Apaay did not think the Sea Mother's sadness was a lie, as twisted as her affections were, "our task will be much easier with him out of the way."

"Friends," Nanuq began in that musical tone, speaking to those few who still lived. "Today, you've witnessed a momentous occasion: the death of the North's most notorious demon." His eyes crinkled at the corners. "But this is not the end. Indeed, our journey has just begun. General."

A man stepped forward from his station against the wall. "Yes, Great One?"

Apaay, caught between horror and grief, could only listen as Nanuq spoke of what would unfold. "In three days' time, a sacrifice will be made public. Tell your men we march for Sinika. Yuki, send word to your forces in the east. The time has come to make the North whole and unbroken once more. Mark my words, general. Before winter's end, Sinika, the last stronghold of the Central Territory, will kneel."

51

"Hello, Tulimaq." Tears coursed swiftly down the woman's cheeks, her bone structure clearly feminine now that it was no longer concealed behind the mask.

Tulimaq stood like a pillar of stone. His features: ashen. His mouth: slack. His grasp on the staff had loosened, for here stood a nightmare, a memory, the deepest pain suddenly returned to him. His mother. Dead, he had believed, now wearing the garb of a man.

"Kill her," Malina growled, the words vibrating through Ila's body from where their arms touched.

No. Her left hand cut the air. Her right hand, which held the blade against the woman's throat, was the steadiest it had ever been. If the last few months had taught her anything, it was that nothing was certain. She had learned to remain flexible in the face of adversity, to flow like water, to follow the path until its farthest point and, if needed, make a new one. Apaay had taught her that. Tulimaq's mother was an unexpected blessing.

With a gesture to Malina, she and her pack sisters switched places so Ila could communicate unhindered. *What we need*, Ila said, *is time. And Tulimaq is going to give it to us.*

It spoke of Tulimaq's control that his only reaction was the twitch of his fingers around the weapon's haft.

You are going to order your armies away from Unana. In return, we promise not to harm your mother.

As soon as they blew the Horn of Amaroq, alerting any and all possible allies of the Wolf Kingdom's return, Nanuq's kirn would descend on the den. They needed time to flee via the tunnels.

The former combat master lifted his chin in acknowledgement. He had yet to shift his focus from his mother's gaunt face. "What you ask of me is impossible. It has taken days to fill this city. It will take days more to empty completely."

Malina sneered. "Then you should probably order them to run."

Ila stepped forward on soundless feet. *You will do as I say.*

"And if I refuse?"

Then your mother dies. They had leverage, but it would not last forever. They must strike while they still could.

When Tulimaq's gaze finally slid to Ila, her stupid, weak heart plunged to the pit of her stomach. He looked colder than ever. The tallest peak of the most remote mountain. But there—a ripple of emotion. And Ila wondered if it might not be too late for Tulimaq to pull through. "I don't believe you. You have too much heart for that."

That was before his men had carved open her skin with blade and whip. Before she had learned what, exactly, there was to lose. She was Matilaqaa, and this was her kingdom, her land, her responsibility, as intimidating as it might be. They had come too far to roll belly-up. Tulimaq would not take this from her. He'd already taken too much.

You can train your body to become strong, but if your heart is weak, it will make no difference.

He'd sunk a blade into her heart, and its name was vengeance.

Tulimaq lunged, but Ila, who had anticipated the strike, dodged out of reach. She spun, aimed, and plunged her talq into his mother's arm. The woman screamed.

He jerked in place, his mask shattering piece by piece to reveal a man who had spent his life running from the boy he'd been. Ila's gut rolled over, and she reminded herself he had done so much worse to her.

Tipki and Saniraq circled to the front, weapons drawn, warning him to keep his distance. White flared around his eyes like an animal scenting fear.

Without shifting her attention from Tulimaq, Ila yanked the talq from his mother's arm. The woman whimpered, sagging in Malina's hold. Ila wiped the blood on her trouser leg before returning the weapon to the small of her back. Malina glanced at Ila in concern.

She did not want to hurt innocents, but this was war. She would sacrifice one for the good of many. She would save those she loved. These women standing at her sides, each represented a piece of her heart, which she would protect at any and all cost.

Drop your staff, Tulimaq.

He tightened his hold on the weapon. The last resistance from which he could not bear to be parted.

Drop your staff, Ila repeated, *or your mother dies.*

Fury lashed across his composed manner. It was a victory, however small. "I did not think you were one to stoop to so low a level."

Did he not know?

You taught me that.

His nostrils flared.

"Do what they say, Tulimaq." His mother looked at him sadly. "It will all be over soon."

Another moment passed before Tulimaq made his decision and dropped the weapon. Tipki retrieved it, her mouth parted in wordless awe at the power thrumming through it. An awesome responsibility. And a burden.

Without his staff, Ila noticed how small he looked, and how alone, with his men dead at his feet. He had thirty thousand blades to fight for him, but not one man to fight *with* him.

Tipki and Saniraq forced him to his knees, where the pool of blood ran between the stones, like the cracks between broken teeth.

"I told you," he said. "It will not work."

They began to bind his wrists using a piece of rope when, too quickly to track, he moved. He was kneeling, twisting, lunging to his feet. Tipki hadn't time to draw her dagger. He'd already snatched it, and the edge glinted as it left his outstretched fingers, slicing a path that ended with the blade buried hilt-deep in Malina's shoulder. She released her grip on Tulimaq's mother with a harsh cry.

Ila barely had time to process it all. When it was done, Tulimaq restrained Malina with an arm banded around her chest, her back to his front, his staff recovered and its blade digging into the hollow beneath her ear where the blood flowed hot and thick. Saniraq had the foresight to grab Tulimaq's mother before she could escape in the commotion. Ila blinked. She had forgotten how quickly he could move.

"I'm going to extend you the same courtesy," Tulimaq said. "Do as I say, and no harm will come to your friend." A pause to make sure she understood the severity of the situation. "Follow me. All of you."

I'll take her, Ila signed to Saniraq, who passed Tulimaq's mother over. Tulimaq watched the exchange with a cool gaze before gesturing them down the hall.

Ila followed in fear of what would happen if they lost sight of Malina. At her side, Tipki's nostrils flared, her fingers twitching every so often, as if to grab for their packmate. Tulimaq led them to a portion of the wall that had blown out, which led to a crumbling, derelict balcony overlooking the city square, in plain sight of the gathered army.

Malina thrashed harder, blood seeping from where the dagger protruded from her shoulder, and Tipki lunged toward her. Only Saniraq's firm grip on the woman's arm stopped her from sentencing Malina to certain death. Tulimaq's unruffled demeanor rested on his mother. Ila had halted at the threshold of the balcony, hidden in the shadows cast by what remained of the wall.

"I did not tell you to stop," said Tulimaq, his attention shifting to Ila. Another step backward, and another, moving nearer to the balcony edge where the railing had cracked and ripped away in chunks.

Fear for her packmate sent Ila forward, and Tipki, Saniraq. And now thirty thousand pairs of eyes locked onto them from below.

Nanuq's force rippled like a stone dropping into still waters, the rings extending farther out with each pass as they spotted their commanding officer standing above them on the cracked balcony atop the exposed cliff face. The world expanded beneath him, ten armies having gathered, cloaking the entirety of the city.

The roar of noise shuddering the air died to an ebb, a trickle, and then, nothing.

Tulimaq stood with Malina near the ledge, the force with which he slotted the blade beneath her chin forcing back her head.

"Kirn of the Empire," he cried. "Today, the Wolf Kingdom has attempted to infiltrate their ruined city. They have attempted to weaken our influence. They have attempted to destabilize everything the Great Bear has worked so tirelessly to achieve. And so I ask you this. Will you stop those who stand in our way? Will you help us reclaim this victory?"

The air ruptured with the force of the army's screams.

One hard shove sent Malina over the railing.

52

Ila screamed as Malina toppled into the void.

Time slowed.

As was the last leaf of a tree come autumn, the fall was gradual. A graceful, arched back and limbs outstretched, a tumble of head over feet. Malina's eyes widened, and the mask slipped from her face and fell down, down, the sun sinking at her back.

Ila had not thought one of them would die today.

It was not even a question of what choice Ila would make. Tulimaq's mother meant nothing. Malina was pack. Shoving the woman aside, Ila lunged, reaching for Malina's outstretched hand, vaguely aware of Tipki and Saniraq unleashing an attack on Tulimaq in the background. Palm pressed to palm. Fingers clasped and tightened. And as Malina's fall hit sudden resistance, Ila's shoulder caught fire from the force of her packmate's weight, and she screamed, falling to her knees. Someone's hand clawed the back of her parka, and with a mighty heave, helped pull Malina back onto solid ground.

Chaos broke out below—men heeding the call of war. The crowd was alive. Ferocity gave it flesh, a skeletal structure, and it lurched, snapping out toward the den like an asp. The first line of Nanuq's kirn reached the cliff and began to climb. Another unit broke away from the mass, having transformed into their animal skins, and lumbered up an incline in the distance to attain higher ground.

Planting herself in front of Malina, Ila joined Saniraq and Tipki in their fight against Tulimaq. Saniraq fell from a kick to the back, and Tipki leaped forward with furious swings and nimble footwork. But she was unfamiliar with Tulimaq's style of combat, and eventually fell to the same fate. That left Ila, fury tightening her skin, a feeling of swelling power thumping alongside her heart.

She whipped out her talq and sliced in a furious downward arc toward his abdomen. Tulimaq sidestepped with ease. Again, Ila swung, and he ducked beneath the screaming blade, and launched himself upward, hitting her pressure points so she lost feeling in her right side. Ila gasped. A kick hit her square in the chest. She tripped over Malina's body. Another step backward. She thought there was more ground, but she hadn't realized how close to the edge she had gone.

And so she stepped back with nothing to catch her fall. Ila's stomach plunged. She was falling.

Tulimaq's hand snagged the front of her parka, jerking her to a halt.

The toes of Ila's boots clung to the ledge, but she was leaning too far back to shift her balance forward. Without Tulimaq's grip, she would tumble down into the abyss. A part of Ila wished he would let go. Then there would be no confusion as to his true feelings toward her.

Do it. Her eyes burned. *Let go.*

"I can't," he said, fingers twitching. The wind buffeted her back, and the soldiers swarmed below. He hauled her closer, furious, despairing, *wanting*.

Why?

Strands of hair had pulled free of Tulimaq's braid and whipped around his flushed cheeks. Sweat dampened his forehead despite the chill. Everything about him was stiff and unyielding and pained. "You know why."

Ila thought it to be the same reason she couldn't let go either.

You care for me. She curled the fingers of one hand around his wrist, the bones slender and delicate, his pulse surging beneath her touch.

In one swift motion, he hurled her around so her back slammed into the broken railing. The impact punched the breath from her lungs. Ila's legs folded. One hand closed around the wooden staff where it had dropped during Tulimaq's attempt to stop her fall, and power crackled up her arm, scorching her skin and flaying open her veins, and Ila was screaming as her body surged with energy, bright and painful as a storm.

Tulimaq wrenched the staff from her grip. She lay there, panting, her skull throbbing so intensely she wouldn't be surprised if it had split open.

"Get up," he demanded.

She was back in the Atakana. It was winter. Mud and snow caked her legs and smeared her face. Her body ached from the long, hard hours spent sparring against Tulimaq, a man who could not be beat. No matter how many times she fell, he never failed to speak those words.

Get up.

Ila climbed to her feet. Her fist shot out, a feint, and as Tulimaq sidestepped, her elbow cracked against his temple. An unexpected blow. He stumbled toward the edge. She hit him again while he was still reeling from the first blow. Another step. His boot slipped over loose shale, the crumbling of solid ground, and as he fell, only a last desperate reach allowed him to catch the ridge with his fingertips. He hauled his upper body partway onto the ledge, his legs and feet dangling. Ila stood over him, looking down.

You care too much, she said, *and you hate it. You think caring for someone makes you weak.*

Tulimaq flinched. Ila pressed forward, relentless in her mission. He had saved her from certain death, but he hadn't wanted to save her. And therein lay the difference.

Demand your soldiers stand down.

He bared his teeth. "Never."

With a furious scream, Ila slammed her boot into Tulimaq's face.

Bone crunched beneath her heel. His head snapped back, blood spraying. His hands slipped free.

Something died inside her as she watched him fall.

Below, a group of soldiers caught his body, setting him neatly on his feet. Tulimaq stood amongst the kirn, relatively unharmed except for the broken nose. She turned her attention to Malina, who was miraculously letting Tipki tend to her shoulder wound. Tulimaq's mother had vanished.

Malina glanced at Ila over Tipki's shoulder, the fresh tears that spilled down her cheeks. Her usual scowl made a slow reappearance. "Are you crying?"

A sob broke in her chest. *Over you? Never.*

The older woman looked extremely uncomfortable over that possibility. "Well, good."

Ila bit her lip. Her facial muscles wobbled with the need to fold and let loose the fear and overwhelming realization that she had almost lost someone dear to her. But there was the army currently clambering up the cliff face, and the tower awaiting in the distance, tucked against the mountain's base, connected by an overgrown, threadbare path that descended through a narrow gorge. There wasn't time.

Together, the four women raced back through the corridor, taking the stairs to the first level and exiting out a side door. To their right, the first wave of men completed their climb, transforming into polar bears before their eyes.

They hit the trail and followed it over the uneven terrain, each pounding stride bringing them nearer to the great horn with its song that would cleave the world in two.

The earth rose and pinched the sky on either side of them, and the land sloped and narrowed. In single file, they raced through the twisting gorge, Malina in the lead, followed by Ila, then Saniraq, and lastly, Tipki. Stone crumbled each time their shoulders brushed the sides. Then the earthen walls sank, and the sky opened, and they emerged from the ravine, the tower like a beacon in the distance. Ila forced her cramping muscles faster. But after a few footsteps, she realized Saniraq and Tipki had fallen back.

A glance over her shoulder showed they remained at the ravine's entrance.

"Go," said Tipki, mouth set. "We'll hold them off."

Ila hesitated. Saniraq, her sweaty hair plastered across her forehead, dipped her chin in silent acknowledgement, as though to send Ila off with her blessing. When Malina jerked her backward, she trailed her pack sister up the grassy incline, the green already beginning to frost over.

At last, they reached the tower. Built of dark gray stone, it soared many hundreds of feet into the air, its roof pointed like a spear tip. Malina tilted back her head. "You'll need to climb up to the windows. I'll hold them off for as long as I can. Once the horn is blown, take the tunnel through the trapdoor. It will lead you to Lun."

Ila froze. Something had changed, and she had not been aware of it until now. *What about you, Tipki, and Saniraq?*

Malina's gaze was steady as she replied, "Someone needs to stop Nanuq's forces long enough for you to get away."

When did you decide this? she demanded. Beyond Malina's shoulder, Tipki used her stolen club to bash a man's head in, the bodies piling up in the narrow gorge opening, slowing the number of soldiers able to pass through. The men, however, had begun clambering over the corpses. One slipped through and sprinted toward the tower.

This woman, whom Ila had fought for every crumb of respect she had been willing to give, struggled to neutralize the rise of emotion in her features. "We had hoped it would not come to this, but we agreed last night while you slept that if it did, we would make sure you reached Lun safely."

She gripped Malina's wrist hard enough to feel the slide of skin over bone, then dropped it. *That wasn't the plan.*

"Neither was getting caught, but plans change."

I'm not leaving you.

Another soldier managed to slip past Tipki and Saniraq. He neared the base of the hill. Once there, he would begin to climb.

"Someone needs to blow the horn. It must be you."

No. She mouthed the word, felt its frail shape, the dissipation on her tongue. She would not let this woman sacrifice her life, or Tipki, or Saniraq. Malina, prickly on the best of days, and harsh, yet dear to her.

The older woman covered Ila's hand with both of hers, sheltering it like an injured bird. "My duty is to the Wolf Kingdom, and you are its heir. I am proud to die for my nation. My choice has been made. Do not take this from me."

And what of me? Ila signed. Her throat squeezed, for there was no more breath in her lungs. *What about what I want?*

"Ila." Grave, grave eyes watched her with calm acceptance. "When we first met, I admit I was angry, having believed you had abandoned us. I did not think you were worthy of your station. But you have proven to be a far greater leader than I could have hoped for, someone who is selfless and whose compassion runs deep. But as a leader, you must think of your people. You must think of the world." Malina closed her eyes, and a tear squeezed from one corner, trailing down her cheek. "Thank you," she said, "for bringing me home."

Ila clamped down on a sob, but it bubbled up. The air burned as she sucked it in. *Damn you,* she signed. Sometime during their long journey, this woman had become her friend, and now she was leaving her, like everyone else. *You can't die, do you hear me? If you die, I'll . . . I will personally come for you in the spirit world.* She swiped at the tears coursing down her face. *I need you. Tipki and Saniraq need you.*

Malina glanced over her shoulder at the approaching enemy. "Maybe you did once." Tipki and Saniraq struggled to staunch the flow of kirn. There were too many. The men, those that managed to fight past, broke like water on rocks and reformed, rippling over the trodden grass and gaining ground. She turned back to Ila. "But you are no frightened child, no caged animal, no woman without a purpose or name. You are Matilaqaa, first daughter of the Vaal and Narg and rightful leader of this nation. You know what to do."

We'll fight, she argued. *All of us.* Ila reached for her talq when Malina stilled her hand.

"The North has waited long enough," her packmate said. Then, clumsily, she signed, *It's time.*

As she pulled away, Ila, stunned by the sight of Malina using sign language, reached for her. *Wait—*

Malina squeezed Ila's hand, then released it. "I will tell Pili you said hello."

Battle lust cracked like a hard glaze across her eyes as she unsheathed her weapons, and Ila knew this woman's mind would not change. Twenty years Malina had awaited this day. She belonged on the battlefield with her packmates, meting out her vengeance against Nanuq's kirn.

With a final nod, Malina turned and trotted a few paces down the hill to meet the surge of kirn that had broken through the gorge at the bottom of the hill, a dagger in one hand, a nigana in the other. Tipping back her head, she howled the song of their people, its sound vibrating through the threads that bound them as pack, and it poured strength into Ila's limbs, for the sound was a warning and an exultation, a pure, elated cry of *here I am* and *come get me* and *I am free, I am free, I am free.*

The army spread, toppling the rise and crawling higher, over rocks and crags, leaving disturbed earth in its wake. Nanuq's kirn, and the heir of the Wolf Kingdom. Then there was Malina: a single woman who stood between.

The first soldier to reach her swung. Malina caught the club in the tines of her nigana and drove her knife into the man's stomach once the weapon had been wrenched free of his hand. Her second opponent met the same fate. They came, the soldiers, the men, in their open-jawed hoods, teeming like hundreds of insects across the hilly ground. Tipki and Saniraq had abandoned their attempts in blocking the gorge and now fought their way to Malina's side.

Ila couldn't watch any longer. The last task had fallen to her, and she could not fail. The tower rose at her back, a rectangular pillar constructed of interlocking stones. Ila climbed. Hand over foot over hand, she climbed, straight toward a sky blinding in its purity. She did not stop until she reached the top and pulled herself through one of the open windows.

She took everything in at a glance. A spacious room with four walls, dusty weapons stacked in one corner. Large square windows punched through on three sides, with the fourth wall carved from the mountain itself. An enormous, curved instrument sprouted from the mountain face, larger than her body, its end flaring outward like a blossoming flower.

Ila closed her eyes as the enormity of this moment hit with crushing force, a declaration of today, the promise of tomorrow so tenuous. Beyond the windows, Nanuq's army poured more blood into the earth.

For her people.

For her pack.

For Apaay.

For freedom.

Leaning forward, Ila touched her mouth to the Horn of Amaroq, and blew.

← 53 →

In the Central Territory, in the City of Trees, a woman with chin-length white hair and a man with an eye for innovation conversed in low voices, away from prying eyes. The quiet of early evening fractured then, pierced by a sound they had not heard in nearly two decades. It was a plea and a lament and an earth's cry of pain, and it came from the west.

← →

In the Northern Territory, deep in the stone halls of Nigun, the Council of Nine gathered around a table of finest oak. A current shuddered through the underground river, sent ripples across the surface of a sacred hot spring. The Council wondered if their sister city, Nalwa, had heard the horn's call, too, and promptly sent for a messenger.

← →

In the Southern Territory, in the capital of Nur, a demon lay in a pool of spreading blood, at the knees of a red-eyed woman whose world was coming apart. On a dais, there sat a man and woman, a goddess and a king. The man heard the horn's cry, and smiled.

← →

And in the Banished Lands, across the swift black waters of Tor, a figure with pale eyes and a mask of bone studied the eastern horizon, waiting. The tides dragged out, rushed in, moving to the rhythm of the sea. When the call struck, the Pale One calmly abandoned their place on the docks, and went to inform the island's inhabitants that the Wolf Kingdom had returned at last.

ACKNOWLEDGEMENTS

Writing a book amidst a global pandemic is a first for me (and hopefully a last). My productivity definitely suffered at times during those long months of quarantine, but I'm incredibly proud of the finished product—a book!—and I couldn't have done it without the help of certain individuals.

Auriane: Your keen editor's eye helped bring *Hunt* to a new level, and for that, I thank you!

Beth: As always, your feedback has been invaluable. Thank you for always taking the time to read my work.

Claire: Thank you so much for your detailed feedback. In a way, *Hamilton* brought us together, so a big thanks to Lin-Manuel Miranda as well!

Faryn: Another amazing cover! Time and again I'm left in awe of your work. Thank you for bringing my books to life through your art.

My family: Your support means more than I can say. Thank you for never expecting me to be anyone other than myself.

Alexandria Warwick is the #1 fan of *Avatar: The Last Airbender.*
She is the author of *The Demon Race* and the North series.

www.alexandriawarwick.com
IG: @alexandriawarwick

Lightning Source UK Ltd.
Milton Keynes UK
UKHW010652090223
416681UK00007B/1991